FEARLESS 3

ALSO BY FRANCINE PASCAL

FEARLESS

FEARLESS 2

FEARLESS
3

REBEL · HEAT · BLOOD

FRANCINE PASCAL

SIMON PULSE
NEW YORK LONDON TORONTO SYDNEY NEW DELHI

This book is a work of fiction. Any references to historical events, real people, or real places are used fictitiously. Other names, characters, places, and events are products of the author's imagination, and any resemblance to actual events or places or persons, living or dead, is entirely coincidental.

Produced by Alloy Entertainment
151 West 26th Street, New York, NY 10001

SIMON PULSE
An imprint of Simon & Schuster Children's Publishing Division
1230 Avenue of the Americas, New York, NY 10020
This Simon Pulse paperback edition February 2014

Book design by Angela Goddard

The text of this book was set in Dante MT Std.
Manufactured in the United States of America
10 9 8 7 6 5 4 3 2 1
Library of Congress Control Number 2013946876
ISBN 978-1-4814-0270-5
ISBN 978-0-7434-3411-9 (*Rebel* eBook)
ISBN 978-0-7434-3412-6 (*Heat* eBook)
ISBN 978-0-7434-3413-3 (*Blood* eBook)
These books were originally published individually.

CONTENTS

REBEL

To Thomas John Pascal Wenk

GAIA

Honesty is a funny thing. People always tell you that they want you to be honest with them. But they're lying. Nobody wants that. Honesty sucks. That's why the word *honesty* is always preceded by other words, like *brutal* and *painful*.

I keep all of my secrets for just that reason. They'd hurt too much if anybody knew. And I don't mean they would just hurt the people I told. I mean they would hurt me, too.

So I keep them to myself. And it's not all that hard. After all, dishonesty kind of runs in my family.

Just look at my father. He ditched me without ever telling me where he was going or why—and he did it on the worst night of my life. And my uncle has apparently been watching over me my entire life, but he never even bothered to introduce himself. He only shows up when I'm about to get shot in the head or stabbed by some crazed serial killer. Great, thanks. But I can take care of myself.

Come to think of it, everybody I know seems to hide the truth somehow. Sam. Ella. Even Mary. In fact, the only person I can think of who *doesn't* hide the truth is Ed Fargo. He's honest about everything.

But as far as keeping secrets goes, I have to admit, I really take first prize. I've never told Sam how I feel about him. And that's just scratching the surface. I've never told him or anyone else about my total inability to feel fear. Or why I'm trained to kick almost anyone's ass in about three seconds flat. Or why I'm stuck with George and Ella.

And here's the biggest one of all. I've never told anyone about my dad or about my mother's death. But I have a good reason. If I were totally honest with my friends about my past . . . well, I'd put their lives in danger. I already have. More than once.

Maybe everyone has a reason for hiding the truth. After all, honesty seems to create more problems than it solves. It can hurt. It can even kill. I guess that's why people are afraid of the truth.

But I wouldn't know about that. I'm not afraid of anything.

HER KIND OF GAME

HIS BODY WENT LIMP. HE WOULDN'T TRY TO MOVE. SHE KNEW IT. HE'D TASTED AN EXCRUCIATING PAIN. . . .

THE THREE WISE MEN

Skeletons.

That's exactly what the trees in Washington Square Park looked like at this time of night: spindly, grotesque skeletons. At least that was how they looked to Gaia Moore. It was amazing how a place could feel like an amusement park one month and a cemetery the next. But that was New York City. It was constantly changing, and often not for the better. That could be said of a lot of things, actually—Gaia's life included.

"Why does this park totally die right before Christmas?" Mary suddenly asked of nobody in particular.

Gaia smirked. One of the coolest things about Mary Moss was that she had an uncanny knack for saying exactly what Gaia was thinking. She also shared the same intolerance for bullshit.

"Because there's no action down here," Ed said. His breath made little white clouds in the frigid December air. "The real action is in Midtown. I say we buy some little red suits and pom-pom hats, then go volunteer to be elves outside some big megastore, like Macy's."

"I'm too tall to be an elf," Gaia replied.

"Me too," Mary added.

Ed shrugged. Dead leaves crunched under his wheelchair. "Then we'll get some fake beards for you guys. Instead of being elves we'll be the three wise men."

Gaia had to laugh. The three wise men. That was funny. A wheelchair-bound ex–skate rat, a female ex–coke addict, and . . . *her.* Whatever Gaia was. She probably *could* pass for a man. Easily. She wasn't beautiful and skinny like Mary. Nope. Forget a wise man; Gaia had the body of a prize-fighter. She didn't even need the beard. All she needed was a little five o'clock shadow. Now that she thought about it, the only remotely feminine aspect of her appearance was her unkempt mane of blond hair. But there was probably a direct correlation between one's freakish looks and the swirling mess inside one's head, wasn't there?

"I guess it's too cold for any Christmas pageantry, anyway," Ed mumbled.

Ed was right. It was too cold for anything. Even chess. Gaia had never seen the park this quiet or deserted. Usually *some* die-hard chess fanatic was out at the tables, trying to hustle a game, no matter what the weather. Like Mr. Haq. Or her old friend Zolov. But Gaia hadn't seen a whole lot of Zolov since he'd been slashed by those neo-Nazi idiots who used to hang around the miniature Arc de Triomphe on the north side.

She almost *wished* a few skinheads were around just so the place would feel more like home. In fact, she wouldn't mind at all if one of them jumped out of the shadows and tried to attack her. She'd walked this park many times for that exact reason. But seeking combat wasn't a group activity. It was something she did on her own. In secrecy. Besides, at this moment she wasn't really craving a good fight. No, what she really missed right now were the sounds and smells of months past: the gurgling of the fountain, the laughter of the NYU students, the sweet odor of roasted peanuts. . . .

Mary abruptly stopped in her tracks.

"You know what? We *should* do something to liven things up." She adjusted her black wool cap and brushed a few wayward red curls out of her eyes. "It's winter break. We're free. I say we create a little excitement of our own."

Gaia met Mary's gaze. She knew that gleam in Mary's green eyes all too well. It whispered: *Let's do something crazy.* And in a way, Gaia could empathize. After all, courting danger was one of her favorite pastimes, too. But Mary's reckless tendencies led down a much more self-destructive path than Gaia's own.

Then again, some people might argue that deliberately looking for fights was a hell of a lot worse than snorting a big fat line of white powder up your nose. But Gaia had never paid any attention to other people's opinions. Ever.

"Why don't I like the sound of that at all?" Ed muttered.

Mary laughed. "Come on, you guys. We're here in New York City. By the looks of things, we basically have the place to ourselves." She waved her hands at the empty benches and frozen pavement. "I mean, everyone else is holed up in their apartments or vacationing in the Hamptons or doing whatever it is that normal people do."

"Your point being?" Ed asked.

"That I'm bored!" Mary cried. "I don't do drugs anymore, so I have to find *something* to do, right?" She laughed.

Gaia kept quiet. Unfortunately, the joke wasn't very funny. Mary had only been off cocaine since Thanksgiving, and Gaia knew enough about drugs to know that a lot of addicts relapsed in those first precarious weeks of clean living. Especially when they were bored.

"I don't know," Ed said quietly. He fidgeted in his wheelchair, tapping his gloved fingers on the armrests. "If you ask me, a little boredom is a good thing. Anyway, aren't we supposed to be going to Gaia's house right now?"

Ed was right. They *were* on their way to the Nivens' house (Gaia never thought of it as her own, and she never would), but there was really nothing to do there. Gaia shook her head. Poor Ed. Part of her agreed with him. Ever since he'd met Gaia, Ed's life had been a little too exciting. Kidnappings. Serial killers. Random acts of violence. Part of her wanted to protect him—to shield him from the danger that surrounded her at all times.

But the other part of her—she couldn't ignore—was just

as bored as Mary. Besides, if Mary was looking for a way to keep her mind off drugs, Gaia was all for it. After all, Mary had appointed her to help out with getting involved in "good, clean fun." Whatever that was.

"What do you have in mind?" Gaia asked Mary.

Mary raised her eyebrows. "A little game," she said. She smiled down at Ed, then back at Gaia. "What do you guys think about truth or dare?"

Ed snickered. "Ooh. That sounds *really* exciting. Can we play spin the bottle next?"

Mary ignored him. "Gaia?" she prompted. "What do you say?"

"Sure," Gaia said. It actually *did* sound exciting—at least to her. The fact of the matter was that she had never played truth or dare before. *Or* spin the bottle. Or any other games that normal kids would have played, the ones who didn't have twisted secret agents for fathers.

But that was the great thing about hanging out with Mary. She introduced Gaia to all kinds of normal experiences. And always in a very abnormal way.

WOOF, WOOF

Ed Fargo's biggest problem wasn't what most people might think: namely, that his legs would never work again. No. He'd learned to deal with that. Or at least *accept* it. It was just another part of his life now. An unpleasant part, sure—like suffering through history class, or seeing his ex-girlfriend Heather Gannis every single day, or forcing himself to smile back at all the phony bastards who pretended to take pity on him. But it wasn't *torture.* No, Ed Fargo's biggest problem was that he couldn't say no to Gaia Moore.

That was torture.

Even more tortuous (or pathetic) was that he was completely, utterly, one hundred percent in love with her. And she had absolutely no clue.

On more than one occasion he'd almost mustered the courage to tell her. He'd even gone so far as to compose a few e-mails and letters, but he always tore them up or deleted them at the last minute. A voice inside inevitably reminded him that it was better to live with delusional hope than crushing rejection.

God. One of these days he was really going to have to shut that voice up.

But for now, it looked like he was resigned to following Gaia around like a dog and catering to her every whim.

Unfortunately, this frequently involved getting into fights, or ducking bullets, or discovering secrets that were probably best left buried.

As every lame-ass soap opera was quick to point out, love sucked.

"So what do you say we get started?" Mary asked.

"Can we at least play at Gaia's house?" Ed groaned. His teeth started chattering. It wasn't from cold, either. The park didn't exactly fill him with a sense of safety and well-being. He'd almost been *murdered* here. He peered into the shadowy tangle of barren tree limbs that lined the path on either side. "We're all freezing our butts off, in case you forgot."

Mary shook her head. "I say we start here. Gaia?"

"No better time than the present," Gaia agreed.

It figured neither of them would listen to him. And he wasn't about to leave without them, either. He really *was* a dog. Woof, woof.

"So who goes first?" he grumbled.

"We'll shoot for it," Mary said. "Rock, scissors, paper." She stuck her hand behind her back. "On three . . ."

Great, Ed thought. He hated rock, scissors, paper almost as much as truth or dare. With his luck, he'd probably lose—and they would dare him to strip naked and streak up Fifth Avenue in his wheelchair.

Mary smiled. "One . . . two . . . three . . ."

Ed extended a fist: rock. It always seemed safest, although

somebody smarter—like Gaia—might disagree. His eyes flashed to Gaia's hand. *Ha!* Scissors. He glanced at Mary. Rock, too. Unbelievable.

Gaia Moore had actually lost.

It was probably the first time he'd seen Gaia lose at anything. He couldn't help but smile. Maybe this wouldn't be so bad after all. It would be nice to see her do something ridiculous, wouldn't it?

"Oh, Jesus." Gaia moaned.

"Now, don't be a sore loser," Mary teased, winking at Ed.

"So which is it?" Ed asked gleefully. "Truth or dare?"

Gaia pursed her lips. "Dare. And you don't have to ask me again. It's dare for the duration of the game."

Mary clapped. "Perfect."

She turned back toward the arch. A solitary figure was sitting on one of the benches, wrapped in a scarf with a hat pulled low over his eyes—a skinny and grizzled older man Ed had never seen before. Ed's excitement began to fade. He could see where this was going. He should have known Gaia would never pick truth. He also should have known Mary would dare Gaia to take some inane, meaningless risk. Why did the two of them have to *create* trouble? Why did they have to pluck it out of thin air? He held his breath as Mary raised her hand and pointed at the figure.

"I dare you to go kiss that guy," she said.

THE GOOD THING ABOUT RATS

Truth or dare was right up Gaia's alley. She could tell right away that she would be able to add it to that short list of loves that made her life tolerable. Everything else on the list was food related. Well, she loved a good chess match. And Sam. But there was no point in dwelling on *that*.

What she really loved were diversions.

She loved anything that distracted her from the dismal specifics of her existence. And kissing some random stranger in the park certainly qualified as a diversion, didn't it?

She walked toward him on the darkened path, waiting for him to look up and notice her. But he didn't move. He was slumped on the bench. His legs were spread in front of him, his skeletal chest rising and falling in the even rhythm of sleep. Icy puffs of breath drifted away from his open mouth. Gaia's nose wrinkled. *Yuck.* Maybe he was drunk. Or *something.* She'd be sure to ask him if she could just kiss him on the forehead—

Wait a second.

He wasn't asleep. He was just pretending.

Only someone with Gaia's acute awareness in sizing up a potential opponent could detect the subtle clues of consciousness: the exaggerated way he exhaled, the concentrated stillness of his eyelids. So he was lying in wait. Setting a trap. The asshole was waiting to attack her.

A familiar electric energy shot through Gaia's body—the jolt that always came in place of fear. This was going to be even more fun than she had expected. How come she'd never thought of playing this game before? It was tailor-made for somebody with Gaia's unique condition: somebody who felt only a sublime emptiness in the face of any threat.

Let's see what you can do, she silently taunted as she stepped in front of him.

She placed her feet squarely between his own. A smile played on her lips. Yes, she could see the tension building in his arms as they lay at his sides. His breathing quickened—just a little. He was getting ready to make his move. To take her by surprise.

Gaia glanced back at Mary and Ed. They were a good thirty yards away, silhouetted against the leafless trees. Their expressions were unreadable in the darkness. She gave them a quick thumbs-up. Then she caught a whiff of bourbon and winced. Disgusting. But she had to get it over with. Otherwise she would lose—and losing was something she was not prepared to do. Fearlessness had to serve *some* purpose, even if it was for a game. And besides, this jerk needed to be taught a lesson. Gaia *lived* for teaching bullies lessons. She was committed.

"Excuse me, sir?" Gaia bent over to look into his eyes.

Two hands clasped around her wrists.

"Gotcha!" the man cried.

She almost laughed. "Give me a break," she mumbled disappointedly. It figured he would grab her by the arms. It was the most obvious and idiotic form of attack. But she'd let him enjoy the illusion of control for a second or two. His thick fingers dug through the fibers of her coat.

"Now what do you think you're doing?" he asked.

She didn't answer. Instead she just gazed into his haggard face. Talk about disgusting. His skin looked like an oil field. He must have been fifty years old. His beady black eyes were rheumy with alcohol.

"You wanna play with me?" he hissed, laughing. He gave her arms a sudden yank, pulling her closer. "Well, it's your lucky night, sugar. I'm gonna warm you up. I'm gonna give you something you'll never forget."

Gaia rolled her eyes. She only had to remember creeps like Charlie Salita and his rapist friend, Sideburns Tim, to feel a surge of anger. But this guy was just too pathetic for any kind of major confrontation. And even though she wanted to prolong this encounter—just for the sake of excitement—the stink of this guy's breath and body were enough to make her puke. Too bad. Sighing, she stamped the heel of her combat boot on the man's toes.

"What the—"

A shocked whimper escaped his lips. His hold on her instantly loosened. Quick as a flash, she clasped his right hand against her left forearm. His eyes bulged. With a single deft maneuver she flipped him off the bench to the ground at her feet—flat on his back.

"What the hell?" he gasped.

He tried to wriggle free, but Gaia held his hand fast. She bent it back slightly.

"Ow!" he screamed.

His body went limp. He wouldn't try to move. She knew it. He'd tasted an excruciating pain. That was the beauty of this particular grip. She could snap his wrist in a second, but there was no need to injure him. It was the essence of true kung fu and one of the first lessons her father had taught her: the art of intimidation—the art of threatening torture without actually having to inflict it more than once.

"Now, you aren't going to try this with anyone else, are you?" Gaia asked calmly.

He didn't answer. He gazed up at her, wild-eyed. His breath came quickly. Even though the temperature was below freezing, she could see beads of sweat forming on his bulbous nose.

"Are you?" she persisted.

"No!" he grunted, cringing. "Come on! Lemme go! Lemme go, you bitch!"

Gaia frowned. "What did you call me?"

"Nothing." His eyes squeezed shut. "Just lemme go," he pleaded. "I'm sorry. . . ."

"That's better," she said. "Now I'll let you go. Just as soon as you promise me you won't try to grab some other girl who—"

"Gaia!" Ed's voice sliced through the night air.

Oh, brother. Once again her self-appointed Superman was swooping in to save the day. Why did Ed always try to get involved? He was undeniably brave and undeniably sweet, but he must have had a short-term memory problem. He'd seen her kick a dozen scumbags' asses, and *this* situation was certainly under control—yet he was still racing down the path as fast as the chair would carry him, with Mary close on his heels. They made quite a rescue party. She almost smiled.

"Come on," the guy at her feet murmured one last time.

Gaia glanced back down at him. "Fine," she said in a soft voice. "But if I ever see you in this park again, I'll think twice about letting you get off so easy." Her tone was very matter-of-fact, as if she were explaining the rules of chess. "Got it?"

He nodded. His face was etched with what Gaia knew, intellectually, was fear. She let go of his hands, then leaned over and lifted him by the lapels of his coat. Jesus. He even was heavier than he looked. She shoved him out on the path and watched as he scurried away.

A rat, she realized. That's exactly what he looked like. A big, fat rat.

But one who'd learned never to proposition another teenage girl again.

Yes. The good thing about rats was that they could be easily trained. All they needed was a little negative reinforcement.

"Gaia?" Ed gasped breathlessly, skidding to a halt. "Are you all right?"

She turned around. "I think I'll live," she said, trying not to smile.

"Holy shit!" Mary cried delightedly. She doubled over beside Ed. Her lungs were heaving. "That was *awesome.* What did he try to do to you, anyway?"

Gaia shrugged. "He told me he'd give me something I'd never forget," she replied. But as she spoke the words, a wave of exhaustion swept over her.

Without thinking, she slumped down on the park bench.

Her face twisted in a scowl. It was ridiculous: Even after a fight as pathetic as *that* one, she still felt completely drained. She supposed she should learn to expect it. Her body was like a balloon. In combat it would fill up with adrenaline and strength—and then *pop!*—it would deflate. Instantly. For a few minutes she would be unable to move. And somehow this peculiar handicap always managed to slip her mind when she was fighting someone. Maybe because she'd never understood it.

"Are you *sure* you're all right?" Ed asked, peering at her closely.

"Fine," she whispered. She shook her head.

After a few seconds her strength began to return. It flowed slowly into her arms and legs, filling them like a thick potion.

She dusted off her hands and stood.

She found herself smiling again.

In spite of the stench, kissing that guy had been a lot of fun. In a very weird way. It had been very diverting, too. She hadn't thought about Sam or her father or any other stupid crap at all during those precious few moments. Truth or dare was *definitely* her kind of game. It helped her to forget. And forgetting was a very, very good thing.

"So," she said, glancing at Ed and Mary. "Whose turn is it now?"

PANDORA'S BOX

Under normal circumstances, Ed would have loved hanging out with two beautiful girls.

But circumstances involving Gaia were never normal.

At least he'd convinced them to leave the park and retreat to the cozy warmth of Gaia's brownstone. That was *something.*

Now, however, he would probably drive himself crazy staring at Gaia and Mary as they lounged side by side on the overstuffed living-room couch. Any beautiful girl had a habit of driving Ed crazy these days—and not just Gaia. Yup. The needle was continuously popping into red on the Fargo lust-o-meter. But he was good at hiding his lecherous thoughts. It was a skill he'd cultivated carefully since the accident. That was something, too.

"All right, Ed, it's your turn," Gaia announced.

He shook his head. "You actually want to keep *playing?*"

"Why wouldn't I?"

"Gee, I don't know," he said, with as much sarcasm as he could manage. "Maybe because somebody just attacked you."

"Oh, please." She waved her hand dismissively. "That was nothing."

He wanted to argue, but there probably wasn't much point. For Gaia, flipping that guy on his ass and scaring the hell out of him *was* nothing. He'd seen her do a lot worse.

"I say we go back out there," Mary said. She sat up straight, peeking distractedly through the windows out to Perry Street. "Being cooped up inside is so lame. It's not *that* cold. As long as we keep moving around, we'll be fine."

Ed slouched back in his wheelchair. "Um . . . haven't you

guys forgotten about the truth part of this game? If everyone picks truth, we'll be fine. We won't have to do anything stupid."

"Forget it," Gaia stated. She shook her head vehemently. "You can't tell people what to pick. That ruins the point of the game." She smiled at him. "And for making such a lame suggestion, I say that you have to go next."

Mary turned away from the window. "I second that motion," she said, grinning wickedly.

Ed sighed. So much for trying to be clever. He should know better by now.

"Fine." He groaned. "Then I pick truth."

But as soon as he closed his mouth, he began to regret his decision. This was probably going to suck. Big time. Gaia wasn't going to sugarcoat a "truth" for him. No. She never sugarcoated anything. She wasn't the least bit concerned about sparing his feelings.

Of course, that was what he loved most about her.

Other people acted extra kind because he was in a wheelchair. Or they just pretended to ignore the chair altogether. But Gaia did neither. She was too honest to be polite. So was Mary. It was no wonder they got along so well.

"Truth, eh?" Gaia asked. She exchanged a quick glance with Mary. There was a sparkle in her eye. "All right, Ed Fargo." She looked him straight in the face. "Did you and Heather ever do the nasty?"

His jaw tightened.

Dammit.

He was starting to remember why he hated this game so much. It figured Gaia would mention Heather. Right. It figured because he never would have expected it. Why *would* she bring up Heather? Gaia hated Heather. And vice versa. They had a perfectly reciprocal relationship. Yin and yang.

And there was also the unpleasant fact that Heather was currently dating Sam, the guy whom Gaia loved.

But that was Gaia for you. She was a Pandora's box of surprises. Always walking that fine line between psychopath and friend. She never seemed completely satisfied unless the air was thick with tension—or if she was in danger of getting herself hurt.

"Well?" Gaia prodded.

Ed chewed his lip. There was another reason this question sucked so much.

He'd never told anyone about his sex life.

He and Heather *had* lost their virginity to each other, only weeks before the accident . . . but they had made a pact to keep it secret. It was their business. Theirs alone. And in spite of the fact that they had broken up over two years ago, Ed still treasured the memory enough to honor that pact. He wouldn't violate it for the sake of a stupid game, even if it pissed off Gaia.

"I changed my mind," Ed finally said. "I want to pick dare."

"No way," Mary interjected. She shook her head. "That's against the rules."

Gaia blinked. For an instant Ed caught her gaze.

Her face softened. "No, that's all right. We'll let the rules slide this time." She grinned. "But just this once."

Ed sighed, relaxing a little bit. That was Gaia for you, too. Just when you thought you'd lost her to the dark side forever, she pulled off some little miracle to let you know there was a heart in there somewhere—buried deep under that impenetrable shell.

"You know what? I actually think I've gotta split," he lied. "It's late. My parents start worrying. You know?"

"Sure," Gaia said softly.

"I don't know," Mary teased. "Sounds like a cop-out to me."

Whatever, Ed thought. Let Mary think it was a cop-out. At this point he didn't really care. Gaia understood. That was all that mattered.

He turned his chair toward the door. Luckily, Gaia's brownstone was one of the tiny minority of houses in Manhattan that were actually wheelchair friendly. Making a quick getaway would be easy.

"Hey, wait a second," Mary said. "What do you say we pick up where we left off tomorrow? That way we can play outside again—when it's light out and warmer." Her voice became excited. "We can use all of New York City as a playing field."

Ed glanced over his shoulder. "I don't know," he said doubtfully. "I mean—"

"Come on, Ed," Gaia interrupted. "What else are you gonna do?"

That was a good question. He knew the answer, too. He was going to sit alone in his house all day long and think about her. And that was just too sad to think about. Not to mention pathetic.

"So are you in or are you out?" Mary demanded impatiently.

Ed sighed. "I'm in," he mumbled.

At the very least, he'd be able to keep an eye on her. Maybe he'd even be able to keep her from doing something incredibly risky or stupid.

Maybe he'd even save her life.

Yeah, right. He could try, anyway. The way he always did. That was also something. Wasn't it?

TO: L

FROM: ELJ

DATE: DECEMBER 22

FILE: 776244

SUBJECT: Gaia Moore

LAST SEEN: Perry Street residence, 11:23 P.M.

UPDATE: Subject observed again with new companion, Mary Moss. Seems to be developing an emotional attachment. Preliminary intelligence indicates Moss is a recovering substance abuser. My own observations lead me to believe she nurtures subject's disregard for authority or personal safety. Advise.

TO: ELJ

FROM: L

DATE: DECEMBER 23

FILE: 776422

SUBJECT: Gaia Moore

DIRECTIVES: Continue to monitor Moss's interaction with subject. I will monitor as well. Neutralization may be required if she places subject in danger. Await further instructions.

MARY

I used to think that having a best friend or soul mate or whatever you want to call it was a load of fairy-tale crap. Best friends exist only on TV shows. As far as I was concerned, nobody could get close to another person in real life. People are just too phony. Or evil. Or self-interested. If somebody becomes your friend, it's usually because they want something in return.

As I said, that's what I used to think. But that was back when I was doing about three grams of coke a day.

It's funny, because I had a lot of friends back then. Tons. They just weren't real. Some of them knew about my habit, and some didn't. It didn't matter, though. I was high all the time. I put on an act with everybody. I used to feel like I had a magic bag full of invisible masks—and I just would change into a different one, depending on the situation. My real face never showed. To be honest, I didn't even know what my real face was or if I even had one.

But then I met Gaia Moore. Or to be more specific, she exploded into my life.

For starters, she beat the crap out of Skizz, the asshole coke dealer who was about to pump a bullet into my stomach. I've never seen anything like it. She was like some kind of fighting machine. There I was, trapped in the park—facing down the barrel of a gun—and all of a sudden this mass of blond hair appears out of nowhere, belts Skizz a few times, and then sends him running away. Then she collapsed. Quite an introduction, huh? At least she let me buy her a cup of coffee.

But after that, I felt like there was a magnet pulling me toward her. I couldn't stop thinking about her. I was fascinated—and a little confused, too, because she didn't seem to want anything from me. She never has. Except for me to quit doing drugs.

It's strange. Those first few days after I stopped using cocaine, I used to think that there was no way I'd be able to function without it. I was convinced I would have to hide myself away from the rest of the world for the rest of my life.

But when I'm with Gaia, something happens to me. It's almost as if all my fear just melts away and evaporates into thin air. Seriously. I'm fearless. I can do anything. And the rush I get from hanging out with her is a hell of a lot more real and intense than the buzz I got from doing a couple of lines.

Not to say that life is peachy. My problems aren't over. For one thing, my family doesn't trust me. Why should they? I lied to them for years. They thought I was the perfect daughter. Little did they know. So now they watch me the way a guard would watch a dangerous prisoner. A nice group of guards, but still.

And even though I left the world of cocaine behind, other people haven't. I still owe Skizz five hundred bucks. People like Skizz don't forgive debts. It's bad for their business.

I guess that's another reason I like hanging around with Gaia so much. She makes me feel safe.

THE COOLEST THING

FOR A TERRIBLE INSTANT HER BODY STIFFENED—
PETRIFIED IN THE FREEZING DECEMBER AIR.
I'M DEAD, SHE REALIZED.

THE FACE IN THE CROWD

"Truth or dare?" Mary asked.

Gaia rolled her eyes. "I *told* you, Mary. You don't need to ask me. I'm not gonna pick truth. Ever. Under any circumstances." She smiled. "Got it?"

Mary shook her head. She glanced down at Ed. She could tell that he was getting frustrated, too. This was ridiculous. They had been wandering around downtown for almost three hours, and Gaia still hadn't picked truth. What would it take, anyway? A gun to her head? Well . . . no, that probably wouldn't work, either.

The problem was, the girl had a pathological aversion to revealing any information about herself. The only reason Mary had suggested this game in the first place was to answer all the tantalizing Gaia questions that had festered in her mind over the past seven weeks. Like why Gaia's parents were out of the picture. Or where she had lived before New York. Or how she had learned to fight like Wonder Woman meets Jackie Chan. Or what the *real* deal was between Gaia and Heather Gannis's boyfriend, Sam Moon . . .

Or why she seemed so certain that she could die at any moment.

"So?" Gaia prompted, clearly enjoying herself. "What's it gonna be?"

Mary glanced at Ed again, who shrugged. They were having fun, but this was starting to bug the hell out of her. There was only one solution. She had to dare Gaia to do something so over the top that there would be no *way* she could pull it off. But that posed another problem. So far, Gaia had eaten a dozen doughnuts in less than a minute (without barfing) and done a handstand on the median of the West Side Highway (without dying). And smiled the whole time.

She had to have a breaking point, though. Everyone did.

Mary shoved her hands into her pockets and glanced into the northwest entrance of Washington Square Park. Somehow they always managed to end up here. She didn't have the slightest clue why, either. The place wasn't exactly hopping with action. It was gray and cold and miserable. The sun was beginning to fade. A few heavily bundled old men were huddled around the chess tables, but that was it.

She supposed she could always dare Gaia to kiss one of them and watch another fight. Nah. Been there, done that . . .

"I got it," Ed said. He turned his wheelchair back toward Waverly Place and pointed at a little Italian restaurant on the opposite corner, La Cocina. It wasn't more than a hundred feet away. There was a table full of thirty-something yuppies in the window: bloated Wall Street types who had probably left work early to get a head start on the night's drinking. The West Village was filled with people like that at this time of year—people who had a convenient excuse to get drunk earlier and more often than usual because it was "the holiday season." Mary knew all about that excuse, which was another reason she wanted to get out of here. The holiday spirit could get ugly fast. Guys like that inevitably got rowdy and leered at her. Or worse.

Ed glanced back at Gaia. He smiled. "I dare you to streak those guys."

Mary laughed. She hadn't been expecting *that.*

"But it's, like, twenty-eight degrees outside right now," Gaia said, frowning.

"Chicken, huh?" Ed lifted his shoulders. His smile widened. "Then I guess you lose."

Gaia started laughing, too. "You really want me to take off all my clothes and run past that window?"

"I wouldn't ask you if I didn't," he replied casually.

"But . . ." Gaia glanced at Mary.

"But what?" Mary folded her arms across her chest and raised her eyebrows. No way was she going to cut Gaia any slack. Ed was a smart guy. If Gaia refused to do this, then she would have to pick truth.

"What if I get arrested?" Gaia protested.

Mary waved her hands around the street. "I don't see any cops." She looked at Ed. "Do you?"

Ed shook his head. "Nope."

"Fine," Gaia grumbled. She quickly ducked into the park and disappeared behind some bushes.

"I don't believe this," Ed muttered.

Mary shook her head. "Neither do I, really."

She stared at the mass of prickly leaves—the only trace of green left in the park—wondering if Gaia was really stripping off all her clothes back there. It *was* freezing. Mary rubbed her arms against her sides. Maybe this wasn't such a hot idea. If Gaia really did go through with this, there was a very good chance that she'd catch pneumonia.

Mary's eyes narrowed. She took a step forward. Gaia was definitely doing *something*—

"Holy shit!" Ed yelled.

Before the image could even fully register in Mary's mind, she saw Gaia in midair: jumping over the fence onto the sidewalk—wearing nothing but her hat. Mary's jaw fell open. She heard Ed gasp as she stood gaping at the pale, muscular frame and the wild mane of blond hair trailing behind it.

Without pausing to look for any oncoming traffic, Gaia sprinted across the street to the window, knocked on it, and jumped up and down a few times.

Every single guy at that table looked like he had just been slapped.

"Awesome!" Ed yelled. He clapped and clasped his stomach, laughing hysterically.

In spite of her shock and mild horror, Mary found she was smiling, too. So were the guys at the table. Then *they* started clapping. It figured. But Gaia had already beat a hasty retreat back behind the bushes. The whole trip had taken no more than ten seconds.

Damn, that girl was impressive. There was nothing Gaia Moore wouldn't do. Absolutely nothing.

Mary sighed. She glanced around to make sure there were no cops in sight. It was probably a good idea to get out of here. Maybe they should head uptown. Yeah. To Mary's neighborhood. The Upper East Side. The land of the rich and famous. There was plenty of havoc to wreak up there—

Oh my God.

Mary's heart jumped. In an instant she forgot all about Gaia.

Skizz.

He was here. In the park. Among the chess gawkers. The long, grayish brown beard was unmistakable. His head was down and his gaze fixed to one of the tables . . . but she could still see that tangled mop of hair, those beady brown eyes.

"Mary?" Ed asked. The voice seemed to float to her from another universe. "Are you all right?"

"I . . . I . . ." She shook her head. Her feet were stuck to the pavement. She couldn't move. Did Skizz know she was here? Had he been spying on her? He could have been following her this whole time, waiting to make a move—

Something brushed her back. She flinched.

"Whoa," Ed murmured. He raised his hands. "Sorry. I

just wanted to see what you were looking at." He moved closer to Mary in an effort to follow her line of sight. "What is it?"

Finally she willed herself to take a few steps back. "We—uh, we gotta get out of here," she stammered. "It's not . . . it's not . . ."

"It's not *what*? he whispered.

"Safe," she croaked.

Ed cleared his throat. "Um, Mary? You're starting to freak me out a little. Did a cop see Gaia?"

Mary couldn't answer. She could only stare at the beard and that fat, foul stomach.

A moment later Gaia ducked back out from behind the bushes—flushed and slightly disheveled. Her coat was unbuttoned, and her shoes were unlaced. She raised her hand in triumph, then paused.

"What's going on?" she asked.

"We gotta split," Mary found herself answering.

"What do you mean?" Gaia asked, glancing back toward the park.

Mary swallowed. It was getting dark. The sun had already sunk below the horizon. Twilight was settling over the park. Her eyes remained pinned on Skizz.

"Mary?" Gaia's voice grew urgent. "Do you recognize somebody over by the chess tables?"

"I . . ."

Skizz lifted his gaze.

He looked directly at Mary. For a terrible instant her body stiffened—petrified in the freezing December air. *I'm dead,* she realized.

As if reading her mind, he smiled and lifted his hand.

Then he drew his forefinger across his throat, very slowly.

"No," she whispered. She squeezed her eyes shut, half convinced that this was some terrible hallucination, some all too vivid nightmare.

Mary forced herself to open her eyes again. She blinked a few times. *What the—*

He was gone. Just like that. Vanished. Somehow that was even more terrifying than if he had hung around. Her gaze darted from face to face among the group at the chess tables, then up and down the various paths. She caught a glimpse of a hunched figure who might have been him, scurrying up toward Fifth Avenue . . . but she couldn't be sure. *Jesus.* Pent-up air flowed from her lungs. Her shoulders sagged.

"Can you please tell us what's going on?" Ed demanded.

Mary leaned on the back of his wheelchair for support. Her knees were wobbly. "It's nothing," she whispered. "I'm sorry. He . . . uh, he's not there anymore." She couldn't keep from shivering.

"Who?" Ed asked impatiently.

Mary glanced at Gaia. Had she seen?

There was no reason to dig up the past. They were having

so much fun. There was no reason for Ed and Gaia to know that she was paranoid about drug-crazed stalkers from coke deals gone bad.

Gaia chewed her lip for a moment. Her blond hair flapped in the bitter wind.

"Are you sure you're okay?" she said finally. She flashed Mary a quick smile. "Do you want to get out of here?"

And at that moment Mary realized something that she never had before: Having a friend meant being able to communicate without having to speak a word.

MIRACULOUS ZIT-RELATED PROMISES

"Riding the subway at night is dangerous."

It was one of those myths about New York City that Gaia had never understood. Like the one about how all New Yorkers talked with a ridiculous accent, like mobsters. Almost all of those myths were lies. She could hardly think of a safer place than the Uptown East Side number six local train. For one thing, there was plenty of light. The glare of those harsh fluorescent lights was practically blinding. And the subways were always *somewhat* crowded, no matter what the hour. They were also crawling with cops.

On the other hand, some lunatic could shove you onto the tracks or a pickpocket could snatch your wallet. And the cops were mostly slobs—stuffed to the gills with doughnuts and coffee. A lot could go wrong if a person was unprepared. Maybe it wasn't so much that the subways were dangerous. Maybe it was just that they were a playground of the unexpected.

That was why Gaia loved them so much.

"Do you think Ed's pissed at me?" Mary asked over the rhythmic roar of the train wheels.

Gaia shook her head, leaning back in the plastic seat. The only drag about the subway was that it was impossible to get comfortable. She inevitably found herself getting mushed next to somebody with terminal BO. And her butt always went to sleep. But at least the car was relatively empty.

"Why would he be pissed?" Gaia asked.

"Because I want to go uptown. And, you know . . ." She didn't finish.

Yes, Gaia knew. Mary felt guilty because going uptown meant ditching Ed. It was nearly impossible for guy in a wheelchair to ride the train.

"Believe me, Ed is psyched we left him behind," Gaia said.

"He was looking for an excuse to go home. I think he's had about enough of truth or dare. He probably would have been bummed if we'd taken a bus or a cab because that would have meant he had to come with us."

"Maybe." But Mary didn't look so sure. She sighed, gazing up at one of the glowing, plastic-encased advertisements above the seats facing theirs. Call Doctor Fitz Right Now! His Miraculous Laser Surgery Will Rid You of Acne Forever!

"What's wrong?" Gaia asked.

"Nothing." Mary shrugged. She seemed to be shaking off an unpleasant thought. "Uh, it's just . . . I've been spending a lot of time with Ed lately, you know? And he and I used to be friends. Not *best* friends, but on and off since we were kids." She paused. "Before the accident. It's just weird."

Gaia nodded. Something about Mary's tone struck a strange chord inside her. Had there been some history between her and Ed?

"I mean, we didn't go out or anything," Mary added quickly, answering Gaia's unspoken question. "But we hung out a lot. The thing is, I never feel comfortable around him anymore. And it's all because of that stupid-ass wheelchair. And I know it's ridiculous. It's all in my head. He's still the same person—"

"Don't worry," Gaia soothed. "That kind of thing is natural."

Mary sighed. "Yeah, I guess you're right," she mumbled.

"I just wish I had the freaking guts to tell him exactly what was on my mind. . . ."

Gaia kept nodding, but Mary's words floated past her. She was overcome by a sudden and shocking thought: I feel normal. Yes. It was incredible. Here she was, talking to a girl—a *friend*, no less—about another friend. Listening. Offering comfort and advice. The way a normal kid would do. *Her.* Gaia Moore. The freak of nature.

When was the last time she had comforted or advised *anyone*?

Her throat tightened. For a second she was worried she might burst into tears. Jesus. She had to get a grip on herself. This was *not* a big deal. Most people had these kinds of conversations every single day of their lives. But the worst problem with her inability to feel fear was that certain other feelings became exaggerated—probably as some kind of perverse compensation. And in this instance it was gooey sentimentality.

". . . boring you to death, aren't I?" Mary was asking.

"Huh?" Gaia shook her head and forced a smile. "No. Sorry. I was just zoning out."

"Well, *I'm* bored to death," Mary said. She raised her eyebrows. "Besides, aren't we forgetting something?"

The train began to slow down.

"What's that?" Gaia asked.

"The *game*, dummy. It's still your turn, right? Why—"

"Seventy-seventh Street!" a voice blared over the loudspeakers.

An impish smile spread across Mary's face. "This is our stop," she said. Suddenly she pointed at Dr. Fitz's miraculous zit-related promises. "I dare you to steal that poster."

The wheels screeched loudly.

Gaia laughed. No way. Mary had to be kidding. It would be impossible to pry that poster from its frame and still exit the train in time. Besides, getting that poster would mean flexing her muscles, which would mean revealing her very abnormal strength to a bunch of strangers—which she hated about as much as she hated being in the presence of Heather Gannis. On the other hand, she always *did* like a challenge.

Impatient-looking commuters gathered by the doors.

"It's now or never," Mary taunted, hopping up from her seat.

The train lurched to a halt.

Gaia's eyes darted around the car. She could do this. She was smiling now, too—smiling in a pulsating, euphoric state of readiness. So Mary thought she could get the best of her, huh? Fat chance.

Her limbs tensed.

Amazing how a simple dare could turn a normal subway exit into a potentially dangerous offense. She had about five seconds. There was only one way to do it. . . .

The doors hissed open.

Before her thoughts were even fully formed, she sprang from her seat and grabbed one of the subway poles, using the momentum to deliver a lightning-fast jump kick. Her leg lashed upward in a blur. The people at the door gasped. The tip of her sneaker struck the plastic with such force and precision that the entire plate instantly shattered.

Whoops.

Senseless vandalism wasn't exactly something Gaia approved of, but this Doctor Fitz sounded like a rip-off artist. Definitely. No way some quack could rid a person of acne forever. She was performing a public service by destroying his false advertising. Well, maybe not. But it was too late to second-guess herself. As she landed, she swiped the crumpled poster from its broken frame—tearing it in half in the process.

Whoops again.

Whatever. Half the poster was good enough. She caught a glimpse of Mary's mile-wide grin. Why wasn't she running? This was no time for horsing around—

"Hey!" a gruff male voice barked. "What the hell do you think you're doing?"

Speak of the devil. A pudgy cop with powdered sugar stains on his blue uniform was at the opposite end of the car. Gaia hadn't even noticed him. But he posed no problem. She was already using the remaining force of her movement to propel her out the door. With her free hand she grabbed Mary's coat sleeve and yanked her out on the platform.

"Freeze!" the cop cried. His face reddened. "You two girls! Don't move—"

The doors slid shut, silencing him.

He was still yelling and gesturing frantically—but Gaia knew there was nothing he could do. The train was pulling from the station. The piercing shriek of the wheels drowned out any other noise. Watching him was like watching a movie with the sound off.

Within seconds he was gone.

"Wow, Gaia!" Mary cried breathlessly. She started cracking up. "Damn! That *ruled*!"

Gaia shook her head. She laughed, too—but she wasn't quite sure how she felt. She glanced around the station. Several onlookers were glaring at them. Bad sign. Time to haul ass out of here before one of them called another cop. She didn't exactly feel like spending the night in a jail cell. Or explaining to George and Ella why she had been arrested . . .

"Come on," she whispered, tugging Mary toward the exit. She broke into a jog. Mary scrambled after her. Their shoes clattered on the concrete. "We gotta split."

"I think that was the coolest thing I've ever seen," Mary gasped.

The coolest? That wasn't the word Gaia would have

used. Silliest was more like it. Or dumbest. But as the two of them hurtled through the turnstiles and dashed upstairs into the wintry Manhattan night, she had to admit something.

The thrill of being bad was undeniable.

She laughed again despite herself. That had been a lot of fun. More fun than she would have expected. Best of all, her real life—the one filled with loneliness and rejection and uncertainty—seemed very, very far away.

PRODUCT IMPROVEMENT

The Moss girl *was* a danger.

Loki knew that now. Her danger lay in her stupidity. And apparently, judging from Gaia's latest stunt, that stupidity was contagious.

He scowled as he stood on the corner of Seventy-seventh Street and Lexington Avenue, watching Gaia and her new friend vanish into a mob of pedestrians. This behavior was unacceptable. Absolutely. Gaia's sudden penchant for delinquency called attention to herself. And it had the potential to give her a name and a face among the local authorities—at the very moment he most needed her to be anonymous.

He pulled a cell phone from his overcoat pocket and punched in a series of ten digits, then turned and abruptly strode east toward Third Avenue.

Loki often managed to forget that Gaia was a child. More specifically, that she was a teenager: a swirling vortex of hormonally fueled contradictions. He'd always thought of her as a *product*. He viewed her as the sum total of her unique genetic makeup, of her early environment—but most of all, of her training. Yet it was now clear to him that her training hadn't been rigorous enough. His brother had done a worse job than he'd previously suspected.

But he would show her the value of discipline. She would learn to exercise better judgment. Emotion and insecurity were not supposed to cloud reason. Not in someone of Gaia's . . . caliber.

He paused on the corner of Seventy-seventh and Third.

The intersection was very well lit. Christmas lights in apartment and shop windows cast the street in a multicolored glow. A few passersby jostled him. He surveyed his surroundings just to make sure he wasn't being watched or followed. Security checks were usually unnecessary; still, one could never be too careful. It was a lesson he'd learned from the very beginning. He never forgot it. *His* training had been effective.

He heard the sound of the black Mercedes long before it rolled to a stop beside him. The engine had a distinct timbre, like a person's voice. It was his home away from home. His traveling headquarters.

Under normal circumstances the driver opened the door for him. But he was too cold and too annoyed for formalities. He ducked inside.

The red-haired woman behind the wheel glanced in the rearview mirror.

He slammed the door. The car pulled into the traffic and began to speed downtown.

"Your instincts were right," he told her.

She nodded. "How do you want to proceed?"

"We wait," he stated.

"But . . ." Her brow grew furrowed.

"I want to see how far she can be pushed. I want to know exactly what she's capable of. Peer pressure was a factor I'd never even considered. I'm sure she'll snap out of it."

The woman's lips tightened. "You think so? I think—"

"I don't like your tone," Loki interrupted. "Remember our little talk about focus?"

She didn't reply.

"If she allows herself to be manipulated to the point of

real trouble, we'll have to intervene on her behalf," he said, mostly to himself. "We don't have the time to sit back and watch her training deteriorate further. My hope is that she'll come to her senses." He sighed grimly. "I don't want to have to deal with her friend. Her psyche is fragile enough. An accident now will just complicate matters."

THE CHRISTMAS SPIRIT

MAYBE IT WAS TIME FOR ANOTHER WHACK. GAIA HAD VOWED NEVER TO PUNCH HER EVER AGAIN—BUT HEY, PEOPLE BROKE PROMISES ALL THE TIME.

NEXT YEAR IN JERUSALEM

Tom Moore longed for a piece of paper and a pen. But in Moscow even the most basic luxuries were sometimes impossible to find. The hotel could provide him with vodka, with bad coffee—but on the day before Christmas, they were out of everything else. Even lightbulbs. His spartan room had a desk, but no desk lamp. And he needed light, too. The days were short at this time of year, and the sun hadn't risen. The only light in the room came from a flickering lamp by his bed, which looked like it had been manufactured during World War II. It was too dim to read or write by.

He shook his head.

Why did they have to assign him to Moscow? Why did they have to torture him?

But the answer was simple enough. He knew the language. He knew the culture. He stretched out on the mattress. It reeked of mothballs.

He closed his eyes and thought of Gaia. He was halfway around the world from her today . . . not too far from where her mother's family had lived for hundreds of years.

The thought made him draw in his breath, wincing involuntarily.

"Katia," he whispered. It had been five years since her death, but her beautiful face floated in black space before him as clearly as if he were staring at a photograph . . . so much like Gaia's. He shook his head. His lids remained tightly shut. Whenever he came to Russia, Katia's memory clung to him like a shroud, smothering him.

He wondered if Gaia could remember how much Katia had loved her. How she lit up whenever her daughter walked into a room. He wondered if Gaia blamed him for her death—something he'd wondered a million times before. Surely she at least blamed him for disappearing from her life. How could she ever understand he had done it for her safety?

Tom shivered. The hotel room was cold. Outside, a blizzard was raging. It was probably twenty degrees below Fahrenheit out there. But he knew the room wouldn't get any warmer than this. The radiator was turned up as high as it would go, clanking and hissing noisily in the corner. When he'd turned it on, he'd sent cockroaches scurrying.

God, he hated the solitude. He was half tempted to fly to New York immediately, to rush to the Nivens' house and sweep Gaia in his arms—just to have the chance to gaze upon her face . . . but that was impossible. Even watching from afar placed her in jeopardy—

The cell phone at his feet rang. His jaw tightened. Even on Christmas Eve they wouldn't leave him alone. Of course not. He had a job to do. He snatched at the phone, struggling to shake Gaia from his mind.

"Yes?" he croaked.

"Package arriving at eleven hundred, sir," a clipped female voice stated.

"Understood," he replied.

"Sir, it's imperative that we intercept—"

"Understood," Tom repeated again, and disconnected the line.

He forced himself from the mattress. His limbs creaked as he stood in the cold room. He felt a quick flash of anger but thrust it aside. After all his years of service his colleagues and underlings still felt the need to remind him of how "imperative" it was that he perform his duties. He'd personally thwarted over two dozen assassination attempts, bombings, and coups. Yet they always spoke to him as if this were his first mission.

He knew that they were only doing their job, of course. And he knew better than to let his mood affect his work. This was a particularly sensitive matter. The "package" contained plutonium—several million dollars' worth. It was being smuggled from nuclear bases outside Moscow to Afghanistan, then places unknown. If it were to fall into the wrong hands . . .

He knew all of this. He knew that if he failed, there was a chance he could endanger millions of lives. Still, it was amazing how the threat of nuclear terrorism could seem so unimportant in the face of the fact that he couldn't hug his own daughter on Christmas.

THE ARMED TRUCE

It was nearly one o'clock by the time Gaia tiptoed up to the brownstone on Perry Street.

She prayed that Ella and George were asleep. She had a feeling they weren't. Or at least Ella wasn't. The living-room light was on. It was strange: The emotion Gaia felt as she turned the key in the front door was probably the closest she would ever come to fear. She wasn't scared, of course. But she felt an undeniable reluctance. It was the reluctance of having to occupy the same general space as Ella—and in the worst-case scenario, actually engage in dialogue with her.

As quietly as she could, she pushed open the door.

"Where the hell have you been?"

Gaia bowed her head. The reluctance was justified.

"Look, Ella—"

"You can't go on treating us this way."

Please. Gaia closed the door. Ella was standing in the middle of the narrow hall. Arms folded across her chest. Nostrils flaring. Wearing that absurd leather miniskirt. Maybe she needed another reminder of how *not* to deal with Gaia. The last time they had gotten into a screaming argument, Gaia had punched her. It had been a reflex; Ella had said something so cruel and horrible that it couldn't be forgiven . . . but at least after that, she had contented herself with being a normal, run-of-the-mill bitch. The blow had frightened her. Maybe it was time for another whack. Gaia had vowed never to punch her ever again—but hey, people broke promises all the time.

"Answer me!" Ella barked.

"What's the question?" Gaia asked.

Ella's green eyes narrowed into slits. "Do you really think you can keep on waltzing in and out of here any time of day or night? Do you have any idea what the consequences will be?"

Here we go again, Gaia thought. She slipped out of her coat and hung it in the front hall closet. Ella *did* need another reminder. The Evil Twin was back.

Sometime in the past couple of months Ella had been afflicted with an acute case of multiple-personality disorder. Sometimes she was the surrogate mom. Sometimes she was the doting wife, who pretended to hang on George's every word. (That personality was particularly nauseating.) But other times, like now, she was the Evil Twin. The Wicked Witch of the West Village. A psychopath. Someone out of control.

There was only one reason for the switches, Gaia figured. The woman had a hidden agenda. She was obviously a schemer—and occasionally all the deception took its toll. Maybe she was stealing George's money. It would make sense. There was no way Ella could support herself without him. She was supposed to be this up-and-coming photographer, but Gaia hadn't seen *one* picture she had taken—other than the lame ones in this house. And they certainly weren't of publishable quality. Yes, maybe she was embezzling from George, siphoning his funds into various offshore bank accounts—and then *poof!*—she'd disappear.

Maybe she would even do it sometime soon. George would be a lot better off. Gaia could always hope.

"Don't you have anything to say for yourself?" Ella demanded.

"Like what?"

"Like why you're wandering the streets two days before Christmas?"

"I didn't realize Christmas Eve *Eve* was such a big deal in the Niven household," Gaia replied evenly.

Ella's face darkened. "Well, maybe if you actually spent some *time* here, things would be different," she snapped.

"I spend lots of time here," Gaia muttered. "I probably spend more time here than *you* do. You're the one who's never around."

"That—that . . . that's completely untrue," Ella sputtered.

Gaia suppressed a smile. For once, Ella didn't have a comeback. Of course not. She knew that Gaia was absolutely right.

"You are so goddamn selfish," Ella whispered. "George worries about you so much, and all you do is torture him with your—"

"You know, it's funny, Ella," Gaia interrupted. "You're always yelling at me about how I torture George. But he and I get along fine. When he's actually here."

Ella shook her head. She looked like she could spontaneously combust.

"Besides," Gaia added calmly, "I'm not the one torturing him. You are."

"*Excuse* me?" Ella barked.

"You're hiding something from him," Gaia stated.

Ella's eyes turned to ice. Neither of them moved. It was as if they were on-screen, playing roles in a film that had been paused in the middle of a scene.

Gaia met her gaze unflinchingly.

"You're obviously up to something," she said. "And it's something you don't want George or me to know about. This *act* you play around the house isn't the real you. I don't know what is."

Ella blinked.

The mere batting of eyelashes could betray so much. In that instant Gaia knew that her suspicions were right: Ella *was* a fraud. Something in her face had changed—very subtly and only for the briefest moment. It was as if a mask had slipped. And the expression underneath registered an emotion Gaia had never seen in Ella before. Fear. The fear of being exposed.

"You have no idea what you're talking about," Ella

whispered. But the words were flat, unconvincing.

"Look, I don't know what kind of scam you're running," Gaia grumbled. "And to be honest, I really don't care. I just want to be able to cohabitate in peace, all right? We owe George that much at the very least. Even *you* can appreciate that."

In a flash the mask was back in place. Ella took two quick steps forward. "I will *not* be accused of this . . . this *crap* in my own house!" she snarled.

Oooh. Scary. If only Ella knew that she intimidated Gaia about as much as a newborn puppy, they could avoid these cheesy showdowns.

Gaia took two steps forward as well. Their faces were now only inches apart.

"Then let's do something about it," Gaia murmured.

Ella blinked again. "What are you talking about?"

"I propose a bargain," Gaia said. "In keeping with the Christmas spirit. An armed truce. Like what the opposing armies did in World War I."

"Like *who* did?"

Sometimes Gaia had a hard time remembering that age and ignorance were not mutually exclusive. Ella probably didn't know jack shit about World War I. She didn't seem to know anything about history, or literature, or politics—or anything that mattered, really. The sum total of her worldly knowledge was limited to the careers of Mariah Carey and Celine Dion.

"It was Christmas Day in 1916, in France," Gaia explained impatiently. "The Allies and Germans came out of the trenches and played soccer with each other. They acted like friends. Then the next day they went back to their trenches and started killing each other again."

Ella snorted. "You're not making any sense, Gaia."

The woman's thickness was astounding. "Fine." Gaia moaned. "Then let me spell it out for you. On Christmas let's just put all this BS behind us. Let's act civil. I won't tell George you're playing him for a chump, and you won't tell me how to live my life. For twenty-four hours we'll act like a normal family." She flashed a big, fake smile. "Deal?"

Before Ella could respond, Gaia brushed past her and marched up the stairs.

"There's only one problem," Ella called after her. Her voice was mocking.

"What's that?" Gaia asked, rolling her eyes.

"You said an 'armed truce.' But we're not armed. Not unless you're hiding a gun in your room. Which wouldn't surprise me."

Gaia paused on the top step. *Oh, please.* A month ago Ella thought she was hiding drugs. Now guns. What next? Uranium?

"We're armed with our secrets," Gaia said without turning around. "I'd say that's plenty of ammunition, wouldn't you?"

FROM: gaia13@alloymail.com
TO: maryubuggin@alloymail.com
RE: Why Christmas sucks
TIME: 1:34 P.M.

Mary—
You would not believe the shit I had to deal with this morning. George bought me a pink cashmere sweater that could barely fit a five-year-old. It was nice, but I'm worried he thinks everyone under forty dresses like his wife. That's George for you. Sweet but clueless. Then Ella screamed at me for (a) not buying George a gift and (b) not being more appreciative. I told her that I didn't celebrate any Christian holidays, as I worshiped the devil. She didn't find it funny. So how was your morning? Merry Christmas, by the way.

FROM: maryubuggin@alloymail.com
TO: gaia13@alloymail.com
RE: Holidays with the ex-coke fiend
TIME: 2:34 P.M.

Get this, Gaia. The only presents I got were books about the dangers of drugs and alcohol. It was like a comedy skit or something. *Drinking: A Love Story*, *Go Ask Alice*, *Smack* . . . My family must have bought out the Addiction & Recovery section of the bookstore. It's enough to make a girl want to freebase. Just kidding. Anyway, ready for some more truth or dare? How does tonight sound? I can't wait to get out of this apartment. Everybody keeps trying to get me to confess all the terrible things I did and to talk about my feelings. I feel like I'm on *Oprah*.

FROM: gaia13@alloymail.com
TO: smoon@alloymail.com
RE: [no subject]
TIME: 3:01 P.M.

Hey, Sam. I was just writing to say Merry Christmas. I haven't seen you in a while. By the way, did we kiss on Thanksgiving, or was that just in my head? I didn't
«DELETE»

FROM: gaia13@alloymail.com
TO: smoon@alloymail.com
RE: [no subject]
TIME: 3:03 P.M.

I love you. I love you. I love you. I
«DELETE»

FROM: gaia13@alloymail.com
TO: smoon@alloymail.com
RE: [no subject]
TIME: 3:05 P.M.

Hey, Sam. Want to play chess sometime? I think you need a good ass kicking.
«DELETE»

DÉJÀ VU

NEVER BEFORE HAD SHE SO LONGED TO BE SOMEONE ELSE, IN ANOTHER PLACE—A MILLION LIGHT-YEARS FROM THIS LIVING HELL.

LIGHTNING STRIKES

Sam Moon was not a superstitious kind of guy. He didn't believe that he would be cursed for all eternity if a black cat crossed his path or that he would be stricken with cancer if he walked under a ladder. He didn't believe in *any* of that garbage. Life was not about luck. And contrary to *Forrest Gump,* life was not a box of chocolates, either. Life was a game of chess. Life was about strategy. About seeing the big picture. Fate played no part in it. He'd learned that at a very young age, when he'd first started hustling chess games.

So why had he come back to New York?

Good question. Why had he left his home in Maryland and taken the train all the way back to Manhattan on Christmas night? Because he honestly believed that if Gaia had miraculously appeared in his dorm room on Thanksgiving, there was a chance she might show up on Christmas as well? Was that *really* the reason?

Yes. It was pitiful and wrong and self-defeating, but that *was* the reason. He was actually hoping fate would bring him and Gaia together again. In spite of everything. In spite of the fact that she'd stated very clearly that it wasn't going to happen between the two of them.

So he was actually relying on luck. He was relying on her to change her mind. Him. Mr. Strategy.

He stood outside the grim dormitory building on West Eleventh Street, gazing up at the rows of darkened windows. He'd told his parents that he had to come back early to make up a physics lab assignment. Which was partially true, in a way. He *did* have to make up a lab assignment. Just not until after New Year's Day.

He should have stayed at home. He'd known that the moment he left, and still he'd come all the way back. His teeth were chattering. A light snow was falling. He was freezing his ass off. There was no *way* Gaia would come here tonight. As the cliché said: Lightning never struck twice in the same place. He could have been sitting by the fireplace right now, sipping a nice, hot mug of cider (his mom made *killer* cider), playing chess with Dad. . . .

The old, familiar anger returned.

He *should* be home. He shouldn't be thinking about Gaia at all. She was with her boyfriend. Whoever the hell *he* was. How could she have sent him that e-mail? Because she didn't have the guts to blow him off in person or even over the phone? Yes. She was a coward. A phony. And how could she have been so cold? Couldn't she have said something different? Like: *Dear Sam, Thanks very much for the beautiful chessboard you gave me. I'm sorry I have a boyfriend, but I'll cherish it always. Love, Gaia.*

But no. For all he knew, she had thrown his gift in the garbage. It was a special gift, a *personal* gift, and she didn't care. She didn't care about anything else, either. Like the fact that he'd gotten her to the hospital that Thanksgiving night—the night they kissed. The night he thought they were destined to be together. He'd never experienced a more perfect, magical moment. It was the greatest kiss of his life. . . .

In *his* mind, though. Not hers. A not so subtle distinction.

Clearly she'd been delirious. She probably had no memory of the kiss. No, she probably *did* remember it—but now was so ashamed and humiliated that she was doing her best to avoid him. She probably cringed every time she thought of it. Kicked herself. Made a sour face.

But even as images of Gaia's rejection whirled through his mind, he couldn't help but long for her even *more.* The less she wanted him, the more tantalizing she became.

He shivered again. He'd catch pneumonia if he stayed out here any longer. So he figured he had two options. Option one: He could go upstairs, sit alone in his squalid little dorm room, and stay up all night, thinking about Gaia. Option two: He could go to Heather's house and forget about Gaia altogether.

Gritting his teeth, he turned away from the dorm and headed in the direction of the subway. He'd cut through the park and get there in no time. Yes. This was the right decision. It was time to finish the process he'd started three weeks ago—the process of making up with Heather. Of recognizing how lucky he was for having such an amazingly beautiful girlfriend. They were finally back on track. They were enjoying each other in a way they hadn't since they first started going out. Besides, the Gannis family would probably *love* to see him on Christmas night. And Heather would be thrilled. Of course.

Unfortunately, he happened to catch a glimpse of his distorted reflection in the windshield of a parked car. Shit. He wasn't exactly looking his best. *Would* Heather be happy to see him? His skin was pale. His nose was bright red. His tousled brownish blond hair was matted and covered with snow. And his new wool overcoat made him look like a desperate old pervert. Which in a way, he was—

Wait a second.

He heard laughter. *Familiar* laughter. Coming from the park. He rounded the corner of Eleventh and Fifth, peering through the snowflakes at the Arc de Triomphe. Yes . . . somebody was in there, behind the arch, weaving in and out of the leafless trees. Two people, in fact. Girls. Young. NYU students, maybe, like him. He picked up his pace, crossing Tenth Street in a hurry. His eyes narrowed. One had red hair. . . . They looked like they were chasing each other.

Another round of giggles echoed off the buildings. Whoever they were, they were having fun. But what were they doing out here on Christmas night?

Actually, the better question was: What was *he* doing

out here on Christmas night? Yes. That was the better question. As usual, he was looking for Gaia. But Gaia didn't want his company. No, it was very obvious that she'd found a new scene. A new boyfriend, to be specific. Or an old boyfriend—"from before"—as her e-mail said. Whatever. Either way, she'd moved on. No wonder she hadn't thanked him for his gift. She'd left Sam Moon behind for better things—

"Sam?"

He whirled around. His eyes bulged.

Maybe he *would* start being superstitious.

Tonight might just be his lucky night.

NO WORDS NECESSARY

If Heather Gannis had any doubts that Sam would be happy to see her, they immediately vanished. His face was lit up like an electronic billboard. Before she knew it, he was sweeping her into an embrace. He practically cut off circulation to the lower half of her body. Well. *This* was a surprise. She wasn't sure if they had officially made up. All their conversations since Thanksgiving had been so . . . *uncertain.*

"What are you doing here?" he cried.

"I called you at home to wish you a merry Christmas," she said. She took a deep breath and gently extricated herself from Sam's arms, brushing a few strands of long, dark hair out of her eyes. "Your parents told me that you came back early. I figured you'd be here. I thought I'd surprise you."

"I'm glad you did," he murmured.

She stared into his eyes. Ever since their troubles started, it seemed the best response she could get out of him was a strained smile and faraway look. But now she saw something new. Or something old, really. Focus. He was entirely *here.* With her. In the moment. Just like when they first started going out all those months ago. It had been so long since he'd been able to gaze at her the way he was gazing at her now. Even when they had made love that one time, he'd seemed distant—as if his brain were disconnected and his body was on autopilot. And then when Gaia Moore walked in on them, it was clear that his mind *had* been elsewhere.

But maybe he had finally gotten over her. The psycho. The bitch who had single-handedly nearly destroyed Heather's life. Of course, there was no point in thinking about Gaia right now. Wherever she was, she wasn't with them—and that was good enough.

"So what are you doing out here in the cold?" she asked. "It's freezing."

"Going to look for you," he answered.

"Well, you found me," she whispered. He couldn't have given her a better reply if she had scripted it herself. Her pulse picked up a beat. She saw something else in his eyes, too. Desire. Yes. It had been a *very* long time since she'd seen that. For all of Heather's popularity and good looks, for all of her supposed confidence and charm, she knew she was very insecure at heart. A strange pain stirred in her stomach. That was probably why she'd allowed herself to end up in bed with Charlie Salita a couple of weeks ago. But there was no point in thinking about *him*, either. Or the fact that she still didn't know if he'd raped her. . . .

Sam bit his lip. "Heather, I—"

"Let's not talk," she interrupted. Her voice was barely a whisper. "Let's just be together. We don't need to say anything. Not yet, anyway."

He nodded.

Without a word, he took her hand and led her back down Fifth Avenue to his dormitory.

TRAINING SCHOOL FOR BADASSES

"Hey! Gaia! Wait up!"

Mary's lungs were about to explode. There was no way she could keep chasing that girl. For one thing, Gaia was in superhuman shape. For another, Mary's own body was still rebounding from years of drug abuse. She wasn't exactly in marathon condition.

"What's the matter?" Gaia taunted from the end of the block. "I'm not too fast for you, am I? Come on. How badly do you want your wallet back?"

Go ahead and keep it, Mary wanted to answer. But all that came out of her mouth was a pathetic little gasp. She leaned against a lamppost, struggling to catch her breath. She sucked in huge gulps of freezing air. It felt like ice was tearing into her chest. She couldn't get enough oxygen. Whoa. She was actually kind of dizzy. Her head throbbed. Purplish dots swam before her eyes.

"Mary?" Gaia called. Her tone suddenly became serious. "Are you all right?"

Mary shook her head. No. *All right* would not be the phrase she'd use to describe herself right now. But in spite of the fact that she was mildly afraid of dropping dead, she couldn't help but feel embarrassed. This was so lame. Here she was, a seventeen-year-old girl, in the prime of her life—and she was legitimately worried about heart failure. Christ. But that was what she deserved, she supposed. It was amazing she *hadn't* dropped dead yet.

On the plus side, all the running around had taken her mind off Skizz. Because there was a very good chance Skizz would be lurking around the shadows here somewhere, trying to sell his product. Or looking for her.

Gaia ran back down the street. Her face was creased with concern. "Hey," she called. "What's the matter?"

"Nothing, nothing," Mary mumbled. Gradually her dizziness faded. Her rattling pulse slowed. She straightened, using the metal pole to hoist herself up. "It's just . . . ah, I guess I'm kind of winded. That's all. It'll pass."

"Are you sure?" Gaia asked, peering into Mary's face.

Mary nodded. She forced herself to forget about Skizz. "You know, I should have known better than to dare you to steal something valuable of mine," she muttered with a smirk. "It figures you'd be a great pickpocket."

Gaia raised her eyebrows, pretending to be offended. "Oh, yeah? Why's that?"

"It just goes along with your other talents," Mary said. Her breathing finally evened. "Did you, like, go to some special training school for badasses when you were a kid?"

"Hey," Gaia protested, wagging a finger at her. "No truths, remember?"

Mary rolled her eyes. "But that's just a question. It's not part of the—"

"Uh-uh," Gaia interrupted. "Anyway, you can't ask me anything. It's your turn." She handed Mary's wallet back to her. "So what'll it be? Truth or dare?"

"Well, I'm way too spent for a dare," Mary mumbled, shoving her wallet back into her inside coat pocket. How *had* Gaia managed to swipe it, anyway? But there was no point in asking herself that question. Gaia would never tell her. "I think you're gonna have to truth me."

Gaia smiled. Her eyes sparkled in the pale light of the streetlamp. She glanced around the deserted street, tapping a gloved finger against her chin. "Hmmm. Let's see. . . . Let's see. . . . Okay, I got one. Truth: What's the worst possible thing you could dare me to do?"

Mary had to laugh. "You know, I'm starting to worry about you," she said. "Thanks to all the books I got for Christmas, I'm an expert at recognizing the symptoms of addiction. And you, my friend, are definitely a dare addict."

"Who, *me?*" Gaia asked sarcastically. She shook her head. "Mary, that's not it at all. It's just that it's about minus fourteen degrees out here with the windchill factor, and I want to keep moving. Truths are way too inactive." She hopped up and down and rubbed the sleeves of her coat for dramatic effect. "So? What is it?"

"What's what?"

"What's the worst possible thing you can dare me to do?" Gaia asked impatiently.

Mary thought for a moment. Now that her cardiovascular system had reached a relative state of normalcy again, she was beginning to realize that Gaia was right: It *was* freezing out here. Whatever this dare was, it would have to involve warmth. And it would have to involve Mary, too. And maybe some more layers of clothing . . .

Aha. Yes. There was a simple way to satisfy all three needs.

"You know, it occurs to me that a lot of NYU students live around here," Mary said, glancing up at the row houses on MacDougal Street. "And I bet they're all gone for the holidays. So here it is. I dare you to sneak into somebody's room and steal all their clothes."

Gaia pursed her lips. "Mary," she said with a groan. "Come on. We shouldn't steal from people, you know? I feel bad enough about the subway thing—"

"You can return the clothes tomorrow," Mary interrupted. "They'll never know the difference. And I'll come with you. That way if we get caught, we'll both share the blame."

"Yeah, but . . ." Gaia still didn't look convinced.

"Hey," Mary said, shrugging nonchalantly. "You asked me what the worst dare is I could think of, and that's it. Go and steal somebody's clothes. And it's not even that bad. I mean, I'm coming with you." She grinned. "Now, does this mean the great Gaia Moore is wimping out on me? Does this mean I won the game?"

"You wish," Gaia said. She started smiling again, too. "All right. So which dorm?"

"Any one you want," Mary said. "There's a bunch over on Eleventh Street."

All at once Gaia's smile vanished.

"What is it?" Mary asked.

"Uh . . . nothing. I was just thinking that Sam Moon lives around here. He . . . uh, he lives on that block. I could take *his* stuff."

Mary hesitated. "Wait a sec. This wouldn't be an excuse to piss Heather off, would it?"

Gaia laughed grimly and shook her head.

"Well, okay," Mary answered uncertainly. She studied Gaia's face. Something strange was going on here. For the first time ever, Gaia did not look supremely confident. No. She looked . . . well, *sad*. She was clearly hiding something. Not that this was anything new. But usually when somebody mentioned Heather's name, Gaia became *angry*—not sad. So . . . this wasn't about Heather. This was about Sam. There obviously *was* some kind of history between Sam and Gaia.

So . . . maybe this would be a good way to find out what was going on. Maybe Mary could actually pry a truth out of Gaia without having to actually truth her. It was worth a shot.

"Ready?" Gaia asked.

"I'm ready if you are," Mary said.

THE ANSWER

Gaia still wasn't sure exactly *why* she'd decided to break into Sam's dorm. It was an undeniably stupid thing to do. But in a crazy way, she was actually sort of hoping that Sam would be there. Because then she'd finally get the answer to the question that had been gnawing at her sanity for a month: *Did we kiss or not?*

And then she'd be able to get on with her life. For better or for worse.

Getting past the security guard was no problem at all. Gaia had come up with a foolproof system for sneaking into Sam's dorm on Thanksgiving night. She'd tripped the guard's car alarm. The piercing siren was the only thing that could get the guy to leave his post. He always parked his car right outside the building—probably so he could keep an eye on it.

Sure enough, Gaia saw the car the instant she and Mary turned off Fifth Avenue onto West Eleventh Street. It was a fairly nondescript American sedan—but the telltale sign was its ridiculous vanity plate: RANGERFAN.

Why was it that all macho meatheads had sports-related vanity plates?

"Stay back a sec," she instructed Mary.

Mary paused on the sidewalk. Gaia crept along the side of the building and peered around the corner into the entranceway. There the guard was, sitting in the lobby, his pudgy face lit up with a bluish glow from the flickering light of the TV screen. She almost felt bad for him. Nobody should have to work on Christmas night. It was just too depressing.

Oh, well. At least she would liven up his shift.

Mary tiptoed up behind her. "What's going on?" she whispered.

"We gotta get past the guard," Gaia whispered back.

Ducking down, she scoured the ground for something to throw at the car. . . . *Bingo.* There was an empty forty-ounce bottle of malt liquor near the curb. She scuttled over and grabbed it, then ran back to Mary.

"What are you gonna do?" Mary asked. Her forehead was wrinkled, but she was smiling. "You aren't gonna crack that over his head, are you?"

"Please," Gaia moaned with a giggle. "I'm not into victimization, remember? All you have to do is follow me into the building as fast as you can. Ready?"

"Uh . . . I guess so. . . ."

Gaia hurled the bottle directly at the license plate. It spun end over end and smashed into the car just over the rear fender, exploding in a loud shatter. Almost instantaneously the car alarm erupted. The sound of the siren tore through the icy night.

"Jesus!" Mary hissed. She bit her lip, trying to keep from laughing.

Three seconds later the guard came bounding out the door.

So predictable. Like clockwork. He ran right up to the rear fender and scowled at it, then glanced out onto the street—in the opposite direction of Gaia and Mary. Perfect. Gaia tapped Mary's shoulder and bolted into the lobby. The blast of heated, indoor air washed over her like an invisible tidal wave—sending much needed relief to her chilled bones. Mary followed close on her heels. Gaia pulled her into the stairwell.

"What floor?" Mary whispered.

"Fourth."

Excitement fizzed in Gaia's veins as she hurried up the flights of stairs. She was barely conscious of Mary's wheezing behind her. A dozen disjointed memories swirled through her mind: sneaking into Sam's room and taking a shower . . . the time she walked in on him and Heather in bed . . . the dream of that wonderful kiss and his words in her ear: *"I love you"* . . . she shook her head. Goose bumps rose on her arms.

"This is it?" Mary whispered when they reached the fourth-floor landing.

Gaia nodded.

"Good," Mary said. "Because I'm about to pass out again."

As quietly as she could, Gaia crept into the hall outside Sam's suite—then stopped in her tracks. The door was open. Was somebody there?

"What is it?" Mary asked.

Gaia shook her head. The faintest scrap of conversation drifted past her ears. It was completely unintelligible; she couldn't even tell if it was a boy or girl—but *somebody* was there. She took another two steps forward—

"My God, Sam," a girl's voice whispered. "That was incredible. . . ."

Oh, no. Not her.

Gaia's knees turned to jelly. The sound of that voice was like a sword, shredding her insides. Never before had she so longed to be someone else, in another place—a million light-years from this living hell.

The voice belonged to Heather Gannis.

Gaia was sure of it. There was no doubt in her mind.

And in that instant she had her answer. Her throat tightened. Sam *hadn't* kissed her that night. He might have brought her to the hospital; he might have even bundled her up in his clothes—but that was it. Why had she come here? It was like déjà vu. She had walked in on the boy she loved most in the arms of the girl she hated most. She didn't even have to *see* them to know that they were together in bed. No, Heather's few husky words painted a perfectly clear picture. And there was nothing Gaia could do to stop them. Sam Moon didn't love her. He loved Heather Gannis. Period.

"Gaia?" Mary whispered.

She turned around, her lips trembling.

Mary was still standing by the stairwell door. She looked very afraid.

"I don't think I can do this," Gaia choked out. "I think I have to get out of here. . . ."

She was barely aware of Mary's leading her back down the stairs and into the freezing night. It was hard to see through the tears.

BAD DEBTS

SKIZZ CHUCKLED. HIS LAUGH WAS VERY EASYGOING AND FRIENDLY—WHICH SOMEHOW ONLY MADE IT MORE TERRIFYING. "THEN WE HAVE A PROBLEM," HE SAID.

CALL NUMBER ONE . . .

If Mary could count on *one* thing in life, it was that Gaia Moore would end up okay. Gaia Moore would always find a way to survive, no matter how bad things got. So there was no point in worrying. Right?

Wrong, a silent voice answered.

In the old days, Mary used to tune out that voice by doing a quick blast of coke. She shook her head. Bad to think of coke. Very bad. She paced the floor of her vast bedroom, kicking through the clothes that were strewn everywhere. Amazing how depressing the place looked when she wasn't high. Even after a month of sobriety, she still hadn't managed to clean it. But the mess used to be a comfort; she felt like she could hide in it—as if the heaps of dirty laundry were actually enchanted mountains in a magical, secret world. When she locked the doors and sliced out a couple of lines in the mirror, everything around her became transformed. . . .

"Stop thinking about drugs!" she hissed out loud.

She glanced at the clock on her desk. It was already past six. A whole day had come and gone—and she still had heard no word from Gaia. Nobody had picked up at Gaia's house when Mary had tried to call there, either. But it wasn't as if they had made definite plans or anything. After they bolted from that dorm last night, Gaia had just kept on running.

She hardly even said good-bye. She didn't even look back. For all Mary knew, Gaia had gone upstate on some foster family outing.

Yeah. Sure.

A person didn't have to spend a lot of time with Gaia Moore to know that foster family outings played no role in her life.

But at the very least, Mary had made an important discovery last night. There definitely *was* some history between Gaia and Sam Moon—

The phone on her desk rang.

Finally, she thought. She ran over to grab it—but unfortunately, there was no place for her to sit. All of those stupid Christmas books were stacked on her desk chair. Jesus. She was definitely going to have to trade them in for some *real* gifts. With an impatient swat, she shoved them onto the floor, then snatched up the phone and plopped down into the soft, cushiony seat.

"Hello?"

"I want my five hundred dollars, bitch."

The blood drained from Mary's face. It wasn't Gaia.

"S-S-Skizz?" she stuttered.

"Hello?" her mom answered on another phone.

Shit. "I got it, Mom," she said quickly. "I got it—"

"Okay, dear." Her tone was cheerful. "Dinner will be ready in five minutes, so keep it short, okay—"

"I *got* it," she hissed.

There was a fumbling click.

"Aw," Skizz said, his voice gravelly. "Ain't that sweet? Well, don't worry, *dear.* You're gonna make dinner. We ain't got much to talk about."

Mary's breath started coming fast. "How did you get this number?" she whispered.

Skizz started cracking up. "Damn, girl, you musta been more messed up than I thought. You don't remember giving it to me?"

No, she didn't. Then again, she wouldn't be surprised if Skizz were lying right now. That was one of the many two-sided problems with drugs: you did things you couldn't remember, but you also hung out with con artists who made up lies about you. And since your brain was fried most of the time, you could never provide any evidence to contradict those lies. You never knew the truth. But it was always safe to assume the worst.

"Well, that's okay," Skizz went on. "I won't take it personally. All I want is my money. Then you won't have to worry about me calling you again. Ever."

Mary swallowed. Her eyes kept darting to the door. What if her mother decided to come in right now? She should have locked it; but then, she wasn't *allowed* to lock it anymore. That was one of the conditions of her cleanup program.

"I don't have your money," Mary said finally.

Skizz chuckled. His laugh was very easygoing and friendly—which somehow only made it more terrifying. "Then we have a problem," he said.

"Look, just give me a couple of weeks to get it together, all right?" Mary whispered frantically. She could feel herself starting to panic. "I swear to God, I'll get it to you. It's just . . . I don't—I mean, my family will be suspicious if I start taking money out of the bank in huge amounts, so—"

"I don't need your life story, sugar," he interrupted coldly. "I just need that five hundred bucks."

She shook her head. "I . . . I . . ."

"Don't think you can hide. I know where to find you. I can come up to that swanky Park Avenue apartment, or I can wait for you downtown. Makes no difference to me. And this time if that psycho blond bitch tries anything, I'll be ready."

"Don't touch her," Mary whispered instinctively. God, why did he have to drag Gaia into this mess? Well, actually, she knew the reason. Gaia had kicked the shit out of him once already. His reputation would be severely damaged if rival dealers found out he'd been beaten up by a girl—*twice.*

He laughed again. "Fine. You got twenty-four hours. You know where to find me. If you don't, I'm coming to find *you.*"

Mary opened her mouth to plead with him one last time. But the line was already dead.

CALL NUMBER TWO . . .

Sam fully expected the raging battle in his head to be over. He'd made his decision. Or rather, *Heather* had made his decision for him. She'd been incredible. Like some kind of wild goddess. A month on the rocks did wonders for a relationship. Especially the physical part. There was no way anybody could top the way Heather made him feel last night. None. He still couldn't quite believe it. Even in memory it seemed more like a crazy, erotic dream than reality.

So why was he miserable?

Well, for one thing, he was stuck in his dorm room the day after Christmas. Aside from him and the security guard, the entire place was deserted. And he couldn't go to Heather's because she was up visiting relatives in Connecticut. Loneliness always made a person depressed. Then there was the fact that his dorm room had no windows and was the size of a prison cell—and was seriously beginning to reek. He hadn't changed his sheets since . . . well, it was best not to think about that.

But he was lying to himself. He knew it. He was just making up reasons to be bummed out. Anything to prevent him from seeing the truth.

The battle wasn't over.

He stared at the phone, half buried under a pile of papers next to his computer. He could just call her. Right now. He could at least find out if she'd kept the chessboard. If she hadn't thrown it out, then he would finally know for sure if it was even worth this agony.

She doesn't give a shit about the stupid chessboard, you idiot.

Whatever. Impulsively he grabbed the phone and punched in Gaia's number, sending the papers flying.

"Hello?" a woman answered after two rings.

"Um . . . hi." Sam cleared his throat. It must have been her foster mom. He suddenly found his palms were moist. Maybe he should have waited a little longer and planned exactly what he was going to say. "Is Gaia there, please?"

"May I ask who's calling?"

"This is, uh . . . this is Sam," he said.

"Oh, hi." Her voice suddenly brightened. "I'm Ella."

"Uh . . . hi," he answered awkwardly. Why did she sound so pleased to talk to him? She didn't even *know* him. His mouth was dry. "How are you?"

"Very well, thanks. And you, Sam?"

Was it his imagination, or was her tone a little . . . flirtatious? She was speaking very quietly and intimately. It kind of gave him the creeps.

"I'm fine," he said. "So . . ."

"I'm sorry, sweetie. Gaia isn't here right now."

He bit his lip. "Do you know where she is?"

Ella sighed. "With that boyfriend of hers, I imagine."

Snap. Ka-boom. Thermonuclear detonation. Mushroom cloud. A red haze filled Sam's brain. Nervousness turned to rage. "Who is this guy, anyway?" he found himself demanding.

"I don't know. But whoever he is, I'm sure he isn't half as cute as you." She sighed again. "Gaia's not known for her judgment, though."

No. She sure as hell wasn't. And Sam was going to give her a piece of his—

Hold on. Did Gaia's foster mom just call him *cute*? Yeah. She did. But how could she even know if he was cute or not? She'd never even *seen* him. Blood rushed to his face. This was more than creepy. . . .

"Sam? Are you there?"

"Uh . . . yeah—yeah," he stammered clumsily. "Listen, can I ask you something?"

"Anything," she answered in a sultry whisper.

His skin was starting to crawl. "I just want to know if you've ever seen her with, um, a new chessboard," he said. "You know, playing chess."

"I sure haven't. I think she plays chess in the park—"

"Thanks," he cut in, slamming the phone down on the hook.

Well. There it was. Not a lot of gray area. Nope. Gaia had thrown away the gift.

Gaia was out of the picture.

So. It was probably about time to give his amazingly hot, ready-and-willing girlfriend a call in Connecticut.

CALL NUMBER THREE . . .

"Ella?" Gaia yelled from the top of the stairs. "Did somebody just try to call me?"

Gaia could have sworn she'd heard the phone ring while she was in the shower. She wasn't the type to imagine things. Well, she *had* imagined that Sam had kissed her—but that was due to a traumatic head injury. She tightened the towel around her body and ran a hand through her soaking hair.

"Ella!" she shouted. "Are you—"

"Quiet!" Ella barked. She stamped loudly up the stairs to the third-floor landing and glared up at Gaia. "We have neighbors."

Then why are you yelling? Gaia wondered, but she kept a

lid on her anger. She wasn't in the mood for a fight right now. "Sorry," she murmured with as much politeness as she could manage. "I was just wondering if that call was for me."

Ella raised her eyebrows. "Why? Are you expecting to hear from someone?"

Gaia's jaw tightened. Asking meddling, inappropriate questions was Ella's specialty. She'd probably guessed correctly that Gaia *was* hoping to hear from someone. Namely Sam—so he could explain why the hell he went back to his heinous girlfriend after what had happened between him and Gaia . . . whatever it was.

She drew in a sharp breath. She would *not* think about Sam. Never again. It was her New Year's resolution, and it was coming a little early. Besides, Gaia didn't want to hear from Sam, anyway. She wanted to hear from Mary, so she could have the opportunity to explain why she had freakishly bolted from Sam's dorm the night before. But Ella had been online half the day. And Gaia had been too embarrassed to call Mary herself. She just hoped Mary wasn't mad.

"And would you please put something on your feet?" Ella demanded in the silence. You're dripping all over the place. Water is bad for the carpet."

Unbelievable. But Gaia simply plastered a big, fake smile on her face. Sometimes the best offense was passive resistance. Ella always got the most frustrated when Gaia refused to engage in an argument.

"No problem," Gaia said sweetly. "I'll put something on my feet just as soon as you answer my question. Was that call for me?"

Ella blinked. "No. It wasn't." She turned and marched back down the stairs.

Gaia rolled her eyes. Obviously it *was*. Good thing Ella Niven was a wanna-be photographer and not a covert agent, like her husband. She was probably the worst liar Gaia had ever met. And it wasn't a good quality for somebody who was trying to play her husband for a chump, either.

It was strange, though. There was no possible reason Ella could have for preventing Gaia from getting phone calls. Then again, Ella wasn't famous for making sense.

Gaia trudged into her bedroom (not that she really thought of it as *hers*; it was just the room she temporarily inhabited), picked up the phone on the desk, and dialed *69.

But instead of ringing, she heard three painfully loud and atonal beeps—the sound of a nonworking or disconnected number.

"We're sorry," a computerized female voice answered. "At your request, this feature has been deactivated. If you wish to have it—"

Gaia hung up the phone. She scowled in bewilderment. Why the hell would George and Ella deactivate the *69 feature? Why would anyone . . .

CIA, Gaia suddenly realized. George probably wanted to

make sure that none of the incoming calls from the agency could be traced—for security purposes. Now that she thought about it, her father had done the same thing. Deactivating the *69 feature was probably company policy. Wonderful. Just her luck. For all Gaia knew, that could have been Sam, calling to confess his love for her. She laughed miserably. Yeah. Chances of that were approximately one in four zillion.

But it wasn't as if she had to launch a massive investigation. Only two people in the world would possibly call her. Mary or Ed. She decided to try Mary first.

"Hello?" Mary's mom answered after two rings.

"Hi, Mrs. Moss," Gaia said. She realized she felt a little funny about calling—and not only because she had some explaining to do to Mary. No, it was also because the last time she'd spoken with Mary's mother had been Thanksgiving night: the very same night Gaia had discovered Mary hunched over a pile of cocaine in her room and bolted from the scene. She wondered for a moment if Mrs. Moss thought that *she* did cocaine too. "It's Gaia Moore. Is Mary around?"

"Oh, hi, dear!" Mrs. Moss exclaimed. "She's in the middle of dinner. I'll have her call you as soon as she's finished."

"Uh . . . thanks," Gaia murmured. She breathed a little sigh of relief. "I'll be home all night."

"You know, Gaia, I never had the opportunity to thank you," Mrs. Moss said. "If it weren't for you, Mary never would have gotten on the track she is now. We owe you."

Gaia's face grew hot. She'd never been good at accepting compliments—mostly because she rarely got them, except from old drunks who liked her blond hair. "No . . . it was, it's uh, nothing," she mumbled clumsily.

"If there's anything we can do for you, just let us know," Mrs. Moss said.

"That's really nice of you. But I'm fine. Thanks. Bye." Before Mrs. Moss could get another word in, Gaia quickly hung up the phone. Jesus. She had nothing to do with Mary's sobriety. *Mary* did. She hated the idea of somebody's being indebted to her—almost as much as she hated the idea of being indebted to somebody else. Debts made it very hard to pick up and leave at a moment's notice. That was part of the reason she'd been so reluctant to be friends with Mary in the first place. Ed too, for that matter.

She sighed. Clearly Mary hadn't called; she was eating. That left Ed. But after two rings, the answering machine picked up at his apartment. "Hello, you've reached the Fargo residence. . . ."

She dropped the phone down on the hook. So Ed wasn't home, either.

Who the hell had called her, anyway? Was Ella telling the truth? Was the call really for somebody else?

Gaia shook her head. No. The idea of Ella's being honest was far too disturbing.

CALL NUMBER FOUR . . .

Ella was just beginning to feel relaxed when she felt the silent buzz of the cellular in the front pocket of her sweater. Her face twisted in a scowl. Loki always picked the worst times to call. She could never enjoy a single moment's peace.

Oh, well. She stood and grabbed her leather coat from the hall closet. For an instant her gaze fell on a small, red package—tucked back amid a bunch of junk that Gaia would never think to search. Sam's gift. Ella allowed herself a little smile. Poor, poor Gaia. The girl would never know just how much the boy cared for her. It was Ella's secret. And she had to be careful. If Loki found out that Ella was interfering so dramatically in Gaia's personal affairs, she would probably wind up at the bottom of the East River.

But a woman needed her diversions.

Ella stepped quickly out into the brisk December night and fished the cellular phone out of her pocket. She walked west on Perry Street toward the Hudson. Christ, it was freezing. Her nose burned in the biting wind. She probably could have stayed at home, but Loki insisted that she never communicate with him in the Niven household. He was obsessive about security. Too obsessive. But she couldn't afford to take chances. He very well may have been watching her right at this moment.

"Yes?" she answered.

"The Moss problem may solve itself," Loki stated.

Ella paused, smiling confusedly. She glanced up and down the block just to make sure she was alone. "How's that?"

"She owes money to a drug dealer. He's nothing more than a street thug, but he's dangerous. He's given her an ultimatum. Twenty-four hours."

Ella's smile widened. She began walking again, rounding the corner onto West Fourth Street to escape the wind. "What should we do?"

"Nothing. See how it plays. I'll contact you later. Keep an eye on Gaia, though. Make sure she doesn't get involved."

"Right." Ella clicked the phone shut and shoved it back into her pocket. Poor, poor Gaia, indeed. So there was a good chance she would lose her boyfriend *and* her best friend. All within the space of a few days. It was turning out to be a merry Christmas after all.

ED

Top Ten Reasons I Should Avoid Gaia Moore Like the Plague and Never Speak to Her Again

1. She nearly got me killed by a bunch of skinheads.
2. She nearly got me killed by a serial killer.
3. She pisses me off.
4. She's in love with Sam Moon.
5. She's involved with something really bad and mysterious that she can't talk about.
6. This bad and mysterious thing will probably get her killed.
7. This bad and mysterious thing will probably get me killed, too, if I keep hanging out with her.
8. She has no redeeming social skills.

9. Every time I think about her, I get a headache.
10. I'm in a wheelchair, and she isn't.

Top Ten Reasons I Should Keep Hanging Out with Her

1. She does a kick-ass imitation of that little kid from *The Sixth Sense.*

That's about it. Oh, yeah. I'm also in love with her. Does that count?

BEARDED CLONES

HE'D LEARNED A LONG TIME AGO THAT IT WAS WISE TO BE PARANOID WHEN HANGING OUT WITH GAIA.

THE NEW GAIA

Ed wasn't sure exactly what drove him to accept Gaia's invitation and meet her and Mary in Washington Square Park that night. He sure as hell wasn't psyched to play more truth or dare. No, he figured there were probably two reasons—a desperate need to be in Gaia's presence and utter boredom.

Pretty much the usual.

Plus he had been spending *way* too much time with his family the past few days. Christmas was already forty-eight hours behind him, and his parents were still planning holiday events—as if dragging him to New Jersey yesterday to visit his grandparents wasn't torture enough. For some reason, his mom and dad really seemed to believe that there were actually twelve days of Christmas—and each of those days required some kind of painfully awkward family gathering.

At least he'd escaped for a while. And it was a little warmer, which probably explained why the park was so crowded at this late hour. Well, that and the fact that all the I'm-too-hip-for-words NYU students were coming back early from Christmas break so they could be in the city for New Year's Eve. Ed snickered to himself as he entered from the southeast. He almost felt sorry for these people—the kids on the benches in their leather jackets and baggy jeans, huddled around each other in tight circles for warmth. All of them wanted to pretend that they were native New Yorkers. But no amount of body piercing could alter the fact that most of them grew up in lame states like Iowa or Kansas or Montana.

He rolled slowly along the brightly lit pathway, scanning for signs of Gaia. There was a lot of action at the chess tables, but he couldn't see—

"Yo! Ed! Over here!"

There she was—standing by the fountain with Mary, waving furiously. God, the more those two hung out together, the more they started to dress like twins. Gaia had bought the same black wool hat as Mary—and Mary had bought Gaia's overcoat. Their outfits were practically identical. It was kind of scary.

But what was even scarier was that Gaia was smiling.

This had been happening a lot lately. It was a fairly strange development, as far as Ed was concerned. Before she'd met Mary, her facial expressions were pretty much limited to various forms of anger. Ed had gotten used to it. He'd come to *expect* it. The fearsome, unsmiling Gaia was the one he had fallen for. But Mary seemed to have some kind of bizarre normalizing effect on her, in a way that he never had. The new Gaia didn't seem to take life as seriously. The new Gaia acted like any other run-of-the-mill seventeen-year-old. . . .

He shook his head. Maybe Gaia was just smiling because she was psyched to see him. Or she was full of Christmas cheer. He should be happy that *she* was happy. So why wasn't he?

"What's up, guys?" he called as he rolled toward them. "You thinking of auditioning for a Doublemint commercial?"

Gaia smirked. "Very funny."

"Hey, my grandma bought me this coat for Christmas," Mary said. "It was out of my hands. I swear."

Ed shook his head, slowing to a stop in front of them. "Yeah, sure," he said with a lopsided grin. "Grandmothers never buy anything that cool. Trust me. I know. Mine gave me a pair of polyester 'slacks.'" He made little quotation marks in the air with his fingers. "Her word, not mine."

Mary laughed. "So how was Christmas, anyway, Fargo?"

"Boring," he grumbled. "Why do you think I came out here to hang with you guys?"

"Because you want to be seen in public with two amazingly hot chicks," Mary joked.

Ed flashed a fake smile. *Actually, yes,* he thought. *You're right.* The really sad thing was that Mary had no idea how beautiful she was. And neither did Gaia. They suffered from the opposite problem that Heather did. *She* thought she was God's gift to men. How could certain people be so insightful about others and yet so utterly stupid about themselves?

"So do you feel like getting back in the action?" Gaia asked, rubbing her gloved palms together. "You've got a lot of turns to make up. We've been on a pretty wild ride so far."

"I'm sure you have," he mumbled.

"Let's get out of the park, though," Mary said quickly.

"Let's go someplace we hardly ever go. Like Chinatown or something."

Ed stared at her, his brow furrowing. Mary seemed a little jumpy again. Her eyes kept flitting from one group of people to the next. And she couldn't stand still. She kept shifting her weight from one foot to the other.

"We just got here," Gaia pointed out.

"Yeah, but . . . I—I don't know," she stammered distractedly. "It's just kind of dull."

"What's the matter?" Ed asked.

Mary shook her head—a little too emphatically. "Nothing," she said.

Ed exchanged a quick glance with Gaia. She shrugged.

"We can split," Gaia said. "Whatever. I've never been to Chinatown before."

Before Gaia had even finished, Mary was already hurrying toward the north exit, straight under the arch. Gaia jogged after her.

Ed frowned. Okay. Mary was freaking out about *something.* He was not imagining this. He followed them slowly, peering to his left into a darkened clump of trees. Maybe she had seen an ex-boyfriend, or—

Him.

Ed's chair jerked to a stop. There was a guy. A fat guy with a beard—standing under a tree, hidden in the shadows not thirty feet away. He was staring directly at Gaia and Mary.

Ed shivered. The night didn't seem as pleasant as it had before. He was freezing, in fact. Cold air nipped at his nose and ears. That guy looked familiar. Ed had definitely seen him around the park before. In fact . . . yeah, *he* was the guy who'd been staring at Mary the other day. So he must have been the reason she was freaking out. Ed's gaze flashed back to the two girls. They vanished briefly behind the right side of the Arc de Triomphe. He turned back. . . .

The guy was gone.

For a few moments Ed craned his neck, trying to spot him—but all he saw were tree branches, swaying in the winter wind under the ghostly lights of the park. Had the guy figured out that Ed had noticed him? More important, was he following Mary? Or Gaia? That was a distinct possibility. In fact, it was a *probability.* He'd learned a long time ago that it was wise to be paranoid when hanging out with Gaia. Any real danger always ended up exceeding his wildest fears, anyway.

"Hey, Ed!" Gaia called. "Are you coming or what?"

His head whipped around. Gaia and Mary were already halfway down the block, heading east. His eyes darted around the street on the other side of the park fence. The guy was nowhere to be found. As quickly as he could, Ed sped out of the park, nearly tipping as he whipped through the arch and around the corner onto the sidewalk.

"Jesus." Gaia looked at Mary, frowning. "Are you all right?"

"Did you see something, Mary?" he interrupted, skidding to a halt beside them. His icy gasps filled the air.

Mary and Gaia exchanged a quick glance.

"What do you mean?" Mary asked. Her forehead wrinkled.

"A guy," Ed whispered. He glanced back over his shoulder. But the street was deserted. "A guy with a beard. A long beard."

Mary's face seemed to go blank. She blinked several times.

"What?" Gaia demanded.

Ed held his breath, waiting.

"Uh . . . nothing," Mary said. Her voice was subdued. She shook her head and cast a brief glance back at the park. "No. I didn't see a guy with a long beard."

"Do you *know* a guy with a long beard?" Ed asked.

Mary didn't say anything. All at once Gaia started laughing.

Ed grimaced. "You mind telling me what's so funny?"

"Nothing," she muttered, shaking her head. She pulled her hat down tightly over her tangled mop of blond hair. "I just didn't know that you had such strong feelings against guys with beards."

"Uh . . . we should go," Mary said. She turned back down the block and started walking east again. "It's too cold to be standing still."

Ed glared at Gaia. Obviously Mary knew this guy—whoever he was. Obviously she was scared of him. So why the hell was Gaia still smiling? Why was she turning this into a joke?

"*What?*" Gaia asked defensively.

"Excuse me for being uptight, but I just get a little anxious when I know somebody's stalking us," he grumbled.

Gaia's shoulders slumped. "Give me a break, Ed. Nobody's stalking—"

"Come *on*, you guys," Mary called impatiently.

Gaia opened her mouth to say something else, then closed it and turned to follow Mary.

Ed's lips turned downward. He shook his head. Hanging out with Mary all the time *was* having an effect on Gaia. She never would have acted this careless in the past. The old Gaia would have told everyone to go home. Then she would have sought out the bearded guy and kicked the crap out of him.

After that, they could have all enjoyed the rest of their winter break in peace.

But not the new Gaia. No. She opted for being a major pain in the ass. Before she met Mary, she used to listen to Ed. Now she didn't. Like when he'd told her about Charlie Salita. Had she paid any attention? No.

Now she was doing the same thing all over again. By not listening to Ed, she was walking right into another stupid situation. . . .

But apparently the new Gaia didn't learn from past mistakes.

THE FREAKS COME OUT AT NIGHT

All of Chinatown smelled like one giant fried dumpling. Gaia's mouth couldn't stop watering. Every storefront window on the narrow street was packed with a brightly lit display of food: either a rack of hanging meats or ducklings or doughy pastries. Most of it looked fairly gross, of course, but the smell was incredible. She sucked in deep, huge breaths of the cold night air. She couldn't believe she'd never discovered this neighborhood. Chinatown was tailor-made for somebody like her—somebody who could pretty much live on desserts and fried foods until her heart gave out.

"I didn't know it was going to be so crowded," Mary said, raising her voice as she led Gaia and Ed through the throng of pedestrians on the sidewalk. She laughed once and glanced over her shoulder. "This is ridiculous. It's like Mardi Gras or something."

Gaia nodded, smiling. Coming here *was* like entering a foreign country. All the street and shop signs were in Chinese. The moment they turned off Mott Street onto Canal Street, every last trace of English vanished. And food was hardly the only exotic item being sold: There were all kinds of little trinkets and statues and electronic gadgets. . . .

"The freaks come out at night," Ed grumbled. "What are we even *doing* right now?"

Gaia didn't answer. Ed's sour mood was getting more irritating by the second. So he'd seen a guy with a beard in the park. Big deal. Even if the guy *had* been watching them, they were far from Greenwich Village right now. And it was hard to think of any place safer than a well-lit city street, packed with tourists.

"I'll tell you what we're doing," Mary stated, stopping in front of a butcher shop. The glass window featured a particularly nasty display of fatty sausage links hanging from the ceiling. "We're playing truth or dare." She turned around and shot Gaia a quick smile over Ed's head. "And Ed?" She nodded at the window. "I dare you to eat one of those sausages."

Gaia laughed. *That* would teach him not to complain.

"Don't I get to pick?" Ed protested. "I mean, it's truth *or* dare, right?"

Mary sighed disappointedly, folding her arms across her chest. "Fine, Ed. If you want to be totally boring . . ."

"If you ask me, those sausages look pretty good," Gaia joked.

Ed scowled up at her, but the faint beginnings of a smile appeared at the corners of his mouth. Finally, she thought. Maybe he was starting to lighten up a little. Maybe he could actually enjoy himself.

"Are you sure they're even meant for human beings?" he asked, rotating the wheelchair so that he faced the window directly. His eyes wandered up and down the display case. His face soured. "I mean—"

Without warning, he spun the wheelchair a full one hundred eighty degrees—so fast that the leg rest nearly grazed Gaia's shin.

"Jesus, Ed," she gasped, jumping back.

His eyes were wide. His face was a ghastly white.

"That guy!" he hissed.

Gaia exchanged a baffled glance with Mary. "What are you—"

"I j-just saw him," he sputtered. He tried to push himself higher up in the chair to get a better view. "In the window. I saw his reflection. . . ."

"Are you *sure?*" Mary asked.

"Positive," Ed whispered. His voice was trembling. "He was right behind us—two seconds ago." He jerked a finger toward the intersection. "Walking that way."

Gaia stood on her tiptoes—scouring the mob with her eyes. But all she saw was the same swarming sea of tourists and Chinatown locals. "I don't know, Ed," she murmured. "Maybe—"

"I *saw* him, all right?" he yelled. "I'm positive. He's following us."

Gaia glanced back at Mary. "Did you see him?"

Mary shook her head, but she was a little pale, too. Gaia sighed. This was just great. Ed was making Mary paranoid, too—and Mary was edgy enough already. There were tons of scuzzy guys with long beards in New York, and most of them looked exactly alike: an army of bearded clones.

"I'm outta here," Ed announced. He spun his wheelchair onto the street with a quick, jerky motion. It rattled as it bounced off the curb.

"Come on, Ed." Gaia groaned. "If this guy's following us, how come he hasn't tried anything yet? I'm sure—"

"Maybe Ed's right," Mary interrupted quietly. "Maybe we should just go home." She wrapped her arms around herself. "It's pretty cold, anyway. And it's getting late."

Gaia sighed, waving her hands hopelessly. It wasn't that cold. Besides, it was never late in New York. Something was always happening. And Chinatown was a hot spot. For the first time since Gaia had moved to the city, she felt like she was a *part* of it—discovering it, unlocking all of its potential. More important, she wasn't focused entirely on herself and her own messed-up life. Sam Moon hadn't crossed her mind once. She didn't know when she'd get the opportunity to feel so Sam-free again. She wasn't about to let anyone blow it for her.

"What about the game?" she asked.

"The game is supposed to be *fun*, Gaia," Ed replied through tightly clenched teeth. "Even if I *am* imagining things, I'm not having fun. So there isn't much point in my playing, right?"

"That's true," Mary muttered, staring down at the ground.

"What are you *talking* about?" Gaia protested. "I'm having fun."

Ed sneered. "And everyone knows that Gaia Moore's fun takes precedence over all."

Gaia's eyes hardened. "What's *that* supposed to mean?"

"Nothing," he muttered. "Look, if you guys want to get shot or stabbed or raped, be my guests." He released the brakes on his wheelchair and struck out into the crowd. "I'm gone."

"Oh, come on," Gaia called after him. "I didn't mean . . ."

"Let him go," Mary said, grabbing Gaia's arm. "We shouldn't have invited him along, anyway. Let's just go back to my place, all right?"

Ed vanished into the night.

A queasy emptiness settled in Gaia's stomach. Maybe she had been a little harsh. She had thought she would never get into another serious fight with Ed Fargo—not after the whole Charlie Salita thing. And he'd been right about Charlie. But he was definitely wrong about this mysterious bearded stalker. No way would somebody follow Mary halfway across town without Gaia or Mary noticing. It was just too far-fetched. Besides, Ed was just overprotective. How many times had he proved that already?

By the time Ed rolled the mile or so up Broadway back to the West Village, his fury had subsided to a dull rage. His neck was starting to ache from shaking his head so much. He knew he must look like a lunatic, gesturing and muttering to himself, but he couldn't care less. His mind was in a haze.

He'd always known Gaia to be reckless. But never *stupid.* Even when she'd insisted on tracking down "the Gentleman"—that whacked-out serial killer who turned out to be the new kid in their class—she'd showed some kind of *logic.* Some kind of rational thinking.

All right, maybe not. It was hard to call vigilantism rational under any circumstances. But at least she'd been mildly concerned with her personal safety. Even when she'd agreed to go out with Charlie Salita and Sideburns Tim, she didn't believe she was making a bad choice. It had been stupid, yes, but not irrational.

Now she just didn't seem to give a shit about anything.

Whatever. It wasn't his problem. Nope. If she and Mary wanted to get killed at the hands of some fatso drug dealer, he'd just find a couple of other hot chicks to hang around with. This was a big city, right? His wheelchair bounced as he turned off Broadway onto Bond Street. Here were plenty of nice young women around. Normal women. Women who wouldn't endanger his life.

Maybe he could even meet some right now.

Sure. The Atomic Diner was just up the block on the right. He loved that place. It was one of those retro fifties joints, with minijukeboxes at each booth and an old-fashioned soda fountain. It was a favorite haunt among the hip Greenwich Village high school crowd.

He used to hang there a lot himself when he was going out with Heather. And he'd always secretly noted that she wasn't the only beautiful girl who liked to eat bacon and eggs at 10 P.M. on a Friday. . . .

He jerked to a stop. His eyes narrowed.

Speak of the devil.

Sitting right there, in the first window booth of the Atomic Diner, was none other than Heather herself.

She was stuffing her face with french fries and talking animatedly with somebody just out of view of the window frame. Probably Sam Moon. Ed bowed his head. Tonight was really his lucky night, wasn't it? First he got blown off by Gaia. Then he saw his ex-girlfriend whooping it up. Clearly Heather's being here was a sign. Yes. A sign that he should go straight home and lock himself away for the rest of the holiday season—

There was a loud rapping on the window.

Ed glanced up. *Oh, brother.* He should have moved more

quickly. Heather had spotted him out there on the sidewalk, and now she was furiously waving at him, beckoning him to come in. He tried to force a smile. There were about a million things he'd rather do than hang out with Heather and Sam—including hard labor, prison time, calculus homework. . . . But it was no use: She'd trapped him. He nodded and sighed.

Wait a second. He did a double take as he scooted past the window.

Heather wasn't with Sam. She was with her older sister Phoebe. Ed's spirits immediately lifted. He hadn't seen Phoebe since the summer, when she'd come home for a break from college. He waved. She waved back. Whoa. She looked amazing. Didn't girls usually put on weight in college? If anything, Phoebe looked like she'd *dropped* fifteen pounds. She looked older, too, somehow—mature and exotic and skinny. Her long, brown hair hung far down her back, and she was wearing a wild-looking, floral blue dress.

He picked up his pace and rounded the corner, pushing through the diner door. The delicious odor of fried food wafted over him. Maybe this wouldn't be so bad after all. It was nice and warm in here . . . and besides, he'd always liked Phoebe. Yes. Phoebe was always very cool. She had an edge, and it was probably for that reason that she and Heather had never gotten along all that well, but deep down she was a lot more mellow and easygoing than her sister.

And way out of your league, bozo, he reminded himself, knowing full well where these thoughts were taking him. *Even before the accident. And she's a sophomore in college. Not to mention the fact that she's your ex-girlfriend's sister—and therefore necessarily in the "untouchable" category.*

"Hey, Ed!" Phoebe called as he rolled down the narrow aisle to their booth.

"Hey, Phoebe. What's up? You here for Christmas break?"

"Yeah." She smiled at him. "I see nothing's changed. You're still roaming the streets at night like a hoodlum."

"Looking for fights, no doubt," Heather chimed in brightly.

Ed smirked at Heather. "What are *you* so happy about?"

"Don't ask," Phoebe said, rolling her eyes. "She just came from her boyfriend's dorm."

"Oh." Ed cleared his throat. He felt a quick pang of two conflicting emotions—the same jealousy he always felt when he pictured Heather and Sam being together, but also a strange sort of relief. He'd thought that Sam and Heather were on the rocks. But if Sam was hanging out with Heather, that meant that he wouldn't be hanging out with Gaia. So Gaia would just have to find someone else to fall in love with.

Like me, for instance.

Ed shook his head. He was supposed to be *mad* at Gaia. Not obsessing over her.

"What's wrong?" Phoebe asked.

"Huh? Oh, nothing." He glanced at her dress, shoving Gaia from his thoughts. "What's up with the new threads? You aren't turning into a hippie on us, are you?"

She laughed. "As if. Why? You don't like it?" Ed was surprised by the question. Phoebe wasn't the type to care what people thought. She'd always been too confident for that. In fact, she'd always been a tad *over*confident.

"No, no, I like it a lot. It's just not your usual style."

"She's being brainwashed by her friends at SUNY, Ed," Heather remarked dryly, her mouth half full of fries. "I mean, look at what she's eating. She actually ordered a salad. I mean, who goes to a diner and orders a salad?"

"Good point." Ed leaned over and frowned at her plate. Not only had Phoebe ordered a salad; she'd barely touched it. Then again, he couldn't blame her. That heap of wilted green lettuce didn't look very appetizing. "Did you join some kind of vegetarian cult or something?"

"Very funny," Phoebe muttered. She grinned. "I just decided to go on a little diet. Besides, do you know how many years *one* order of Atomic Diner fries can take off your life?"

Ed laughed. "Is that the kind of thing they're teaching you in college?"

"That, and how to dress in clothes that went out of

fashion before the first Woodstock," Heather replied. She shook her head in mock disdain.

"Hey, I like this dress," Phoebe said, giving her sister a playful kick under the table. "Besides, none of my old clothes fit me anymore."

"I like it, too," Heather grumbled with a smile. "I'm just jealous."

"Well, then, you'll just have to go to school in the fabulous metropolis of Binghamton, New York, too," Phoebe said. "I'll put you on a strict wheat germ diet and take you shopping for secondhand clothes, and we'll look like twins from a Doublemint commercial."

"Oh, goody!" Heather cried. "Just what I always wanted!"

Ed laughed again. It was amazing to see Heather and her sister actually getting along. And not only that—*he* was enjoying himself. He didn't think such a thing was possible. Especially tonight. Here he was, sitting with Heather and her sister, chatting and laughing. There wasn't any tension. None. For a few blissful, fleeting seconds he'd even managed to forget that he was in a wheelchair.

It was a good thing he'd ditched Gaia after all.

Well . . . no, it wasn't. But at least he could pretend it was for the next few minutes.

HIGH SECURITY

Skizz.

There was no doubt in Mary's mind: Ed had seen Skizz. The pig hadn't been kidding about coming to find her. He'd probably been following her all day. For all Mary knew, he could be lurking outside the apartment building right now.

She stood at her bedroom window, staring down at the lights of Park Avenue. She didn't see any people out there—but Skizz was clever. The twenty-four hours he'd given her to pay him back had long since expired. At least this was a high-security building. Her door was dead bolted. Besides, there was a doorman. There were video cameras. All the doorman had to do was press a button, and the police would rush right over. . . .

". . . should call him," Gaia was saying.

"Huh?" Mary tore her attention from the street below and glanced back at Gaia's sprawled form on the unmade bed. "Sorry. What was that?"

"Maybe I should call Ed," Gaia murmured, staring up at Mary's ceiling. "I feel bad. I guess I just kind of got caught up in the game."

Mary walked over and sat on the edge of the mattress. "You know, Gaia, we don't have to keep playing." She bit her lip, debating whether or not to tell Gaia about Skizz's call. No. It was best not to think about it. Besides, there was a chance that his threats were empty. And even if they weren't, this was *her* problem. Not Gaia's. She didn't want to drag Gaia into the middle of it—especially after Skizz's warning about the "psycho blond chick."

"But I *want* to keep playing," Gaia stated.

"But maybe for Ed's sake . . ." Mary let the sentence hang.

"You don't believe him, do you?" Gaia asked. She sat up straight, her eyes narrowing. "Did you see something too?"

"No." Mary sighed and shook her head.

"Then what are you worried about?"

"It's just . . ." Mary lowered her eyes. It felt terrible to keep her feelings bottled up inside her. She could at least let Gaia in on her thoughts without going into all the gory details. And as a friend, Gaia had a right to know why she was acting so strange. "Remember that guy you beat up the night we met?"

Gaia nodded. "How could I forget?" she murmured.

"Well, I owe him money . . . ," she said.

"Is that it?" Gaia asked.

Mary frowned. "Well, yeah, but—"

"Don't worry," Gaia said soothingly. "He won't try anything. That guy is *useless.* In case you've forgotten, I kicked his ass in the span of about five seconds."

Mary didn't look convinced.

"Besides," Gaia added, "I'm sure he's heard that you're clean now. So you're of no use to him, you know?"

"Maybe," Mary said dubiously. "But Skizz doesn't forget about things like money."

Gaia was silent for a moment. "How much do you owe him?" she finally asked.

"Five hundred," Mary whispered.

"I bet that's a drop in the bucket to guys like that," Gaia reassured her. "Trust me. And if you're thinking about all this because of Ed . . . don't. He's the most paranoid guy on the planet."

Mary tried to force a smile. But the sad fact of the matter was that her friend had no idea what she was talking about. And Gaia had the benefit of thinking she was invincible—a trait Mary didn't share. She would be safe inside her room or with Gaia around to protect her—but someday, at some moment, she'd find herself alone on the streets.

That was when Skizz would strike. She was sure of it.

ANONYMOUS TIP

Red Square was packed with people, but Tom Moore knew that this was to be expected. He welcomed the crowds. Witnesses would ensure the safety of this meeting. Not that he was worried about security, but he knew that his contact had some concerns. Debra (at least that was her alias) was still new to this theater of operations, new to the job itself. And young. In fact, she reminded him a little of Katia. Beautiful and innocent. Naive . . .

He thrust the thoughts aside. He would not think of Katia. Not now. He would concentrate on the task at hand.

As he hurried across the cobblestones in the direction of the multicolored spires of St. Basil's cathedral, he was surprised by how many American voices he heard. Of course, the week after Christmas marked the height of the tourist season—in spite of the frigid temperatures. And since Russia was no longer a closed and communist society, tourism was one of the few industries that kept its economy afloat.

Tourism and terrorism, of course.

He raised his eyes in the biting wind, glancing up at the cathedral. Even after having seen it so many times, he was still struck by its fairy-tale beauty: the brilliant reds and greens and golds, all of the different turrets and ornate fixtures. . . . It looked less like a place of worship and more like an enchanted castle. He snaked his way through a mob of students toward the southeast entrance: the rendezvous point. But then he paused.

Debra wasn't there.

Protocol dictated that she should be the first to arrive. For a moment he stood still and sized up his surroundings. As far as he could tell, he wasn't being watched or followed. There was no need to panic . . . not yet. There was a chance that she could have been held up in traffic. Public transportation in Moscow was notoriously unreliable.

He stepped closer to the cathedral's massive arched doorway. The biting wind stung his ears, but he hardly noticed. A few people jostled him. Where *was* she? The entire operation hinged on this one exchange. She *knew* that. The agency was counting on her. She had managed to acquire a copy of the smugglers' safety deposit box key. The box contained the money they would exchange for the plutonium.

But Debra didn't know the location of the bank. Only Tom knew that. Each member of the unit was entrusted with one vital piece of information; that way the entire operation wouldn't be compromised if one of them were caught. Still . . . if she failed to deliver the key in time, then Tom would be unable to prevent the smugglers from leaving the country. And they were leaving soon. This afternoon, in fact. They would have all the cash they needed to buy anything they wanted—

A muffled beep rang from deep inside his coat pocket. He scowled. That was probably Debra, calling to explain why she was late. He fished out his cell phone and flipped it open.

"Yes?" he muttered.

"Hello, Tom."

He stiffened. It wasn't Debra. It was a man. And whoever he was, he wasn't part of the agency. The agency never addressed its operatives by name over the phone.

"Tom?" the man asked. "Are you there?"

"Yes," Tom croaked, feeling a sudden dreaded certainty that Debra would never arrive, that she had been killed. The voice was American . . . but Tom couldn't place it. From the static, he judged the call was coming from overseas.

"I'm listening."

"It's about Gaia."

Jesus Christ. It took all of Tom's years of training, all of his carefully honed self-control, not to display any emotion. But he could no longer breathe. He gripped the phone as tightly as he could. He felt like his heart had been set ablaze.

"Go on," Tom choked out. He barely recognized his own voice.

"Your brother's moving against her," the man said.

Tom drew in a deep, quivering breath. Loki. He should have known. He was clever. Obviously he was well aware that Tom was halfway around the world, unable to stop him.

"He's placed someone very close to her," the voice went on. "An operative whom Gaia would never suspect."

"Who?" Tom hissed. "I don't have time—"

The line went dead.

"Hello?" Tom barked. "Hello?"

He stared at the cathedral door. Still no sign of Debra. It could mean only one thing. She was dead. She had to be. Tom dialed the agency's emergency number as quickly as he could.

"Go," a voice answered.

"Three, zulu, alpha, four, seven," Tom whispered—the code for a failed operation. It was surprisingly easy.

"Understood," the voice replied.

Tom folded the cell phone and jammed it back in his pocket. Suddenly nothing mattered anymore—nothing but Loki and Gaia. The rest of the world ceased to exist.

Without so much as a backward glance, he turned and hurried from Red Square.

Hang on, Gaia, he silently implored. *I'll be there soon.*

ED

I used to think that I was lucky in a way because I had already experienced the worst possible thing that could ever happen to me. Some people coast through life—then when they're forty or something, they're suddenly hit with a disfiguring disease or a heart attack or they lose all their money. And since their lives have basically been gravy up to that point, they're totally unequipped to deal with it. They have a complete mental breakdown. It's institution time. Electroshock therapy. Straitjackets. The works.

Not me, though. I figured since I already suffered one of the most major catastrophes known to man, the rest of my life would be pretty good by comparison.

Nothing could make me feel any lower than losing the use of my legs. Especially since my entire life was pretty much devoted to skateboarding. To quote the old cliché: When you've hit rock bottom, there's no place to go but up. I guess it helped me deal with the last two years. Thinking that way kept *me* out of an institution.

Now I know that I was wrong.

No matter how much pain you endure, something else can come along to knock you back down. Something totally different and unexpected. It doesn't even have to be physical pain. It can be something as simple as getting into a fight with somebody.

But there's no point in dwelling on the negatives. You'll just drive yourself crazy.

OVER THE EDGE

WELL, NOT TONIGHT. HER HEART POUNDED. OH, NO.

IT WAS TIME TO MAKE DADDY PROUD AGAIN.

FEAR

Gaia could see the fear clearly etched on Mary's face. It was right there: right in her creased forehead and downcast eyes. They had been speeding downtown on the number six local train for nearly fifteen minutes, and Mary hadn't spoken once. She was more worried about this drug dealer than she'd admitted. Probably thanks to Ed.

Gaia knew all about fear. She'd seen it enough on people's faces to know the signs. And she'd also studied it. Scientifically. She'd read that the best way to overcome it was to confront it directly, head-on . . . to embrace it.

It was a lesson from the *Go Rin No Sho*—the "Book of Five Rings"—a Japanese guide to martial arts. Her father used to make her read it all the time. Most of the books were about as thrilling as the yellow pages and about as heavy, too—like *Leviathan* and *The Iliad.* Her dad was a stickler for the classics. But the *Go Rin No Sho* was different. Gaia had loved it from the time she was a little girl. It was beautifully written, like poetry. It taught that a person would never be complete unless they explored both good and evil. Darkness and light.

It made perfect sense. To her, at least.

Maybe that was why she remembered the lesson about fear so well. Since she didn't feel fear, she could never confront it. But she realized something: Even if *she* was unable to use fear as a tool, she could help Mary use it.

"So we're still playing, right?" Gaia asked over the rattle of the speeding train wheels.

"Huh?" Mary asked.

Gaia shifted in her seat, trying to get comfortable. It was impossible. Even though she generally loved the subways, rush hour was always a nightmare. Somehow she found herself mushed between Mary and some businessman's designer leather briefcase. The sharp corner was starting to dig into her sides. But they were almost at Astor Place—the stop closest to Washington Square Park. She could endure a few more minutes of torture.

"The game?" Gaia prompted.

"Oh—yeah, yeah. Of course." Mary nodded as she stared down at the forest of legs rising from the grimy subway floor. "But do you think we can avoid the park? Just for tonight? We can go back tomorrow."

"And why would we avoid the park?" Gaia asked gently.

"Because I'm scared of running into Skizz," Mary admitted.

"I think that's exactly why we *should* go to the park," Gaia countered. "Look, chances are he won't even be there. And even if he is, he won't try anything. And even if he *does*, I'll kick his ass, all right?"

Mary smirked. "I guess I don't have a choice, do I?"

"No," Gaia replied dryly. The train began to slow. She glanced out the window. The lights of the Astor Street station swam into view. The wheels squeaked harshly. "So here's what. I dare you to go back to the spot where we first met—and sing a song of your choice by Hanson at the top of your lungs."

For a moment Mary looked at her as if she were completely insane. Gaia couldn't blame her. She didn't even know where that dare had come from. It had just sort of popped out of her head.

"Hanson?" Mary started laughing. "But that's not fair. I don't even *know* any songs by Han—"

"Then make one up," Gaia interrupted. "Or sing a song by Michael Jackson. Any ridiculous song will do." She grabbed Mary's arm and pulled her up along with her, then began snaking her way through the crowded car.

"What if I want to pick truth?" Mary asked.

Gaia looked her straight in the eye as the doors slid open. "You don't really want to pick truth, do you? I mean, this is a chance to sing in public, right?"

"I don't know, Gaia. . . ."

"Look, by daring you to do something silly in the same spot where you last saw Skizz, you'll see that you have nothing to worry about. And once you see that you're safe, you'll realize that you can start getting on with your life."

LIGHTBULB

What the hell am I thinking? Mary wondered.

Here she was, about to sing a song (she didn't even know *what* song)—and there was a very good chance that by calling attention to herself, she would send Skizz running straight for her, like a moth to a lightbulb.

She walked silently with Gaia down Eighth Street, with her head down to protect her face from the bitter wind. The air was so cold that it felt antiseptic, bluish. The night was eerily quiet. Her eyes smarted. Her nose burned. She kept her gaze pinned to the sidewalk. She couldn't believe she had actually let Gaia talk her into this. If Skizz was anywhere in the city, he'd be *here*.

But at the same time, in spite of her anxiety, she couldn't help but feel a peculiar anticipation. And somewhere in the dim recesses of her consciousness, she knew that the anxiety and anticipation were all bound up together in the same feeling. It was a feeling all her own—a *selfish* feeling, one that was bent on seeking pleasure, no matter what the risk. It was the same one she used to get when she diced out a line of coke. Or met Skizz on some dark corner to make a score . . .

It was the one she got knowing that she was putting herself in harm's way.

And that was the root of her problem. Of all her problems, really. Very simply put, the closer she was to danger, the more she felt alive. That was bad. Very bad. She had to suppress that feeling. She shook her head as they turned south onto Fifth Avenue. Once she started slipping down that slope, there was no telling *what* she could do.

"Piece of cake," Gaia murmured, patting her shoulder.

"Yeah," Mary whispered. "Right." She glanced up. The Arc de Triomphe loomed ahead of her at the end of the block, brightly lit against the purplish, starless sky. Behind the white marble the park was a shadowy black abyss. She swallowed.

"All you gotta do is go in there and sing," Gaia said with a perfectly straight face. "I mean really open up. Let the entire West Village hear your dulcet tones."

Mary had to laugh. But she found she was trembling. Of course, that was the weather's fault. The chill tonight soaked through her coat, down past her skin, all the way to the center of her bones. She paused on the corner opposite the park entrance.

"And why, exactly, am I doing this again?" she asked. Her question billowed from her mouth in a frozen white cloud, then vanished under the streetlamps.

Gaia raised her eyebrows. "Because I dared you to," she said with a smile.

EXORCISM

Gaia knew that Mary was afraid.

But as she watched Mary trudge into the park alone, she knew that the more fear she felt, the better it would be in the long run. The greater the risk, the greater the reward.

Besides, Mary was in no real danger. First of all, the park was completely deserted. Only a lunatic would be hanging out there on a night like tonight—a night so cold that the tips of your fingers and toes went numb after about three minutes. Also, as Gaia had told Mary, if some creep *did* try anything, she would be right there. Ready to knock him flat. From where she was waiting on MacDougal Street, she could see the entire park—and Mary would never be out of her sight, not even for an instant.

She smiled as Mary sat on a park bench in a circular pool of pale light. Good. By singing a ridiculous song and freezing her butt off in that exact spot, she would drive out her fear of Skizz. It was like a ritual, an exorcism. And Mary Moss would emerge from it a new woman.

CLOSE

This wasn't the exact spot where Mary had last seen Skizz face-to-face, but she figured it was close enough. Gaia wasn't that nitpicky. She hunched over and squeezed herself, struggling to fight the cold. Her teeth chattered uncontrollably. So. She had to rack her brain for a song. The problem was, she didn't *listen* to Hanson. But she had to sing something—or Gaia would never let her out of the park. For some reason, though, she couldn't seem to think of anything. Her mind was a complete blank.

Mary had never been the creative type. She always hated this kind of thing, being forced to perform on the spot. That was probably another reason she'd loved coke so much, now that she thought about it. Up. One little bump, and your thoughts moved at the speed of light. For those five minutes you were a genius. Not only a genius; a world-class singer, too. No song, no matter how out of tune and excruciating, was ever *that* bad when you were wired. Of course not. It was brilliant. . . .

She shivered, frowning. As usual, thinking about cocaine was getting her nowhere. The sooner she started singing, the sooner she could get the hell out of this frozen wasteland.

"If you wanna be my lover," she sang quietly. She knew it was lame, but she couldn't help herself. It would have to do. *"You gotta get with my friends—"*

Suddenly she felt a presence behind her.

"Gaia?"

She looked behind her—nothing. Mary glanced toward where Gaia stood at the edge of the park. Her friend was there, hugging herself and shivering but also grinning from ear to ear.

At least one of them wasn't completely paranoid, Mary thought. She turned back toward the empty park.

"Uh, *friendship lasts forever . . .*"

A finger tapped her on the shoulder. Mary smiled. Gaia had finally realized this was cruel and unusual punishment.

She took a bow toward the empty square, but as she stood up to turn, she noticed she could still see Gaia way over at the edge of the park, fiddling with her coat buttons.

Mary opened her mouth to scream Gaia's name, but it only came out in a whisper.

HIM

Gaia didn't see the shadowy male form creeping up on Mary until it was right behind her. She was concentrating too hard to hear whatever the hell it was that Mary was singing. Jesus.

Where had he come from? She was *trained* to spot people in the night.

She sucked in her breath and bolted across the street, hurtling the low park fence in one fluid motion. Whoever he was, he must have been hiding. Waiting. And whoever he was, he was large. Fat, almost. And familiar . . .

Shit. There it was. The beard. Even with his back to her, she could see a tangle of greasy hairs flapping in the wind. She broke into a sprint.

It was him.

PANIC

"I . . . I . . . ," Mary sputtered in horror.

She couldn't move. Her teeth stopped chattering; her body stopped trembling. Her limbs were too tense, frozen solid. For all her fear and worry, she just hadn't truly believed Skizz would be here. It was just too *obvious*, somehow—too predictable. Like walking into a trap. A trap laid expressly for her. Life wasn't that simple.

"Who's Gay-uh?"

Mary could only shake her head. Skizz looked even more foul than she'd remembered. His skin was blotchy, covered with scabs. His beady eyes bore down on her from within the fat folds of his face. And the wispy ends of his beard spread in every direction. Instinctively her eyes flashed to his hands. Both were jammed into the pockets of his down jacket. *Oh God.* Something besides his hand was also stuffed in the right pocket. Something pointy.

"I'm asking you a question," he growled.

"Sh-She . . . she's nobody," Mary stuttered, unable to tear her eyes from the pocket.

"Look at me," he barked.

She flinched. Her eyes darted to his face.

All at once he smiled—revealing an uneven row of yellow teeth. "I'm sorry, baby," he murmured. "I'm being rude. It's none of my business. So let's just take care of *our* business, and I'll be on my way. Then you can go back to your little birthday celebration."

Mary opened her mouth, but panic had robbed her of speech.

Skizz looked up for a moment, glancing furtively in either direction down the darkened path. He withdrew his right hand from the coat. Clutched in his chubby fingers was a small, shiny pistol—no bigger than a toy, a water gun. It glittered in the cold light of the park lamps.

A last gasp of air escaped Mary's lungs. She couldn't breathe anymore.

"Now, I'm assuming you came here to pay me back," he whispered. He laughed humorlessly. "There ain't no other reason a rich girl like you would come out in this cold. Gotta be drugs or money. So let's see the cash. *All* of it."

But I don't have it, she answered silently. *I swear—*

He cocked the pistol. "Now."

RAGE

The instant Gaia saw the glint of metal, her pace doubled. She was barely conscious of the ground flying under her feet. Her mind was totally focused on the figure of the drug dealer, hunched over the back of the bench where Mary sat.

Time slowed to a crawl.

Gaia was sick with rage. It was *her* fault that Mary was in danger. *Her* fault that Mary might get killed. *She* had pushed Mary into this situation—back into the world Mary had left behind, and now she might die because of it. Never before had Gaia felt such anger. And all of it was directed at herself. If he pulled that trigger . . .

But no. She wouldn't allow it. She was almost upon him. Her muscles tensed. She knew exactly how she was going to strike: a flying sidekick to the back that would send him flipping over the bench.

Her legs pumped to a fever pitch—then lifted from the ground, slowly and gracefully, like the retraction of a plane's landing gear after takeoff. For a wondrous instant she was airborne. She thrust out her right leg, straightening so that the side of her foot would connect . . .

Now.

RESCUE

"AAAH!"

Mary heard Skizz's bloodcurdling scream at the exact same moment she realized he was no longer standing behind her; he was flying *over* her.

She threw her hands over her head and cringed, watching

in terror as he tumbled through the air and landed flat on his back. The gun clattered away from him into the shadows.

And then she saw Gaia—gracefully somersaulting across the pavement.

Warmth surged through Mary's body. She should have known Gaia would come to her rescue. Gaia would teach Skizz about trying to collect on a debt from a recovering addict. It was ass-kicking time. And not a moment too soon.

TRICK

Gaia crouched over the drug dealer's body in the most basic kung fu stance—legs bent, arms up, right hand poised above the left. Her breathing was slow and even. The electric fizz tingled in her veins the way it always did before combat, but there was something different tonight.

She was oddly calm.

Her rage hadn't subsided. Yet it gave her an edge. Almost as if she were watching the events unfold from a distance . . . watching as this fat, middle-aged piece of shit staggered to his feet. How could she have been so stupid? She'd forgotten the rules of combat she'd had pounded into her head since she could remember. *Always* be ready. *Always* be alert. Instead she'd been reckless and self-indulgent, using her skills for petty pranks and leading her friend into a deadly trap.

All those years of her father's painstaking training were going to waste.

All those afternoons spent in their backyard—repeating kick after kick, block after block. . . . She was supposed to be disciplined. A *machine.* She'd allowed her dear father's education to slip away. She'd lost the very thing that had turned her into a monster. Yes. There was no denying it. She'd become sloppy in her teenage years.

Well, not tonight. Her heart pounded. Oh, no. It was time to make Daddy proud again.

She smiled at the drug dealer.

He straightened, wincing—clutching his back. Suddenly he froze. His eyes narrowed. "*You,*" he spat. "You're that bitch."

"That's right," Gaia murmured. "I'm that bitch."

He lunged forward, swinging with his right hand.

Gaia almost laughed. He'd telegraphed that punch so blatantly that she didn't even need to block it. She simply ducked out of the way, sidestepping him. The force of his own effort sent him staggering across the pavement.

He whirled around. His eyes smoldered.

He was breathing heavily, filling the air with white vapor. "You just better pray you don't get hurt," he hissed. "You don't know who you're messin' with."

I think I do, Gaia thought. But she kept silent. Talking during a fight was a distraction. Besides, silence instilled fear in an opponent. Not that she needed any advantages over him. He was scared enough. With good reason. He had no idea what was coming.

"Careful, Gaia," Mary murmured from the bench. "There's a gun on the ground."

The drug dealer grinned.

Oh, please. Did he really think Gaia was that stupid? Obviously he didn't know where the gun was. Otherwise he'd be looking at it.

Again he jumped forward and threw his right fist at her face.

How original, Gaia thought. There was no need to block *this* punch, either—but she wasn't interested in toying with him any longer. She shifted to the left and grabbed his wrist in midair, simultaneously kicking his right shin. It was classic kung fu. One of her patent moves. The force of his own punch in combination with the kick sent him flying off balance. But she didn't let go of his hand. Instead she twisted it, holding him in place—supporting almost all his weight. She grunted. Damn, he was heavy.

They were face-to-face.

Gaia grimaced. She could smell his rancid breath. Still, she savored the moment. By now he'd guessed that he couldn't possibly defeat her.

She let go of him. He nearly fell.

In the split second that he fought to regain his balance, she decided to switch from kung fu to karate. With an almost clinical detachment she chose to end this boring fight with a technique straight out of the *Go Rin No Sho*. A trick.

She raised her right fist.

He stared at it, backing off slightly.

She struck with her left.

The hand whistled audibly as it sliced through the frozen air toward his neck.

Contact. All of her years of training went into that strike—straight to the pressure point. She felt his collarbone shatter, heard the soft cracking sounds. It felt like gravel under the soft layer of his blubbery flesh.

"Uhh!" he gurgled.

He sank to his knees. His eyes were wide in shock. His mouth fell open. He gaped up at her, shaking his head. But she felt no pity. He deserved this—for torturing Mary when she was trying to get clean, for hooking others on drugs, for making the world a sadder and more desperate place. They *all* deserved this . . . everyone who caused suffering, everyone who profited from other people's misery.

"Gaia?"

Mary's voice drifted out of the night. But it was as if Gaia heard it in a dream. Time slowed again; there was no future, no past—only a continuous present in which she needed to finish her opponent. That, too, was a lesson from the *Go Rin No Sho.* She could recite the lines word for word. She could almost see the page in front of her as she drew back her left leg: *"Strike with the left side, with the spirit resolved, until the enemy is dead. . . ."*

The drug dealer lifted one hand, using the other one to clutch his ruined shoulder. "No," he wheezed. His lungs labored heavily. "Please, stop—"

Her leg lashed out in a powerful kick. The tip of her toe connected just under his chin. Blood splattered from his mouth. But amazingly enough, he didn't cry out. He made absolutely no sound. His body hung in midair, with his head thrown back, eyes staring at the sky—then he collapsed backward, hitting the pavement with a sticky smack.

"Gaia!" Mary shrieked.

Gaia stared down at him. The drug dealer's eyes were closed now. He lay perfectly still.

"What are you doing?" Mary's voice rose. "Stop it! Stop it!"

Gaia turned to answer her friend—but at that moment the ground beneath her seemed to open up and swallow her whole.

NIGHTMARE

Two dead bodies. Two.

That's what I'm dealing with.

Mary sat on the bench, still unable to move. Her eyes flashed from one crumpled form to the other. Time to rewind. She couldn't understand what had just happened. Gaia suddenly went into psycho kung fu mode, and then . . . *what?* Both she and Skizz looked like ghosts. They were bone white. Skizz's blood glistened in black puddles on the pavement. His mouth was open. Several teeth were missing. Neither he nor Gaia seemed to be breathing. Mary knew *she* was breathing because her breath was quite visible—exploding from her nostrils in a rapid, doglike rhythm. She was practically hyperventilating—

There!

A faint, grayish puff drifted from Skizz's unmoving lips.

Mary held her breath.

A few seconds later there was another puff. Then another. Skizz groaned.

Okay. Mary swallowed. *He isn't dead. This is good. Very good. Fatally injured, maybe—but not dead. Not yet, anyway. That left Gaia. . . .*

Mary jumped up and crouched beside her. She couldn't panic. No. The last time Gaia had beat up Skizz, she had also keeled over—for no apparent reason. Mary had thought that Gaia was on coke, actually. At the time it seemed like the only reasonable explanation for her inexplicable behavior.

Of course, that beating had been a slap on the wrist compared to this.

But maybe Gaia's passing out was some kind of physical problem. Like an allergic reaction or something. Yeah. The harder Gaia pounded on somebody, the worse she suffered. And now Mary remembered that Gaia had avoided the subject of that first collapse—

"Oh, man," Gaia mumbled.

"Yes!" Mary whispered. Hot tears welled in her eyes. She reached out and grabbed Gaia's hand. *My God.* The skin was so cold. . . .

Gaia opened an eyelid. "Are you okay?" she croaked.

"Me?" Mary hissed, glancing around. The question was almost funny, it was so absurd. But the situation was far from humorous. The park was still deserted. Her eyes fell on Skizz. He wasn't moving. He was still breathing, though. Barely.

"Yeah," Gaia answered. "He didn't do anything—"

"We gotta get out of here," Mary hissed urgently. "I think you hurt Skizz really bad."

Gaia clutched at Mary's arm and tried to pull herself into an upright position. She coughed a few times. She blinked at Skizz.

"Oh, no," she murmured shakily. Her entire body quivered. Mary couldn't help but notice that her neck was dotted with goose bumps. "I didn't mean . . ."

Mary shook her head. "It—it doesn't matter," she stammered. She could feel her pulse rising, feel her face getting hot—even though the temperature must have been close to zero. Gaia looked so disturbed, so unsure of herself. What the hell had happened, anyway? What had pushed her so far over the edge? The entire evening was starting to feel less like reality and more like some horrible nightmare. Mary fought to stay in control. "We gotta get out of here, Gaia. I mean it. This is really bad. . . ."

Gaia slumped against her. "You're gonna have to help me," she gasped.

"All right." Summoning all of her strength, Mary grabbed Gaia by the waist and hauled her to her feet. "Do you think you can walk?"

"I'll . . . try." Gaia flung an arm around Mary's shoulders. She felt like a giant rag doll in Mary's grip—floppy and out of control. But Mary squeezed her as tightly as she could.

"All we have to do is get to your house, okay?" Mary pleaded urgently. "It's not far at all. We can figure this all out when we get there."

Gaia nodded. "We gotta call 911. He's in really bad shape. . . ."

"We will. We will." Mary shambled down the path toward

the south exit, struggling to drag Gaia beside her. The girl could barely move. She was like a zombie. Catatonic.

The two of them nearly stepped on Skizz's face.

"I'm so sorry, Mary," Gaia whispered. "I'm so sorry—"

"It's all right," Mary interrupted.

But she was lying. It wasn't all right. Nothing was all right.

GAIA

Until now, I never understood the worst part about being fearless.

It's that I'm not afraid of myself. And I should be. I should be terrified of myself. Especially after what I did to that drug dealer in the park.

I just pray he lives. No, *pray* is the wrong word. I don't believe in prayer. I don't believe you can petition a higher power (if there even is a higher power, which I doubt) by clasping your hands together and getting on your knees.

But I hope the guy lives. I really do.

And I wish I could tell Mary what happened out there, why I did what I did, but the truth is that I have no idea. That ought to scare me too.

It doesn't, though. How can it?

PROBLEM SOLVED

LOKI SMILED AGAIN. EVERY OPERATIVE KNEW WHAT IT MEANT TO BE REMOVED FROM AN ASSIGNMENT. IT MEANT REMOVAL FROM EXISTENCE.

PARTIAL CONFESSIONAL

"I don't see anything about it in the paper," Mary mumbled. "So maybe he's okay."

Gaia sat slumped at the Nivenses' little kitchen table, staring across a soggy bowl of Froot Loops as Mary feverishly scoured the newspaper for any word of Skizz's death. Harsh winter sunlight streamed through the windows. Gaia didn't feel like mentioning that *The New York Times* probably wouldn't bother to report the death of a drug dealer. She didn't want to upset Mary any more than necessary. But the truth of the matter was that drug dealers got beat up and killed all the time in New York. It was a hazard of the business.

Still, if Mary believed that Skizz was okay, then she might calm down. And if Mary was calm, then maybe Gaia could convince herself that Skizz was okay, too.

Yeah. Sure.

I might have killed a man.

She'd been up all night, repeating those same words to herself over and over again, like some kind of twisted mantra. She hadn't slept. The fight had left her utterly spent—but she couldn't stop thinking about that look on his face after she'd kicked him. . . .

But he'd been breathing. Yes. She definitely remembered seeing his feeble gasps in the night air. So there was a chance he could have lived. Hopefully their call to 911 hadn't been too late.

"The problem is, I don't know his real name," Mary murmured distractedly, flipping through the Metro section to the obituaries. She held the paper up in front of her face. "I think it was James something. . . ."

Gaia's bleary eyes fell to the brightly colored mush in her cereal bowl. Blech. For once she had absolutely no appetite. George had left a carton of minidoughnuts out on the counter as well—but even *those* didn't look tempting. She sighed and grabbed her bowl, then dumped its contents into the garbage and tossed it in the kitchen sink.

Mary flinched at the clatter.

"Sorry," Gaia mumbled.

"It's okay." Mary folded the paper and laid it in front of her. Her hair was stringy, disheveled. Her face was still as pale as it was the night before. Her freckles seemed to stand out in relief on her white skin. Dark circles ringed her eyes. Jesus. She looked as bad as Gaia felt. "Hey, are George and Ella going to be coming back anytime soon?"

Gaia shrugged. "Who knows?" She sighed and sat back down. The important thing was that they were gone. There was no *way* she could deal with either of them right now. George would probably try to have some misguided heart-to-heart, and Ella would probably bawl her out for wasting a serving of breakfast cereal. But there was no point in getting angry over imaginary events. She had plenty to worry about in real life. She nodded at the paper. "You know, I don't think you're gonna find his name in there even if he *did* die," she muttered.

"I know," Mary whispered. "I was just . . ." She didn't finish.

"Maybe we should go look for him," Gaia suggested.

Mary nodded grimly. "Yeah. I was thinking about that."

Gaia ran a hand through the tangled blond mess on her head. "The problem is . . ."

"If we find him, and he *is* okay . . ."

Their gazes met across the table. There was no need to complete the thought. If Skizz had indeed survived that attack—and if he was out of the hospital and out on the streets—well, then, he would have only one mission in life. Revenge.

"Gaia?" Mary's voice was soft, shaky. She leaned across the table. "Look, I know you hate talking about yourself and revealing your deep, dark secrets or whatever, but . . . but the thing is . . . I mean, what made you freak out like that?"

Gaia stared back at her. She blinked a few times. She'd known Mary was going to ask that question sooner or later. It was actually pretty amazing that Mary had waited so long. And she deserved to know. Even though Gaia hated confessionals more than she hated hanging out with Ella, she figured she owed Mary *some* kind of explanation.

At the very least she had to soothe Mary's fears that such an attack would never happen again. And if she tried to articulate what she did, then maybe she would understand her own actions better herself.

"I really don't know," Gaia whispered, staring down at the newspaper. "It was just a lot of things, really." She drew in a deep breath and raised her eyes. "But mostly . . . mostly it was that I felt responsible for putting you in danger. I was mad at myself. I just took it out on him."

Mary shook her head. "But it wasn't your fault. I mean, I didn't *have* to go into that park. I could have said no—"

"But I pushed you," Gaia insisted. She tried to smile. "And the thing was, I thought I was actually doing you a favor. I know that sounds crazy, but it's true. I thought that if you went into the park and nothing happened, you wouldn't be scared of Skizz anymore." Any trace of her smile vanished. "And look what happened."

"You saved my life, though," Mary pointed out. She swallowed, drumming her fingers on the wooden tabletop. "I mean, even in the worst-case scenario, you know, even if he doesn't make it . . . you *were* protecting me. He had a gun. It was self-defense."

"Right," Gaia whispered emptily. "Self-defense." Guilt chewed through her like some kind of flesh-eating disease. Mary's words were a lie. Gaia didn't have to defend herself; she could have scared that guy off with one punch.

"It *was,*" Mary stated. But she might just have been trying to reassure herself. She slouched back in her chair and eyed Gaia curiously. "You know, you never told me. Where did you learn to fight like that, anyway?"

"My father," Gaia grumbled.

"Really?" All at once Mary sat up straight. Her gaze took on a new intensity. "The way you talk about him, it sounds like he knew everything about everything."

Gaia couldn't help but laugh. "Yeah. Sort of." She didn't try to mask the bitterness in her voice. "He instructed me in a lot of things."

"Like what?"

"Like . . ." Gaia hesitated. Amazingly enough, discussing her father wasn't nearly as painful as she would have imagined. It actually felt *good* to talk about him. And it wasn't as if Mary was trying to get information from Gaia for any sinister purposes; she simply wanted to know as much as possible about her friend. It was perfectly natural. Especially since Gaia hardly ever talked.

"Well, he made me read a lot," Gaia continued. She lifted her shoulders. "He basically made me do things that most kids shouldn't have to do until they're a lot older. Or not at all."

"Why?" Mary persisted.

Gaia laughed again. "Beats the hell out of me. I'd like to ask him myself."

"Why can't you?"

"Because I haven't seen the son of a bitch in five years."

The words flew from Gaia's mouth even before she was aware of saying them. *Damn.* She blinked. She hadn't realized the depths of her own venom. She was surprised. But most of all, she was surprised she had revealed so much. Had she made a mistake? Mary didn't need to know all the specifics. And Gaia certainly didn't need to discuss them. It had been a reflex; she couldn't help it—

"What happened?" Mary whispered.

Gaia's eyes fell back to the newspaper. A bitter bile rose in her throat. A stream of disjointed images floated through her consciousness: her mother's flowing dark hair . . . the delighted sound of her father's voice at the chess table in their cozy little wood-frame house: *"Katia! Our little girl is going to grow up to be a grand master!"* . . . a roaring fireplace . . . a terrible, driving snow that obliterated everything—

"No."

Mary blinked. "What?"

Gaia stared up at her. Had she said "no" out loud? She must have. This was not good. Thinking about her father would inevitably lead to her thinking about her mother, about that final night—and she was in no condition to go down that road. Not now. Not ever.

"I'm sorry," Mary murmured. "I don't mean to pry."

Gaia shook her head. "No . . . no, it's just that . . . my—

my father's a lousy guy," she stammered. Her throat tightened. "End of story."

Mary nodded. "I understand."

No, you don't, Gaia thought. Her mind was in a very dark cloud. *And you never should have to understand about people like him—people who desert the ones they're supposed to love. Nobody should have to understand. I sure as hell never will.*

"So what do you say?" Mary asked. Her tone was colorless. "You want to go to the park and see if we can find anything out?"

"Yeah." Gaia nodded. So much for opening up and confiding. She felt nauseated. Trying to determine whether she had killed a drug dealer was far preferable to digging up more of her past. "I do."

EXQUISITE SKILLS

Subject: John Doe, Male, Caucasian, aged forty to fifty. Admitted to St. Vincent's at 10:33 P.M. December 28. Injuries: fractured clavicle, fractured jaw, massive internal bleeding. Preliminary reports indicate assault. Subject is still unconscious. Condition is stable but critical. Fourteen grams of cocaine were discovered on his person.

Loki tossed the report on his desk without bothering to read the rest. There was no point. It merely confirmed what he had witnessed with his own eyes.

He'd been wrong to doubt Gaia's discipline. Very wrong. A smile spread across his face as he leaned back in his leather chair, basking in the sunshine that streamed through the giant windows of the loft. He didn't understand why Ella was upset. She stood by the door, pacing the wooden floor in small circles. But then, the woman's motives almost always defied logic.

"She could have killed him," Ella muttered.

"I'd have been that much more impressed if she had," Loki replied dryly. "And he still might die. He's not out of the woods yet."

Ella stopped pacing and shot Loki a hard stare. "She's out of control. If she had—"

"On the contrary," he interrupted, glaring at her. "She's very much *in* control. Had you been there with me, you would know. Her skills are still exquisite." He paused for a moment, furrowing his brow. "And why *weren't* you there, exactly?"

"I'm married," Ella snapped. She looked down at the floor. "In case you forgot, that takes up a lot of my time." Her voice softened. "George is a smart man. I've been playing this charade for five years, and if—"

"You're complaining?" Loki demanded.

Ella lifted her eyes. Her jaw twitched.

"Because if you're not satisfied, I can simply have you removed from the assignment," he remarked. His tone was casual.

She didn't answer. Loki smiled again. Every operative knew what it meant to be removed from an assignment. It meant removal from existence. Permanently. She would envy "John Doe" in her final breathing moments.

"All I'm saying is that her behavior has been erratic," Ella murmured after a moment. "You said so yourself. One day she's out vandalizing, the next she nearly kills someone."

Loki shrugged. "I know now that it shows she has a highly developed sense of loyalty. All we have to do is manipulate that loyalty when the time comes."

Ella threw her hands in the air. "Well, when *is* that time?" she cried. "We've been—"

"That's none of your concern," Loki interrupted. "You *know* that. And if anyone's behavior has been erratic, it's been yours."

Again she was silent.

Loki's eyes fell back to the report. With the drug dealer out of commission—indefinitely, it seemed—Mary Moss's life was no longer in jeopardy. They would have to come up with an alternate plan should it become necessary that she be neutralized. But he needed to observe her a few more times before he made that decision. It would have to be made soon, though. Ella's impatience notwithstanding, time was getting shorter.

Yes. The new year would bring many changes. For Gaia most of all.

Ella placed her hands on the back of Loki's neck. "I'm tired of waiting. And I'm tired of watching," she whispered, rubbing his shoulders—at first tentatively . . . but then slowly, sensuously.

"Most of all, I'm tired of not getting what I want. What I know you want, too." She leaned down and kissed his lips softly, stroking his cheek.

For a moment Loki let himself be kissed. It had been a long time. Too long.

He pulled her onto his lap, caressing the small of her back with one hand. With the other he pulled at a strand of her hair. For such an incredible bitch she could be so soft, so delicious, so . . .

Suddenly his senses returned in a blinding flash. What the hell was he doing? He had no time for Ella's foolishness. Loki stood abruptly, dumping Ella into a pitiful heap. He met her eyes with a glare of disgust. After all of the mistakes he had made, how could he ever be willing to let a woman distract him from the task at hand? Especially an inferior specimen like Ella. He knew perfectly well who she could never be. And so did she.

Neither of them had any illusions about that.

TOO DAMN PITIFUL

Four days. That was the longest Ed had ever gone without talking to Gaia. But even *that* seemed like nothing compared to the past two. Of course, the queasiness probably had something to do with it. And the terrible certainty that the two days would stretch to three, then to four . . . and that he might not ever talk to her again.

But he'd made a decision. He didn't care what happened to Gaia Moore. Not as long as she insisted on acting like an imbecile. He wouldn't apologize.

Funny how those kinds of decisions never seemed to stick.

He sat at his desk, staring at his computer. He couldn't bring himself to do anything else. Like turn *on* the computer. He thought about calling Heather, mostly to see Phoebe . . . but she would probably be on her way out to have some fun somewhere, and that would just make him *more* depressed. Anyway, if Heather *or* Phoebe wanted to hang out with him, they would call him. And they hadn't. Seeing him at that diner had probably been enough Ed Fargo to last the Gannis sisters another few years or so—

Stop feeling so goddamned sorry for yourself.

He ground his teeth. All day he'd sat in this exact spot, staring at his distorted reflection in the grayish cube of the blank screen, reliving the events of that night in Chinatown. He couldn't even remember how the fight with Gaia had started. One minute they were staring at a rack of grade F meat; the next, he was storming away from her.

Why? What the hell had she done to piss him off so much?

If anything, *he* should call to apologize. He was the one who had freaked out. He'd been so damn jumpy. For no reason at all, really. Now that he thought about it, he probably had imagined seeing that fat bearded guy in the window. And even if he hadn't, that guy wouldn't have tried anything on a crowded street.

And even if that fat guy *had* tried something—even if by some miracle that guy had suddenly attacked all three of them with a machete or a submachine gun . . . then Gaia would have kicked his ass.

Ed shook his head.

He was to blame. There was a way to end his suffering, though. Several, actually. Turn on the computer. Pick up the phone. Call. E-mail. Apologize. Bada-bing, bada-boom. Over. Problem solved.

But he just couldn't bring himself to do it. Because deep down in his battered soul, a part of him still clung to his old pride—the pride he'd felt when he could walk, when he was known as "Shred," the baddest skater south of Fourteenth

Street. It would be just too damn pitiful if he made the first move to reconcile with Gaia. Yes. If she valued the friendship as much as he did, *she* would have to be the one to call. It was a test. And if she failed—

Bzzzzzt.

Ed jumped slightly. The apartment buzzer was ringing. He rolled his eyes and scooted out of his bedroom into the narrow hall that led to the entranceway. It was probably some guy from Federal Express, delivering a lame Christmas fruit basket from a cousin twice removed in Hackensack that Ed had met only once.

He pressed the intercom button. "Hello?"

There was a crackle of static. "Ed?"

His jaw dropped. That voice. It sounded like . . . *her.*

"Gaia?" he asked, pressing the button again.

"Yeah. Is it cool if I come up?"

"Uh . . . sure."

His arm fell to his side. He glanced around the apartment. His heart immediately started thumping. Gaia Moore was coming up. *Here.*

Maybe he should clean up a little bit. Maybe he should tear down all the Christmas streamers and bulbs and paper angels that were still strewn all over the place. Jeez. He never realized how lame they were. This place was like one giant advertisement for corporate holidays. Speaking of which, at least his parents were at work. That lowered the lameness factor considerably—

He scowled.

Why was he getting so worked up? Almost *everyone* had Christmas decorations, or Hanukkah decorations, or Kwanza decorations . . . probably even Gaia's mysterious guardians. There was no point in trying to mask the fact that his parents weren't hip. Ed rubbed his palms on his jeans. He'd never tried to put on an act with Gaia before. He shouldn't start now. . . .

The doorbell rang.

He took a deep breath. Then he rolled over and opened the door.

Gaia stood before him. She didn't come in. She looked more beautiful than ever. But he didn't know why; she was still wearing those baggy cargo pants, some nondescript gray sweatshirt, and that overcoat-and-hat combo that looked like it had been swiped off a homeless person. Maybe it was her hair. It looked more sultry somehow—hanging in tousled curls across her face. And her cheeks were flushed from the cold, almost as if she were blushing.

"Hey, Ed. Sorry to bother you."

"I . . ." He didn't even know what he wanted to say.

"Look, I don't have a lot of time," Gaia said quickly. She stared down at her sneakers. "Mary's waiting downstairs. I just wanted to tell you that I'm really sorry about the way I acted the other night. It was stupid."

Ed just stared at her. He couldn't believe this. He didn't have a clue as to how to respond. For once Gaia Moore was doing exactly what he'd prayed she would do. It was almost frightening.

She looked up at him. "You were right, too, by the way."

"What do you mean?"

"There was a guy following us. Mary's old drug dealer."

"What?" Ed gasped. "How do you—"

"Look, I can't go into it right now, okay?" she interrupted. She glanced back toward the elevator and flashed him a quick, enigmatic smile. "Just . . . things are a little weird right now. But I just want you to know that I'm sorry. I swear I've learned my lesson this time. Okay?"

He nodded vigorously. "Well, yeah. I mean, I'm sorry, too—"

"I gotta go. See ya." She turned back down the hall.

Ed blinked. But before he could even open his mouth, he heard the elevator bell ring, then the doors open and shut.

He laughed. Well. It looked like everything was back to normal. He was friends with her again, and she was involved in something bad again. Yup. It was just another ordinary day for her. Appear out of nowhere, make Ed experience a dozen emotions in the space of about thirty seconds, and vanish. Classic Gaia.

"Oh, no," Mary croaked the moment she and Gaia turned onto MacDougal Street. She pointed a shaky finger at the park.

Gaia peered through the tree branches, following Mary's outstretched arm—straight to the spot where she had left Skizz on the ground.

Her mind suddenly went blank. She knew why. She should have been scared.

Cops were there.

Part of the path had been roped off with yellow police tape. Two policemen in dark blue jackets were standing on the other side of it, talking to two guys in long trench coats—detectives, maybe. One of them had a camera.

"He must have died," Mary whispered, shivering in the cold. "He must have—"

"Shhh," Gaia whispered gently. She knew she should probably turn and run—but instead she felt only a powerful curiosity. The presence of cops was actually a *good* thing. Now there was a quick way to find out if Skizz had died there last night. She knew police procedure when a body was found in the park. Her face darkened. Oh, yes. She knew it all too well. When "the Gentleman" had murdered Cassie Greenman there a couple of months ago (and tried to make Gaia his next victim), the police had outlined Cassie's body in chalk on the ground, leaving a grim memory of the crime for all to see. So if Gaia had really killed Skizz, there ought to be one of those outlines as well.

"Wait here," Gaia instructed Mary. "I'm gonna go check it out—"

"Are you crazy?" Mary hissed. "Gaia, they could be looking for you."

She shrugged. "Then there's no point in postponing the inevitable, right? I might as well get it over with. Just hang out here. If you see me getting arrested or something, take off." She turned and hurried across the street without waiting for Mary to reply.

Hopefully Mary would follow her advice. Gaia figured she would. After all, Mary had something working in her favor that Gaia didn't. Fear.

Gaia's eyes narrowed as she entered the park. The glare of the winter sunshine made it difficult to see, but from what she could tell . . . no, there definitely wasn't any sort of chalk drawing on the ground. A good sign. Of course, Skizz could have died at the hospital—

"Can I help you, miss?" one of the cops asked as she approached.

She smiled at him innocently. "I was just wondering what was going on."

"Nothing," the other cop replied shortly. "Just move along."

"Did . . . uh, did somebody die?" she asked, staring down at the marked-off area. Several large, rust-colored stains glistened on the pavement.

"Somebody was assaulted," the first cop said. His voice hardened. "Now, please move along. This is a crime scene."

Gaia nodded, then turned away. So Skizz might still be alive. Assault wasn't murder. She glanced surreptitiously back at MacDougal Street. Mary was still standing on the corner, staring at her. Gaia had started walking back toward the park exit when she heard a couple of footsteps behind her.

"Excuse me? Miss?"

The guy with the trench coat and camera was catching up with her. Now that he was closer, she could see that he didn't look like a typical cop. Hardly. He looked more like he belonged at some kind of pretentious gallery opening in SoHo. He was wearing a four-button suit under his coat, and he had a goatee. His black hair was slicked back with gunk.

"Yeah?" she asked.

He leaned close to her and gently took her elbow, steering her farther away from the crime scene. "My name's Jared Smith," he murmured. "I'm a reporter for *The Daily News.* Is it all right if I ask you a couple of questions?"

Gaia hesitated. She glanced back at Mary. Even from

this distance Gaia could tell that Mary was getting more anxious by the second. She kept bouncing up and down on the balls of her feet. But this guy might know something about what happened—something that the cops weren't willing to share.

"I guess so," she mumbled. "What do you want to know?"

"Do you hang out here a lot? In the park, I mean?"

She took a step back, trying not to gag. His cologne reeked. "Um, sometimes," she answered. "Why?"

"Have you ever been offered drugs here?" he asked. He pulled a little notebook out of his trench coat pocket.

"No." Gaia scowled. "What's this about, anyway?"

"The cops think the assault might have been the result of a turf war in the drug trade," he said. He fished for a pencil, then gave her a quick, disdainful once-over. "I was just wondering if you knew anything about that."

Whoever this Jared Smith was, he sure as hell didn't have any manners. Just because she wasn't dressed as if she'd walked straight out of an Armani ad, he automatically assumed that she was a junkie. But at least she knew now that she wasn't a suspect. She supposed it made sense. Who would ever suspect a junkie of kicking a big fat drug dealer's ass?

"Can I ask you something?" she said.

He shrugged, jotting something down in his notebook.

"Is the victim alive?"

"Barely," he answered. "But he'll make it. He's at St. Vincent's. Apparently the cops have been looking for him. He's being arraigned today on three counts of possession with intent to sell, resisting arrest, and assault with a deadly. As soon as he's able, he's gonna be moved to the infirmary at Rikers Island. Why do you want to know? Was he your supplier?"

Gaia ignored the question. She resisted the temptation to punch him in the face. This smug bastard needed some major work on his people skills. Not that she was one to talk, of course. But she was glad to end this little interview. Skizz had survived—and it looked like he'd be getting locked away for a very long time. Mary's worries were over. And so were Gaia's. She felt like a tremendous weight had suddenly been lifted from her shoulders. She *wasn't* a killer. She might be a lot of other things . . . but she still wasn't that. She whirled and strode away from him.

"Hey!" he called after her. "I'm asking you a question!"

"He wasn't my supplier," she answered, without even bothering to look over her shoulder. She picked up her pace in case he tried to follow her.

"Can I get your name? In case I want to quote . . ."

The sound of his annoying voice was lost in her footsteps as she darted back across MacDougal Street to Mary.

"What's going on?" Mary whispered, peering behind Gaia at the park. "What did that guy want? Is he a detective—"

"There's nothing to worry about," Gaia interrupted gently. She grabbed Mary's arm and whisked her around the corner toward Sixth Avenue. "That guy was just some sleazebag reporter. But he told me that Skizz is on his way to jail. The cops think a rival dealer did it."

Mary blinked several times. She looked at Gaia, then stared down at her feet as they walked side by side. "Are you *serious*?"

"Yeah. He's wanted for, like, eight felonies or something."

"But . . . what if he tells the cops who kicked his ass?" Mary asked. She shook her head. "I mean, he can describe the way you look, you know?"

Gaia laughed. Funny. She hadn't even thought of that. But it didn't concern her very much—and not only because she was fearless. She doubted very much that Skizz would rat her out to the cops. He was probably scared shitless of her. And the cops probably wouldn't believe him, anyway. The idea of a seventeen-year-old girl's nearly killing an armed drug dealer was just too preposterous. At least, that was the way it had always worked in the past.

"I guess we'll just have to cross that bridge when we come to it," Gaia said, patting Mary's shoulder. "But for now, I'd say things are cool."

FROM: shred@alloymail.com
TO: gaia13@alloymail.com
RE: 411
TIME: 5:03 P.M.

Hey, G$—
Very psyched you came by. I have to say, I'm a little curious about what you said. What did you mean by "things are a little weird"? Can you be more specific? I know you don't like answering these kinds of questions, but a little info would put my mind at ease. Also, what are you doing tomorrow night? I need to escape my family. Thanking you in advance—
Ed

FROM: gaia13@alloymail.com
TO: shred@alloymail.com
RE: No worries, no plans
TIME: 6:00 P.M.

Hey, Ed—
Forget about what I said. Things aren't going to get weird. As for tomorrow night, I have no plans. Mary and I were talking about watching TV at her house and stuffing our faces with ice cream. Yes, I know it's lame. But if you feel like being lame, too, consider

this an invitation. We're going to get together
around nine.
G$

FROM: shred@alloymail.com
TO: gaia13@alloymail.com
RE: Being lame
TIME: 7:08 P.M.

Hey, G$—
Count me in. I'll be there.

FROM: gaia13@alloymail.com
TO: smoon@alloymail.com
RE: [no subject]
TIME: 10:01 P.M.

Hi. I'm just writing to tell you that I think you're the biggest jerk I ever met and I can't believe you're back with Heather and I hate you and I never want to talk to you again. And everything I just wrote is a lie. I miss you. I want to call you, but I can't. I can't even bring myself to say your name out loud. I don't know why. I'm not scared of you. I don't get scared, in case you didn't know. I just feel confused. So is this what fear feels like? Can you tell me?
«DELETE»

TO GAIA

HE'D ENVISIONED MAKING OUT WITH GAIA COUNTLESS TIMES, IN THOUSANDS OF DIFFERENT SCENARIOS— BUT NEVER ONCE HAD HE IMAGINED THIS.

HOMECOMING

Tom Moore's legs were practically numb. They always went numb in airplanes, even in first-class seats. But his mind wasn't on his own discomfort. His fingers furiously flew across his laptop, searching the agency's databases for Loki's known associates. He'd been awake for almost thirty-six straight hours—and airborne for about half that time—but there was no chance he could sleep. Not until he figured out who had contacted him.

Search: Loki—U.S. Militia Groups.

No match found.

He shook his head. Nothing. Only when he searched for Loki's contacts outside the United States did he come up with any matches: the usual list of terrorists and arms dealers—shadowy characters from groups like Hammas and Shining Path. But the man who had called didn't have the slightest trace of an accent.

So who was he?

Tom rubbed his bloodshot eyes and leaned back in his chair, staring out the round window at a wall of blackness. The plane was somewhere over the Atlantic now. It would probably be touching down at JFK within the hour. He had to think. Who would Loki employ that could possibly have access to Gaia? One of her friends? Tom thought he knew them: There was that boy Sam and the kid in the wheelchair . . . and that was pretty much it. For the most part Gaia kept to herself. And there was no way either of *them* could be working for Loki. So was it somebody whom Gaia had met recently?

He hunched back over the screen and typed for what must have been the hundredth time:

Search: Loki—recent communications

The computer hummed for a split second.

2 matches found.

ELJ (identity unknown)

BFF (identity unknown)

He kept coming up with the same two sets of initials over and over again. And he had no idea who either "ELJ" or "BFF" could possibly be. Neither did the agency, apparently. It was a miracle they had found out *that* much. Loki was meticulous in covering his tracks.

Tom's eyes wandered to the window again. There was a possibility, of course, that he hadn't allowed himself to consider.

It was a very obvious possibility. A *probability*, in fact—which was that the call was a trap. Loki might have even made the call himself, masking the timbre of his voice with an electronic device. Loki might well have wanted to lure Tom out of Russia in order to dispose of him once and for all, so that there would be nothing standing between Loki and his twin brother's daughter. . . .

Tom slammed the laptop shut. Speculation was a waste of time. He'd know the answers to all these questions soon enough.

Loki might answer them himself.

A TOAST

"Ella, honey?" George called from the living room. "Don't you want some wine? I'm just about to crack open another bottle."

Better make that two, Ella thought, groaning silently. She sat at the kitchen table, feeling very much as if her life were draining from her body. What the hell was she even doing here? It was two nights before New Year's Eve, for God's sake. The best time of year for parties. The big end-of-the-year blitz. Almost everyone they knew was out on the town. Yet George had insisted on staying at home every single night since Christmas. Socializing with other people was the only remotely tolerable aspect of their sham marriage—but they didn't even have any plans for New Year's Eve itself. Did the old man really believe she *wanted* to be alone with him? Was he really that blind?

Yes. He was. She found herself smiling in spite of her anger. He was that blind because she was such an excellent actress.

"El-la!" he called in a singsong voice.

"Coming!" she answered with false brightness.

He was so goddamned cheerful. She thought of the thirty-eight-caliber pistol hidden behind her night table. It would be so easy to run upstairs and grab it. So easy to twist on the silencer. So easy to shut him up for good. On these nights—the painful, romantic nights, the nights when she had to play the role of a loving wife . . . well, she couldn't take them much longer. The years were beginning to take their toll. No payoff could be worth this agony.

She swallowed. No. The payoff *would* be worth it. She would make sure of it. And it would far exceed anything that Loki had envisioned for her. Oh, yes. In fact, her reward would include Loki himself.

Ella took a deep breath and plastered a smile on her face, then pushed herself from the table and strode into the living room.

"There you are," George murmured. He was leaning back on the sofa, struggling with a corkscrew and a glistening green bottle. At least she lived luxuriously. In a purely materialistic sense, she had everything she needed. For the time being, anyway. That bottle of chardonnay probably cost seventy bucks. Two crystal glasses sat on the mahogany coffee table. Those weren't cheap, either. Wedding presents. How ironic. The logs burning in the fireplace cast the room in a soft glow; few brownstones in New York had real working fireplaces. Her life was good. She should just enjoy it while it lasted.

Pop!

"There we go," George whispered. He laid the corkscrew on the table, then filled her glass with the golden liquid.

"Thank you," Ella murmured seductively. She raised her glass as George filled his own. "Cheers."

He put down the bottle and lifted his glass. "Cheers." He leaned forward, then hesitated. "Wait. I want to ask you a question. Do you have any New Year's resolutions?"

She smirked. "It's not even New Year's Eve."

"I know, but I guess I've been thinking a lot these days about the changes I'd like to make. So?" His smile widened. "What's it going to be?"

"Well . . ." She edged closer to him. "The only change I'd like to make is to spend more time with my loving and very sexy husband," she whispered. He blushed slightly, as she knew he would. It was so easy to control him. "How about you?"

His face grew serious for a moment. "I want to make sure that Gaia is happy. I want to include her more. To really make her feel like part of the family."

Ella nodded. How sweet. And pathetic. And infuriating.

It was almost too much. The mere mention of Gaia's name made her insides twist. But her smile didn't falter. She tilted her glass. "A toast. To Gaia."

"To Gaia," George echoed, tapping her glass with his own.

Yes, Ella thought. May she rot in hell.

THE SCORE

The week between Christmas and New Year's Eve was Sam's least favorite time of the year—at least when he was in New York. True, he'd been here only once in the past: last year. But he already knew the score. Inevitably the entire week meant going from one lame party to the next, night after night, always trying to track down an elusive great time that never materialized—and winding up each time on the street at 3 A.M., freezing, disappointed, and trying to hail a cab back home.

Clearly tonight would be no exception.

For starters, he didn't even know where he *was*. Well, he knew he was at some filthy, cramped apartment in the East Village—but he had no idea who lived here. Kelly? Christie?

Something like that. Whoever she was, she loved red lights and deafening industrial rock and was a friend of a friend of Heather's sister Phoebe . . . and she'd offered some kind of incomprehensible greeting when he and Heather and Phoebe walked through the door. "Welcome, warriors." At least that was what he thought she'd said. Whatever the hell that was supposed to mean. And then she'd disappeared.

So now he found himself drinking a warm beer and wondering where his girlfriend and her sister went. What a blast. Whoopee. He tried to maneuver his way from the tiny living room to the hall by the closet-sized kitchen—but just ended up getting mushed against a wall by a group of heavily pierced strangers. They were all dressed in black. The wall vibrated in time to the music. He scowled and slurped down his beer. Best just to get drunk. At least he'd be able to forget—

"Sam! *There* you are!"

Phoebe was jumping up and down by the kitchen doorway, trying to make eye contact with him. She waved her hands over the heads of the mob.

"Come here!" she called.

Yeah, right. She was only about ten feet away, but he'd need a battering ram to reach her. He shrugged and tried to smile.

"Hold on a sec," Phoebe shouted. "We're coming out . . ." Her voice was lost in the din as she ducked back into the kitchen.

Good luck, he thought. He drained the rest of the beer in one long gulp. *Blech.* He made a face and wiped his mouth with his sleeve—but a pleasant, warm numbness began to spread from his stomach throughout his body. Hopefully if Heather and Phoebe *did* make it out of the kitchen, they'd bring him another drink. It was strange. Usually he wasn't a huge fan of booze. It just made his head swim. It probably made him act a lot more obnoxious, too. A lot of kids in his dorm drank all the time, and if they were any indication of how people acted when they were drunk—

He stiffened. His eyes zeroed in on a tall girl coming out of the kitchen.

Her back was turned to him, but from here it definitely looked like Gaia.

Yes. That hair. That long, blond tangle. Nobody had hair like that. He stood on his tiptoes. His heart began to race. What was she doing here? What . . .

The girl glanced over her shoulder.

Shit. Excitement fizzled out of him like air hissing from a deflating flat tire. Apparently somebody else *did* have hair like that. Somebody a lot less attractive.

He shook his head. Of course Gaia wouldn't come to the same party. And even if she *had*, he would have nothing to say to her. He suddenly found he was extremely pissed off. At everyone. At Heather and Phoebe for bringing him here. At the people in this room. But most of all at Gaia—for dropping off the face of the earth, for finding a new boyfriend, and for dominating his thoughts about ninety-five percent of the time when he *should* be in love with someone else. . . .

"Whoa!" Heather's familiar shriek tore through the crowd. He couldn't see her, but she was obviously close by. He shook his head again, overcome with guilt. What the hell was his problem? He *was* in love with her. Heather was beautiful. Heather was smart. Heather had a cool sister who was *also* beautiful. She was everything a guy could want—

"Excuse me! Sorry!"

A second later Heather burst from between two spaced-out-looking grunge types and nearly fell against Sam. She clutched a plastic cup of beer in each hand. A couple of drops splashed on Sam's flannel shirt.

"Whoops," she murmured, giggling. She handed Sam one of the cups, then used her free hand to try to wipe his shirt. She swayed slightly. Her face was flushed. "Sorry about that. It's just kinda hard to move around in here."

"No kidding," he said.

She took a huge gulp of beer.

"Maybe you've had enough," he muttered.

"Oh, come on." She slapped his arm. Her eyes were heavily lidded. "It's a party. You know, the last time I was this messed up . . ." She didn't finish. Her gaze became glassy.

"What?" Sam demanded impatiently.

She sighed and shook her head. "Never mind." She smiled

up at him. "Iss not worth getting into," she slurred. "So are you having fun?"

"The time of my life," he stated flatly.

"Good." She nodded, somehow oblivious to the biting sarcasm in his voice.

"So where's Phoebe?" he asked, struggling to keep a lid on his annoyance.

Heather shrugged dramatically. "Who knows? She's a . . . she's a free spirit." She burst out laughing, as if that were the funniest joke anyone had ever made.

That was it. Something snapped. He didn't know what it was. Maybe it was Heather's drunkenness, or the crowd, or the stale stink of beer . . . but he'd had enough. He brushed past her and tried to force his way to the door.

"Hey!" she cried, still laughing. She grabbed his shoulder from behind. "What's wrong?"

"Nothing," he muttered, shoving through the grunge kids. "I just want to go home."

"What?" she yelled. "I can't hear you—"

"I want to go *home*," he snapped, turning back around.

She blinked. Then she raised her hands, grinning crookedly. "All right, all right," she said. "Whew. No need to yell. Lemme just get my coat. I'll tell Phoebe we're leaving. This party's kind of lame, anyway."

He opened his mouth—but before he could say anything, she stepped past him and snaked her way into the kitchen.

He was going to tell her that she should just stay here, that he didn't want to ruin her good time, that he was just feeling lousy . . . but those all would have been lies. The truth was that he didn't want to be with her. No matter *where* they were. Not tonight. He wanted to be with someone else.

But it was too late. His girlfriend was coming with him.

He eyed his beer, then lifted the cup and started chugging. Best just to go numb, right?

THE ANTIDOTE

Gaia stared down at the bottom of the empty pint of chocolate chocolate chip ice cream.

"No more." She groaned.

She couldn't believe she'd eaten the whole thing—on top of another pint before that *plus* an amazing dinner (chicken Kiev, care of the Moss's Russian cook, Olga). . . . Her stomach felt like it was about to explode. She glanced up at Mary and Ed. They weren't faring much better. Mary was sprawled on the living-room couch beside her, clutching her belly. Ed was slumped in his wheelchair in front of the flickering, muted television set. He frowned at his own half-eaten bowl of Rocky Road. He looked a little pale.

"I don't know if I can finish this," he said blankly.

"Hey, kids!" Mary's mother called from the kitchen. "Do you want some more ice cream?"

Mary rolled her eyes. "Uh . . . no, thanks, Mom."

Gaia exchanged a quick glance with Ed. The two of them burst out laughing. Gaia winced. She placed her own empty carton next to Ed's bowl and held her sides.

"Stop it," she moaned. "Don't make me laugh. I'm too full."

"How about a little more chicken, dear?" Ed asked, imitating Mary's mom.

"Stop it!" Gaia closed her eyes for a moment and shook her head, giggling. "I mean it. It's not funny. . . ."

"Hey, check it out," Ed suddenly announced, pointing at the TV screen. "They're talking about all the preparations for New Year's Eve in Times Square." He snorted. "You know, I've lived in New York my whole life, but I've never gotten the whole Times Square thing. Who would actually want to *go* there? I mean, who would want to stand out in the freezing cold in Midtown, packed in like sardines with a bunch of strangers, just to watch some cheesy ball drop?"

"To be part of history, Ed," Mary answered dryly.

Gaia smirked. She didn't get it, either. She'd read somewhere that something like a million and a half people had gone there last year. And they had all been stuffed into an eight-block radius. How could they even *breathe*? She had no desire to experience New Year's Eve like that. Nope. She wanted to be someplace like this. Sitting in a cozy apartment, enjoying the company of friends . . . yes. This was perfect. This was right.

All at once Gaia felt a lump forming in her throat—the same lump she felt a few days ago on the subway with Mary. *Oh, Jesus.* She wasn't going to get all weepy and sentimental again, was she? It was not good form. Not for a superbadass chick like Gaia Moore. But she couldn't help it. She hadn't been so content or relaxed since . . . well, since she'd had a real family.

She swallowed.

A real family. The words rang through her mind like the distant cry of some tortured animal. She shook her head. She wasn't going to think about her mother or father. Not anymore. She wasn't going to think about love lost or love turned to hate. None of that mattered anymore. *This* was her family now: Mary and Ed. They were all she needed.

"You know what's even more pathetic than watching New Year's Eve celebrations at home?" Ed asked with a grin. "Watching the *preparations* for New Year's Eve celebrations."

Gaia smiled and turned her attention to the TV screen. There was no need to dwell on the past. It was best just to have a good time. The camera panned up from the streets to the darkened crystal sphere, hovering on a long cord over Times Square. It looked like a giant disco ball. All those people would gather to see *that*? She sighed. Ed was right. It *was* kind of pathetic watching this stuff. Besides, New Year's Eve really didn't mean anything at all. The end of the year was a totally arbitrary date. If they had been using the Chinese calendar, December 31 would be just another day.

"Oh, by the way," Ed said. "I want to take this opportunity to let you both know that I think you're the biggest losers on the planet."

Gaia kicked the back of his wheelchair.

"Hey!" He chuckled.

"How about some cookies?" Mrs. Moss called.

"Mom!" Mary yelled, grimacing.

Ed started cracking up again. "So . . ." He grabbed the remote and clicked off the television, then turned his wheelchair around so that he was facing the two of them. "If we aren't gonna eat cookies, what *are* we gonna do?"

Mary raised her eyebrows. "You know, we never got a chance to finish the game."

"What game?" Ed asked.

Gaia laughed. It figured Ed wouldn't remember. "What do you think, you dope?" she asked. "Truth or dare."

Ed frowned. Then he laughed, too. He slumped deep into his chair, burying his face in his hands and shaking his head. "That's what I get for opening my big mouth. . . ."

"Look, Ed, we won't leave the apartment this time, all right?" Mary said. "It'll be strictly indoors. It's too cold, and we're all too full—"

"But I thought the game was over," Ed interrupted. He looked up. "Besides, isn't it customary that a game of spin the bottle always follows a game of truth or dare?"

"Where?" Mary asked dryly. "In Fargoland?"

Ed shrugged and smiled. "Hey, I'm just trying to liven things up a little bit."

"So whose turn is it?" Gaia asked, suddenly excited. *This* was the good time she'd been looking for—the antidote to thinking about all the crap in her life.

Mary smirked at her. "Are you volunteering?"

Gaia nodded and sat up straight. "You got it."

"Okay." Mary leaned back. She looked very pleased with herself. "I think I've got a dare that'll liven things up Fargo style. Gaia?" She paused dramatically. "I dare you to make out with Ed."

For a moment Gaia was stunned into silence. She could feel a flush creeping up her cheeks. This was certainly something she hadn't expected. But then again, she should have expected no less from Mary Moss.

"That's it?" Gaia asked, filling her voice with bravado. Jeez. Did Mary think that kissing Ed was some kind of big deal? It was like kissing a brother, if she'd *had* a brother. . . . She glanced over at him.

Okay, not *quite* like kissing a brother. Gaia had to admit it, Ed was actually a *guy*. Her friend, yes. A complete freak sometimes. But a *guy*. And when it came to kissing guys, her track record was pretty lousy.

Gaia roused herself out of her thoughts long enough to notice that Ed was scowling at Mary. For some reason, it sent a small pain stabbing into her chest.

"You scared or something?" she asked him, pretending to be offended.

READY

Ed couldn't answer the question. He couldn't answer it because he *was* scared. And ashamed. And a little crestfallen, too. He'd envisioned making out with Gaia countless times, in thousands of different scenarios—but never once had he imagined *this*: exchanging a few sloppy kisses for Mary Moss's benefit. On the other hand . . .

Gaia winked at him. At first he thought she'd seemed a little shocked, but it must have been his imagination. Gaia looked completely unruffled as always. "You ready, baby?" she mock whispered.

He barely heard the question. His heart was thumping so fast that the sound of his pulse filled his ears; he felt almost like he was buried under a thick, gauzy blanket. He no longer felt uncomfortably full, either. His stomach felt strangely empty. Regardless of whether or not this moment conformed to any fantasies he'd had, he realized that it was actually happening.

He was about to kiss Gaia Moore.

He really was. He gaped at her as she approached the wheelchair. Events unfolded way too fast when Gaia got together with Mary. One second he was watching TV; the next—

"And when I say make out, I mean make out," Mary said, giggling. "No half-assed, closed-mouthed smooching."

"I know," Gaia murmured. She stood in between his legs and leaned over him, gripping the wheelchair's hand rests to steady herself. Her face was now barely three inches from his own. He could see every detail of her porcelain skin, every fleck in her blue eyes. . . . He could even detect a slight tremble in her lips. He couldn't believe how soft they looked, how moist, how . . .

"Uh, you sure you want to do this?" he asked, swallowing.

Instead of answering, she simply covered his lips with her own.

TURN-ON

Gaia felt like she was floating. Her eyes were closed. Her lips felt the texture of Ed's lips; her tongue explored his mouth. For the first few seconds the motions were mechanical. Her body was acting independently of her thoughts. Her mind drifted back through all the kisses she'd experienced in the past. But then, without warning, she shifted back to the present.

She was enjoying this.

The way Ed kissed her . . . it was *tender* somehow. Caring. Loving. Sensual.

Did Ed feel the same way? She couldn't help but wonder what he was thinking. And then she stopped wondering. She forgot about Mary. She forgot about everything.

Ed's fingers brushed against her arm.

A little tingle raced down her spine.

Whoa. What was going on here?

She *was* enjoying this. She tentatively let her fingers travel to his soft, thick hair, noticing that his hands had moved to her lower back. The sensation it caused was dizzying.

Without thinking, she pressed her body toward him. She wanted to stretch the moment as long as it would go. Ed responded, pulling her closer to him and pressing his lips more urgently onto her own. This was insane.

Suddenly Gaia was hit with the urge to pull back. She

wanted to see Ed. She wanted to know what was going on in his head. She jerked away abruptly, meeting his eyes with her own baffled gaze. His face was flushed. He held Gaia's stare in a look that seemed half pain, half elation.

"Ooh, baby!" Mary cried.

And that was it.

The moment was shattered. Gaia was no longer in a private little world of two; she was back in Mary Moss's apartment, playing truth or dare. She backed away and took a deep breath. Her heart was fluttering.

Ed didn't speak. Their eyes met for a moment.

Whew. Gaia smiled. That was weird. Her feelings of a second before seemed to be floating away—like a wisp of smoke from a candle. It was formless and intangible . . . and then it was gone. What had she been thinking? This was *Ed*. Her friend. She laughed and took a deep breath. It was a good thing it was someone else's turn now.

"So, Ed," she managed to say nonchalantly. "Was it as good for you as it was for me?"

THE DECISION

THAT HAD BEEN QUITE AN ENLIGHTENING LITTLE EXCHANGE. QUITE AN OUTPOURING OF EMOTION. TWO GIRLS, UNITED BY LONELINESS . . .

The night could be worse, Ed realized. It could be a hell of a lot worse.

True, he was playing the annoying game again. But on the plus side he'd eaten a great meal. And he was hanging out in a hot girl's living room. And it looked like he was going to be spending the night here. It was already almost one o'clock.

Oh, yeah. He'd also kissed Gaia Moore.

That minor little thing. The thing that would explain why his heart was about to explode out of his chest. The thing that would explain why he could hardly breathe.

The weirdest part of it was that the memory was already fuzzy. It had happened only seconds ago, but it felt like a dream. Of course, he hadn't seen anything; his eyes had been closed. The only part of it that was clear was the sensation of her lips against his.

And that had been pretty nice. Pretty damn nice.

He shifted in his wheelchair and gazed at Gaia, stretched out on the couch beside Mary.

Yes. It *had* been nice. Hadn't it?

So why did Gaia look totally unaffected—as if nothing had happened at all? Hadn't she felt *anything*? She had pretty much initiated it by volunteering. . . .

Then he remembered. It was part of a game.

Right. A joke. Nothing more than that. A little comedy routine between friends. Actually, in a way, the kiss had been pretty symbolic of the way Gaia felt about him. She liked to push him. She liked to get him riled up. But only to make him laugh. In her eyes, he was the funny guy. The sidekick. Somebody whom she loved and wanted around—but not somebody she would ever take seriously, at least in a romantic way. That was why she had gone so far. She never would have kissed Sam Moon like that. Not in a game, anyway.

No silly dares or pranks or stunts would ever change the way she felt.

And the truly ironic (meaning shitty) thing was that she had no idea that he didn't *like* being the sidekick. She had no idea that he wanted something more out of their relationship. So. When he looked at it from that point of view, the kiss had sucked. But everything sucked from a certain point of view. What else was new?

"All right, Ed," Gaia said. "Your turn. You've ducked this for way too long. Truth or dare?"

He thought for a second. He could feel a sour mood creeping up on him, but he fought it back. He'd been having a lot of fun up until this point—and he wasn't going to let *his* problems ruin *their* good time. It wasn't Gaia's fault that she wasn't head over heels in love with him.

"Truth," he said.

Mary leaned over and whispered something in Gaia's ear. The two of them giggled.

Uh-oh. Ed's face grew hot.

"Good," Gaia said. She sat up straight. "If you could have sex with anyone in the world right now, who would it be? And it has to be somebody you actually know. Not a supermodel or Madonna or anything like that."

Ed stared back at her. *You, you moron,* he felt like shouting. But there was no point. She was smiling—mischievously, of course, but innocently, too. And he could see it in her beautiful blue eyes: She honestly didn't know that she was the only one he would *ever* want to have sex with . . . in a real kind of way. Even after that kiss, she had no idea. Of course, he'd be happy to have sex with a number of other girls in a not so real way, but it wasn't the same.

There was no way he could tell her. He'd known this all along, but only now did he really see *why* he couldn't confess his love for Gaia Moore. It wasn't the fear of rejection. He could live with rejection.

It was because he knew he'd hurt her.

If she found out how he really felt, she'd be horrified. On a variety of levels, too. One, because their relationship would never be the same; two, because she would realize that she was causing him pain; three, because there would be no way she would ever reciprocate. . . .

"There is someone," he found himself saying.

"Really?" Gaia's eyes widened. She leaned forward. "Who?"

Mary bolted upright beside her. "Yeah," she said eagerly. "Who?"

"You . . . you'll probably think it's a little weird," he said, swallowing. His pulse picked up a beat. It would be so easy to tell the truth. So easy to get it off his shoulders once and for all—

"That's okay," Gaia prodded. "Weird is good. So?"

"Phoebe Gannis," he said.

The name just popped into his head; he hadn't even been sure he was really going to say it until he uttered the words.

Gaia's face soured. *"Who?"*

"Heather's sister?" Mary asked. She smiled, cocking her eyebrow. "Jeez, Ed . . . I hope Heather didn't know about that while you two were dating."

Ed shrugged. In a way, his answer hadn't been a complete lie. He'd always had a little crush on Phoebe. And it had definitely been at its height while he was seeing Heather.

"Wait a second," Gaia said, raising her hands and glancing between Ed and Mary. Her brow was tightly furrowed. "Heather Gannis has a *sister*? How come I didn't know about this?"

"She has two, actually. Phoebe goes to college upstate," Ed said. "She's never around."

Gaia frowned. "Is Phoebe . . . Does she look like Heather?"

Ed allowed himself a little smile. He was almost certain that Gaia was going to ask: *Is she pretty?* But that would mean acknowledging that Heather was pretty, and Gaia hated giving

Heather any compliments—even indirectly. She was jealous of the girl. She had good reason, obviously; Heather was dating the guy of her dreams. But it was nice to know that Gaia occasionally experienced the same kinds of emotions as everyone else. Ed sometimes had a hard time remembering that.

"She's a lot better looking," he said. That wasn't a lie, either.

Mary laughed. "This is *very* interesting. You know, Ed—"

"Oh my God!" He slapped his forehead. "I totally forgot. My mom told me I *have* to come home tonight because we're having my grandparents over tomorrow." He turned and rolled over toward the door. *Now* he was lying. But they didn't have to know that. He was starting to realize that he'd been wrong about this night from the start. It would suck to spend the night here. He wouldn't be able to get any sleep. He'd just lie awake, thinking about Gaia. So tantalizingly close. Forget it. No way. He'd been through enough emotional crap already. "I'm really sorry—"

"But it's almost one o'clock," Gaia protested. "How are you gonna get home?"

"There are tons of cabs," he said, grabbing the doorknob. "It'll be no problem. Don't worry." He smiled over his shoulder. "You guys have fun, all right?"

Mary and Gaia glanced at each other.

"Uh . . . all right," Gaia said reluctantly. "But it's not the same without you."

He smirked. "I'm sure you'll figure out a way to make up

for my absence," he said. He turned and headed into the hall. "See you later."

"Be safe," they called at the same time.

"You too," he said.

Amazingly, he felt pretty good as he rolled through the silent, darkened apartment to the front door. Weird. Things really *could* be worse. He had two good friends. Friends who actually saw past his wheelchair to the person sitting in it. How many people in his situation could say that? And so what if one of them drove him crazy? So what if he would always be in love with her? Being the sidekick wasn't *all* bad. No.

The world wasn't perfect, as he well knew. Far from it.

DEMONS

"So it looks like it's just you and me again," Gaia said with a sigh.

Mary settled in against the opposite end of the couch. "I guess so," she murmured. She was bummed to see Ed go. For the first time in a long while, she felt like she'd made a breakthrough with him—like she was actually hanging around with

Ed Fargo, her *friend*. As opposed to the sad guy who'd suffered a terrible accident. As opposed to the guy whom she pitied but wanted to avoid. And she knew that Gaia was to thank for the change. Gaia was so comfortable and easygoing with him that Mary just couldn't help being that way, too. And it wasn't even an act. She honestly hadn't thought of his wheelchair once.

On the other hand, Ed hated truth or dare. Mary grinned. There was no denying it: The game was a lot more fun when he wasn't around.

"Does that mean it's your turn?" Gaia asked.

"Yeah."

"So?" Gaia turned on her side, propping her head up with her elbow. She smiled. "Truth or dare?"

"I know if I pick dare, you're gonna make me eat another pint of ice cream or something. So I gotta go with truth."

Gaia nodded, but her eyes suddenly grew serious. "All right. Truth." She hesitated for a few seconds. "Why do you think you got addicted to coke?"

Mary blinked. Jesus. *That* wasn't the question she'd been expecting. It wasn't exactly in the madcap spirit of New Year's Eve fun. Mary had been thinking more along the lines of: Are you a virgin? What's the most disgusting thing you've ever done with a guy? Et cetera, et cetera. *Girlie* stuff. The kind of stuff you giggled about at 1 A.M., lying in bed with your best friend.

But then again, if Mary revealed something personal

about herself, then Gaia would be more inclined to do the same. Yes. She could use this truth to her advantage. Besides, her therapist had told her that it was a good idea to talk about her drug experiences. The more she articulated her feelings, the more she opened up about her past—the less she would be inclined to keep her emotions bottled up inside her and find an unhealthy outlet for them. Anyway, it might be nice to share this stuff with a *friend* for once—instead of some concerned-looking, middle-aged woman in a white lab coat.

"I think there were a lot of different reasons," Mary said, lowering her eyes. "One of them, obviously, was that it felt so good. The first time, I mean. You never get the same buzz you do after the first time." She laughed miserably. "Pretty soon you stop getting any buzz at all. You just need it to feel normal. . . ."

She swallowed, shaking her head at the sordid images that were beginning to seep back into her mind: doing a clandestine blast in the parking lot of the DMV before her driving test, running off to the bathroom during final exams last spring, sneaking so much at her mother's birthday party that she got a nosebleed . . . and all the while justifying the behavior to herself by thinking: I'm just tired today. That's the only reason I'm doing it.

The problem was, she was tired every day. And the exhaustion never let up.

"What was it like that first time?" Gaia asked.

Mary took a deep breath. "It was . . . wild. I went to this

party with a guy I was dating—Brian Williams. I was a sophomore, and he was a senior. I guess I was kind of in awe of him." She smiled. "My parents hated him."

"Why?"

"He smoked. In front of my mom. He had long hair and lousy manners, and he dressed like a rock star. Seriously. The first time he came over here, he was wearing leather pants and this ripped black T-shirt. You could see his belly button through it. Which was pierced, by the way." She laughed again. "I thought he was glamorous."

"Go on," Gaia gently prodded.

"Anyway, he took me to this club downtown. I didn't know anyone there. It was all older people, friends of his from outside school. That band Fearless was playing."

"Really?" Gaia sat up straight. Her expression was strangely intense.

"Yeah. Why?"

"I just . . . I don't know." She shook her head. "That band just seems to haunt me."

Mary smirked. "I know what you mean. I'm strangely haunted by men named Chaz. Anyway, I barely heard them. Brian bumped into this friend of his." Her jaw tightened. "Guess who?"

"Skizz," Gaia whispered.

"The one and only." Mary closed her eyes and shuddered, feeling very much like she had been magically transported back to that stuffy, dimly lit basement. She could practically smell the smoke and hear the pounding beat of drums; she could see the creamy look of anticipation on Skizz's face.

"Anyway, he took us into one of the back rooms while the band was playing and got out a little envelope and a little spoon. He offered it to Brian first, then me. I was scared—but curious and excited, too. And I wanted to impress Brian, obviously. Plus it didn't seem like that big a deal. As far as I could tell, it didn't even affect Brian at all. He didn't freak out or anything. . . ."

Gaia leaned back against the pillows. "But it was a big deal." It was more of a question than a statement.

Mary opened her eyes again. "It was like I was suddenly transformed into this different person. I felt so cool. Really sexy, too—which was something I'd never felt before. And I thought I was in tune with everything that was happening around me. We went back out and danced, and I met a hundred different people. I wasn't shy or awkward at all." She cringed. "I probably made an ass of myself, but I had no clue."

Gaia nodded, but she didn't say anything.

Mary shook her head. It seemed so hard to believe that all the pain and lies and misery of the past year started right *there*—right at that exact moment. It was so random, in a way. What if she'd gotten sick that night and had never gone to the club? What if Skizz hadn't been there? What if she'd refused to go off with him? What if, what if . . . there were a thousand variations of the same question. Even when she was at the height of her addiction, she used to drive herself crazy asking herself *what if.*

"Needless to say, once that amazing feeling wore off, I went back for more," Mary continued. "All night long. I barely slept. I spent most of the next day crying. I didn't even know why I felt like such shit. But I had a feeling what could make me feel better." She sighed and glanced at Gaia. "I called Brian, and we hooked up with Skizz the very next night."

"And pretty soon Brian fell out of the picture," Gaia murmured. "Right?"

Mary nodded sadly. It was amazing how Gaia could see so much without having to be told. "I don't even know what happened to him. He just disappeared. You know what the crazy thing is? My parents were really psyched that he was gone. They thought I'd snapped out of a terrible rebellious phase. They had no idea of the truth."

"But they do now," Gaia stated. "That's all that matters."

"Yeah, but . . ." Mary shook her head. She wished she could repeat Gaia's words with the same conviction. But she knew she couldn't. "The problem is, the demons don't go away that easily. They're always right there, right around the corner." Her voice fell to a whisper. "When things get bad, I still think about it—"

"Anytime that happens, call me," Gaia interrupted firmly. "I mean it. I don't care what time it is or where you are or anything. Just call me. I'll come." Her tone softened a little. "I'll come and kick those demons' asses."

Mary tried to return the smile. Her eyes began to smart. A tight knot grew in her throat. What had she done to deserve a friend like Gaia? How could she ever pay her back?

Actually . . . there might be a way.

Yes. She could do for Gaia what Gaia had done for her. She could help Gaia confront her *own* demons. Gaia couldn't go on keeping her entire past a secret. It wasn't healthy. Mary had known all along that something was eating at her friend, slowly destroying her. Everything pointed to it. Her eagerness to fight, her cocky attitude, her reluctance to get close to other people . . . they were all symptoms of something tragic, lurking just under the surface. And no matter how much fun she and Gaia had together, Gaia never lost that aura of wistful sadness—as if she were somehow certain that bad times were never far away.

So it was time for Gaia to tell the truth. And Mary would have to help her.

But she would have to be crafty. Crafty like Gaia. A simple, straightforward question wouldn't work. Gaia would never answer it. Plus they were still playing truth or dare. Mary would have to trick Gaia in the context of the game. Right. She'd have to trick Gaia in the same way Gaia had tricked *her* that night they'd snuck into Sam Moon's dorm. . . .

"So I guess it's your turn now, right?" Mary asked.

Gaia nodded.

"And you're obviously not gonna pick truth, right?"

Gaia nodded again, smiling.

"Then I *dare* you to tell me the truth," Mary said. She looked Gaia straight in the eye. "I dare you to tell me why you don't live with your family anymore."

FAIL-SAFE POINT

For a moment Gaia was frozen.

Mary was smart. Gaia had known that from the day she'd met her. But she hadn't expected Mary to be so cunning. She hadn't expected Mary to beat her—fair and square, as the cliché went. There was nothing Gaia could do. She couldn't argue her way out of it; she couldn't fight her way out of it. She had to answer the question. It was too bad Mary didn't know how to play chess. She'd be a hell of a chess player.

This marked one of those few times in Gaia's life that she was very happy to be the freak that she was. Because right now, fearlessness was a good thing. She wasn't afraid of talking about her family history. She wasn't afraid of digging up the past. Objectively, however, she knew it would cause emotional pain that she wasn't equipped to deal with. In a very real sense, it was like staring down the barrel of a loaded gun. She didn't have to feel fear to know that the gun would hurt her.

But for the first time she also knew that she didn't have to face the pain alone.

Until now she'd never been able to share the story of her family's demise because there had been nobody with whom to share it. It was that simple. She'd never had close friends. The string of foster families she'd lived with after her mother's death didn't give a rat's ass about anything except the support check from family services.

She had someone now, though. Somebody who would listen. Somebody who wouldn't judge her. Somebody who had also endured unspeakable suffering and shame—and had emerged stronger on the other side. Gaia owed it to herself to try. And to Mary.

"I . . . uh, it happened five years ago," she whispered.

Mary nodded.

The world seemed to melt away. The entire universe shrank to this room, this moment. Gaia stared into space, seeing nothing. Her mind was dominated by a vision of driving snow. . . .

"We used to spend time at this house in the mountains. We kind of lived there on and off," Gaia continued. "Just the three of us—me, my mom, and my dad. My dad worked—" Gaia broke off, clearing her throat. She wondered how much she should reveal about her father's business. Probably as little as possible, for the sake of Mary's safety. Not that Gaia had any concerns that this conversation would ever leave this room. She trusted Mary absolutely. Still, it was always best to be as cautious as possible. "My dad worked for a federal agency."

"Doing stuff he wasn't allowed to talk about, right?" Mary asked.

Gaia sighed. "Right." Mary understood perfectly. "So, anyway, the three of us lived in this cute little old house, way out in the boondocks. My mom always loved the country." Gaia swallowed. Her voice grew strained. "She . . . ah, she was from Russia originally. She grew up on a farm. Way up in the north. She loved the winters. . . . It was her favorite time of year." She shook her head, trying to wipe the image of her mother's face from her mind. "Anyway, my mom and dad never talked about my dad's work, although now I know that my mom must have been involved somehow. Or at least she *knew* everything. I mean, if she didn't know . . . she probably would have wondered why my father spent so much time teaching me all these exotic martial arts and forcing me to learn calculus."

Mary laughed softly. "That makes sense."

"Yeah." Gaia blinked several times. Again she saw that blanket of driving snow against a starless night sky. She felt like she was floating in a giant tub—and the drain had just been unplugged. She was swirling closer and closer to a dank black hole. "So . . . there we all were, living up in this house . . . and—and it was winter, and . . ."

"It's okay," Mary murmured. "It's okay."

Gaia felt the wetness on her cheeks even before she realized she was crying. But she couldn't stop now. She was going to tell the whole story. Even if it killed her. She'd passed the fail-safe point. There was no turning back.

"It was night," she choked out. "There was a blizzard. We'd just finished dinner. My dad was setting up the chess table by the living-room window. We always played . . ." She sniffed. "We always played chess after dinner. My mom was in the kitchen, cleaning up. I was sitting across from my dad. Just looking out the window. I didn't see anything. Just snow. I didn't hear anything. Not a sound. I didn't . . ."

"It's okay," Mary repeated.

Gaia squeezed her eyes shut. No. It wasn't okay. It was anything *but* okay. The words seemed to come from somewhere else, as if Gaia were listening to a recording of herself speak. "There was a noise in the kitchen. A little twang, like the sound of a string being plucked. It was nothing. I didn't even think about it. Just a little twang. But my dad got this look in his eye. . . ." The pitch of Gaia's voice rose; the words came faster and faster. "He dove across the table and tackled me. All the chess pieces went flying. I screamed. I heard shooting. My dad was shooting at somebody. It was so loud. I tried to get up, but my dad held me down. I know it sounds stupid, but I thought I could help. I didn't know who was trying to hurt us or why, but I knew I had to save my mom and dad. Then the bullets stopped. My father got up. And—and . . ."

The next thing Gaia knew, she had collapsed into Mary's arms. She was sobbing uncontrollably. Her body shuddered. Her breath came in great heaving gasps. Mary said nothing. She simply held Gaia against her. Her grasp was very tight.

"I heard the sound of somebody running," Gaia wept. "But the thing I remember most was looking up—just for a second. Looking up, and seeing my dad in the doorway. And he looked at me. He was holding a gun. But his face . . . his face; there was nothing there. It was like a mask. Totally blank. His eyes were dead. . . ." She couldn't go on.

"What about your mom?" Mary whispered. "What happened to her?"

Gaia sniffed again, burying her face against Mary's shoulder. "I knew she'd been in the kitchen when the whole thing started. So I stood up and walked in that direction. I didn't see her at first. I thought maybe she was hiding, but . . . then I noticed the blood. It was all over the floor, leaving a trail that went behind the counter. When I turned the corner . . . she was just lying there. I sat next to her. I just put my head against her cheek and cried. My dad came in a little later, and—I don't know; we just waited. I don't really remember much else. An ambulance came and took us to the hospital. I rode up front. But it was too late. My dad and I just sat there in the waiting room all night, waiting for nothing. . . ."

Mary squeezed her tightly. "At least he was there for you."

Gaia struggled to take a breath. She shook her head. "He

was there for me. But then he wasn't. When the doctors came out and told us that my mom had died, he didn't say anything. He just sat there, with those same dead eyes. Then he hugged me. It was a weird hug, though. It was like he was pulling me toward him and pushing me away at the same time. Neither of us spoke. And then . . . that was it. He got up and walked away. Of course, I thought he'd be back. I waited and waited. But I never saw him again. And I never found out what happened or why he left. After that, I went into foster care—"

"I'm so sorry," Mary whispered. "I'm so sorry."

Don't be, Gaia thought. Her body slowly started to relax. It was over. The night was over. The tears still came, and the pain still remained—but now there was something else, too. Relief. She never knew how right it would feel to express what had happened, to relive it. For the first time ever, she felt she could get over it. Of course, she knew she would never put it behind her completely—but she felt like she had somehow been set free.

"Are you okay?" Mary asked.

Gaia nodded. She leaned back and tried to smile once she managed to compose herself. "What do you say we stop playing truth or dare?"

Mary laughed softly. "I think that's a good idea." She glanced at the clock. It was almost 2 A.M. "You want to try to get some sleep?"

Gaia shook her head. "Nah. How about I teach you how to play chess instead?"

NEUTRALIZATION

The listening device was good for a range of up to forty miles. Mary Moss's bedroom was no more than one-tenth that distance from the loft, so Loki had excellent reception.

He switched off the receiver and leaned back in his desk chair.

Well. That had been quite an enlightening little exchange. Quite an outpouring of emotion. Two girls, united by loneliness. Two misfits. Two outcasts. He shook his head. The bug had certainly proved its worth. It had been easy enough to plant; it was no bigger than a fingernail and practically transparent. And those so-called high-security buildings on Park Avenue were nothing of the sort. They could be easily penetrated in a variety of ways. Loki hadn't even needed a key. Earlier in the day he'd slipped undetected through the service entrance in the back. A third-rate burglar could have planted this bug.

He glanced up at the window and out at the Manhattan night. The city was alive this evening—crawling with people.

Of course. It was the holiday season.

Holidays meant nothing to Loki. As he saw it, they were arbitrary excuses for human beings to associate with one another. He was glad to be alone. He had always prized his solitude, but on nights like this—nights when he was forced to make an important decision—solitude was imperative.

He knew what would happen if Ella were here. She'd be clamoring for Gaia's head.

She'd insist that Gaia's breakdown tonight was evidence of deep-seated psychological instability and that Gaia would be of no use to them.

And she would be right . . . to a certain extent.

At the moment, in her current state, Gaia truly *was* of no use to them. She was of no use to anyone.

But Ella's insight only went so far. True, Gaia was unstable—but that was only because her environment was unstable. Every aspect of her life needed to be controlled. Rigidly. Certain volatile factors needed to be eliminated. Loki couldn't risk another outburst like that. Gaia was slipping further out of control. Too many secrets were at stake. Too many revelations were pending. So. There was no other possible course of action. He'd postponed the inevitable long enough.

Mary Moss had to be neutralized.

Immediately.

LOKI

It's a shame, actually.

I know I am not what you wanted me to be. You would consider me heartless. And for that, I am a little bit sorry. But unfortunately, it was inevitable that I would become who I am.

Almost inevitable.

Once there was a chance that I could have been more. That chance was you, my love.

Katia.

Katia.

Even now my lips tremble as I speak your name. *Katia.* I would have sacrificed it all for you.

But that is not quite how things turned out. Instead

you were stolen from me. And you went willingly, though I don't blame *you.* We both know who is really to blame.

That night. The last night I could still feel my heart beating in my chest. If only I had seen you there a moment earlier than I did. If only I could take back that one bullet that was meant for someone else. If only you had let me destroy Tom Moore instead of trading your own life for his.

How I wanted to hold you as you lay in that pool of blood. I wanted to kiss those lips and pull your soul into my own. And how I've spent hundreds of nights, playing it over and over again in my head, thinking what I should have done differently.

But as I have learned, there is no time for regret. And there is no time to chide you for loving my brother instead of me. There is only time for revenge.

And believe me, Katia, revenge is what I do best.

HEAT

To Sara Weiss

A LONG WAY FROM A BLIZZARD

GAIA HAD NO PROBLEM UNDERSTANDING HIS BROKEN-NOSE ENGLISH.

A REGULAR FRANKEN-NAZI

The dealer smiled as Gaia came close. "Hey," he said. He took the toothpick from between his yellow teeth and waved it through the snowy air. "You're out awful late, little girl."

Gaia Moore shoved her hands down inside her pockets and walked closer. "I'm not a little girl."

"Yeah, babe, whatever." The dealer replaced his toothpick, stomped his feet, and rubbed his hands together. "So what is it you want? I'm freezing out here."

"How sad." Gaia took a long look at the dealer. He was a big man, maybe six foot three, with big hands, thick arms, an equally thick neck, and hair that had been shaved down to a gray stubble. A regular Franken-Nazi. Exactly the kind of guy Gaia loved to pick a fight with—especially after what had happened over the last couple of weeks. It was easy to see why big boy felt confident enough to be working alone at midnight. Most of the dealers Gaia ran into were wimps, but this guy looked strong enough to pick up a park bench and beat somebody with it.

The dealer scowled. "Hey, girl. You shopping or staring?" His big hands dipped into his pockets and came out with a display of his stock. Clumps of white crystal shoved in tiny bottles. Brown powder in glassine envelopes. "You want something?"

"Yeah." Gaia nodded as she looked at the drugs. "Yeah, I want something." She slowly took her hands from her pockets. "I want you to get out of my park."

The man took a moment to react. "Your park?" He shoved his wares into his coat. "What makes you think this is your park, chicky?"

Gaia jerked her thumb back along the path she had been following. "I live over there," she said. She pointed ahead. "And my favorite doughnuts are over there. I figure that makes everything in between mine."

The dealer was big, but his sense of humor was not. A single, heavy, black eyebrow crunched down over his squinted eyes. "If you're not making a buy, kid, get out of my face."

It was Gaia's turn to smile. "Make me."

The toothpick fell from the big man's lips. "You got some kind of brain damage? Hell, girl, I clean bigger things than you off my boots."

Gaia glanced down at the man's stained coat, then back at his face. "From the look of you, I wouldn't think you ever cleaned anything."

The dealer opened his mouth as if he was going to reply, then he stopped and shook his head. "You want to be nuts, you be nuts on your own time. I got business to do." He turned his big shoulders and started across the park toward the empty, snow-covered chess tables.

"You afraid of a girl?" Gaia called after him.

The dealer kept walking.

Gaia cupped her hands beside her mouth. "Police!" she shouted. "You better come arrest this asshole!"

The dealer froze. He spun around to face Gaia. "Shut up."

"Police!" Gaia shouted again. "You better hurry! He's wearing a black coat, and he's got a pocket full of crack!"

"Shut the hell up!" The dealer stomped back along the snowy path. "You want to be hurt? If that's what you want, I'll—"

"Police!"

For a big man, the dealer moved fast. He charged and swung a knotted fist at Gaia with enough force to drop a horse. Only Gaia wasn't standing there anymore. She stepped left, ducked under the man's arm, caught his thick wrist, and gave a hard tug.

Gaia's move pulled the dealer off balance. He staggered forward past the place where Gaia was crouching. Before he could turn, Gaia planted her hands against the man's broad back and gave a shove. The dealer tripped and fell facedown on the frozen ground.

The big man scrambled back to his feet. There was snow on his stubble-covered head and more caught in his shaggy unibrow. "I hope you like this snow," he said. "Because I'm gonna make you lick it all up."

He lunged at Gaia, but she dodged again. This time she rose up on the ball of one foot, carefully aimed a kick at the man's ribs—and slipped in the snow.

Ten thousand lessons had taught Gaia how to fall. They didn't help this time. Her feet went up, and Gaia went down. She landed on her butt with enough force to knock most of the air from her lungs and send a jolt of pain running up her spine.

The big man was on her in a moment. One big hand closed around Gaia's right arm and jerked her from the ground. The other hand drove into her gut.

The muscles in Gaia's stomach spasmed. What little air remained in her body hissed out between her teeth. Gaia gasped and strained to pull in a breath. The man tossed her back to the ground and gave her a kick that pounded into her shoulder.

He grunted in satisfaction. "I don't think you're going to make any more trouble for me, babe." He drew back his leg and aimed a second kick at Gaia's head.

Gaia rolled, put her hands under her chest, and flipped onto her feet. Before the man had recovered from his missed kick, Gaia spun and planted a punch in the center of his stomach. She punched again, backed away, and followed up with a high kick that spun the man's head around.

Even though it was the guy who was getting hit, Gaia was the one feeling dizzy. She still couldn't breathe. She was fighting on nothing but the oxygen in her lungs, and that was running out fast.

If the drug dealer had been smaller, that kick would have been enough to send him flying. The fight would have been over in five seconds flat. Instead the big man only staggered for a moment, then lunged toward Gaia again.

Gaia dropped onto her hands and swept the big man's legs out from under him. As he was falling, she landed a fresh kick square in the middle of his face. Blood sprayed from his shattered nose. It arced away from the blow and laced across the snow in a dark red line.

For a moment Gaia froze. She looked at the snow with its stain of blood, and her mind went spinning back. A gunshot echoed through her memory. She saw her mother lying on the kitchen floor. . . .

The oxygen gauge in Gaia's body reached *E.* She dropped out of her memories and onto her knees. Air. She needed air.

The dealer groaned and started to get up. He fumbled at Gaia with sausage-sized fingers.

Gaia's stomach muscles relaxed, and she managed to grab a lungful of air. She threw off the guy's hand, rolled away across the snow, and got up. She squeezed down another breath. The oxygen flowed into her muscles like cool water.

The dealer stood and faced her across the snow. "Ooh liddle bidch," he said.

Gaia had no problem understanding his broken-nose English. She pulled in enough air to answer him. "Let's get this over with. I want to get my doughnuts."

The big man came for her. He was more cautious this time. Gaia could see the way his eyes danced back and forth as he tried to anticipate her move. It didn't help.

Gaia waited until he grabbed for her, slipped away, and drove a kick into his side. Before he could turn, she drove another kick into his back. It was a kidney shot, illegal in any karate tournament. This wasn't a tournament.

The dealer made a deep grunt and fell to his knees. Gaia kicked him again. And again.

"Top," said the dealer. "Pweez top."

Gaia took a step back. "You going to get out of my park?"

The dealer nodded, sending fresh blood dripping from his nose.

"And you'll never come back."

"Neba. I swear. Neba."

Gaia nodded. "All right, then, go."

The dealer got slowly to his feet and stumbled away. Gaia stood and watched him until the big man was only a smudge in the snowy distance. Then she fell onto the nearest park bench.

For the space of sixty seconds Gaia was completely

paralyzed. It was the cost of being stronger and faster during the fight—the price she paid for running her muscles at two hundred percent. She lay there on the bench, unable to move a muscle. She was glad that the park was deserted. The only thing worse than being helpless was having someone else see her when she was helpless.

She turned her head and saw the dealer's blood on the ground. Once again, images flooded her mind. Night. Snow. Blood. Her mother.

Gaia shook the images from her head. She propped herself up on her hands, took in a deep, cold breath, and tried to forget.

GAIA

My mom loved snow, but she didn't like snowball fights. Or at least, she'd make you believe she didn't like snowball fights. Oh, no, she only came outside to enjoy the beauty of a winter's day. Snow on the tree branches. The way everything sparkled in the sun. All that shit.

She was a good actress, my mom. And if you believed her long enough to look away—pow! You'd catch a cold one right on the ear.

The best thing I remember about those snows was that the snow stayed white for a month at a time. Cloud white. White like things are in dreams. All clean and perfect.

I know that things can seem a lot better when you're

remembering than they really were. But those snows really were great. Really.

City snow is not pretty snow. That's the truth. And that's the closest thing to a poem you're going to get out of me.

Back when I was a kid. Before my mom . . . I mean, before my dad . . . Let's just say before. Before I came to New York City. Back then I used to see real snow.

I know, this is already starting to sound like one of those stupid stories your fat uncle Pete tells about the good old days. You know, the "when I was a little kid it snowed all year long and I had to walk ten miles to school and we couldn't afford shoes so I had to wear bread wrappers on my feet and it was all uphill both ways" story.

Old people say things like this because they're way into this nostalgia thing. They want to look back at the past and make it so everybody was braver and nicer and better than they are now. They had it tough, but they stuck together. They didn't get anything but an orange for Christmas, and they were happy. They ate dirt six days a week, and they liked it.

My story's not like that. For one thing, I'm only seventeen, so I didn't grow up with dinosaurs or go hunting mastodons. The other difference is, no nostalgia.

Let me tell you right now: Nostalgia sucks.

All those old stories are nothing but dressed-up lies. Who wants to look back, anyway? I mean, do you want to look back and see how your mom died? Do you really want to think about how your father disappeared and never bothered to so much as write? Do you want to remember how you got shuffled off from one place to another and end up being forced to live with two people you barely know? No. Believe me, thinking about the past is just plain stupid.

That's why I'm just talking about snow.

It snowed in the mountains. Back then, I had a mom and a dad just like a regular girl. That part of the story seems like a fairy tale now, even to me, but it really did happen. I had a mother. I even have the pictures to prove it.

Of course, if you look at the pictures, you probably wouldn't think they were very good evidence. On one side you have my mom: always stylish, completely charming, totally beautiful. And then there's me. I'm . . . not my mother.

Even back in those days of yore, the Moore family wasn't exactly typical. First off, my dad was like a major government spy. Half the time he was off to some jungle or desert or foreign capital. I never knew which one because he could never talk about it. Then when he was home, Dad dedicated himself to my little problem. The Gaia-don't-get-scared-of-anything problem.

Which wouldn't have been such a problem at all except my dad was afraid that I wouldn't get scared when I should. Which was completely wrong. Just because I'm fearless doesn't mean I'm stupid. I don't go jumping off cliffs. I don't get into a fight with more than two or three idiots at a time. Usually.

But Dad made me study every martial art in creation so I could stomp the crap out of the people I should have been afraid of but wasn't. By the time he was through, he had turned me into the muscle-bound freak girl I am today.

Snow. This is about snow.

In the mountains it snowed for weeks at a time. Not wimpy little flurries. Serious snow. And when it stopped, we would build snowmen and snow forts and snow anything else you could think of. My dad would even stop telling me about "the sixteen deadly pressure points on the human body" long enough to come outside and take part in snowball Armageddon.

Of course, not every snow was perfect. I mean, it was snowing on that night too. The last night.

Blood melts into the snow. You might think it would spread out and fade. Maybe it would even turn some shade of pink. It doesn't. Blood is dark against the snow. That night, that last night, it looked almost black.

Okay, now let's talk about city snow. Let's talk about snow in New York.

First off, it doesn't snow that much here. People talk about this place like it's the north slope of Alaska, but we're lucky to have two decent snows a year. Every little flurry here is treated like an emergency. Two flakes get together, half the city runs for home.

When the snow does fall, it starts out white, just like mountain snow. But give it two hours on the ground, and it turns into certified City Snow™, pat. pending.

City Snow is not a product of nature. It looks like a mixture of wet cement and motor oil. Ever see a Coke Slurpee? That's pretty close. Not the kind of stuff you want someone to wad up and throw at you.

I guess you could make a snow fort in the park—if you worked fast enough to get it done before the snow turned to goo. You might get in a few decent snowballs. Maybe make a snowman, too.

But some jerk would probably come along and mug it.

AN UNFORESEEN EFFECT

JUST ONE LITTLE LINE WOULD BE LIKE TEN POUNDS OF DOVE DARK CHOCOLATE.

HER NATURE

Ella dropped the glowing stub of a pastel-colored cigarette and heard it hiss into the snow at her feet. She shivered as she tightened the sable-edged hood around her face. The plush fur coat kept her arms and body warm, but it did nothing for the frigid wind that crept under her skirt.

There were at least a hundred decent restaurants in the city and another hundred that were passable. Ella fantasized about a plate of steaming alfredo at Tony's. Perhaps some black crab cake at Opaline. To get out of the wind, she would have settled for coffee at the nearest Chock Full o' Nuts. Instead she was stuck, shivering in the park, watching a little idiot who didn't have the brains to get in out of the cold.

"All right," she said. "Your little protégé finished her fight, and now she's eating her dessert. Do we have to stay out here and freeze all night?"

Beside her, a tall form shifted in the deep shadows of the winter trees. "We're watching. Isn't that your assignment?"

Ella glanced at the girl resting on the cold park bench. Was there some law that said Gaia couldn't go inside like a civilized person? For the ten-thousandth time, Ella wished she had never taken on this assignment. Not that she had been given any choice.

"I watch Gaia every day. How long are we going to stay out here?" she asked.

"As long as we have to," said the tall man.

Loki stepped forward, and the light from a distant streetlamp cast sharp shadows across his rugged features. He stood with his hands jammed into the pockets of his black trench coat and his deep-set eyes focused on Gaia. "We wait until we know what we need to know."

Ella scowled. "But she's not doing anything," she said, allowing a note of complaint to creep into her voice. It irritated Ella that Loki would rather spend time out here just watching Gaia when they could be spending that time in a much more intimate way.

"Exactly." Loki turned his face toward Ella for a moment. In the dim light his eyes looked as dark as the winter sky. "And that's what we're here to observe."

"Nothing?"

Loki made an exasperated growl. "You've had months to study this girl," he said. "How many times have you seen her sit quietly and do nothing?"

Ella thought for a moment. "Not many," she said carefully.

"Not many? Try none. Not even after a fight like that. She's usually up and running as soon as she gets her energy back." Loki nodded toward the distant bench where Gaia sat in the falling snow. "The girl is restless. Headstrong. It's part of her nature." He pulled his hands from his pockets and ran gloved fingers along the rough bark of an ancient elm. "Gaia goes hunting for something to eat. Gaia goes looking for another fight. Gaia does not sit quietly and think."

Ella shivered again. "She just finished beating up some guy three times her size. Isn't that enough for you?"

Loki made a noise of disgust. "Did you see how she fought? She was slow. Clumsy. Her heart wasn't in the fight." He shook his head. "That fool should have been no problem, but Gaia came close to being seriously injured."

That thought made Ella smile inwardly. If only Gaia would hurry up and get herself killed. Ella was so tired of hearing Loki talk about the little blond-haired beast. If the girl got herself shot or stabbed or, even better, slowly and painfully beaten to death, Loki would be angry for a time, but he would recover. Best of all, Ella could leave her sham marriage and be with him all the time. That was sure to speed his recovery.

"Maybe she's sick," said Ella.

"If she has an illness, it's not caused by any bacterium or virus," replied Loki. "No. I have a good idea of what's gone wrong with our girl."

She's not my *girl.* Ella knew that Loki had something in

mind. She wished he would just spit it out. It was far too cold for drama. "What is it?" she asked.

"Mary Moss."

It took Ella a moment to place the name. "The little junkie girl? Is that what you're worried about?"

Loki was slow to reply. "The relationship between Gaia and this Moss girl is certainly something that we must consider." Loki put his hands back into his coat pockets. "Moss and the other friends that Gaia has made. They're making her . . ." He paused for a moment, a frown turning down the corners of his mouth. "They're having an unforeseen effect."

Ella stared at him. Loki was hiding something. That wasn't surprising—Loki was always hiding some secret. It was part of his job. But this secret involved Gaia, and that made it Ella's business too.

She clenched her teeth in frustration. Ella couldn't see what difference it made that Gaia had picked up a few pitiful friends, and she certainly didn't like the idea that Loki wouldn't tell her what was going on. "The Moss girl is nothing but a whining little addict, and that other kid, Fargo, is a cripple. Neither of them seems dangerous."

"They're far more dangerous than you know, my dear." He turned to Ella and took a step toward her. "Have you forgotten the goal of this project?"

The intensity of the look in Loki's eyes made Ella take a step back. "No, I—"

"Then you'll understand that for things to end up as they should, Gaia must not feel close to anyone," he said. "It's important that she not form any deep attachments."

"I understand." The explanation sounded reasonable enough, but Ella still had the feeling that Loki was hiding something. Something serious.

Loki nodded. "I have to admit that I underestimated this problem myself. I was looking for physical dangers to Gaia, not for this sort of difficulty."

A fresh gust of wind blew in among the trees. Ella shook from head to toe. "Now that we've seen her, couldn't we go somewhere?" Ella stretched her hand toward Loki's. "We don't get enough time together. We could go to your place in the Village and—"

"Not now," said Loki.

No matter how many times Loki rejected her, it always seemed to sting. Ella tried to look unaffected, but she could feel anger settling over her features. She could see no reason for them to stand there being cold. It wasn't as if Gaia was suddenly going to jump up and do something interesting.

Ella started to point this out, but quickly shut her mouth. Making Loki angry was definitely on the list of very unhealthy activities. She had already pushed her luck far enough.

"Maybe I can help solve this problem," Ella suggested.

Loki had already turned his attention back to Gaia. "And how will you do that?" he said without looking at her.

"I could forbid Gaia to go out to see these friends," Ella suggested.

Loki laughed. It was a sound as cold as the snow around them. "And exactly what good would that do? Do you really think Gaia would obey your order?"

Ella felt her face grow warm. She didn't like being reminded of the way Gaia refused to respect her commands. And she especially didn't like the tone of Loki's voice. He seemed amused by the whole idea.

"Maybe I could talk to the parents of the Moss girl," she said. "I could hint that Gaia might have trouble with drugs herself. They might keep Mary—"

"No," said Loki with a sharp shake of his head. "That kind of intervention would only cause Gaia to rebel further. I believe that in this case direct action may be required."

That was an answer Ella had no trouble interpreting. "Then what should I do? I could follow Moss and—"

"Leave the girl to me," Loki interrupted. "No, I have something else for you to do." He stopped abruptly and scanned Ella from head to spiked heels. "There's another of Gaia's relationships that concerns me. One that I think you may be particularly well suited to handle."

A LOT OF LITTLE THINGS

Criminals were all big babies. Just because it was dark, cold, and snowing, they were all off somewhere keeping their little toes warm. The whole park was deserted.

Gaia folded her legs beneath her, chomped half a chocolate doughnut in a single bite, and watched the snow fall.

The weather doofus on the eleven o'clock news was calling for six inches, but at the moment the snow was barely there. Big, heavy flakes drifted down slowly from a sky that was half clouds and half stars. It was more than a flurry but a long way from a blizzard.

Spots of cold moisture appeared on Gaia's face as the snow stuck and melted. Snowflakes caught in her hair and snagged on her eyelashes. Slow streams of melt water made their way down her cheeks, and damp spots even dared to appear on her sacred doughnut.

Memories of childhood snow were one thing, but Gaia quickly decided that getting hit in the face by real snowflakes wasn't particularly romantic. Instead it was cold and wet. Still, Gaia sat facing into the night until the collar of her sweater was damp and her long, pale hair was a wind-whipped mess.

She felt weird. There had to be a word for the emotion Gaia felt, but she wasn't sure what that word would be. It wasn't fear. She could be sure of that much. She didn't feel afraid. If her father was right, she *couldn't* feel afraid. Not ever. But if she couldn't be afraid, she could still feel sadness. And loneliness. And guilt. In Gaia's opinion, it wasn't a very good deal.

Except this feeling wasn't one of those familiar aches. This was an actual, honest-to-whatever good feeling. This was a lot of little things that added up to something that might almost be happiness. At least Gaia thought it was happiness. She didn't exactly have a great basis for comparison.

Gaia shoved the second half of the doughnut into her mouth, opened her eyes, and watched as the last of the stars vanished behind the advancing clouds. For what seemed like a century, Gaia had been holding all her secrets to herself. Now, for the first time since being forced to move to New York, she had friends she could share with.

They probably weren't friends her parents would have approved of, but Gaia's parents were long gone. Out of the picture. Mary Moss was a recovering coke addict with something of a wild streak. Ed Fargo had been a daredevil nutcase on a skateboard until an accident cured him of being crazy and left him in a wheelchair. They weren't perfect people.

But that was a good thing. Gaia could never have been comfortable with perfect people. No matter what they had been or what they had done, Ed and Mary were what Gaia needed. People that she could relax with. People that made her almost feel normal.

Only the night before, Gaia had gone so far as to tell Mary about what had happened to her mother. It might not sound like a big step, but for Gaia it was huge. Gaia never talked about her mother. Never. Not to anyone.

Talking to Mary had been one of the hardest things she had ever done. Gaia had spent so many years training to fight that taking out some half-stoned mugger barely took an effort. Her father had forced her to study so hard as a kid that high school was more like kindergarten. But telling someone else about her emotions, letting someone in on the things that had happened to her—that was hard.

Now that Gaia had slipped out a little of her past, she felt surprisingly good. Strange, but good. A little bit of the monster-outsider juice had been drained. A little of the pressure in her head was gone.

The world wasn't perfect, of course. Gaia was still an overmuscled freak. She was still stuck living with her foster parents, the Nivens, and particularly with Superslut Ella.

And of course there was the one least-perfect thing in Gaia's world. The one that divided possible happiness from undeniable joy.

Sam Moon.

It was probably the best thing that Gaia didn't have Sam. She had only kissed him once. At least, she thought she had kissed him once. Only she had been half dead at the time, and there had been this major blow to her head, and it might possibly have been nothing but a hallucination. Anyway, one maybe kiss and Sam had already become this incredible obsession.

Gaia had already spent enough time thinking about Sam to learn a new language or become a piano virtuoso or develop a new theory of relativity. If she actually had him, actually had Sam Moon all to herself, she might short-circuit or blow up or rip his clothes off and—

Yeah, *obsession* was definitely the right word.

Thinking of the no-Sam situation took the edge off Gaia's good mood. He was probably spending his time with Heather. The insidious, ugly, ultimately evil Heather Gannis.

The image of Sam being somewhere with Heather was enough to finally pull Gaia out of her doughnuts- and snow-induced coma. She unfolded her cold legs and slid off the snow-crusted bench. It was very late. If Ella was still awake, she was going to have a fit when Gaia came in.

Gaia didn't care. She leaned back her head and whispered up to the gray clouds, each word emerging in a puff of steam.

"Come on," she said. "For once let's have some real snow."

MOONMAN

Sam Moon leaned back into the cab to pay the driver, careful to give a good tip. After all, it was the holiday season. People were supposed to be cheerful and generous.

"Thanks for the ride, Mr. Haq," Sam said as he handed over the money.

The cabbie took it from him with a grin. "Thank you so much, Samuel," he said in English so exact, it could have come straight from the pronunciation guide in *Webster's*. A look of concern crossed the man's wide face. "Are you all right, Samuel? I haven't seen you at the tables as much as usual."

Oh, I'm fine. It's just that I'm having sex with one girl while I'm totally obsessed with another. Sam tried to smile. "Sure, Mr. Haq. As soon as the weather clears up, you'll see me in the park."

"Perhaps we will play a game then?"

Sam nodded. "Absolutely. I'll be looking for you."

"Good! Very good," said Mr. Haq. "I will be quite happy to take even more of your money." He laughed, gave Sam a final wave, and pulled away from the curb.

Sam turned and walked slowly up the steps to the concrete bulk of his dorm at NYU. The trouble with Gaia—the Gaia problem, as he had started to call it—was not exactly the kind of thing he could discuss with Mr. Haq. And it was definitely not the sort of thing he could discuss with his parents. His parents weren't big believers in problems.

There really isn't *a problem,* he told himself as he came to the door of the dorm. *I'm with Heather, not Gaia. I'm supposed to be happy now.*

Sam pushed open the door, stepped inside, and stomped the snow from his shoes. *I've got to stop thinking about Gaia. Gaia Moore is not a part of my life. Enough already.*

There was more life in the building than there had been the night before. When Sam had come scrambling back on Christmas night—in the futile hope that Gaia might stop by—the place had been all but empty. Since then a trickle of students had turned up every day. It was still more than a week before classes started up again, but already the dorms were nearly a third full.

Sam yawned as he tromped up the stairs to his room. It had been a long day. He had called Heather first thing that morning to see if she wanted to get together, but she had said she wasn't feeling well. Considering how much alcohol she had downed the night before, Sam wasn't surprised. With Heather out of action and Gaia out of the picture, Sam had decided to hustle back home and spend a day with his parents. He didn't know if the few hours he had been able to spend at home were worth it, but at least it made him feel a little less guilty for running off on Christmas Day.

It was close to two in the morning, but when Sam walked out onto his floor, there was the familiar thick, sudsy odor of beer in the air and the ultrasonic thump of a subwoofer jolting through the walls. Someone down the hall was having a party. It shouldn't have been a surprise. The period between semesters was nothing if not an excuse to party. But Sam was way too tired to participate.

He fumbled into the quad and opened the door to his dorm room. Inside, he dropped his things, shrugged off his heavy coat, and staggered to his bed.

He wondered where Gaia was at that moment. Which

was a stupid thing to wonder. Obviously Gaia would be asleep. Like any normal person would be at this hour. And wasn't he going to stop thinking about Gaia, anyway?

Sam took off his boots and lay back against the pillow. The bass from the nearby party pounded up through the bed like some huge heartbeat. Despite the cold outside, the room suddenly felt stuffy and hot. Sam peeled off his shirt and lay on top of the sheets. He balled up the pillow and pushed it over his ears. He kept his eyes closed and did his best to think about absolutely nothing.

The sound of the bass beat kept pounding through the bed. *Thump. Thump. Thump.* Gaia. Gaia. Gaia.

Heather, thought Sam. *Not Gaia.*

Gaia. Gaia. Gaia.

Heather. I love Heather.

Liar. Liar. Liar. You. Love. Gaia.

Oh, shut up.

With a groan Sam got out of bed and walked over to his computer. If he couldn't sleep, he had to do something, and there was only one thing he could think of that might take his mind off the Gaia problem.

Sam had been a chess geek since grade school. Only that inner geek could save him now. He logged on to the Internet and went to the pogo.com game site. From there he logged in as Moonman and proceeded to the chess area. Sam bypassed the "blue" chess rooms. Those places were full of beginners and low-rated players. Even though he had been on the site only a few times, Sam's rating was already edging three thousand. If he was going to find a challenge, he would have to do it in the site's "red" room.

Sam yawned while the site loaded. It was funny how as soon as he got out of bed, he started to feel like he could sleep. He wasn't fooled. One quick game to clear his mind, then he would give the bed another try.

A scrolling list of chess games appeared on the screen. Even at this late hour most of the tables were already occupied with games in progress. At others a single name beside the board indicated someone waiting for a challenger. Sam passed up a couple of players with ratings under two thousand. He flipped to the bottom of the list and was happy to see the small silhouette of a waiting player who was rated at 2,950. It was a perfect number, within ten points of Sam's own rating.

Sam reached for the mouse and was about to join the game when he noticed the name of this perfectly matched player. *Gaia13*. He froze. It could be a coincidence. There had to be other girls in the world with the name Gaia who liked chess.

Sam's fingers began to literally tremble above the mouse button. He wanted to join the game. There was a chat facility that let the two players send messages to each other while playing. If it really was Gaia—his Gaia—Sam would have a chance to tell her some of the things that he had been thinking for the last few days. He was going to press the button and go in. He was.

It's not her. It can't be her.

His finger touched the plastic of the button. All he had to do was click the button. All he had to do was . . .

The icon that represented a waiting player suddenly disappeared. *Gaia13 has left.*

Sam leaned back in his chair and closed his eyes. It wasn't her. The name players used on pogo was only a nickname. Just because some player used the name Gaia didn't mean it was Gaia Moore. It wasn't her.

Sam didn't believe that for a second.

MOVIE OF THE WEEK

Whois? Query Results

Moore, Katia

No Records Found.

Whois? Query Results
Moore, Gaia
No Records Found.

Mary Moss frowned and gave her mouse a shove that sent it sliding across the desktop. She had tried a hundred different search engines and a dozen different queries, and she was still no closer to finding out what she wanted to know. There were a zillion people named Moore and at least ten thousand named Katia. But nowhere could Mary find that combination—the combination that was the name of Gaia's mother.

Ever since Gaia had decided to share the story of her mother's death, Mary had been obsessed with finding out more. The story had everything. There was violence. Murder. Mystery. And, of course, heartbreaking tragedy. Gaia Moore was a regular walking movie of the week. And Mary was a sucker for drama.

But of course, it was more than that. Gaia was Mary's friend. Gaia had saved Mary's ass, both physically and emotionally, on more than one occasion. Maybe this was Mary's chance to finally do something for her best friend.

Mary leaned back in her chair and ran her fingers through her ginger-red hair. There had to be some way to get the information she was after. There had to be someplace she could go, someone she could ask.

If I only had a little blast of coke, I'd be able to think so, so much better. The idea of the drug was enough to make Mary shiver. A little cocaine would be like a glass of cold water after crossing a desert. Just one little line would be like ten pounds of Dove dark chocolate. It would be like . . . like . . .

It would be like setting your hair on fire and trying to put it out with gasoline.

Mary knew well enough that there was no such thing as just one little line of coke. One line of coke could turn into a thousand miles of white powder. Mary had only started fishing her life out of the toilet she had fallen into after her last tangle with drugs. The last thing she needed was to jump inside and flush.

Another idea occurred to Mary. She selected another site from the menu and waited until the search box came up.

ALTAVISTA ADVANCED QUERY FACILITY

moore AND katia

—No results. Try another query.—

ALTAVISTA ADVANCED QUERY FACILITY

moore AND death AND fire

—1 Result Found—

Mary almost typed a fresh query before she realized that she had gotten a hit. Quickly she snatched back her mouse and clicked on the link.

The page turned out to be the archives of a small upstate paper. The article was so different from the story that Gaia told, Mary thought for a second it was just a mistake. Then she realized it wasn't a mistake. It was a lie.

Local Woman Dies in Fire

The West County home of Mr. and Mrs. Thomas Moore burned down in the early morning hours this Tuesday. Mr. Moore, an employee of the State Department, and his young daughter escaped the blaze, but Mrs. Moore was unable to leave the home in time. The county coroner's office indicates that Mrs. Moore died of smoke inhalation.

The article continued for half a column, but there was no mention of any guns. Mary ran her finger along the monitor glass. The article didn't agree at all with the story that Gaia had told her. Not even the stupidest coroner in the world would mistake a gunshot wound for smoke inhalation. And Gaia had never mentioned her house burning down. That meant either the paper was wrong or Gaia was lying.

Mary was willing to bet anything that Gaia had told the

truth. That meant someone had created this story. Someone with enough pull to get just what they wanted planted in a local paper. Someone with enough power to convince local officials to lie.

Mary smiled. This story was getting better.

A MAN-SHAPED SHADOW

MARY'S HEART BOUNCED IN HER CHEST.
FEAR RAN THROUGH HER BODY LIKE STRONG ACID.

BOILED IN BEER

There was nothing like a sleepless night to make morning look like the bottom of a litter box.

Sam brushed his teeth for a solid ten minutes and still couldn't manage to dislodge the fur that was growing on his tongue. He stared at the face in the mirror and winced. He was supposed to meet Heather in only an hour. If he didn't manage to look a little less like a refugee from *Night of the Living Dead*, the Gaia Problem was going to turn into the No-Girlfriend-At-All Problem.

Sam found he could think a little more clearly about Gaia now that the sun was up. It was clear to him that Gaia had moved on. Maybe she once wanted to be with Sam. Maybe she had never given him a passing thought. Maybe she had only kissed him because someone had massaged her brain with a blunt object. One thing was sure—Gaia wasn't thinking about Sam. According to the phone conversation Sam had held with Gaia's stepmother, Gaia had a boyfriend.

Gaia hadn't even bothered to thank Sam for the Christmas present he had bought for her. If there had been a chance for Sam and Gaia the couple, that chance was over.

There were absolutely zero odds that he was ever going to be with Gaia Moore.

So why do I keep obsessing about her?

He splashed cold water on his face and scrubbed it off with a slightly stale towel. It was like he was haunted by Gaia. He wondered if he could find a priest willing to do an exorcism.

At least I have Heather, he told himself. Then he gave himself a mental kick for having the thought. It wasn't like Heather was some sucky consolation prize. Heather was undeniably and totally beautiful. Half the guys at school were chasing Heather, and the other half didn't even feel worthy enough to try.

Oh, yeah, and there was sex. Only a few nights before there had been sex. It wasn't like Sam had a terrific amount of experience with sex, but sex with Heather was fun. It was good, no, *great*. Great sex. Any guy should feel lucky to have Heather. Having Heather was still the best thing in his life. His Gaia-free life.

Once he was cleaned up and dressed, Sam felt a little better. Less like a zombie and more like he was only terminally ill. He slipped on his coat, took a last dismal look into the mirror, and started out the door.

Before he could get all the way into the hall, another door down the way flew open and music spilled out. A short, wide-shouldered guy with curly brown hair and a broad grin stumbled into the hall. "Sam!" he cried in a voice loud enough to be heard in Brooklyn. "My favorite person in the world!"

Sam winced at the volume. "Hey, Brian." From the

slurred, overloud voice and the unsteady walk, Sam could tell that Brian Sandford had a very low percentage of blood in his alcohol system.

The other student took a swaying step. "Man, it's good to see you."

Sam forced himself to smile. Something was badly wrong here. Brian Sandford was obviously drunk, but Sam didn't think he was drunk enough to forget one fact—Brian and Sam hated each other.

Brian was a local who had wandered over to NYU from the Village School. He seemed to have the same set of friends as Heather, though Sam knew Brian wasn't in the class of people that Heather would have considered the top rank. It had taken Sam several meetings to figure out that Brian had the flaming hots for Heather Gannis. He seemed to consider the fact that Heather was dating Sam as some kind of personal insult.

From the broad smile on his face, it seemed that Brian had finally recovered from his jealousy. "It's been a long time, huh?"

"I saw you two nights ago, Brian. At the Kellers' party, remember?"

Brian nodded enthusiastically. He stumbled down the hallway toward Sam and put a hand on the wall to steady himself. "Yeah," he said. "Good party. Too bad you left so soon." Brian's breath was so strong that it made Sam's eyes water. It was clear that Brian hadn't been leaving any parties early. He didn't smell like he had been drinking beer. He smelled like he had been *boiled* in beer.

"I'm glad you enjoyed it," Sam said. He closed the door to his room and zipped up his coat. "I'll be seeing you."

A heavy hand came down on Sam's shoulder. "Too bad about you and Heather," said Brian.

Puzzled, Sam turned and looked into Brian's flushed, smiling face. "What?"

"You know," said Brian. "How you guys are breaking up and everything."

He's drunk, Sam thought. *He's drunk and he doesn't know what he's talking about.* "Did Heather say something to you?"

"Heather? Nah." Brian's red eyes closed for a moment, and his mouth gaped open. Sam could practically see the two sober brain cells in Brian's head scrambling to dredge up the memory. "It was the guys, man. They were saying how Heather was doing maid service."

"Maid service?"

"You know. Going from bed to bed."

A flash of cold ran up Sam's back, and he felt a sudden, metallic tightness in his guts. "They're lying."

Sam tried to put some kind of authority into his voice, but it wasn't enough to stop the flow of words that spilled from Brian's beer-saturated throat. "That's not what Charlie says."

The coldness in Sam's back began to spread into his legs and arms. There was a buzzing noise in his head. "Charlie."

"Charlie Salita. You know Charlie."

Sam did know Charlie. Charlie was a jock and a standard at all the parties Heather attended. "You're saying that Charlie Salita slept with Heather."

Brian's smile grew even wider. "Charlie says she's really hot," he said.

"He's lying."

Brain leaned in closer. "He's got details, man. He knows things about Heather."

"He's making it all up," Sam insisted.

"Charlie says your old girlfriend is a real bunny in the sack."

Sam Moon wasn't a violent person. He played chess, not football. He couldn't remember being in a real fight since junior high. None of that mattered.

He raised his right hand, carefully folded his fingers, drew back his arm, and drove his fist straight into Brian Sandford's grinning face.

LIKE A FAMILY

The trail of blood stretched across the frozen ground. Gaia bent and touched her finger to a bright red splash. Cold. The blood was as cold as the snow it was staining.

Gaia stood and looked ahead. The snow was falling so thickly that she could barely see twenty feet, but somewhere up there she could see shadowy movement. Gaia hurried along, jumping over one splash of blood after another.

Cold wind streamed through her tangled hair and brought goose pimples from the bare skin of her arms and throat. Gaia tried to remember why she was outside in such cold weather without a coat. Or shoes.

The blood trail led into a grove of stark, black-trunked trees. The shadowy figure was closer now, and the blood spots were closer together. Gaia moved faster. She had to catch up. She had to catch up before . . . she didn't know what. Something was going to happen, something bad, and Gaia was the only one who could stop it.

A new shape loomed up out of the snow. It was a building. A house.

Gaia ran ahead for a few steps, then skidded to a stop in the ankle-deep snow. It wasn't just any house—it was her house. Not the brownstone she shared with the Nivens. Her real home. The house where she had lived with her parents. With her mother.

No sooner had the thought of her mother crossed Gaia's mind than a figure ran up the steps and into the house. Gaia had only enough time to tell it was a woman before the front door opened and closed with a bang.

"Mom?" Gaia ran toward the door. "Mom!"

Snow dusted the steps leading up to the door and was drifted against the sides of the house. There was blood here, too. Lots of blood. There was blood on the steps. On the porch. On the door.

Gaia pulled at the door, but it refused to open. "Mom!" she shouted. "Mom, let me in!" There was no answer from the house.

She began to hammer on the door. *Bang. Bang.*

Gaia smashed her fist against the door. The whole thing looked too fragile to stand, much less hold up to blows. Gaia struck out again, and the door rattled in its frame. She jumped and planted a solid kick. The bare sole of her foot clapped against the wood. Dust flew into the blood-stained snow.

Thump.

The boards held.

Gaia gritted her teeth. The door didn't look strong. But no matter how she battered at the aged boards, they wouldn't break.

"Gaia," called a voice from inside.

"Mom?" Gaia froze. "Mom, is that you?"

"Gaia." The voice was soft and familiar.

Gaia put her ear against the door. "Mom. It's me. Will you let me in?"

"Gaia!" This time the voice was a scream. And it wasn't Gaia's mother.

Gaia leaped back from the door. "Mary?"

"Gaia!" screamed the voice inside the house. "Gaia, help me!"

Gaia leaped, spun, and kicked the center of the door with all her strength. With a loud crash the door jumped in its frame. A thin crack split the center board from top to bottom. Fragments of wood rained down. Gaia kicked again. And again. Then followed up the kicks with a blow from a stiff right hand.

The crack widened.

"Hang on!" Gaia shouted into the opening. "I'm coming!"

She spun and directed another kick at the door, but before her foot could reach the wood, strength drained from her legs. The blow landed as only a weak thump. Gaia tried again, but this kick was even weaker.

She staggered and fell against the door. Her muscles were failing. This was supposed to happen after the fight, not in the middle. She couldn't collapse now, not when Mary was still in danger.

Gaia pushed herself away from the burned boards, drew in a deep breath, and pounded against the door with everything she had. Left hand. *Thump.* Right hand. *Thump.* Kick. *Thump*.

Blood began to pour out from under the door. Not a few spots of blood or drops of blood. Streams of blood. Buckets of blood.

The blows did nothing. Gaia was weak. Too weak to help Mary. Too weak to help anyone.

Gray fog closed in at the edge of her vision. Gaia was completely drained. Helpless.

"No," she whispered. "No, I have to get it open." She brought her hand down against the wood over and over.

Thump.

Thump.

Knock.

Thump.

Knock.

Knock.

Gaia's eyes flew open. She came off the bed in a fighting crouch, jumped into the center of the room, and searched for the nearest enemy.

Only there were no enemies. No corpse of a house in the middle of the snowy woods. No locked door. There was only a bedroom with an unmade bed and several careless heaps of clothes.

Gaia stood there for a moment, her breath coming hard. A dream. It had only been a dream.

The knock at the bedroom door came again. "Gaia? Are you up?"

Gaia groaned. It was Ella's voice. "Yes," she admitted. "I'm up."

"Good. I've got breakfast ready."

Gaia frowned at her bedroom door. This seemed real, but she had to be dreaming. "What did you say?"

"Breakfast is ready."

Gaia wondered if that sentence had ever before passed between Ella's overly red lips. Domestic was not Ella's middle name. Gaia decided she would rather face another nightmare than eat breakfast with a bimbo. "No, thanks," she said.

"You're sure you won't grace this event with your presence?" Even through the door Ella's voice carried enough sarcasm to cut steel. "There's French toast."

"No, thanks, I . . ." Gaia blinked. Wait a minute. Replay that last statement. "Did you say French toast?"

"Yes, but if you don't want it—"

Gaia's stomach grumbled. "I, um. I mean, okay. I'll be down in a minute."

"How wonderful." From outside the door came the sound of Ella's high heels going down the steps.

Gaia looked down at her stomach. "Traitor," she mumbled. Eating breakfast with Ella was against all of Gaia's principles. Most days Ella was a bitch, pure and simple. She treated Gaia with all the warmth usually reserved for a social disease.

So what did it say about Gaia that she was willing to ignore those principles just for a little bread and syrup? "I really am weak," she said to the empty room. At least when it came to food.

She peeled off the oversized T-shirt she had worn to bed and slipped into a pair of worn cargo pants. As she rooted through the pile of clothes on the floor in search of a sweatshirt that had been worn less than three times, Gaia's thoughts returned to her nightmare.

Gaia was not a big believer in dreams. Somewhere among the thousand and one books that her father had force-fed to her, she had even digested Freud's book on dreams. Gaia wasn't buying it. Dreams were just little movies in your head, not predictions about the future. If you dreamed you were falling, it didn't mean you were going to fall. If you dreamed you hit the ground, it didn't mean you were about to die. If you dreamed a friend was trapped, it didn't mean they were really in danger. And no matter what Mr. Freud said, not everything was about sex.

Gaia had been concerned about Mary—concern seemed to come from a different place than real fear. Which was probably why Mary had been in the dream. But there was no reason to worry about Mary anymore.

Skizz, the drug dealer who had been threatening Mary, had been on the receiving end of a patented Gaia Moore ass kicking. He had survived, but he was in the hospital. And when he got out, the police were waiting. There was no way Skizz could be a threat.

Gaia finally managed to locate a khaki green sweatshirt and tugged it over her head. She dragged her long hair free of the shirt and shook her head. It was just a dream. Dreams didn't mean anything.

She exited her room and made it down to the second-floor landing before the smell of cooking stirred her into hyperdrive. From there she took the steps two at a time.

Cooking was definitely rare behavior on Ella's part. When she did cook, Ella usually made obnoxious gourmet dishes with all the taste of old sneakers. Gaia only hoped that Ella's idea of French toast didn't involve bread and snails.

Gaia reached the bottom of the stairs and slowed her walk as she reached the kitchen. No reason to look too anxious.

George Niven sat at the breakfast table with the Sunday edition of *The New York Times* heaped in front of him. He looked at Gaia over the top of the national news section and smiled. "Hey. How are you doing this morning, kiddo? Going to have some breakfast with us?"

Gaia shrugged. "Guess so." She walked across the ceramic tile floor and sat down across the table from George.

Gaia liked George Niven well enough. George had worked with her father at the CIA for years. He had only one serious flaw. For some reason unknown to science, George was in love with Ella. And in Gaia's opinion, that was a pretty big flaw. It made her wonder just how good an agent George could really be when he couldn't even tell that the woman he had married was the world's biggest slut.

Ella marched across the room, her heels snapping on the tiles like rifle shots. Even though it was barely eight in the morning, her scarlet hair was swept up over her head, her makeup was there in all its Technicolor glory, and she was decked out in a teal dress so short, it barely qualified as a blouse.

"Here," said Ella. She inverted a pan, and two slices of browned toast fell onto a plate. Gaia grabbed for the syrup and doused the toast in a maple-flavored flood. She was a little cautious on the first bite, but the food was actually good. Wonders would never cease.

"So," said George. "You have any plans for New Year's?"

Gaia shrugged. "I'm not sure."

George folded his paper and put it on the edge of the table. "Why don't you come with us?"

Gaia paused with a forkful of French toast halfway to her mouth. "Come where?"

"With Ella and me," said George. "I have an invitation to

a New Year's Eve event down in Washington, D.C. It would be great if we all went together."

"All together," Gaia repeated.

George smiled. "Like a family."

A shiver went through Gaia, and the syrup in her mouth seemed to turn sour. Gaia barely held down her breakfast. "Uh, I . . ."

She was saved from answering by the ringing of the phone in the kitchen. A moment later Ella called from the other room, "Gaia, it's for you."

Gaia jumped up from her chair, ran into the kitchen, and took the phone from a scowling Ella. "Hello?"

"Hey," said Mary's voice at the other end. "I dare you to meet me in the park."

"I told you I'm done with truth or dare," Gaia said, smiling. "But you don't have to dare me to do that. You have something planned?"

"I'm going on an errand," said Mary. "And then to do some shopping. Come along and help me pick out something outrageous."

Gaia wasn't exactly the queen of shopping. In fact, she wasn't the princess or the duchess or the lady-in-waiting of shopping. Gaia was a shopping peasant. The trouble with shopping was that it usually involved trying things on. Trying things on usually meant looking at yourself in a mirror.

Looking in a mirror meant facing the fact that your legs were as big as tree trunks and your shoulders looked like they were ready for the NFL.

"How about I skip the shops and meet you after?" Gaia suggested.

"Okay," said Mary. "Just as long as you don't try to get out of our plans for tonight."

Gaia winced. Tonight. She had almost forgotten. "Not the dancing."

"Absolutely the dancing," Mary said. "You promised."

"That's what you say. I don't remember any of it."

"You said you would go."

"I was talking in my sleep."

"It still counts," said Mary. "I better get moving if I'm going to find the perfect thing to wear tonight."

"Mary, why don't we try something else tonight? I mean, dancing, that's just not—"

"Hey, do you hear something?"

Gaia frowned. "What?"

"On the phone," said Mary. "I thought I heard something."

"Like what?"

"I'm not sure. Weird." Mary sighed. "Anyway, see you in the park around three?"

"Sure," said Gaia. Meeting in the park would give her at

least one more chance to talk Mary out of her plans for the evening.

Gaia hung up the phone and went back to her breakfast. She managed two forkfuls of syrup-soaked toast before George returned to his earlier question.

"So, what about it?" he asked. "A family outing?"

"Uh, that was my friend Mary on the phone," Gaia said quickly, suddenly seeing her way out of the worst New Year's Eve on the planet with George and Ella. "I forgot I already promised to do something with her."

George frowned, but he nodded. "All right," he said. "But I'll keep the offer open. We need to do something to make this family gel."

Gaia dropped her fork and stood up from the table. A family? With Ella? One thing was sure, that was never going to happen. There might be some paper in an office across town that listed Ella as Gaia's foster mother. But paper was as much of a relationship as they would ever have.

The only thing that made Gaia feel a little better was the expression on Ella's face. From the way her forehead was wrinkled and her lips drawn down in disgust, it was clear that Ella liked the idea of Gaia as her daughter just about as much as Gaia wanted this red-haired bimbo as a mother.

THE BAT CAVE

The New York Public Library wasn't exactly Mary's favorite place. The building was a little too official. A little too *People's Court*. The last time she had been here was on a field trip back in fourth grade. Or maybe it was third. Whenever it was, all Mary really remembered was the lions.

She stopped to pet one of the stone beasts on its cold marble nose and looked up at the huge building. "Wish me luck, Leo. I'm going in."

Mary hurried up the long staircase with a cold wind blowing at her back. Inside, the library was nearly as cavernous as a football stadium. The place wasn't quite as ominous as she had expected or remembered. Inside there were colorful displays, banks of computer monitors, and lots and lots of people.

She wandered through the stacks until she found an information desk. After getting directions, she spiraled down a winding marble staircase, walked past an acre of book stacks, then continued downward to a smaller staircase of black wrought iron. It seemed to Mary that the stairs went down a long way. Much longer than they should have. They twisted on and on, past doors marked Archives and Records and Acquisitions, until Mary was sure that she must be several floors below ground level. It seemed to her that the weight of the whole city was pressing down on her head.

Finally, around the time Mary was beginning to wonder if the next door might be marked China, the staircase ended. The hallway she now saw had none of the intricacy or character of the building above. It was just a plain gray hall, with a concrete floor and bare walls.

Mary walked ahead cautiously. The whole place smelled of damp paper and dust. The dim light left shadows along the walls.

If I see a rat, I'm going to scream.

There were no rats. Or at least, the rats stayed hidden.

Another twenty feet along the hall Mary reached a door labeled Research. She let out a relieved breath and rapped her knuckles against the door.

"Yes?" said a muffled voice from inside.

"Aunt Jen?" Mary called. "Is that you?"

There was a rattle, and the door opened just enough to admit a head with ringlets of copper hair and round, rimless glasses. "Mary!" she said excitedly. "What are you doing down here?"

Mary shrugged. "I was on my way to the center of the earth and thought I would stop in." She rolled her eyes. "I came here to see you, of course."

"That's great," her aunt replied. Her expression suddenly changed from a smile to a look of worry. "You're okay, aren't you? You're not in trouble?"

Mary sighed. It was clear that her parents had already passed along the terrible story of Mary and her drug addiction. "No, Aunt Jen, I'm not in trouble." She held up a small manila folder. "I wanted to see if my favorite aunt could help me find some information."

Relief spread over her aunt's face. "I'm your only aunt," she said, "but I guess you can come in anyway." She swung open the door.

Mary stepped in, but as soon as she was through the door she stopped again. "Wow! It's the Bat Cave."

Jen laughed. "Just a few simple tools."

"Yeah, right." Everywhere Mary looked, there was another computer or monitor or some other piece of electronic gear. The whole place glowed. "It looks like I came to the right person."

Aunt Jen plopped into a padded office chair and waved to another. "Have a seat and tell me what's up."

Mary sat down and opened her folder. She hesitated for a moment. What Gaia had told her was a secret. She knew that Gaia would be upset if she knew Mary had told someone else. On the other hand, Mary couldn't help Gaia unless she knew what was going on. She reached into the envelope and pulled out several sheets of computer printout. "I have this friend," she said. "Something happened to her parents."

Mary watched her aunt take the papers and study them with a frown. Aunt Jen had the same hair as Mary's mother, but that was where the resemblance stopped. Aunt Jen was ten years younger and thirty pounds heavier than her mom. And when she smiled, she looked closer to twelve than thirty-two. Even if Mary had a dozen aunts, this one would still be her favorite.

"What do you think?" Mary asked after a minute of silence.

Aunt Jen shook her head. "I don't know what to think." She flipped through the papers one more time, then looked at Mary. "I'm a library scientist. I study how to organize information. I'm not a detective."

Mary leaned forward in her chair. "Yeah, but you've got access to every piece of paper in the world."

"That's not quite true."

"It's close." Mary smiled hopefully. "Can't you make a few searches? Check a few files?"

"For what?"

"Anything you can find."

Aunt Jen gave an elaborate sigh, but there was a smile on her round face. "All right," she said. "I'll see what I can do." She glanced at her watch. "But it will have to be later."

Mary grinned. "That's fine." She got out of her chair and hugged her aunt. "Call me as soon as you find anything."

Aunt Jen led her back to the door. "You stay out of trouble."

Mary nodded. "Don't worry. I'll be fine." She turned and

headed back down the gloomy hallway. Once again she felt that terrible sense of being buried under tons of earth.

I'll be fine if I don't have to come back down here, she thought with a shiver. *If I worked down here, I would have to be drugged.*

UNSEEN

Loki waited on the third landing. He could hear the girl coming closer, her leather-soled shoes clapping against the metal stairs. She was three twists of the stairs below, but she was climbing steadily. This girl had young legs. She would reach him soon.

He flexed his fingers. This would be a good opportunity to prevent any further threat from Mary Moss. A quick push and she would go screaming back to the bottom of the stairs. The fall was only thirty or forty feet, but Miss Moss would not survive. Loki would see to that.

The footsteps were closer now, still rising to meet him. Loki leaned over the railing. He could just make her out—two turns down.

Gaia shouldn't have told her about Katia. True, he still might have been forced to kill the Moss girl eventually. Her friendship with Gaia, if it continued, was too much of a threat. But the knowledge Gaia had shared with Mary had completely sealed her fate.

Loki squeezed his eyes shut for a moment. No one could know the truth. It was unlikely that this girl could learn anything of importance. Unlikely, but not impossible.

Mary was one turn below now. Her head was barely a foot beneath Loki's boots.

Kill her. Stop her from asking any more questions. It was the cleanest way to solve this problem.

Mary rounded the last turn and headed up to the landing.

Loki faded back into the shadows. He moved with absolute silence, and his clothes blended with the darkness. He stood absolutely still. He didn't breathe. He didn't even blink.

Mary passed within five feet of him. She could have reached out and touched him. He could have reached out and sent her to her death. But Loki had decades of experience in being unseen. Mary went on without pausing.

Loki waited until the girl had passed, then started after her. Mary would live through the day. He had decided that he didn't have enough information to act at this point. His surveillance of Mary Moss was incomplete. She might have informed others of Gaia's story.

He would have to tighten the noose around Mary. He

would find out exactly what she knew and who she had told. Once those questions were answered, Loki would see that Mary Moss met with an early and tragic end.

BIZZARO HEATHER

Ed Fargo hated salt.

Not salt on food. As far as Ed was concerned, salt was in its own food group with an importance level that put it right below the all-powerful sugar-and-chocolate group and just above the equally vital grease group. Food salt was good. Unfortunately, not every grain of salt was lucky enough to end up decorating a giant pretzel.

As soon as there was the least hint of snow, the storefronts around the Village began to apply liberal amounts of salt to the sidewalk. Not little dashes of salt. Not handfuls. *Tons* of salt. Whole bags of coarse, milky rock salt. So much of the stuff that Ed wondered if there was actually more salt than snow.

There were several reasons to hate the stuff. Most of the

year, being in a wheelchair was at least quiet. Now that it was salt season, every pump of his arms crunched so loudly that he sounded like he was rolling over a bag of potato chips. There was also the cleanliness factor. The salt from the wheels got all over his hands and on his clothes. And then there was the mechanical safety factor. Ed could only imagine what all the crud was doing to the chair. Salt rusted cars, and cars were covered over with nice layers of paint and all kinds of expensive antirust coatings. Ed's chair was nothing but bare metal. He wondered if the whole thing was going to melt into a puddle of rust one day and dump him in the middle of an intersection.

Ed was so involved in staring at the salt clinging to the spokes of the wheels that he almost ran over a beautiful girl.

"Hi, Ed."

Ed looked up to see Heather Gannis standing on the sidewalk in front of him. As usual, Heather was dressed wonderfully, with a cream-colored sweater peeking from under her jacket and a matching cap of soft wool pulled down over her mass of thick brown hair. And as always, Heather looked great.

"Heather," he said. "You, um . . . You look great." *Another brilliant, insightful observation by Ed Fargo.*

Heather gave a halfhearted smile. "Thanks." She looked past Ed for a moment. "I wish I felt better."

Ed searched for the right thing to say. Back when Heather

was his girlfriend, he knew what to say. Even after he and Heather had broken up, he had his patented collection of smart-ass remarks. Now that Heather was actually being nice to him again, Ed wasn't sure how to play it.

"Well," Heather said with a disappointed tone in her voice. "I guess I'd better—"

"Wait," said Ed. He gave up looking for something clever to say and went for the simple question. "What's wrong?"

Heather shrugged and looked off into the distance. "I'm not sure."

"You feeling okay? You're not sick or anything?"

"It's not me," she said. "I was supposed to meet . . . someone . . . down here, and he didn't show up. And then I saw you and I thought . . ." She stopped again and shook her head. "I probably shouldn't talk about it."

Ed stared up into Heather's face. She was pretty. Maybe even prettier than Gaia. Of course, Heather didn't have the quirky beauty of Gaia Moore, but there was only one Gaia Moore—and that was probably a good thing for the sanity of everyone involved.

Still, there was no doubt that Heather was very pretty, and at one time Ed had been convinced he loved her. Maybe he really had loved her. He had hated her, too, for the way she had left him after the accident. He wasn't sure that either one of those feelings was completely gone.

"I better go," said Heather. She licked at her lips and fidgeted with her wool hat. "It's getting late."

Ed nodded, but as Heather started to step past him he reached out and caught her by the arm. "How about some coffee?"

Heather shook her head. "I don't know if I should."

"Come on," Ed urged. "Let's have a little latte and talk."

For a long second Heather stood with her head hanging down. Then she nodded. "All right," she said. "I guess I need to talk to someone."

Ed followed her down the street to Ozzie's. It was a place famous in Ed's memory because it was the place where Gaia and Heather had first met—the place where Gaia had doused Heather with a full cup of steaming coffee.

"What are you smiling about?" asked Heather.

Ed pushed back the memory and shook his head. "Nothing," he said. "I'm just glad you decided to come with me."

For once he seemed to find the right words. Heather smiled at his response. "I'm glad you asked me."

While Heather grabbed a spot at one of the tables, Ed went to the counter and ordered for both of them. He had no trouble remembering what Heather wanted. She hadn't been Ed's first girlfriend, but she had been his first really serious girlfriend. And his last. Ed could probably remember almost everything Heather had ever ordered on their dates.

With two steaming double lattes clutched carefully in one

hand, Ed rolled over to the table where Heather was waiting. She took her drink without a word and lifted the foamy brew to her mouth. As she put down the cup, she sighed. Her eyes slipped closed for a moment. "Thanks," she said. "I needed this more than you can know."

Ed took a quick sip from his own latte. He knew that Heather had been through a lot over the last couple of weeks. In fact, Ed might be the *only* one who knew everything that had happened. For some reason, Heather had trusted him with some pretty heavy secrets. Still, it wasn't like Heather to let down her guard out in public. Heather lived at the top of the high school food pyramid with the truly popular people. It was a nasty place up there, a place where you didn't dare let people know that you were less than perfect.

"Okay, now that we're stocked on caffeine and sugar, are you ready to tell me what's up?" Ed asked.

Heather put her elbows on the edge of the table and rested her face in her hands. "I don't know if I should," she replied, her voice escaping through her slim fingers. "It's not one thing. It's a lot of things. Some of it's not even really my problem."

"If it's bothering you, then I guess it is your problem."

"Maybe." Heather nodded and gave another sigh. "Maybe I do need to talk about it."

"Then tell me." Ed looked at her with what he hoped was a confident solid expression. Your trustworthy friend Ed. "You know you can tell me anything."

The tightness in Heather's face relaxed a notch. "I always could." Heather lowered her hands and looked around her, as if afraid someone else might hear, but the coffee shop was nearly empty. Finally she looked back at Ed. "Part of it's about Phoebe," she said softly.

"Phoebe?" Ed flushed. A wave of embarrassment washed over him that almost knocked him out of his chair.

Phoebe was Heather's older sister. If anything, Phoebe was even more beautiful than Heather, though until recently she had been a little bit heavier. Not now, though. Ed had seen Phoebe only a few days before, and she had looked fantastic.

What made Ed red with embarrassment was the memory of what he had said about Phoebe. In the middle of an intense game of truth or dare, Ed had said that he wanted to sleep with Phoebe more than any woman in the world. It had been a lie, of course, and Gaia and Mary were the only ones there to hear him. Surely neither one of them would have talked to Heather. Would they?

Ed swallowed hard and tried not to look too terribly guilty. "Is Phoebe still in town?"

Heather nodded. "Just for a couple more days, though. Then she's going back to college."

A little bit of relief edged through Ed's near panic. Heather didn't *sound* like she knew about Ed's big sex-with-Phoebe confession. "So what's wrong?" he asked.

There was a long moment of silence, then Heather shook her head. "I can't talk about it. At least, not yet." A sad half smile settled on her face again. She reached across the table and took Ed's hand. "Thanks for asking me in here," she said. "I really appreciate it."

Ed tried out another reassuring smile. Anybody else at school might not recognize this soft, vulnerable person. This couldn't be Heather Gannis. Where were the biting remarks? Where was the absolute confidence? They would think this girl was bizzaro Heather. Most of the students at the Village School probably thought Heather's family was rich and Heather was a pampered princess. Ed was one of the few who knew how hard Heather worked to keep up that illusion.

"So if you can't talk about Phoebe and she's only part of it, what's the rest?"

Heather picked up her coffee, took a long drink, then set the cup down hard on the table. "Sam."

Once Ed had seen some science show where people's brains were monitored while someone read words from a list. Different words caused activity in different parts of the brain. If someone had clamped one of those helmets on Ed, the word Sam would have blown out the circuits.

"You and Sam are having trouble?" Ed hoped his voice didn't show as much strain as he felt. He didn't know whether he wanted Sam and Heather to be apart or not. On the one hand, if Sam stayed with Heather that meant Sam wasn't with Gaia. But Ed wasn't completely sure that he was over Heather. All things considered, Ed decided the world would be better if Sam Moon experienced spontaneous combustion. "Sam was the one who was supposed to meet you."

Heather nodded. "Over an hour ago. We were going to have lunch and maybe see a movie. Everything seemed fine."

"Except he didn't show."

"No," said Heather. "He didn't." She looked over Ed's shoulder toward the street outside. "You don't think that he knows about . . . you know."

Ed knew. "Charlie."

Heather looked around the coffee shop again, then brought her face close to Ed's. "Do you think Sam knows?"

Ed wasn't sure what to say. Charlie had gotten Heather into bed. He had bragged about it and had even used Heather for "points" in the little sex game some of the jocks had put together. "I think it's possible," Ed said carefully. "I mean, Sam's not around the Village School, but he's not on the other side of the world. What are you going to do if he finds out?"

Heather closed her eyes and put her hands against her temples. "I don't know what to do," she said. "I mean, no matter how big a jerk Charlie was and no matter what really happened, I went with him into that bedroom. Nobody made me do that."

Ed reached out and touched his hand gently against Heather's cheek. "It's okay," he said. "Sam probably doesn't know, and even if he does, I'm sure he'll understand."

Heather covered Ed's hand with one of her own and leaned against his palm. "You think . . ." She hesitated for a moment, then ventured a tentative smile. "You think you would be interested in getting something to eat?"

Ed grinned. "When have I ever turned down food?"

Heather's smile brightened. "And after that—"

"A movie," Ed finished. "Sure. I'd love to."

Heather's smile grew wider and lost some of its sad edge. "I can always count on you." Then, much to Ed's astonishment, she leaned across the table and kissed him on the cheek.

THAT TONE

Mary Moss held the handle of one shopping bag with her teeth, put another between her knees, and bent down to jab her key into the lock. She managed to turn the doorknob and stumble inside before everything tumbled to the floor.

"Little help here!" she called out, but the apartment was dark and quiet. Mary dragged her stuff inside and let the door swing shut.

Actually, it was probably good that her parents weren't home. For one thing, it showed that they were beginning to trust her again—even if it was for only a few hours in the middle of the day.

Since learning of Mary's drug habit, her parents had been smothering her with everything from videotapes and brochures on rehab centers to books from famous users who had kicked their addictions. Even her Christmas presents had been heavily loaded with an assortment of such uplifting material.

Mary didn't feel uplifted. She was off the drugs, and it wasn't because she had gone to any trendy center or been inspired by some has-been celebrity. She had kicked cocaine on her own. Well, maybe having Gaia around had helped a little. Maybe more than a little. But the point was, Mary was off the coke. If her parents were looking for the right time to give her books about drugs, they had missed it—by years.

The other reason it was good to find the apartment empty was that now her parents wouldn't see what she had bought.

Mary hefted the bags and made her way up the stairs to her bedroom. She had just enough time to get her things together before going out to meet Gaia. If she was lucky, she might even squeeze in a call to Aunt Jen before she left, in case there was any news on the Gaia's-parents-mystery front.

She gave the shopping bags a shake. Even though most of her Christmas presents had been of the ex-druggie-book variety, there had still been some cash slipped in among the pages. Not as many bills as in previous years, but then, her parents were probably afraid that if they gave her a big wad of cash, she would shove it up her nose.

Even the reduced cash supply had been enough to add some serious punch to Mary's wardrobe. She emptied the contents of the first bag onto her bed and studied the results. There were blouses she had liberated from Classics, a retro clothing store south of the park. There were some jeans that were completely too squeezy at the moment but that Mary hoped to wear as soon as she had battled off the holiday bulge. There were three pairs of shoes and a lace camisole in a violet so deep, it was almost black.

Mary smiled down at the pile. The clothes represented four hours of dedicated shopping, but they were definitely worth it. If you knew where to shop, a little bit of cash could buy a big chunk of cool.

She reached down, picked up the camisole, and carried it across to the mirror on her dresser. She held it up and was just imagining what her mother would say if she tried to wear it sans shirt when she heard a noise from the hallway.

Mary turned. "Mom?"

There was no reply.

"Mom? Are you guys home?"

For several long seconds Mary heard nothing. Then there was a soft creaking sound—the sound of boards shifting under someone's weight.

At once Mary's throat drew tight. "Mom?" she tried again, but this time it was only a faint whisper.

Slowly she let the camisole slide from her fingers and fall into a dark puddle on the floor. Moving as quietly as she could, Mary took a step toward the door. Then another. She peered out through the opening.

There was no sound from the hallway. No creaking boards. But there was a shadow. A man-shaped shadow. Just outside the limits of her sight, someone was standing in the hallway. Even without the shadow Mary didn't have to see him to know he was there—she could *feel* him.

She thought of making a run for the front door, then remembered the phone by her bed. Keeping her eyes on the hall, she slid toward the nightstand.

There was another noise, not so soft this time. A footstep, followed by the sound of something—of someone—brushing against the wall.

Mary's heart bounced in her chest. Fear ran through her body like strong acid. With trembling fingers she lifted the receiver of the phone and brought it up to her ear. In the silence the dial tone seemed impossibly loud. Surely whoever was out in the hallway would hear it. Surely he would know what Mary was trying to do.

Another footstep from the hallway. Louder this time. Closer.

Mary brought her fingers to the dial and pressed down on the nine. The tone was so loud, it made her jump. She had to close her eyes for a second and draw a breath before moving her finger over to press the one. She raised her finger to press the button again.

There was a sudden noise from downstairs. A clatter followed by the squeak of the door being shoved open.

"Mary, honey?" called a voice from downstairs. "Are you home?"

Mary felt a wash of relief so strong, she almost fell. "Dad!" she called out. "I'm up here." But as soon as she spoke, Mary realized that her parents could also be in danger. "Watch out!" she shouted. "There's someone else up here!"

Footsteps sounded from the stairs. "What did you say?" called her father.

Mary let the phone drop and jumped to her door. "Stay back, Dad! There's someone—"

But there was no one. In both directions the hallway was empty.

Her father reached the top of the stairs. "Who did you say was here?"

Mary looked along the empty hall and shook her head. "I

heard . . . I mean, I thought . . ." She paused, then shrugged. "Nobody, I guess."

Her father's face turned down in an expression of concern. "Are you okay?"

The tone of his voice made Mary wince. It was a tone she had heard all too often lately. No matter what the words, anytime her parents asked her a question in that tone, she knew what they were really asking—was she on drugs?

"I'm fine," Mary said. "Just fine." She backed into her bedroom and closed the door.

A LITTLE PIECE OF PAPER

There had to be a better phrase than jet lag. Jet lag sounded so harmless. "Oh, I'll be okay in a little while. I just have a touch of jet lag."

What Tom Moore felt wasn't jet lag. This was something more like jet flu, or jet attack, or maybe jet coma.

For almost twenty hours he had been on a series of planes. Moscow to St. Petersburg. From there to Munich.

Munich to London. And finally on to New York. By the time the small government Starcraft jet taxied onto the tarmac at JFK, Tom had to look up at the sky to tell if it was day or night. He felt like someone had beaten him on the head with a rock or drugged his coffee. Or both.

As usual, there had been men in dark suits waiting as soon as he stepped from the plane. The debriefing had gone smoothly. Tom's mission in Russia had gone reasonably well—despite a few setbacks and that botched rendezvous right before he'd left. And despite the fact that the whole trip had been overshadowed by memories of the time he had spent there in the company of his wife. The agency people weren't interested in Tom's memories. All they cared about were the dry facts. They wanted to know about the contacts he had seen and the timetable of the assignment.

Tom stayed awake long enough to accept dry congratulations on the completion of the latest mission, then fell into the backseat of a bland government-issue sedan and gave the driver directions to his latest apartment. Before the car even started to move, Tom fell into a gray haze.

Even in the backseat of the sedan, his mind was haunted by images of Katia. Moscow had been her home and the place where she and Tom first met. Going back there left Tom with a heavy weight of memories that clung to him like cobwebs. He wasn't even sure he wanted them to go away. Katia was gone. Memories were all Tom had.

At least he could still see his daughter, even if it did have to be at a distance. Meeting with Gaia wouldn't be safe for either of them, but Tom *had* to see her and make sure that she was all right. See Gaia. That thought cheered him as he climbed out of the car and walked the last couple of blocks to his apartment.

The apartment wasn't much, just a small one-bedroom place tucked above a corner fruit stand. It was far from fancy, but it provided an adequate base for Tom—especially since he was rarely in town. When he considered some of the other places he had called home over the last few years, it was practically paradise.

The fruit stand was doing slow but steady business. Tom waved at the owners as he walked around the building and made his way up the wooden stairs along the side. Even in December the air was scented by peaches and limes from the store.

Tom was nearly asleep on his feet, but he wasn't so tired that he didn't check the door before he went in. Before leaving, he had placed a small scrap of paper at the bottom of the door. Nothing special, just a little piece of newspaper that he had torn off and wedged against the door frame. If someone wasn't looking for it, they would never know it was there. Which was exactly what Tom was counting on. If someone had opened the door while he was away, the paper would have fallen out. He had fancier methods of detection available, but Tom was a great believer in simple methods.

He bent and inspected the door. The paper was still in its place.

Tom smiled in relief. The bed, and eight hours of solid sleep, were waiting inside.

Except.

Tom had his hand on the doorknob before something started to tickle at his brain. For a half a second his tired mind tried to sort out what was wrong. As he did, his fingers continued to turn the knob.

The paper was still there, so everything had to be okay. Only it wasn't, because . . . because . . .

Because the paper was turned the wrong way.

Someone had been there. Someone had gone inside, done whatever they wanted, and come back out. They had been careful. They had seen the little scrap of paper and put it back. Only not perfectly.

The doorknob clicked under Tom's hand, and the door cracked open. For the space of a heartbeat he stood there, staring into the darkness on the other side of the door.

Instantly the sleepiness and exhaustion he had felt since leaving Moscow vanished. Before his heart could beat a second time, he had started to turn away. Before a half second had passed, the suit bag had slipped from his left hand and he was at the top of the stairs.

The explosion came before he could take another step. There was no noise because the force of the blast instantly stunned his ears into silence. It lifted him, stole his breath in white-hot heat, then flung him downward like a singed rag doll.

He hit the bottom of the steps, bounced, and was instantly forced against the wall by an inferno wind.

When it was over, Tom fell. He fell down into darkness. And silence. And the smell of peaches.

ABOUT TONIGHT

EVEN GAIA HAD HER LIMITS.

A SMART BOY

Sam put his finger against the pawn and shoved it forward on its rank. "It wasn't like I did anything."

"Yah." A black knight jumped in from the side of the board to trample the unprotected piece.

"I mean, sure, I thought about someone else. I'll admit that." Sam pushed his bishop toward the center of the board.

The black queen slid up beside the bishop. "Der is nothing wrong with thinking."

Sam reached for his one remaining rook, hesitated, then drew back the bishop instead. "Okay, maybe I even kissed someone else," he said. "But that's not nearly as bad as what she did. Not even close."

"Yah, of course." The knight jumped again, and the rook left the field.

Sam scanned his diminished army and frowned. He shoved another pawn toward the opposite ranks. "And the first chance she gets, the very first chance—"

The black queen swept forward. "Dat is checkmate."

"It is?" Sam blinked and looked across the board. Usually he had a good grasp of the board, but now the chess game seemed as remote as another planet. He had lost. Again. He unzipped his heavy coat, fumbled in his pockets, and came out with a ten.

Zolov reached across the board and took the bill from his hand. "Thank you," said the old man. He stared down his long nose and studied the bill carefully, as if expecting to find a forgery. After the personal inspection Zolov held the ten up in front of two battered Power Rangers that sat beside the chessboard. "What you think?" he said.

Apparently the little plastic people gave their approval. After a few moments Zolov crumpled the bill and shoved it into the depths of his old tweed coat.

Sam shook his head and stared off across the frozen park. "I don't know. I thought maybe Heather really was the one. Now she's completely lied to me, and Gaia doesn't care if I live or not, so—"

"Be good to Ceendy, you," Zolov said suddenly. The old man's face reddened, and he waved an ancient, arthritic finger at Sam. "I like dat girl."

"Cindy?" Sam leaned back in surprise. "You mean Gaia?"

Zolov's bushy eyebrows drew together. "Dat girl, you should be lucky to have her." The old Russian glared at Sam for a few seconds longer, then picked up his chess pieces and began to put them back into position for a new game. "She is not like the others."

Sam tried to think of something to say. He couldn't be sure—maybe Zolov was thinking of Gaia, maybe he was thinking of someone else entirely. Maybe he was thinking of someone who had been gone for half a century. Zolov was never very clear on much. Except for chess. When it came to chess, Zolov was still as sharp as ever.

The Russian finished arranging the pieces and looked over at Sam. If the old man had been angry before, there was no trace of it remaining on his face. "We play again, yah?"

Sam did a quick calculation. Considering the difficulty he was having concentrating on the game, he was sure to lose. Even on his best days he could rarely match Zolov. But he could afford to lose another ten, and he certainly had nowhere better to go. "Sure," he said.

Zolov held out his hands. Sam picked one at random. The Russian unfolded his fingers to reveal a white pawn. "So," he said, you go first."

Sam started playing again, moving the pieces through a standard opening. He glanced across the board and decided to risk Zolov's anger. "What is it that makes Gaia different?" he asked.

Zolov snorted. "You not know that, you not know Ceendy, do you?" He jumped a knight over a rank of pawns.

Sam had to smile. He still couldn't tell if Zolov was talking about Gaia or just talking. But this was better than sitting around brooding about Heather. "I guess Gaia is special."

Zolov grunted and shoved a pawn forward.

Sam studied the board for a moment before moving in reply. Just because he knew he was going to lose didn't mean he wanted to make it easy. "It doesn't matter how special Gaia is. She isn't mine."

Zolov started to move, stopped, and looked across the board at Sam. "You don't know?"

"Know what?"

The Russian shook his head. "Think he is a smart boy, but he doesn't even know."

"Know what?" Sam repeated.

"Doesn't know Ceendy loves him." Zolov looked down, pushed up his queen, and smiled. "Dat is check!" he cried.

MUSIC FROM MARS

As expected, the snow had wimped out again. No more than a dusting remained along the hedgerows that bordered the park. The parks department, which had absolutely no appreciation for snow, had already completely cleared the main paths. Still, Gaia couldn't find much to complain about. The clouds had broken, the day was bright, and she didn't have to spend it *(a)* going to school or *(b)* sitting around the brownstone with Ella.

Gaia was due to meet Mary by the central arch in half an hour, which gave her plenty of time to cross the park. Normally she walked fast no matter where she was going, but now she strolled along the path at a leisurely pace, watching the people as they passed and the kids slipping down the metal slides on the playground.

She was near the center of the park when she heard a scratchy, warbling music drifting along the path. It was a strange sound. Gaia could make out a man's voice, but the words and the tune were utterly alien. Like music from Mars. She picked up her pace and angled toward the source of the weird sound.

A few twists in the path brought Gaia to a small group of people and a contraption just as strange as the sounds it was making. Mounted on what looked like a large version of a kid's red wagon, the thing spouted odd, angled lengths of plumbing pipe and a cone that looked like it might have come from a large desk lamp. At the heart of the mess Gaia could just make out a large—and very old—phonograph.

The record playing on the device wasn't any easier to understand from close up than it had been from far away. The singer's voice rose and fell, and alien words poured out. Gaia couldn't tell what the man was talking about, but there was no mistaking the message. This song was sad. This song was lonely. The singer sounded like he had just discovered he was the only person left in the world.

Standing there in the park with her hands in her pockets and her face chilled by the cold breeze, Gaia knew how he must have felt. She'd felt that way for a long time. But instead of thinking of her mother, the image that appeared in Gaia's mind was Sam. What was he doing right now? Did *he* ever feel this lonely? Did *he* ever hear songs that made him think of *her*?

Gaia wondered if she should walk over to the chess tables. She hadn't played in a while, and she really should keep in practice. She might get a chance to talk to Zolov. She might even run into Sam.

That was ridiculous, of course. Sam was with Heather. He was not only with Heather, he was sleeping with her. And Gaia should know: unbelievably, she'd witnessed them having sex not once, but twice. Although she could be a glutton for punishment, even Gaia had her limits. It was time to accept that Sam was never going to be part of her life. It didn't matter how Gaia felt about him because Sam didn't share those feelings.

"Is this song really that sad?" asked a voice at her back.

Gaia spun to find Mary looking at her. "You're early."

"So are you," said Mary. She tilted her head a little to the side and looked at Gaia. "Is something wrong?"

"No, nothing." Gaia was embarrassed to find there were tears blurring her eyes. The combination of the music and her own thoughts of Sam really had been getting to her. Gaia blinked away the tears and smiled. "How did your shopping trip go?"

Mary's lips turned up in a wicked grin. "Great, of course. I found exactly what I need for tonight."

"About tonight," said Gaia. "I don't know—"

"Oh, no, Ms. Moore," said Mary. "You're not getting out of this." She took Gaia by the arm and drew her away from the phonograph cart. "Come on, let's get somewhere we can talk without yelling."

Gaia followed as Mary led the way toward the north end of the park, where a re-creation of the Arc de Triomphe loomed over the people strolling the paths. The music from the weird phonograph faded until it was only a melancholy hum in the winter air. "Where do you want to go?"

Mary waved a hand ahead. "Doesn't matter. Somewhere we can continue our conversation."

"Which conversation is that?"

"You know." Mary gave Gaia a sideways look. "The conversation we were having about your mother."

Gaia stopped dead in her tracks. Mary was the first person she had ever told about her mother's death. Sharing had made Gaia feel better than she expected, but she was definitely not ready to say more. "That wasn't a conversation," she said. "That was a dare."

"I know," Mary said. "But I thought it might help you feel better to tell me more about it. I'm here for you, Gaia."

"There isn't any more to tell," said Gaia. Images of snow and violence danced on her brain for a painful moment. "I told you everything."

"Everything?" Mary paced back and forth on the sidewalk. "What about your dad? And how did you end up with the Nivens? And why was your mother killed?" She shook her head. "You've barely even started."

Gaia started to answer, stopped, opened her mouth to reply, then shut it again. The problem with most of Mary's questions was that Gaia didn't really know the answers. And even when she did know, there were still things she wasn't ready to tell. "The truth or dare game's over now," she said. "Let me catch my breath before we get into more."

Disappointment creased Mary's forehead, but she nodded. "All right," she replied. "It's just that it's all so . . . so . . . sad and . . . I wish I could help."

Sad wasn't the first word that came to Gaia's mind when she thought about her own life. *Try tragic. Heartbreaking.* "Let's try another subject. Tell me what you found to wear tonight."

Mary raised her chin and struck a pose. "Only something perfect."

"How nice for you," Gaia said with a laugh. "At least one of us will look decent."

"That's the really good news," said Mary. She held up her

left hand and revealed a small plastic shopping bag. She let the bag dangle from the tip of her finger and swung it back and forth. "Now for the even better news. I found something for you, too."

"You bought something for me?" Gaia looked at the bag and got a tight feeling in her stomach. "Something to wear?"

Mary nodded. "Something perfect for tonight." She held the bag out where Gaia could take it. "Come on. Take a look."

Gaia squinted at the bag suspiciously. "I don't know about this. I don't think I should even go."

"You promised."

"That's what you say," Gaia replied. "I don't even remember you asking."

Mary shrugged. "So you were mostly asleep. A promise is still a promise." She held up the bag and gave it a little jiggle. "Just look."

Gaia took the bag and peeked inside. "What is it, a top?"

Mary sighed in exasperation. "It's a dress, of course." She grabbed the bag back from Gaia, reached inside, and pulled out the garment.

Gaia's eyes went wide. "You're sure that's a dress?"

"Absolutely," Mary said with a nod. She shook out the dress and held it up against herself. "It's a little black dress. A genuine LBD. A staple of any decent wardrobe."

"Your wardrobe, maybe." Gaia shook her head. "I don't think that's my size."

"It's exactly your size," said Mary. She held the dress toward Gaia. "It'll look great on you."

Gaia took the dress from Mary and stared at it. It made her feel a little queasy to think about wearing the thing. Not that she didn't want to. Gaia could imagine what Mary or another girl might look like wearing the dress. A normal girl.

"You wear that tonight," said Mary, "and every guy in the place will be looking at you."

Yeah, it'd be a regular freak show. "This thing doesn't even have any straps." Gaia turned the dress over in her hands. "What's supposed to hold it up?"

Mary laughed. "You are."

The thought of that was enough to make Gaia want to drop the dress. "Thanks, but no." She started to hand the dress back, but Mary pushed her hands away.

"You're not getting out of it that easy," Mary said. "You're going to wear that dress, and you're . . . you . . ." Mary's voice trailed off, and she stared off into the distance.

"Mary?" Gaia turned and tried to see what had upset Mary, but Gaia couldn't see anything but a handful of people walking along a path. "What's wrong?"

Mary continued to stare for a moment, then shook her

head. "Nothing. Nothing's wrong." She raised one hand and pushed her red hair back from her face. "I'm seeing ghosts. That's all."

Gaia frowned. "You're not still looking for Skizz, are you?"

"No, I—" Mary stopped and shrugged. "Maybe. I don't know."

Gaia wasn't sure what to say. She knew that Mary had been afraid of the drug dealer. And Mary had been right to be scared. Skizz really had tried to hurt her to get back the money Mary owed for drugs. But there was no reason to be scared of the dealer now. Gaia wasn't proud of the beating she had given him, but there was no way he would be a problem to anyone.

"Skizz is in the hospital," said Gaia. "You know that."

"Yeah, I guess so." Mary still looked doubtful. "It's just that this morning . . ."

"What?"

Mary shook her head. "Nothing." The grin returned to her face. "Let's get back to an important topic, like how you are so going to wear that dress tonight."

Gaia thought about it for a second. She could wear the dress. She would look about as attractive as a football player in a tutu, but she could wear it. "I think I'll find something else."

"You won't even try?" asked Mary.

"Not this time."

Mary's bright green eyes locked onto Gaia's. "Coward."

Gaia took a step back. "What?"

"You heard me," said Mary. She jerked the dress from Gaia's hands and shoved it back into the sack. "I buy you a great dress, and you don't even have the guts to wear it."

Anger started to tighten down on Gaia. "If it's so great, why don't you wear it?"

"Maybe I will." Mary narrowed her eyes. "At least I'm not too scared."

"I am not scared," Gaia said in a near shout. "Believe me, I'm not afraid."

"Yeah?" Mary held out the bag. "Then prove it."

CHECKING WITH UNDERTAKERS

Ed was on his way out the door when the phone rang for the two hundred and a thirty-seventh time that afternoon. He groaned. Every time his parents were gone, it seemed like he spent all his time answering junk phone calls.

He rolled across the kitchen, grabbed the phone, and started talking. "Look, this is an apartment. We don't need insulated windows. "We don't need siding. I don't need insurance because I don't own a car, and I don't donate to anybody who calls me on the phone. Clear enough?"

"That's great, Ed," said the voice over the phone. "Now, are you ready to listen?"

Ed fumbled the phone, dropped it, caught it, and shoved it back against his ear. "Gaia?"

"I need a favor," said Gaia. There was a burst of music and background noise.

"What kind of favor?" asked Ed. "Where are you, anyway?"

"I'm at Eddie's."

"Who's Eddie?"

"Eddie's the restaurant," Gaia said. The music started up again, and Ed had to strain to hear her over the driving beat. "I'm here with Mary."

"Yeah?" In his mind's eye Ed had no trouble picturing Gaia and Mary. Gaia's hair was long and pale, buttery blond. Mary's was shorter, wavy, and copper red. Both of them were beautiful. Together the two girls were the hottest pair Ed had ever seen. Just a couple of days before, Gaia had kissed him. True, it had been an exceptional situation, but it had been a kiss. A real kiss. Right on the mouth. He wondered what Gaia was wearing. He wondered what Mary was wearing. Maybe Mary would—

"Ed? Ed, are you there?"

"Uh, yeah." Ed tried to shake off the daydreams and listen. "I'm here."

"There's something I want you to do for me."

"Sure. What is it?"

Gaia made a reply, but Ed couldn't hear her over a sudden increase in noise from the restaurant.

"What was that?"

"Skizz!" Gaia shouted into the phone.

"What?"

"Skizz. Mary's old dealer. I want you to find out where he is."

Ed stared at the receiver. "How am I supposed to do that?"

"Check the hospitals."

"Why would he be in a hospital?"

"Because," said Gaia, "I put him there."

"Oh," said Ed. Then, "Oh!" as he realized the meaning of what she had said. "You sure I shouldn't be checking with undertakers?"

"No. Or at least, I don't think so. If you can't find him, check and see what you can learn from the police."

Ed grabbed a pad from the kitchen counter and made a couple of quick notes. "Okay," he said. "I'll see what I can find. But remember what happened last time we tried to play detectives?"

"We're not talking about going up against a serial killer,"

said Gaia. "I just want to be sure this particular scuzzy drug dealer is still out of the picture."

"Gotcha. I'll see what I can find out." Ed cleared his throat. "So, Gaia. If I find some information, maybe we can get together and—"

"Thanks, Ed," said Gaia. "I'll check in soon." The phone clicked and went dead.

Ed hung the receiver back on the hook and scowled. "Great," he said to the empty kitchen. "One kiss and she thinks I'll do anything for her."

Then he pulled a phone book out of the cabinet and started to look up hospitals.

WITH A *K*

Mary held the phone close to her mouth. "Aunt Jen? Can you hear me?"

She waited for the reply from the other end and frowned at the receiver. Clearly the tales of Mary's terrible drug addiction were still affecting the opinions of her favorite aunt.

"Aunt Jen . . . Aunt Jen . . . Aunt Jen! Look, I'm okay. I'm not at a party. I'm at a restaurant."

Mary shifted around on one foot to see if Gaia was watching her. "Eddie's. *E-d-d-i-e-s.* It's near the campus. NYU, okay?"

She nodded as she listened to her aunt's reply. "No party. No drugs. Just a greasy restaurant. I'm having a cheeseburger."

Even this information generated a lengthy response. Mary began to wonder how many people went back on drugs just because so many people pestered them about staying off. "Look, Aunt Jen, I only wanted to see if you found out anything about that stuff I brought you."

Mary listened for a moment, gritted her teeth, and squeezed her eyes shut. "Yes, I promise it has nothing to do with drugs. Can we please forget the drugs?"

Mary took another glance toward the table and saw that Gaia was looking at her. She cupped her hand over the mouthpiece and tried to speak as softly as she could in the noisy diner. "Yes, I know what the name Gaia means. Uh-huh."

Mary dragged a small pad of paper from her pocket. *Thomas Chaos,* she wrote on the pad.

THE MOSS SITUATION

Loki directed the laser sensor at the window of Eddie's diner. In proper situations the device was a wonder. It could take the tiny vibrations that sound caused in the window and use those vibrations to re-create the original sounds. This was not a proper situation. The noise level inside the place made it nearly impossible to sort one sound from the sea of babble. With some difficulty Loki finally managed to locate the voice of the Moss girl.

". . . is Gaia . . . what that means . . . father . . ."

Loki lowered the device in frustration. It was clear that the girl was discussing Gaia, but he couldn't tell what she was saying. Not even Loki could bug every phone in the city.

The situation was becoming intolerable. The girl had information about Katia, and she had shared that information with others. Possibly several others.

Loki dropped the laser detector back into his pocket, took out his phone, and pressed a single button.

"Yes," said an emotionless voice from the other end.

"We'll have to move faster than expected on the Moss situation," said Loki. "She presents too much potential risk."

"I understand," replied the flat voice. "Measures will be prepared."

"You handle the aunt," said Loki. "I'll take care of the girl myself."

STEP TWO

Ella picked up the phone on the first ring. "Yes?"

"Hi," said the voice from the other end. "This is Sam Moon. Is Gaia there?"

Ella smiled. Sam was a beautiful boy. Nearly perfect, in Ella's carefully considered opinion. He was far better than anything that Gaia deserved. "No, Sam," Ella said sweetly. I'm afraid Gaia is out."

"Do you know when she'll be back?"

"Not until late. She's out on a date with her boyfriend."

"Oh."

Ella ran a lacquered nail down the side of the phone. This was working out so well. "Do you want me to take a message?"

"No. No, I guess not."

"Should I tell her you called?"

"No," said Sam. "Thanks."

The sadness in his voice was absolutely delicious. "You're welcome, dear."

Ella set the phone back on its hook and brushed her fingers through her scarlet hair. The call couldn't have gone better if she had planned it. Now it was time for step two.

HER OWN HEARTBEAT

HIS FINGERTIPS PRESSED INTO HER,

PUSHING HER AGAINST HIM.

ELLA WEAR

"You look great."

Gaia squinted at the image in the mirror. "I look ridiculous."

Mary rolled her eyes. "Are you kidding?" She moved around Gaia, inspecting her dress from all angles. "I wish I looked half as good as you."

Gaia tugged at the top of the dress. "Half my size is more like it. This thing might fit you, but it's *way* too small for me."

"Are you nuts? It's a perfect fit."

Gaia turned away from the mirror in disgust. "Okay, you've seen me wear the dress. You have to know I can't go out in this thing."

"All I know is that it fits great, you look great, and you should wear it." Mary flipped back her red hair and studied Gaia for a moment. "But if you're too scared—"

"I'm not scared," Gaia said between gritted teeth. "Being scared has nothing to do with it."

Mary nodded. "You just don't want to be embarrassed."

"Exactly."

"You're afraid somebody will make fun of you."

"Right . . . I mean, no." Gaia drew in a deep breath and blew it out through her mouth. "I am not afraid."

"Good," Mary replied brightly. "Then you won't mind wearing the dress."

Gaia lowered her face into her hands and shook her head. She wondered if being a sociopathic loner was really such a bad thing. On her own, she managed to get into fights only with armed criminals. Somehow that didn't seem nearly as disastrous as wearing this dress out in public. "Please tell me we're going somewhere that nobody knows me."

"Absolutely."

Gaia raised her head. "And we'll never go there again."

Mary shrugged. "If that's what you want. Wait till you get there before you decide something like that."

"Then all right, I may be crazy, but I'll wear the dress." Gaia went to the closet, pulled out her longest coat, and pulled it over the snug dress. "I'm not saying I'll stay long. Once everyone's had a good laugh, I'm leaving."

Mary shook her head. "You really don't see it, do you?"

"See what?" asked Gaia.

"Believe me. When the guys see you in that dress, there is not going to be any laughing." Mary pulled her coat on over the translucent top and short black skirt that made up her own outfit. "Let's get moving."

Gaia wasn't afraid. She *couldn't* be afraid, but she was definitely not looking forward to this evening. Her mood wasn't improved when she saw that Ella was waiting for them at the bottom of the stairs.

Ella folded her arms and leaned back against the stair rail as the girls approached. "Well," she said. "And where are you two going?"

"Dancing," Mary answered before Gaia could open her mouth. "Want to come along?"

Gaia winced. She could read the sarcasm in Mary's voice. She had no doubt that Ella heard it, too. But that didn't mean Ella wouldn't say yes just because she knew how much Gaia would hate it. Gaia looked back over her shoulder and glared at Mary, but Mary only smiled in reply.

Ella gave a short laugh. "I do love to dance," she said, "but no. I'm afraid I have my own duties to attend to tonight."

"That's too bad," Gaia said quickly. "Well, I'll see you later."

She started to step past, but to Gaia's surprise, Ella reached out and laid her hand on Gaia's arm. "Do be careful, dear," she said.

Concern wasn't usual for Ella. "Sure. All right." Gaia walked on, and Ella's fingers slipped away.

"Please tell me you weren't serious," Gaia whispered as she and Mary reached the door.

"What? About Ms. Niven coming with us?" Mary grinned. "It would be something, wouldn't it? I'd love to see if she even can dance on those heels she wears."

"It would be something, all right," said Gaia. She pushed open the door and stepped out into the cold night.

It wasn't until she was outside the brownstone that Gaia realized how happy she was that Ella couldn't see what she was wearing under the coat. For the first time since she had come to New York, Gaia was wearing a shorter dress than her foster mother. *Oh my God. I'm dressed in Ella wear.*

VODKA

"Twenty-three?"

Sam nodded.

The woman behind the bar was thin and thirty something, with pink hair piled on her head, a neat gold hoop through the side of her nose, and deep lines around her eyes. She looked skeptically at the ID card, then at Sam, then at the ID again. "You look younger."

"It's a curse," said Sam. He reached out for the card, but the bartender pulled it away.

"I wish I had a curse like that," she said. She gave the card another long look and held it up to the light. "This is a good fake."

Sam jerked the card away from her and put it back in his pocket. "It's not a fake!" he said.

The woman held up her hands. "Hey, don't get so worked up. I didn't say I wasn't going to serve you." A phone rang. The bartender turned and picked it up.

While she talked, Sam spun around on his stool. There was a dance floor in the club, but no one was dancing. Not yet, anyway. Up on the stage a band was just beginning to set up and a couple of men were arranging lights. Sam wasn't sure what kind of music the band played. He thought about asking, but after a moment he decided it didn't matter. He hadn't come into the club for the music.

He pulled out the ID card he had used to get in. These days, with color laser printers, there was almost nothing that couldn't be faked. Making the ID hadn't taken ten minutes.

The bartender finished with her phone call and strolled back over to stand in front of Sam. "You're getting an awfully early start, kiddo."

"Sam."

"Whatever." The woman leaned one elbow on the bar. "What's it going to be tonight, Sam?"

Sam stuffed the fake ID down in his pocket and studied the bottles behind the bar. The range of beverages was a little intimidating. He wasn't a regular drinker. In fact, he usually skipped both the beer and the shots available at campus parties. He just didn't enjoy it that much.

But this time Sam wasn't drinking for enjoyment. He was drinking to take the edge off Heather's betrayal. He was drinking to wash Gaia out of his mind. He was drinking to smother the pain that cut through him anytime he thought of either girl.

He expected it would take a lot of drinking.

Sam stared at the multicolored bottles for a few seconds, then shook his head. "Give me a recommendation," he said.

The bartender took a bottle of water-clear liquid down from the shelf. "If I was you, I would go home," she said. "But if you're going to stay here, then go for vodka."

"Why vodka?"

"Because," said the bartender as she pulled out a glass and set it down on the bar. "Vodka is good when you want to do some serious drinking. It doesn't leave you with such a bad hangover." The woman tipped the bottle and filled the glass nearly full of the clear fluid. "And kid, you look like you're here for serious drinking."

ONE THING HE KNEW

Ed held his fingers against the bridge of his nose and tried to get his temper under control. "I *understand* you still need insurance information. I don't *have* insurance information. No. No. No! I don't know his Social Security number!" He listened for a moment longer, then slammed the phone back into its cradle.

Four hours before, Ed had been on his way out of the house. Instead of leaving, he had been on the phone for hours. He never even got out of his kitchen.

Ed had been trying to get information from St. Vincent's, where Skizz was staying, by pretending to be everything from the police to Skizz's brother. The workers at the hospital weren't stupid, but they were overworked. If you kept at it long enough and pestered hard enough, you could get them to tell you what you wanted. But it sure took time.

Ed glanced toward the windows and saw it was already dark outside. He thought about going out. He could find something to eat. Wander down to see what was on at the movies.

But the sad truth was, despite all the time he had spent badgering people over the phone, Ed still didn't have all the information he needed. He had the first part. It wasn't much, really, just a sentence or two.

And Ed knew one thing for sure—what he had learned so far wasn't going to make Gaia happy.

WHY PEOPLE DANCE

"Come on!" Mary took Gaia by the hand and started dragging her toward the dance floor.

Gaia put on the brakes. "Wait."

"Wait for what?" Mary let go of Gaia's hand and swayed from side to side in time to the music. "Come on. Let's get out there."

People pushed past them on both sides. The band had been playing for only a few minutes, but already the floor was getting crowded with couples, singles, and assorted groups. The close press of people made Gaia feel more than a little trapped. She was used to being alone, prowling around the park or hiking down the streets at night. Being in the crowded nightclub made her so squeezed, that Gaia almost forgot about the way she was dressed. Almost.

"Gaia!" Mary called. Even from two feet away she had to shout to be heard over the driving music. She spun around on her high-heeled shoes and flashed a bright smile. "Aren't you going to dance?"

Gaia shook her head. "I don't think so. Dancing isn't on my resume."

Mary grabbed her hand again. "You know how. You just don't know that you know." She pulled Gaia toward the center of the floor.

Gaia let herself be pulled. First it was the skimpy dress. Now it was dancing. She wondered if a person could reach a complete overload of embarrassment. A pressure so strong that they collapsed inward, like a star falling into a black hole.

Mary released Gaia's hand. She started to dance slowly, shifting her weight and letting her arms drift back and forth. "Here's the secret," she said. "Guys have to learn how to dance. Girls don't. I mean, sure you have to learn if you want to be really good, but if you just want to have fun and get the guys bothered, all any attractive girl has to do is move."

Gaia looked down at her own feet. "That's great for attractive girls. How does it help me?"

Mary stopped dancing and put her hands on her hips. "Gaia, give it up. You know you're gorgeous."

"I'm not—"

Mary waved at the dancing crowd. "There's not a woman

in this place half as hot as you. "Why don't you want to believe that?"

"Because it's not true," said Gaia.

Mary frowned. "Then pretend, okay? For tonight just pretend that you're as pretty as . . . as . . . oh, as pretty as you really are!"

The tempo of the music picked up. Mary smiled and started moving again, swinging her hips and moving her body with the beat. "Come on, dance."

Gaia watched Mary for a few seconds. The red-haired girl moved so well. Her pale face and arms seemed to float above her dark clothing. She wasn't doing anything fancy, but her movements were smooth, fluid. The easy way Mary moved her body made Gaia feel jealous. There was no way she could move like that—and no way she would look as good as Mary did.

For long seconds Gaia stood still in the middle of all the dancing. She thought about leaving the floor. She thought about leaving the whole club. Then she thought about what Mary had said.

Gaia knew that Mary was only trying to make her feel better. She knew she wasn't beautiful—her mother had been beautiful, but not Gaia. But what if she was to pretend? Could she think of herself as beautiful for just one night? Could she imagine what it would be like to be a normal girl? An attractive girl without monster legs? A girl like Mary who knew how to dance.

She closed her eyes. Slowly Gaia began to move. Her feet remained almost still, but her legs moved. Then her hips. Then her body and shoulders and arms.

At first she felt awkward, stiff. Gaia knew how to move smoothly—she had gone through a thousand karate training exercises that were more about moving well than hitting anything. But dancing was different. There was no plan, no path to follow. She had to make it up as she went along.

Gaia picked up speed, bringing herself in time with the music. She started to feel a little better. A little looser. She was sure that if she opened her eyes, half the people in the club would be laughing at her. So she kept her eyes shut.

The more she caught up to the music, the more she could feel it inside her. The drums pounded in her stomach. The guitars sliced along her arms and legs, driving her to move faster, to dance wilder. With her eyes still closed, Gaia raised her hands over her head and spun around.

Maybe everyone was laughing, but it was starting to feel good. Really good. The movements of her body became more confident. There was a jazzy, electric feeling in her limbs. It was something like the buzz she sometimes got before a fight.

When Gaia dared to open her eyes, Mary was gone. Lost somewhere in a sea of dancing bodies. No one was laughing.

But there was someone looking at her.

A young Hispanic man with flashing black eyes and

short-cropped hair was dancing right in front of Gaia. He was smiling at her. And he was dancing at her.

The man wasn't very tall, barely as tall as Gaia, but he was well built, with a narrow waist and broad, square shoulders. Gaia guessed he was somewhere in his early twenties. He wore a black jacket that was hanging open at the front and a snug white shirt that pulled in tight against the brown skin at his throat. He was muscular. Not overmuscled, but smooth, firm, fit.

The man didn't say a word, but his eyes never left Gaia. He looked into her face as he danced. Right into her eyes.

Gaia could barely feel herself moving. It was like she was riding the music. It seemed effortless now, like something she had done all her life.

The tune ended, and the music changed, but Gaia never missed a step. For the first time in a long time she felt like she was part of something bigger than herself.

She understood why people danced.

The man moved closer. He leaned toward Gaia, and she leaned away—but not far away. They moved together, so close that the man's jacket brushed against the cloth of Gaia's dress. As soft as a whisper. Gaia's long blond hair sprayed around her shoulders and spilled across the man's face.

Their bodies were inches apart. Less than an inch. Touching. Gaia could feel the heat coming from the man's skin as if there were a furnace in his chest. She couldn't tell if the beat she felt was the music. Or her own heartbeat. Or his.

The man's hand moved around Gaia and settled at the small of her back. His fingertips pressed into her, pushing her against him.

In that moment Gaia forgot that she was wearing a dress that exposed her bulky legs and arms. She forgot that she was supposed to be embarrassed. For that moment she even forgot about her father, and mother, and Sam.

And when the song ended and the man—the man she had never seen before in her life—brought his face down to hers, Gaia kissed him. Hard.

HOT IN THE THROAT

Vodka did pack a punch. Unfortunately, that punch didn't hit Sam where he wanted. Instead of thinking less about Heather and Gaia, every shot of vodka only seemed to make him think about them more. And it burned more, as if he were pouring the alcohol straight into a raw wound in his heart.

Still, Sam didn't stop. He was sure that if he only drank enough of the cold, clear liquid, he wouldn't be able to think at all.

Sam leaned over the bar and waved an unsteady hand toward the glass. "'Nother one," he said.

The pink-haired bartender gave him a quick inspection. "You sure about that, Sam my man?"

"Sure," Sam repeated with a nod.

The woman frowned. "All right, but just one more." She refilled the glass and waited while Sam shakily counted out the cost of the drink. "Whoever she was, she must have hurt you bad."

A girl with short, honey-blond hair, big silver earrings, and a very small red T-shirt dropped onto the stool next to Sam. She gave him a quick smile as she ordered a beer. "Great band, huh?"

Sam glanced over the sea of dancing people at the trio up on the band platform. He shrugged. The truth was, Sam had barely noticed the music. Ever since his second drink, all the noise in the place had merged into a kind of hum. Even though the music was loud enough to send ripples across his drink, the vodka kept Sam insulated from everything going on around him. The music seemed dull and distant, like something happening in another town.

"They're okay," he said. "I guess."

The blond girl's smile slipped a bit. "You here by yourself?"

Sam nodded. He picked up his glass and took a drink. The vodka was cold in his mouth but hot in his throat. "All alone."

"Aww, that's too bad." The girl looked him over for a moment, then held out a hand. "Why don't you come out and dance with me?"

Sam started to say no. After all, he was supposed to be with Heather, and that meant not being with anyone else. Then he realized how completely stupid that was. There was nothing wrong with a little dancing. Besides, dancing was nothing compared to what Heather had done. He certainly wouldn't be cheating on anyone.

But when Sam started to get up, the room began to swirl around him and the floor swayed like the deck of a ship caught in a storm. He stumbled back against the bar, tried to take a step, and stumbled again.

The girl put a hand on his arm. "Man, you're crashed."

"Am not," Sam replied. He tried to stand up straighter, but that only made the room start to spin faster.

The girl laughed at him. "I don't think you're going to be doing any dancing tonight."

Sam frowned. "I can dance."

"Sure you can," said the girl, "but not with me. Next time hit the dance floor before you hit the bottle." She drained her beer, gave Sam a quick wave, and charged back out onto the dance floor.

Sam watched her go and felt a fresh flood of despair. He carefully sat down on his swaying bar stool and picked up his drink. He was going to be alone forever. That was clear.

He was beginning to think about leaving when someone new settled in next to him. It was a girl—no, a woman, a definite woman—in a skintight emerald green dress. The dress was cut very high on her thighs to reveal long, shapely legs, and it scooped down low at the top to reveal even more pale skin. Long seconds went by before Sam could manage to raise his eyes from what the dress revealed and look up at the woman's face.

She smiled at him. "Hello." Her lips were very full and very red.

"Hi," Sam managed. He ran a hand across his tangled hair and tried to return the woman's smile.

"So why is someone as cute as you sitting over here all alone?" she asked. Her voice was soft. Throaty. Sexy.

Sam had to swallow hard before he could reply. "It's, um, a long story."

The woman leaned toward him, revealing even more of the contents of her dress. "That's all right," she said. "I've got all night."

Ed scribbled down a note. "Thanks, Detective Hautley. That story will be in the paper tomorrow. Oh, absolutely. Page two or better. Yes, I have the spelling. Thanks again."

The phone went back on the hook for the last time, and Ed leaned back in his chair. He had lied so often that night that he felt like he had taken a crash course in method acting. He could probably go to work on Broadway. Or head out to Hollywood.

Or make a real killing ripping people off with a phone scam.

It had taken more hours of pretending to be someone he wasn't, but finally all the lying had paid off. All it took was finding the right person.

The right person turned out to be Detective Charles Hautley. Hautley was a vice cop who wanted to be in homicide, and he was willing to share a few choice details with a reporter who might make the poor, hardworking, clean-living detective into a star. Once Ed got the good detective on the phone, it hadn't taken him ten minutes to find out what he wanted.

Hautley knew all about Skizz. He knew the man's record. He knew about the dealer's trip to jail. And most important, he knew where Skizz could be found.

And now that Ed knew the answer, he wished he had never asked.

GAIA

I always knew that vacation was the best idea in the history of the world. Right up there with the doughnut.

You have to wonder who came up with something so brilliant. It's a shame that this hero isn't in the history books. There should be statues. There should be parades. They ought to give a holiday in honor of the guy who came up with vacations.

Maybe there was some caveman out there who got tired of hunting woolly mammoths. Better yet, maybe it was some cavewoman stuck back home, chewing on mastodon blubber and sewing bearskins. One day she wakes up, looks around, and says, "Hell with this—I'm going to Florida." One smart cavewoman.

Even little vacations are good. Memorial Day. Columbus Day. Dead Presidents' Day. But when it comes to vacation, size definitely matters. Spring break, good. Christmas break, also good. Summer, very, very good.

That's all I knew about vacation until last night.

But I have made a discovery every bit as important as that sun-bathing cavewoman's. Something right up there with fire, electric lights, and Krispy Kreme. I have found the New World of vacations.

Ever hear someone say, "Wherever you go, there you are"? Yeah, it's a stupid saying. Corny. Stupid and corny.

It's also wrong.

Here is my attempt at explanation.

Point 1. I was at the club last night.

Fact B. Gaia Moore got left behind.

I don't want to sound like one of those guys selling self-improvement books on 3 A.M. infomercials, but you really can take a vacation from being you. You can stop worrying about who's looking or who's talking about you or what they might say. Why should I care what anybody there thinks of me? I mean, I don't have to live with those people. I probably wouldn't like them if I did.

If you run hard enough, you can outrun yourself. And the only secret is: Stop running.

Doesn't make any sense, right? That's because you haven't been there.

Actually, I can't claim solo credit for this great, world-shaking discovery. It was Mary Moss who blazed the trail to this hidden continent of vacation. It's because of her that I learned how to stop being Gaia for a few hours and just have fun. She led me to the land of Moss. Mary Land. The place where you don't stress over what other people think.

All my life I've never been afraid, but I think this is what it really means to be fearless. It means doing the things you want to do without worrying about being rejected.

So I think it's time to do something I've been wanting to do for a while. I think it's time to talk to Sam.

GAIA MOORE NAKED

THE REAL DIFFERENCE THIS MORNING WAS THAT GAIA SOUNDED HAPPY.

THE GIRL IN THE MIRROR

Gaia came out of the shower with one of the tunes from the night before running through her head. She walked across the bedroom wrapped only in a towel, but she had a hard time walking. Her feet still wanted to dance.

She had started to rummage through the clothes beside her bed when she noticed the black dress thrown across her chair.

I wore that. I went out in public in that.

No one had laughed. At least, if someone had laughed, Gaia didn't notice them. The guy she had danced with—Inego, his name was Inego—certainly hadn't been laughing.

Gaia paused, stood up, and walked across the room to the mirror. Carefully she studied her reflection in the mirror.

Gaia wasn't prepared to admit that Mary was right—no way was she beautiful. Not by a long shot. Still, maybe things weren't so bad as Gaia had always thought. Sure, her legs were packed with muscle. But were they so awful? Her shoulders and arms were bulked up, too, but this morning they didn't look so terribly hulkish.

Gaia tried to imagine what it would be like if she didn't know that girl in the mirror. What if she were just to meet this girl on the street or maybe at school? What if she didn't know this was Gaia Moore, fearless expert in all things kung fu and girl freak? Would she really think this blond stranger looked that bad? Could she be normal? Could she even be . . .

The phone rang. Gaia was across the room in a flash, leaving her towel behind as she ran. She grabbed the receiver and, for once in her life, managed to answer before Ella could get to the phone downstairs. "Hello," she said.

"Gaia?"

"Ed!" Still naked and damp from the shower, Gaia threw herself back onto the unmade bed and lay facing the ceiling. "How are you? It's a beautiful morning, huh?"

There was a pause of at least five seconds before Ed spoke. "It's cloudy outside."

"Whatever," said Gaia. "How are you doing?"

"I'm not sure," Ed replied. "I was trying to reach a girl named Gaia."

"That's me."

"Gaia Moore?"

"Don't be an asshole, Ed."

"Hmmm," Ed replied. "That sounds more like it. Okay, maybe I did reach the right girl after all. But you sound different this morning."

Gaia sat up on the bed and ran her fingers through her damp hair. "Different how?"

"I don't know. You sound cheerful, and you're not, I don't know—"

"Not what?"

"Not whining, I guess."

Gaia scowled at the phone. "I do not whine."

"Oh, yeah? Whenever you talk about your foster parents, or Sam, or school, or—"

"Shut up, Ed." Gaia bounced up from the bed, jammed the phone between her shoulder and her ear, and started digging through the available clothes. "If you're so tired of me, you could always call someone else."

DANCING GAIA

Ed shook his head, then realized that shaking your head didn't work when the other person was on the phone. "No," he said. "The Gaia report is the high point of my day."

"All right, then," Gaia replied. "Stop complaining. Or should I say, stop whining?"

Ed grinned. Gaia did sound different, but she was still Gaia. The real difference this morning was that Gaia sounded happy. That was a condition that didn't happen nearly as often as it should. In Ed's opinion, Gaia needed to be happy all the time. And of course, the way to see that Gaia was happy all the time was to see that she fell in love with Ed.

He started to say something else, but his voice caught, and his smile collapsed. Gaia was happy.

And he was about to ruin it.

"Ed? You still there?"

"Yes." Ed cleared his throat. "I'm still here."

"Hang on for a second. I need to get something on. I'm standing here naked."

Ladies and gentlemen, Ed's mental theater presents: Gaia Moore Naked. *Now held over for another extremely popular extended run.* Ed considered it an absolute tragedy that the picture phone had never caught on. He thought of telling Gaia that there was no reason for her to get dressed just to talk on the phone, but he didn't want to give her quite that clear a glimpse into the things that churned in his brain.

"Okay," she said after a few moments. "I'm back."

"So, uh, did you and Mary go to the club last night?"

"Absolutely."

"And what did you do while Mary danced?"

"What do you mean, what did I do?" Gaia shot back, doing a pretty decent imitation of Ed's tone. "I went dancing."

"You?"

"What? Is it so shocking that I can dance?"

Actually, it wasn't shocking at all. It was very easy for Ed to imagine Gaia dancing. She had those incredible long, strong legs. Dancer's legs. In his mind Ed could see Gaia spinning and swaying on those legs. Her blond hair flying. He knew without ever seeing it that Gaia would be an incredibly sexy dancer.

"So," she said. "Do you want to hear about it?"

"Sure." *Hearing might not be enough,* Ed thought. *How about coming over and doing a demonstration for me?*

Ed listened as Gaia described going to the club, getting out on the floor, and starting to dance. Every word increased the heat that was growing inside him. He could picture it in his mind almost as if he were really there. A new feature debuted in his personal Gaia Moore multiplex. Dancing Gaia. Of course, in real life Gaia had probably worn clothes while dancing, but Ed thought he could allow a few special effects in his mental movie.

"And when I opened my eyes," Gaia continued, "this guy was there."

The film suddenly broke in Ed's internal cinema and went flipping around the reel. "Sam?"

"No, not Sam. Some guy I've never seen before."

"How bad did you hurt him?"

Gaia made a disgusted sound. "I don't automatically hit every guy I meet. I didn't hurt him. We danced together."

"You danced with a strange guy?"

"Did I mention he was really good-looking?" said Gaia. "And he was a really good dancer. We danced together all night. It was great. Maybe better than great. Incredible. I never really . . . I mean, I never danced like that before."

Ed felt a stab of jealousy. He was immediately jealous of any guy who spent time with Gaia. Having Gaia say that the guy was good-looking only opened that wound a little wider. But what really hurt, what really poured the salt into the cut and rubbed it in good, was the fact that Gaia and this good-looking stranger had danced together.

Ed lusted after Gaia twenty-four hours a day. He was pretty sure that he even loved her. One of these days, if he could show her what a great guy he was and stay close, Gaia might even start to love Ed. After all, she had kissed him, even if it was only once. All he had to do was keep at it and wear down her resistance.

But one thing Ed would never be able to do was dance with Gaia. He would never get to be with her the way the guy from the club had been the night before.

There was a new threat here, a threat maybe even bigger than the hurdle of Sam Moon. It was clear that Gaia liked the dancing. And the guy. If she kept going to the clubs, it would mean she saw less of Ed. And more of the guys who were there—guys who could dance.

"Ed?" Gaia called from the other end. "Are you still there?"

"I'm here." The wheelchair suddenly felt very hard against his back and arms. He adjusted his position, trying to get more comfortable. "So, are you going to see this dancing fool again?"

"No," said Gaia. "At least, I don't think so. I didn't even tell him anything but my first name."

Good. The situation wasn't completely out of control. "So you just left. You and Mary."

"Are you trying to ask if I had sex with this guy?"

"No." *Yes.*

"Well, I didn't. We talked a little bit. And kissed a couple of times. But mostly we danced."

Kissed.

Ed felt like someone had roped a brick to his heart and thrown it in a lake. Gaia had kissed this stranger. Kissing wasn't supposed to be a big deal. People kissed all the time. But Ed had thought Gaia was different. He'd thought that the kiss she had given him was special. Important.

"Ed? You keep going quiet on me. Are you doing something?"

"No." Ed was embarrassed to hear the catch in his voice. "No, just thinking."

"Don't hurt yourself. What's the news? Did you find out anything?"

Ed had almost forgotten the reason for his call. He held the phone away from his face for a second and cleared his throat before speaking. "Yeah," he said. "Yeah, I found out something."

"So, is Skizz still in the hospital?"

"No." Ed picked up a piece of paper and looked at the notes he had scribbled the night before. "According to the nurse I talked to, his injuries weren't as serious as first believed. Plus the guy had no insurance, so they kicked him out."

"I'm not sure whether I should be happy or upset that he's not that hurt," said Gaia. "If he's out of the hospital, I guess he's in jail."

"That's the really fun part," said Ed. He flipped over his page of notes. "It seems that the drugs found on your boy Skizz were judged to be the product of an illegal search. Inadmissible as evidence."

"So how are they going to keep him in jail?"

"They're not," Ed replied. "Skizz is loose."

THE FATHER OF GAIA

Mary bent down and picked up a broken piece of wood. It was no more than a few inches in length, splintered at both ends, and scorched black. It was all that remained of the door to the apartment leased in the name of Tom Chaos.

"So what did he look like?" she asked.

The fruit stand owner scratched at his thinning hair. "I'm not sure I ever met the man," he said.

"Didn't you rent the place to him?"

The man nodded. "I did, but that was over the phone. I never met this Chaos guy in person." The man's face pulled down in a heavy frown. "If I knew what he looked like, I'd be putting up posters. This bastard blew up my stand."

Mary looked across the pile of rubble. "I thought the paper said it was a gas explosion."

The fruit stand owner snorted. "Oh, yeah, some gas explosion." He waved a thick finger at Mary. "That damn apartment didn't even have gas."

"So what—"

"Who knows." The man kicked at a pile of shattered boards and rotting fruit. "You gonna hang around here, you be careful. I got enough troubles with the insurance guys already." He turned and stomped away.

Mary looked at the ruined fruit stand and the shattered remains of what had once been an apartment. There wasn't much left. The fruit stand had been split down the middle. No one had been killed, but the building was twisted in its frame like a broken toy. Bricks from the back wall had landed as far as two blocks away. Only some of the plumbing still remained where the apartment had been, sticking up into the sky like the picked-over skeleton of some dead beast.

No one had been killed here, and there had been few witnesses to the actual explosion. It was a small story, buried deep in the pages of the *Times.* Except for the search that Mary's aunt had made, it might have stayed buried.

Mary pulled out her notebook and looked at the few lines she had scribbled. Thomas Chaos had rented the broken apartment. Gaia's father's name was Thomas Moore. There was no real connection. Only two little facts had made Mary come to the site of the ruins.

First, Thomas Chaos didn't exist. All the information he had provided in renting the apartment had turned out to be fake.

Second, in some versions of Greek mythology, Chaos was the father of Gaia.

If those two bits of information fit together as Mary thought, it made for interesting results. Gaia Moore's father was somewhere in New York.

That was information Mary thought Gaia might find very interesting.

SAM

It's supposed to be a dream. In fact, it's supposed to be the classic dream, something every male in America fantasizes about.

You're sitting alone when this beautiful woman walks up and sits down beside you. You might be drunk enough to think any woman looks good, but you're not drunk enough that you don't recognize gorgeous when you see it. True, this woman might be a little older than you, and she might be a little more slutty than your usual taste, but isn't that part of the way the dream works? This is a woman with a lot of experience when it comes to sex.

This beautiful woman—beautiful, sexy woman—

starts to talk to you. She tells you you're cute. She says she likes you. She tells you she's all alone. She puts her hand on your leg. She brings her face so close, you can smell the flavor of her lipstick. And eventually she asks you if you want to go home with her.

What are you going to say?

So, the two of you end up in a hotel room, and the dress comes off, and she's just as sexy as you thought she would be. Her body is incredible.

She's as experienced as you thought she was. She knows exactly what to do with her hands. And her mouth. And her body. Even if you're half drunk—even if you're ninety-nine and nine-tenths percent drunk—you're not falling asleep on this performance. She moves like no one you've ever met. She bends in places you didn't even know human beings had joints. She keeps you going not just once or twice but until exhaustion catches up with drunk and the room spins. When you fall asleep, she's still pressed against you. Warm, and soft, and sexy.

When you wake up, the woman is gone. There's no note. The hotel room is taken care of. There are no obligations or commitments. You get one night of fantastic sex with one unbelievable woman and the price tag is zero. That's the dream, right? The all-American male sex fantasy.

So why does it feel so much like a nightmare?

THE FEAR OF DYING

MARY HAD ABSOLUTELY NO DOUBT THAT SOMEONE HAD COME TO KILL HER.

THE REAL DREAM

It was after noon before Sam made it back to his dorm room. As soon as he was inside, he stumbled across the room and collapsed on his bed.

Either the bartender was wrong or Sam didn't have the typical reaction to vodka. If there were hangovers worse than the one he was feeling, Sam didn't want to know about it. Already he felt like someone had lifted the top of his skull, poured in a box of thumbtacks, and put the lid back on. Add in the family of gerbils that had taken up residence in his stomach, and Sam was ready to call the Mafia and see if he could hire a killer to come and shoot him.

Sam crawled up the bed until his face was smashed against the pillow and tried to keep his head from exploding. The drums down the hall were silent this time, but they weren't needed. Sam's heart was beating all on its own. On some scale, he knew that the hangover was getting better. The idea that he might actually live through it now seemed like a possibility—not that death wasn't still an attractive option.

The bone-crushing hangover might not have felt quite so bad if Sam hadn't also felt so guilty.

Heather cheated first.

That was true. In fact, once one partner had cheated, could

you even call what the other did cheating at all? Shouldn't it be like getting a free hit?

Of course, Sam had kissed Gaia when he was still supposed to be with Heather. And there was the little detail of his constant Gaia obsession.

Sam worked at trying to get the right feeling of justification, but he couldn't manage to find it. Even memories of the great sex he had experienced the night before didn't help. Sam couldn't get past the idea that the sex was wrong. Great, but wrong.

It didn't matter that Heather had cheated. Heather didn't know that Sam knew that she had cheated. And Sam hadn't said anything to Heather about breaking up. So no matter what Heather had done, they were still an official couple. Which made sleeping with the woman from the bar absolutely wrong. And all of that was way too much thinking to do with a hangover.

The whole thing didn't make a lot of sense. Sam knew that. He was acting like some character from a book. Real people weren't supposed to think like this. Real people slept around. Everybody said so.

But it didn't feel right. Maybe no one in the world would blame Sam for sleeping with this woman after Heather had cheated on him. Hell, every guy in the dorm would probably congratulate him for scoring with this babe even if Heather hadn't cheated on him. It didn't matter. The only thing that mattered was that Sam felt guilty. What he had done was wrong, no matter how many talk show guests and frat dudes might disagree.

He was going to have to talk to Heather. He was going to have to tell her it was over.

There was a knock at the door.

Every rap of the mystery guest's knuckles went through Sam's skull like a chain saw. He winced and pulled the pillow tighter around his exploding head. "Go away!" he shouted as loudly as he dared.

"Sam?" said a faint voice. "Is that you?"

Sam groaned and rolled to the edge of the bed. The world did a little jumping, twisting lurch. "Who's there?"

"Gaia."

"Gaia?" Sam sat up quickly, bringing a railroad spike of fresh pain to his head. He couldn't imagine why Gaia Moore would be at his door. Especially not when she had been out with her boyfriend only the night before. He got up and stumbled across the room over a floor that pitched and heaved like a ship on the high seas. He fumbled open the door and saw that the impossible was true. Gaia Moore had come to call.

"Why are you . . . ," he started, then he swallowed and tried again. "Uh. Hi, Gaia."

"Hi, Sam." Gaia was dressed in usual Gaia gear, cargo pants and a gray sweatshirt, but there was something different about her hair. It almost looked like it had been combed. If Sam weren't drunk, he would have sworn she was blushing.

"I wanted to ask you something," she said.

"What's that?"

Gaia pushed her hair back from her face, glanced at Sam for a moment, then looked away. "I was wondering if you had anything planned for tonight."

"Tonight?" Sam wondered if this was just part of the hangover. Was it possible to have hallucinations from one night of drinking? If he didn't know better, he would have sworn Gaia Moore was asking him out on a date.

"It's New Year's Eve," said Gaia. "So I thought you'd probably be doing something with Heather."

"No," said Sam. "I'm not doing anything with Heather." In his own ears he could hear both anger and guilt in that statement.

"That's great!" said Gaia. "I mean, it's not great that you don't . . . I mean . . . I thought maybe you would want to get together tonight."

Sam felt a moment of dizziness that had nothing to do with his hangover. Gaia Moore *was* asking him out on a date. The last few days had been an incredible roller coaster. First there was the woman at a bar, now this. His life was getting so strange in all directions. "Sure," he said. "Sure, I could do something tonight." Surely by then the hangover would have faded.

"Cool." For a moment Sam caught a glance of that endangered species, a Gaia Moore smile. "I'm meeting Ed and Mary around eight. If you came over around seven, we could walk over together."

"Ed Fargo and Mary Moss?"

"Uh-huh. We're talking about checking out the fireworks in the park. If the weather's not too crappy, we thought we might even do the whole tourist Times Square thing. After all, this is my first New Year's in New York."

Ed and Mary. Sam knew Ed Fargo well enough and had met Mary Moss a few times. If Ed and Mary were coming along, then this wasn't so much a date as a kind of group activity. Nothing serious. Gaia might even be asking Sam more as a let's-be-friends kind of thing, not an I-love-you kind of thing. In fact, that seemed like what had to be going on. Ed and Mary were Gaia's friends. Gaia was just inviting Sam to be part of the gang, not to be her boyfriend.

"Sure," said Sam. "Sure. I'll be there." Being friends with Gaia was better than getting no dose of Gaia at all.

"All right," said Gaia. She bounced on the balls of her feet for a moment. "Okay. I guess I'll see you then."

"Right," said Sam. He managed to make what he hoped was a decent smile in reply.

Gaia hesitated for a moment. Then she spun on the soles of her worn sneakers and padded off down the hall.

Sam watched until the top of her blond head had disappeared down the staircase. Maybe for some guys, meeting a beautiful woman in a bar and having a night of sex was their fantasy. But for Sam Moon, Gaia was the real dream.

REPTILE BRAIN

Maybe I should lie.

Ed stared at the phone and tried to rub away the headache that was building behind his eyes. He had spent so much time on the phone the last couple of days, his right ear felt hot and swollen. If the phone company charged for local calls by the minute, Ed would have been way deep into his college fund.

There was only one more phone call to make now, but Ed wasn't sure he should do it. If he dialed the phone, it would mean putting Gaia at risk. If he didn't dial, it could mean risking Mary.

I could check it out myself, he thought. *I could tell Gaia that I couldn't get the information. Then I could go up there myself and . . . and . . .*

And what? Ed might hate it when people thought he couldn't do something because he was in a wheelchair. But there were a few things that he really couldn't do. This might be one of them.

One dark, deep little part of Ed's brain definitely did not want to make this call. Sure, Mary was pretty. A little wild sometimes, but Ed liked her. And she was a friend. Still, Mary wasn't Gaia. Gaia was beautiful. Gaia had kissed him. He didn't just like Gaia—he was pretty sure he loved her.

The little reptile part of his brain was talking loud and clear. *Forget Mary. Don't do anything that would get Gaia in trouble.*

That reptile brain was hard to resist. The only thing fighting against it was the idea that if he didn't call, he would be breaking Gaia's trust. If he didn't call and Mary got hurt, Ed would have to live with that forever.

Still, it took a good ten minutes before he lifted the phone and reluctantly dialed Gaia's number.

"Hi. This is Ed. I need to speak to Gaia."

A few seconds later her voice came over the phone. "Hey. You going to be there tonight?"

"I'll be there," said Ed. He took a deep breath and continued. "But I found out something that I thought you should know."

"What's that?"

"I found Skizz."

A GREAT AGENT ONCE

"Are you sure you don't feel up to it?" asked George.

Ella summoned up her best suffering-but-devoted-young-wife smile. "I'm sorry, dear. It really does feel like I have a cold coming on." She laid her fingers lightly against her chest. "I shouldn't make a trip right now."

George frowned. "If you're certain."

"I am." Ella nodded sadly, the brave smile still on her brightly painted lips. "You go on. I'll stay here, nurse my cold, and watch the celebrations on television."

George thought for a moment, then shook his head. "Nope. If you're staying here, I'll just stay with you."

Ella sat up quickly. "Now, George, you can't do that. You know you have commitments down in Washington."

"Those commitments can wait." George knelt down beside the couch, and took Ella's hand. "I'm more worried about us."

"Us? What could be wrong with us?" Ella looked at him with mock concern. "Is there something bothering you, dear?"

"What's bothering me is how little time we spend together," said George. Worry creased his forehead. "Half the time my job takes me out of town. And even when I am home, it seems like you have a photography assignment almost every night."

"I'm trying to get established," replied Ella. "It's important that I take any assignment I can get."

George squeezed her hand. "I understand that, but I miss you, Ella. I want to be with you."

Ella reached across with her free hand and patted George softly on the cheek. "Don't worry. We have all our lives to be together." She nodded toward the door. "Now, go on to your party. The last thing I want you to do is to stay here and catch my cold."

George nodded. "All right," he said. "I'll go. But when I get back, we are going to have some reserved time together."

"Wonderful," said Ella. "I can't think of anything better."

With one last look, George turned for the door. "Take care of yourself while I'm gone."

"Don't worry. I'll be waiting right here." Ella waved at him as he went out the front door of the brownstone.

As soon as the door closed, Ella's expression turned into a scowl. She climbed up off the couch and went into the kitchen to wash her hands. It was getting to the point where just the touch of George's hands was enough to make her want to scream. Just the sight of him made her stomach churn.

George Niven was a great agent once. Even Loki said so. But he wasn't anymore. Now he was just weak and stupid. Ella wasn't sure how much longer she could keep up this charade. She had never expected to be with George this long. Loki had promised her that one day this long project would move into the next phase. When that happened, Ella wouldn't have to pretend anymore. Wouldn't have to be with a man she despised more every day.

At least she would get a chance to see Loki tonight. If she was lucky, she would even spend the night in his bed. Now that George was out of town, everything would be fine.

TO: outsider@div13.gov
FROM: insider@div13.gov

****ENCODED TRANSMISSION-256-BIT KEY TO FOLLOW****

Request immediate meeting. Location delta. 1900 hours. Situation degrading.

EVERYDAY EVENTS

Mary looked at herself in the mirror and grinned. She didn't think she was the most beautiful girl in the world. Usually she didn't think much of her looks at all. But she had to admit that the camisole looked very fine.

The flimsy top would definitely not meet with her mother's approval, but then, Mary's mother had already gone off to her own New Year's event. There was no one left in the house to pass judgment on what she was wearing.

Mary thought for a moment about changing into something else. After all, if they really did end up down at Times Square, this outfit was going to be beyond chilly. But she was also going to be standing next to Gaia Moore all night. Gaia might not realize she was beautiful, but to most guys, that only made Gaia more attractive. Unless she looked her very best, Mary could get overlooked.

She was still debating whether or not to change when the phone rang. Mary picked it up, expecting it to be Gaia or Ed. Instead there was only a crackling, humming sound on the line. The phone had sounded funny for the last couple of days. There was always this strange little hollow tone to everything. But this went way beyond the previous problems.

"Hello?"

"Mary . . . you . . . me." The voice was faint and filled with static.

"Aunt Jen?" Mary spoke into the phone. "Is that you?"

". . . trouble . . . Katia Moore . . ."

A chill ran down Mary's back. "Aunt Jen, there's something wrong with your phone. I can't hear you."

". . . government . . . secret . . ." Then the phone gave one last squawk and went dead in Mary's hand.

"Aunt Jen?" Mary called hopelessly into the silence. "Are you there?" She waited a few seconds, then set the phone down.

Her aunt must have been calling from a car phone. That was the only explanation. She must have gone into a tunnel and lost the connection.

It was clear that her aunt was trying to tell her something about the death of Gaia's mother. Mary was surprised that her aunt would be working on the problem so late on New Year's Eve. The information on Katia Moore must have turned out to be particularly interesting.

Mary stood by the phone for a moment, hoping her aunt might call back, but the phone stayed quiet.

Mary went back to getting ready, but the chill of fear that had arrived with the phone call wouldn't go away. It had to be more than an interesting story to keep her aunt working so late. If she was calling from a car phone, maybe she was on her way somewhere. Maybe she was even coming to talk to Mary in person.

Then Mary remembered a flaw in that theory. Aunt Jen didn't even *own* a car. She might have a portable phone, it sometimes seemed like everyone in Manhattan carried one, but there was no way the reception should have been so bad. Not from anywhere in the city.

Mary ran back across the room and picked up the phone. This time there was no strange hollow sound. This time there was no sound at all. The phone line was dead.

Mary's heartbeat was suddenly racing. She was paralyzed for a moment, the dead phone in her hand. One part of her brain was still trying desperately to fit this into the world of everyday events. Phone lines go out. It's New Year's Eve. A million people probably called each other at the same time and blew the circuits. But the rest of her mind didn't buy it.

She put the phone back on the hook and grabbed her coat from the closet. Gaia was expecting to meet Mary in the park. That was still an hour away, but Mary decided she would rather freeze out in the cold or walk over to Gaia's brownstone. Anything but stay here. She slipped into her coat, picked up her purse, and headed out.

Mary had gotten as for as the kitchen when she noticed something strange. There was a little case lying on the kitchen table. A small, leather case that looked something like the case for the flute Mary had once played in junior high band. Curious, she walked over to the case and looked inside.

The case was packed with some kind of dense gray foam.

There were cutouts in the foam just large enough to hold an assortment of objects. Only a few of the slots were full. Two held small objects the size of a fingernail. They looked something like miniature lollipops, slightly squashed lollipops, only inside the translucent balls Mary could see an array of tiny electrical parts, and where the stick should have been on a piece of candy, there was a bundle of wires.

Mary had never seen anything quite like this, but she immediately had an idea of what it was for. There had been a funny sound on the phone all week. Someone had been bugging her phone, listening in on every conversation.

There was an empty opening at the center of the case that was shaped something like a large cigar. Next to it was a shape that was considerably more frightening. There was no doubt about what it was meant to hold. Mary could make out every detail of the outline—the grip, the trigger guard, the long, slender barrel. The third opening was fitted to hold a gun, and that gun was missing.

But even that wasn't the worst thing in the case. The worst thing was two small glass vials. One vial was still in its slot. The other of the tiny bottles was sitting out on the counter. Inside it was a thimble full of snow-white powder.

Cocaine.

The sight of it brought an unexpected wave of desire boiling up from somewhere deep in Mary's guts. It had been *so* long.

One quick sniff. One quick sniff and I'll be able to think this through so much better.

Mary took a slow step back. If there was any time in the world when it was a seriously bad idea to get cranked out of her head, this was the time. She shifted her eyes as far to the right and left as she could without turning her head.

Someone was in the house. That someone was carrying a gun. Mary had absolutely no doubt that someone had come to kill her.

SOME DOGS

The crowd on the F train wasn't the most upscale Gaia had ever seen. There was a high concentration of black dusters and guys with stubbly little beards. Even on New Year's Eve, she suspected more of them were interested in getting drunk or getting high than in celebrating.

Perfect customers for Skizz.

Gaia rode in the front of the front car. If she could have, she would have ridden on the outside. She would have pulled or pushed or done anything to make the cars go faster. There was a tension in her legs. An ache in all her muscles. It wasn't fear, but it wasn't quite the same cold energy she felt right before a fight. By the time the train reached the station, the tension was so great that she squeezed out the door and flew up the stairs before anyone else on the train had taken two steps across the platform.

Skizz was loose. Gaia had expected the scumbag to spend a week or more in the hospital. After that, he should have gone to jail for pushing drugs. Mary should have been safe for years.

Now Gaia would have to take care of him. Again.

Gaia knew she could handle Skizz. She had already kicked his flabby ass twice. Three times would be no problem. That didn't mean there wouldn't be complications. There was no telling what kind of mood Skizz was in. Beating up a guy like Skizz was kind of like kicking a feral dog. He might get scared and run away. He might turn around and bite.

Gaia had one mission, one goal. She had to make sure that a simple message got through the dealer's lice-ridden head: Get near Mary Moss and die.

Gaia reached the street and cut across an intersection toward St. Mark's Place. It was nearly dark, and fat snowflakes were drifting down from a deep gray sky. The sun was still shining on the taller buildings, but already the air felt ten degrees colder.

There weren't as many people on the street here as there were back in the Village. The stores and restaurants along the sidewalks were at least a grade below those near Washington Square. Not the swankiest neighborhood in the city.

St. Mark's Place was a park, but it turned out to be considerably smaller than Gaia had expected, little more than a block of green space and a few knots of trees. Gaia stood in one corner of the cold space for a few minutes and watched as two men passed a bottle back and forth. Two girls with spiked hair walked past, and a cloud of pungent pot smoke momentarily swamped Gaia.

She didn't see Skizz.

According to Ed's source in the police department, Skizz had been spotted at this location twice in the last two days. Both times he had avoided arrest, but the park was a known site for drug traffickers. None of which guaranteed that Skizz would show up tonight.

Gaia bit her lip and did a slow scan of the people in the park. It was getting close to seven. Unless she wanted to miss her meeting with Sam, Gaia needed to get back on the train. It looked like lowlife hunting was going to have to wait for another night.

She was halfway back to the station when she saw a familiar shape on the street corner ahead. A big guy with a round gut and a big, jutting beard. Gaia smiled a hard smile. *Thar she blows.* There was no mistaking Skizz's bulky silhouette.

Gaia thought about her approach. She could go in cool and casual. She could come in screaming and kicking. She could be sneaky. Sneaky won.

She came up behind Skizz, grabbed him by the back of the coat, and pulled.

The man flew back a step, stumbled, and fell onto the dirty snow. Gaia quickly stepped around in front of him and put a foot on his chest. "Hi, there," she said. "Funny mee . . ." She stopped in midword.

She had the wrong guy. This wasn't Skizz. This couldn't be Skizz.

Only it was.

The drug dealer was a wreck. His face was lopsided and swollen. His lips were split, and inside his open mouth Gaia could see several broken or missing teeth. There was a cast on one of his legs and a sling around his left arm. A bandage wrapped his dirty hair. His left eye was covered by gauze and tape. His right eye looked up at Gaia with complete and utter terror.

"You," he croaked. "It's you." His voice shook.

Gaia couldn't feel fear, but she could feel shock. *I did this.* She didn't exactly feel sorry for Skizz. He had only gotten what he deserved. But it was a little stomach twisting to see what she had done to a man using nothing but her hands and feet.

Gaia took a deep breath and tried to get the proper tone

of mean back in her voice. "I came to make sure you stayed away from my friend."

Even as she said it, the statement sounded ridiculous. Skizz couldn't be the one who was after Mary. Skizz couldn't be after anyone.

The dealer pushed his hands against the ground and scooted himself back through the snow. "Don't," he blubbered through his torn lips. "Don't hurt me." Tears streamed from his one good eye and rolled into his matted beard.

Gaia stared down at him for a few seconds longer. Then she put her hands in her pockets and started walking for the subway station.

Some dogs ran. Some dogs bit. Some dogs got broken.

At least Gaia could be sure of one thing. Mary was safe.

MY HERO

Mary moved slowly across the carpeted floor. At every step she paused and looked left and right. She could barely get herself to move. Her knees trembled, and her legs were unsteady. At any moment she expected a bullet to come out of some corner of the apartment. The fear was so bad, she wanted to lie down and just wait until whoever had left the case on the table came to kill her.

She froze at the door to her room and stood trembling there for several seconds, unable to move.

A noise down the hall broke her free from her paralysis. It was a faint sound, but it was enough to propel Mary through the door and into her room. She closed the door behind her and carefully turned the lock.

She didn't have any illusion that the door would actually keep the intruder out. Her parents had managed to open it with nothing more sophisticated than the bent end of a clothes hanger. And the door was thin enough that even Mary could have probably knocked it down with a kick. She only hoped it would buy her time.

Still trying to move as silently as possible, Mary crept across the room and gave the phone another try. No dial tone. Nothing.

That meant there were two choices. Mary could try to go out the front door. She had already passed on that option once. She figured that it was what the intruder expected, and now he would be even more prepared. Hopefully, whoever was in the apartment wouldn't be prepared for option two.

Before she made her escape, Mary had one more little task. She went to the dresser and grabbed the handles for the lowest drawer. Mary pulled the drawer open slowly, an inch at a time. She held her breath. Any noise. Any noise at all might draw the stranger with the gun.

It took only a few seconds to open the drawer and grab the bottle of pepper spray she had hidden inside, but they were long seconds. The fear of dying seemed to stretch out time, making every moment into an hour.

Mary stuffed the pepper spray into her pocket and hurried across the room to the bed. Under the foot of the bed was a small case made of bright orange plastic. It was one of those stupid things that her parents had bought from some salesman. Some stupid thing that Mary had always thought was a waste of money. She had certainly never expected to use it. But she was glad she had it now.

Mary slipped the case from under the bed and popped open the latches on the sides. She shivered as the case opened with a loud click.

Inside, there was only a bundle of wire and thin metal rods. It looked like a mess, but Mary dragged it free from the case and carried it over to the window. Then, with her heart beating high in her throat, she put her thumbs against the window locks and pressed. There was a terrible moment when she thought the old locks wouldn't open, but a second later the locks popped, the glass shivered, and the window swung slowly inward.

A blizzard of cold air swirled into Mary's bedroom. Snow

settled on her head. Wind made the clothes in her closet into dancing ghosts.

Carefully Mary leaned over the edge and looked down. Five floors below, cars hummed past on the street.

She looked at the bundle of wire and located the top. With hands that shook from both fear and cold, Mary hooked the top over the windowsill and hurled the rest out the window. The emergency escape ladder uncoiled with a whine. Far below, she heard the bottom of the ladder clank against the side of the building.

Mary put her head through the window again and looked down. The ladder didn't reach all the way to the sidewalk, but it was close. If she climbed down and hung from the bottom, her feet would be no more than a dozen feet from the ground.

But that climb didn't look too easy. In fact, it looked insane. The narrow ladder seemed as fragile as a bit of spiderweb, and the bitter wind made the whole thing bob and dance. If Mary climbed down the ladder to the bottom and dropped from there, she would probably be okay. But if she fell from the top, or from thirty or fifty feet up, the sidewalk would do the intruder's job as well as any bullet.

Mary stepped back from the window and looked at the bedroom door. Maybe going out the front wasn't such a bad idea after all. Slipping past the gunman suddenly seemed like a much better idea than trying to climb that toy ladder down five floors.

The bedroom door rattled. The knob turned, stopped, then turned the other way. A moment later there was a clicking metal-on-metal sound.

Picking the lock. *They're picking the lock just like my parents used to do when I was sulking in my room,* she realized.

Without another moment's thought Mary was standing in the window. She grabbed the ladder, gave it a tug to see if it would hold, then started down.

The ladder was even more treacherous than it looked. The rungs were so narrow that they bit into Mary's fingers like knife blades. The way the ladder lay up against the side of the building made it nearly impossible to keep her feet in place. Again and again her toes slid from a rung, sending her on a dozen terrifying minifalls. But she was doing it. She was making it down.

The end of the ladder was twenty feet below. Then ten.

There was a sudden jerk from above. Mary looked up to see the silhouette of a figure leaning from her bedroom window. With impossible strength, that person was pulling up the ladder. Instead of going down, Mary was heading back up.

She scrambled for the bottom of the ladder, moving as fast as she could, but by the time she reached the last rung, the end of the ladder was nearly twenty feet above the sidewalk. And it was getting farther away with every passing moment.

Mary let herself dangle from the very bottom of the ladder, closed her eyes, and dropped.

It seemed to take a long time to reach the ground. Too long.

The ground hit her like a subway train. A white-hot lightning bolt ran up Mary's right leg. She was on her side, then her face, then her back, then her side again. A sparkle of lights swam across her vision, and everything in the world shrank to a gray point far down a deep well.

When the world came back, Mary was looking at red taillights streaming past in the slushy street. Her face was lying in cold snow. The rest of her felt kind of numb, like that pins-and-needles feeling you get when your arms or legs fall asleep.

She tried to sit up, but that only brought a new explosion of pain from her leg. Mary bit back a scream and slowly turned herself over.

She was still alive. For the moment that seemed like a miracle.

"Miss?" A man came up at a run. "Miss, are you all right?"

Mary started to nod, then changed her mind. "No. I think my leg is hurt."

The man looked at her for a moment, then looked up at the building. "I saw you come down. That was quite a fall."

"Yeah, tell me about it." Mary squinted up at the window, but she could see no one looking down. The ladder was also missing in action.

"Is there a fire?"

Mary shook her head. "A guy broke into our apartment. I think he's trying to kill me."

The man stood and looked in both directions along the sidewalk. "I think you had better come with me," he said. "We should get you to the police."

Mary's long involvement with drugs hadn't exactly made the police her favorite people, but this seemed like an excellent time to make new friends. "Sure," she said. She tried again to get to her feet. Her right leg didn't cooperate. "I think I'm going to need some help."

The man reached down and helped her to her feet. "I have a car parked on the next block. You think you can make it?"

Mary nodded. "Let's go."

She hopped along at the man's side, leaning against him and keeping almost all of her weight on her left foot. As they passed under a streetlight she saw that the man was older than she thought. Probably somewhere in his forties. He seemed strong, though, and he had a handsome, chiseled face.

"Why would someone be trying to kill you?" the man asked.

"I don't know," said Mary. She stopped for a second to catch her breath, then limped on. "There was this guy who tried to kill me a couple of days ago, but I don't think he has anything to do with this."

"Two different guys tried to kill you in the last few days?"

The man gave a surprised laugh. "You're a popular girl."

"Mary," she said between breaths. "My name is Mary."

The man paused. He supported her weight on one arm and reached across with the other to shake her hand. "My name is Loki."

"Loki? Is that from mythology or something?"

"Exactly."

Mary shook his hand and smiled. "It's a weird name, but you're certainly my hero tonight, Loki."

RAGE

HE TOOK THE DARK, HEAVY BULK OF THE GLOCK PISTOL AND PRESSED THE BLUNT BARREL AGAINST MARY'S BACK.

THE BODY

Sam rang the bell on the front of the brownstone and waited. He was more nervous than he wanted to admit. *This isn't a date,* he told himself. *Gaia probably doesn't even think about me like that. She only invited me over as a friend.*

That didn't do much to help. But at least he was going to get to see Gaia. Since Thanksgiving they had barely spoken. Her visit was the last thing he had expected.

He heard feet coming toward the door at a near run. There was a fumble of latches, and the heavy wooden door swung open. "Sam!" said Gaia. "You came."

"I said I would come," he replied.

"Yeah, but I figured Heather would call, and you would . . ." Gaia stopped and shook her head. "Never mind. Come on in while I grab my stuff. I just got back myself."

Sam followed her inside the brownstone. "Where have you been?"

"I had an errand to take care of," said Gaia. "But it's all worked out now."

Sam nodded and looked around the room. "This is a great place," he said. He looked up at the high ceilings and the heavy molding. The brownstone was authentic and well maintained. Except for some tacky ceramic figures and some modern art pieces that didn't fit the style of the house, it was the kind of a place that made it into the Sunday magazine section on homes.

"Thanks. It's okay," said Gaia.

Sam stopped looking at the room and looked at Gaia. "You look . . . different."

Gaia tilted her head. "If that was a compliment, you need more practice."

"It was," said Sam. "So I guess I do." Gaia did look different. Her hair, which often looked like it had never been introduced to a comb, was glossy and smooth. Her jeans and sweater were nothing fancy, but they were a lot nicer than the baggy cargo pants and sweatshirts that Sam had always seen her wear before. "So, where's the rest of the gang?"

Gaia opened a closet and pulled out a coat. "I told Ed and Mary we'd meet them in the park. We probably should get going."

"Okay," said Sam. He was relieved to hear that the list hadn't been expanded. If Gaia was worried that he might be doing something with Heather, Sam had been equally worried that Gaia might call in the mysterious boyfriend her foster mother had mentioned on the phone. Sam could take being one of Gaia's gang. He didn't think he could stand to see her cuddling with another guy.

A voice called from somewhere in another room. "Gaia? Aren't you going to introduce me to your friend before you leave?"

An annoyed look crossed Gaia's face. She finished pulling on her coat and zipped it closed. "We have to go!" she shouted back. "If you want to meet him, you'll have to hurry."

A woman stepped around the corner into the front room. She was wearing a short teal skirt and a tight white top instead of an emerald dress. But there was no mistaking the legs, the face, or the body. It was the same woman that Sam had met at the bar. The woman he had sex with only hours before.

Gaia gave a sigh. She waved a hand at the approaching woman. "Sam, this is Ella Niven."

The woman walked up slowly, a Cheshire grin on her hungry red mouth. She reached out a hand with nails lacquered to the exact shade of her lips. "Hello, Sam. I'm Gaia's foster mother."

Sam wished that fainting were still in fashion. Falling into darkness and having everything just go away sounded like a wonderful idea. Instead his brain seemed to separate from his body and float up to the high ceiling of the room. He saw his self standing there. The body's mouth was open in a stupid expression. Its eyes were wide and glassy.

Sam watched as Gaia stepped around in front of the body. He saw the woman—Ella—looking at the body with an amazing expression that mingled amusement, playfulness, and a promise that another night might be waiting.

Gaia looked worried. "Sam? You okay?"

The body took a step back. The mouth closed, opened, closed.

From his perch up by the ceiling, Sam thought the body was about the funniest thing he had ever seen. He would have laughed if he still had a mouth to laugh with. It was nice and warm up near the ceiling. He felt fine there. It was good to be free of the body and all the stupid, embarrassing things that it could do.

"Sam?"

The body turned and stumbled to the front door.

Gaia moved after it. "Sam? Where are you going? What's wrong?"

The body made some meaningless sounds. It fumbled at the door, opened it, and fell out into the night.

At once the feeling of floating by the ceiling vanished. Sam was back inside his own skull as he ran down the sidewalk, pushing past people on their way to parties and celebrations. He could feel the cold wind chapping his cheeks and nose. He could feel the freezing tears that streamed from his eyes. He could feel the crushing weight of emotion that squeezed at his chest.

There was no escaping himself. No escaping the awful wreck he had made of his life.

NOTHING BUT A TRAMP

Go after him. You could catch him.

It was true enough. The same thing that made Gaia strong also made her fast. The visit to St. Mark's Place hadn't even been enough to dent the energy in Gaia's legs. She could run down Sam in half a block. But she wasn't sure what to do if she caught him. She had no idea what had made him run in the first place.

"I wonder what upset your friend," said Ella.

Gaia spun around and looked into her foster mother's face.

As usual, there was a faint trace of a smile on Ella's lips. Except when she was angry, Ella always seemed to find everyone else in the world quite amusing.

"What do you know about it?" asked Gaia.

"Me?" Ella shook her head. "Why should I know anything?"

Gaia narrowed her eyes. "I don't know, but you do."

"Please. How should I know anything about this boy of yours?"

Gaia didn't bother to answer. Gaia was smart, but it didn't take a genius to know that Ella was hiding something. Somehow Ella knew something about Sam. And from Sam's reaction, Sam certainly thought he knew something about Ella.

"Where did you meet Sam?"

"Why, I'm not sure that I ever have," said Ella. "I'm not in the habit of associating with boys that young."

Gaia gritted her teeth. Ella might be in her thirties, but she certainly dressed like she still thought she was a teenager. Gaia knew that Ella was going out almost every night that George wasn't home—and sometimes even when he was. Ella wasn't fooling anybody but George. For some reason, George seemed completely blind to the things his much younger wife was doing. He was the only one who didn't realize Ella was nothing but a tramp.

If Ella was cheating on George, who was to say she was actually cheating with people her own age? Ella liked to dress younger. Maybe she liked to date younger, too. Maybe she was spending her nights running around with younger guys. Guys like Sam.

Gaia decided not to think about it. She turned and ran out the door.

OUT OF THE DARKNESS

The United Nations building gleamed in the darkness. Tom Moore walked slowly along the curving rows of flags and hunched his shoulders against the cold wind, sending a ripple of pain through his rib cage.

I shouldn't be out here on a night like this, he thought. *Not in this condition.*

The snow that had started at sunset was falling more thickly as the night wore on. It whipped in between the multicolored banners and drifted up against the curb.

By the time Tom reached the meeting point, the snow had already covered the sidewalks. And was beginning to spread into the streets.

A figure came out of the darkness. Tom tensed for a moment, but as the man came closer he relaxed. Tom put out his hand. "It's good to see you."

George Niven gripped Tom's hand tightly. "It's been too long. Way too long." He looked back over his shoulder. "We better walk."

The two men turned and walked side by side along the icy sidewalk. "This is risky, George," Tom said. "You could have been followed."

"I spent the last hour making sure that I wasn't," George

replied. "But don't worry. I don't intend to make this a regular event. I heard about what happened at your apartment. You look terrible."

"I'm fine." Tom glanced at the older agent, dismissing the subject. "So why are we out here in the snow? Have you seen Loki?"

"No. I have no doubt he's nearby, but I don't know where."

"Then why—"

"I think Gaia's in serious danger." George shoved his hands deep into the pockets of his coat and stared up at the fluttering flags.

"How do you know?" Tom asked.

George nodded. "I found a hidden microphone on one of her jackets." He lowered his eyes and looked at Tom. "I'd picked the jacket up off the banister, and as I was carrying it up to her room, I felt something prick my finger. I have no idea how it got there, but . . ."

"But it's got to be a Loki job," Tom finished.

George waved a hand through the air. "I'm almost positive." He paused and stared off into the darkness. "I have someone checking the device to see if we can trace it. Someone from the agency. But I'm not optimistic."

The implications of what George was saying swirled through Tom's mind. If Loki had been close enough to Gaia to have her bugged, then Gaia was under even closer observation than Tom had thought. Loki knew when she was home and when she was away. He knew everything, from what kind of music she was listening to, to what she ate for breakfast.

"You're right," said Tom. "My daughter is in even more danger than I knew."

George drew in a deep breath. "What do we do now, Tom?"

"I'd love to say that I'll come and get my daughter tonight," said Tom. "But I can't. Not in the shape I'm in. And not while we don't know what Loki's next move will be."

"So we keep waiting."

Tom nodded. "And when we get our chance, we act."

George walked over to the nearest flagpole and leaned against the metal base. "You mean we kill him."

"Yes. We'll do whatever we have to."

Tom pulled a gun from his pocket and studied it briefly before returning it to his coat. Then he shook George's hand again, turned, and walked away.

INNOCENT EXPLANATIONS

The weather had cut down on the crowds, but there were still at least a hundred people milling around near the arch at the center of Washington Square Park. Gaia stood on her tiptoes, looking for Mary—and hoping that she might see Sam—but neither one was among the crowd. Finally Gaia spotted Ed on the far side of the mass of people and hurried over to join him.

Ed was moving back and forth over the same patch of sidewalk. From the deep grooves in the snow, it looked like he had been pacing for some time. He spotted Gaia as she approached and stopped. "Hey, I thought you were bringing Sam with you."

"I was." She shrugged and raised her gloved hands. "He weirded out on me." She started to say something about Ella but stopped herself. She didn't even want to think about it herself, much less give Ed a reason to start making theories. "I guess he's not coming."

Ed grunted. "I guess we're even, then. Mary never showed up."

"Maybe she's still waiting at her place."

"Tried it," Ed replied with a shake of his head. "I've called over there twice. No answer. Did you find our pal Mr. Skizz?"

Gaia nodded. "I found him, but I don't think he's the one

after Mary." Thinking of Skizz's battered face, Gaia thought that looking in the mirror must be the scariest thing he did all day.

"Then where is she?"

Gaia wished she knew the answer. There could be a hundred innocent explanations. Mary was never the world's most organized person. She might have gotten the time wrong or run off to do some other errand before they got together. Somehow Gaia didn't think so.

"Come on," she said. "We've got to go."

"Where?" asked Ed.

Gaia started walking. "We'll figure that out on the way."

A VERY POPULAR GIRL

Mary leaned back into the plush leather seat. "For a government guy, you've got a great car."

Loki laughed. It was a good laugh. Deep and reassuring. "Thanks. It comes with this assignment."

"Nice work if you can get it." The pain in Mary's leg was

beginning to ease. After the terror of escaping the apartment and the freezing air outside, it was great to feel safe and warm. She closed her eyes and listened to the soft hum of the car's big engine. She wondered if it would be too rude if she fell asleep on the way to the police station.

Loki took a right-hand turn at the next intersection. "What do you think they wanted?" he asked.

"Who?"

"Those people who tried to kill you."

"Oh, them." Mary had been so caught up in what the intruder in her apartment had been trying to do that she hadn't put much thought into who or why. The idea that someone was trying to kill her sort of shoved out all the other thoughts. Now that she was thinking about it, she found it was a pretty tough question.

There were a couple of obvious candidates. After all, Mary had been a very popular girl lately when it came to creeps and thugs.

The intruder could have been Skizz. Mary still owed him five hundred dollars for drugs she had taken before Gaia inspired her to drop the coke habit. Only Skizz wasn't exactly the type to bug someone's phone. He would never have been snooping around her apartment in the first place. He might kill her, sure, but the other stuff was too weird to be Skizz.

Mary also gave some thought to the sex-for-points bozos

she had caught at the Village School. Two assholes from the gang had already tried to rape her. Now that Mary had helped to expose the ring, she was sure that they would love to get back at her. Except this thing with the case and the electronics wasn't exactly the kind of stunt that a bunch of dumb high school jocks would pull.

"I don't know," she confessed. "It's not like my family's rich or anything. I can't imagine what . . ." Mary stopped. Maybe she *could* imagine. A memory drifted through her head: Aunt Jen on a crackling phone line.

"Did you think of something?" asked the government man.

Mary nodded. "Maybe. It might have something to do with this friend of mine. A girl named Gaia Moore."

"Gaia?" The man slowed the car and glanced over at Mary. "I know Gaia."

"You do?"

"More than know her. She's my niece."

Mary stared at the man behind the wheel. "You're Gaia Moore's uncle?" The idea excited her so much that she nearly forgot the pain in her leg. It was almost too good to be true. In fact, it almost seemed like it *couldn't* be true. She shot the man a doubtful glance. "Man, what are the odds?"

"Actually, it's not all that coincidental," Loki answered. "I came into town especially to check on Gaia. And her foster parents said she might be with you." The man cast another glance at Mary. There was a tense expression on his face. "So what makes you think that these people who were in your apartment have anything to do with my niece?"

Mary started to blurt out a response but realized there were things she probably shouldn't say in front of Gaia's uncle. "Gaia told me something," she said carefully. "Something about her mom."

The man sighed. "Katia. Gaia told you about how she died." He steered the car through another right turn.

"Yeah."

"And did you share that information with anyone else?"

A twinge of pain ran up Mary's leg. She twisted in her seat. "I told part of it to my aunt Jen. She works at the library. I thought she might be able to find out something that would help Gaia."

"Your aunt. Yes." Loki looked at her with a strange intensity. "Anyone else?"

"No." Mary peeked out her window. It seemed like they had been driving for a long time. "Are we almost at the police station?"

"Soon," said Loki. "You're sure you didn't tell anyone but your aunt?"

Mary nodded. "Only Aunt Jen." A medium-sized apartment building swung into view through curtains of blowing snow. "Hey!"

"What's wrong?" asked Loki.

"That's my building." Mary ignored fresh pain from her leg and brought her face close to the foggy side window. "We've been going around in circles."

"We have?" Loki pulled around a double-parked minivan. "I must have taken a wrong turn."

A tightness began to slowly squeeze Mary's throat. "What police station were you going to, anyway?"

"Actually," Loki replied, "I thought we should do something about your injuries before we went to the authorities."

"Are we going to a hospital?" asked Mary.

"Not necessary." Loki abruptly stopped the car in the middle of the street. He twisted and reached into the car's backseat.

Mary leaned away from him. "What are you doing?"

Loki pulled back a case. A small, leather case, sort of like the one Mary used to carry her flute in for band. Deftly Loki popped the catches at the side of the case and flipped it open.

"I have just the thing for your pain," he said.

Loki reached into the case, pulled out a vial of cocaine, and threw it to Mary.

DEEP BREATHS

Ed's arms had been doing leg duty for over a year, but he couldn't remember his shoulders ever being so tired. "Where are we going now?"

Gaia Moore marched ahead of him, her torn sneakers crunching through the snow. "Back to the brownstone."

Ed groaned. "You can't mean your brownstone."

Gaia nodded without turning. "The one where I stay, yeah."

"But we've already been there," Ed replied. "And we've been to Mary's apartment, and back to the club, and to half a dozen local restaurants and made at least that many trips across the park."

Gaia stopped in her tracks. She didn't say anything at first, but Ed could see her back moving in and out as she took deep, deep breaths.

Somehow I don't think this is going to be good, Ed thought.

"We're going back because Mary might be there," said Gaia.

"I understand, but—"

Gaia spun around and stomped back to Ed. "What's your idea, huh? Where do you think she is?"

"I don't—"

"Because you know what I think?" said Gaia. "I think she's

in trouble!" She leaned over Ed and slammed her hands down on the arms of his wheelchair. "I knew she was in trouble, but I didn't help her."

"You tried to," said Ed. He looked up at Gaia and shivered. There was enough tension in her to light half the city. "Look, I'm sure Mary's okay."

Gaia let out a breath that whistled through her teeth. "How the hell can you know that?"

LOYALTY

Mary looked through the curving side of the small glass vial. The powder inside was so white, so fine.

"Go ahead," said Loki. "You want it, don't you?"

Mary wanted to say no, but instead she nodded. "Yes," she said in a harsh, breathy voice.

She reached over and took the vial from his hands. She did want it. Mary wanted the rush, but more than that she wanted the energy and the feeling of being able to think so much better. "You're not really Gaia's uncle, are you?"

"I am." Loki started the car moving again and took a hard left. "Now, take your medicine like a good girl."

Electric wires. Mary felt like all her nerves had been replaced with tight, hot electric wires. She wanted the cocaine. She needed it.

Mary ran her finger along the black plastic top of the vial. A few loose grains of powder stuck to her fingers. Want it. Need it.

"Take it," repeated Loki. "The sooner you're done, the sooner you can see Gaia."

Gaia.

Mary ran her finger over the glass one last time. Then she dropped the vial on the floorboard of the sedan, raised her foot, and crushed the little bottle under her heel.

"I promised I would stay straight." Mary ground the cocaine into the sedan's dark carpet.

"Promises are very important," said Loki. And then he swung his arm in a lightning-fast backhanded slap that drove his knuckles into Mary's mouth.

The blow was like an explosion. Mary's head snapped back. Incredible pain lanced through her mouth.

"Now," said Loki. His voice was flat calm. "Let's go over a few things again. Did you tell anyone?"

Mary raised a trembling hand to her mouth. Her fingers came back covered in blood.

"Did you tell anyone?" said Loki.

He didn't raise his voice, but his tone left no doubt he expected an answer.

"No," Mary mumbled through her torn lips. "Nobody."

The second blow was blindingly fast.

Mary's head went back so hard, sparks ran across her vision.

"I already know you told your aunt," said Loki. "Isn't that right?"

"Yes," Mary cried. "Yes."

Loki nodded. "So you did tell someone," he said as he turned the car around another corner. "And did you tell anyone else?"

"No."

"You're certain."

Mary nodded. "Yes." She sniffed. "Don't you know that already?"

"If you're referring to the devices I left at your home?" Loki shrugged. "Unfortunately, they don't always pick up everything."

"There was no one else."

Loki nodded. "For the sake of both you and Gaia, let's hope you're telling the truth."

LOKI VP

Loki steered the black sedan around the corner. "Don't worry," he said. "We'll be getting out soon."

Mary sagged against the window. "And then what?"

Loki didn't answer. Instead he pulled the car over to the side of the road and parked. He left the engine at a low, smooth rumble. The windshield wipers continued to drive back and forth, clearing the heavy, wet flakes of snow.

It was time to end the threat posed by Mary Moss. Loki intended to not only ensure that the girl would never share what she had learned about Katia's death but also to put an end to Gaia' s experiment in friendship. When this was over, Gaia would never again dare to share her deepest feelings with anyone—except, of course, her dear uncle.

Loki reached into his pocket and pulled out a black stocking cap. "It's time to get out."

The girl looked at him suspiciously. "I don't suppose that means you're letting me go?"

Loki had no intention of letting Mary go free, but he knew well enough how a little hope could make it easier to keep a prisoner under control. "Come with me and answer a few questions. Then you're free to do as you please."

The expression on the girl's face was one of mingled fear, doubt, and hope. It was clear to Loki that she didn't really believe him, but it was just as clear that she desperately *wanted* to believe. "I thought you were going to kill me."

"Answer my questions, and I'll have no reason to kill you." He pulled the black mask over his face and got out of the car.

The heavy blanket of snow softened his footsteps as he circled the car. Loki checked the area to be sure that no observer was too close before opening the door. There was no one. He jerked open the door, letting in a swirl of snow.

The girl tumbled out and tried to stand. Loki looked down at her.

"Don't try to run," he said. He raised one side of his coat and revealed a heavy black pistol attached to a long tube.

"Silencer," mumbled Mary. "That's what the other thing was in the case."

"Come with me," said Loki. "I'd prefer not to use this if I don't have to."

Mary nodded. She began walking along the sidewalk in slow, small steps. Her feet slipped frequently in the snow.

Loki stayed close. "That's good," he said. "Keep moving."

Mary stopped and shook her head. "No," she said softly.

Loki was on her in one quick stride. He grabbed the front of her coat and pulled Mary toward him. "I said I would prefer not to use the gun. I didn't say I would hesitate."

"Are you really Gaia's uncle?" the girl asked.

"Yes." There was no harm in telling her anything now.

The girl would never have the chance to spread her information.

"And after you kill me, what are you going to do to Gaia?"

Loki gave a tug on her coat. "I've already told you. Talk and you're in no further danger."

The girl gave a weak nod. She started to move again, but two steps down the sidewalk her knees folded, and she collapsed in the snow.

Loki took her by the arm and lifted her. Mary dangled from Loki's hand like a doll.

He gritted his teeth. "Get up." Mary continued to hang limply from his hand. Loki removed the silencer and put it back into his pocket. He took the dark, heavy bulk of the Glock pistol and pressed the blunt barrel against Mary's back. "Answer my questions, and I'll set you free. Stay here and die."

Mary got her feet back under her and stood. She trembled in Loki's grip, but when he gave her a nudge with the gun, she began to walk.

Loki steered his captive along. "Her death was an accident."

Even in the dim light he could see the girl's eyes grow wide. "You killed her?"

"I loved her," said Loki.

He jerked on Mary's arm. They were in the midst of a small grove. Ordinarily they might have been visible from half the park, but the driving sheets of snow closed in around them like walls. Everything more than a dozen yards away was lost in curtains of white.

"Stop here," said Loki. He released his grip on her. "Turn around and face me."

Mary slowly spun around. "You killed Gaia's mother."

Loki put his gloved hand in the girl's hair and shoved back her head. "It was an accident."

"Right, I believe you." Despite her awkward position Mary suddenly smiled. "So, who were you trying to kill?"

Loki took the Glock pistol and leveled it at Mary's forehead. "Gaia's father." His finger slipped inside the trigger guard.

He barely noticed the girl's right hand coming up. It wasn't until her hand was in front of his eyes that Loki realized he had been careless.

And then his face exploded in pain.

A DECENT SNOW

Gaia had read that some blind people developed a better sense of hearing. Or sense of smell. Or touch.

Maybe it was true; maybe it was nothing more than

another urban legend. All Gaia knew was that she couldn't feel fear, but she could feel everything else. Sometimes she wondered if she felt them more than normal, frightened people.

At the moment what she felt was rage. Rage and frustration.

You should know better than to think you're normal. You should know better than to think you can have friends. You should know better than to think you might possibly, one day, be happy.

Ed rolled up beside her. His breath steamed in the light of the nearest streetlamp. "If this snow gets any deeper, I won't be able to move."

Gaia kicked at the path. Six inches of snow and it was still falling. The weather would pick tonight for a decent snow. "It doesn't matter," she said. "I don't know where to go."

"What about the park?" suggested Ed.

Gaia glanced at him. "Why?"

Ed spun his chair around and pointed back the way they had come. "That's where we said we'd meet her. If she's looking for us, that's probably where she'll go."

"I thought you were too tired to move."

"Not yet." Ed gave her a tired grin. "But if it keeps snowing, you might have to carry me home."

MUMMY

Mary ran under the thin, bare branches of the winter trees. She had lost the path. The snow covered everything, obscuring the boundaries between path and field and playground. Everything looked the same. Black trees. White snow.

She struggled along on her injured leg. At every step it seemed that her foot got heavier. After a hundred yards she was limping. After two hundred she dragged the leg behind her, leaving long cuts in the snow like some mummy from an old movie limping across the sand.

"Help!" she shouted, but it seemed that the snow muffled her voice. "Gaia!"

The snow was falling faster than ever. It made it hard to see more than a few feet ahead. Mary knew that she was still in the park, but she didn't know where.

She might be near the chessboards or the fountain. The Arc de Triomphe might be no more than a dozen yards away, cloaked by night and snow.

"Gaia!"

The same thought ran through her head over and over. *I have to find Gaia. I have to warn her about her uncle.*

FIREWORKS

Halfway to the park Gaia got behind Ed and pushed. Even with her help, getting the chair through the deepening snow was a struggle. It was ridiculous to even try it. The only thing that made sense was to help Ed get home.

But inside, something seemed to hammer at her. Hurry. Hurry.

No more than two dozen people were waiting near the arch by the time they reached the center of the park. None of them looked anything like Mary Moss.

"How long do we wait?" asked Ed.

Gaia shook her head. She was all out of answers. *I have to find Mary.*

"Gaia."

The call was so faint that at first Gaia was sure she had imagined it. Then it came again.

"Gaia."

"Did you hear that?" asked Gaia.

Ed raised his head. "Hear what?"

Before Gaia could reply, the fireworks finally started. Sparkles of gold and silver mixed with and lit the falling snow.

Gaia didn't stop to watch. She turned and ran into the night.

CLOSE

Blood was frozen on Mary's cheek. She could barely breathe. Her eyes teared in the bitter cold. Her leg ached from hip to ankle.

When the colors started in the sky, she thought it was an illusion. It was only after the second explosion and the third that she realized it was the fireworks at the center of the park.

Gaia was close. All she had to do was follow the fireworks.

"Gaia!" she shouted again.

She limped forward a step. Another step.

A tall, dark figure appeared from behind a tree. "I have to give you credit," said Loki. "You came very close." He raised the gun over his head and brought the handle of the heavy weapon down in a vicious blow.

This time the fireworks were all inside Mary's head.

BLUNT INSTRUMENT

Loki's eyes were still streaming with tears. He risked removing his mask for a moment, bent, grabbed a handful of snow, and rubbed it across his burning face. Then he carefully replaced his mask. Even with the heavy snow, the park wasn't completely empty. If he were seen, the situation would be severely complicated.

Despite the pain her attack had caused, Loki felt even more regret about killing the girl. Mary Moss had proved to be quite resourceful. It was true that she had become too close to Gaia, but if Mary could be turned, that closeness could become an advantage. Mary might be used to manipulate Gaia in ways that a blunt instrument like Ella could never achieve.

No. She knows about Katia. She can't be allowed to survive.

Mary groaned and rolled over in the snow. Her eyes blinked open. "Gaia," she groaned.

Before she could do anything more, Loki drove the toe of his boot into her side. The girl let out a little yip. A small hand with bright red nails reached toward his ankle. Loki stomped down hard on the pale fingers, then sent another kick into the girl's body.

This time he was rewarded by a low, whistling moan before his victim passed out. Mary Moss would be giving him no more trouble.

Loki once again put his fingers in the girl's red hair. He pulled her unconscious form to her knees, moved around behind her, and put the Glock at the base of her skull. It would look like a drug hit. That's what the girl's parents would think. That's what the police would think. Most important, that's what Gaia would think.

And Gaia would learn a very important lesson—don't get too close. Otherwise you might get hurt.

Loki put his finger on the trigger.

"No!" came a scream from his left.

Loki felt a sense of movement. The sense of something rushing toward him out of the darkness and snow.

He pulled the trigger.

FROZEN MOMENT

Gaia collided with the man just as the gun exploded. For the tiniest slice of a second the muzzle flash lit the snow around her, freezing the motion of every snowflake like the world's loudest strobe light.

In that moment of light Gaia could see everything. She could see the wool knit of the man's mask. She could see the black pistol in his gloved hand. She could see the bruises on Mary's face, and the blood on her split lips, and how her ginger hair was blown aside by the bullet on its way to her brain.

The frozen moment ended. Gaia's momentum knocked the man from his feet and sent him sprawling in the snow. Gaia didn't go down. She landed on her feet, skidded, and jumped again to find the man already getting up.

Gaia put a sneaker in his hidden face. The man sat back down in the snow. Gaia launched another kick.

When fighting, Gaia usually worked hard not to cause permanent damage. This wasn't usually. She aimed her blow at the man's neck and delivered it with enough force to send his head bouncing all the way to Eighth Street.

The man blocked. It was a fast, efficient flip of his left arm, just enough to send Gaia's foot grazing past its target.

The missed kick sent Gaia flying over him. She tucked down her head, did a quick tumble, and rolled back to her feet. By the time she turned around, the man was also standing.

Gaia circled left, faked right, and went in. She sent a stiff right hand aiming for his face. Blocked. A spin kick at his side. Blocked. A sharp uppercut at his chin. Blocked.

She took a step back and studied the man. He held his hands low, almost too low, but he was fast. Gaia gritted her teeth. He wasn't fast enough. No one was.

Gaia went back another step, then came forward in an electric rush. She flew into the air with her stiff right leg aimed at the man's head.

The man raised an arm to block, but Gaia adjusted her aim midflight. She lowered her foot and drove it square in the center of the man's chest. He staggered back, but before Gaia could follow up her attack, she was forced to duck a whistling right hand that shattered the air only inches from her face.

This guy was good. Most of the idiots Gaia fought were completely clueless. Some of them had packed on a lot of prison muscle, and they probably looked pretty tough. Gaia wasn't impressed by looks. Even the tough guys were slow and easy. Not this guy. He was big and fast. More than that—he was trained.

The man feinted a kick, then withdrew another step.

Gaia followed. She threw a punch. Blocked. Kick. Blocked. Punch. A solid blow to the man's gut. Kick. A glancing shot to his hip but still enough to make him take another clumsy step. Leg sweep. The man in the black ski mask went down.

Gaia took her time. One more shot. That was all it would take. When it came right down to it, people were so easy to kill.

There was movement on her left. Gaia whipped around to face this new attack.

It was Mary. Her outstretched right hand clawed at the snow.

The man in the mask hadn't managed to touch Gaia a single time, but one look at Mary hit her like a bus. Gaia took a step toward her fallen friend. Then she remembered the man in the mask. Gaia turned back to face her enemy.

He was gone.

Gaia hurried forward. There were footsteps in the deepening snow. If she followed, she could catch the man. She was sure of it. All she had to do was leave Mary.

That was not an option.

She ran back to where Mary lay. Blood was spreading in the snow. It was splashed around Mary and speckled for a dozen yards in all directions. Mary's hand had stopped its fitful clawing at the earth. Mary's legs were still.

Images flashed through Gaia's mind. A house in the snow. Her mother. Blood and snow. Over and over, blood and snow. Gaia moved toward Mary as if she was wading through all her worst nightmares.

She's dead. She had to be dead. There was so much blood.

Gaia knelt in the stained snow. Tears made her vision waver, and her hands trembled as she reached out to touch Mary's cheek. Above her, shifting, sparking colors appeared as a fresh round of fireworks burst over the park. "Mary?"

To Gaia's astonishment, Mary's eyes opened. Her face was a mask of blood and pain, but her eyes immediately locked on Gaia's face. "Gaia?" she said in a weak, weirdly distorted voice.

"It's me." Gaia ran a hand over her friend's hair. Her fingers came back warm and sticky with blood. "Don't worry. You're going . . . You'll be okay."

Mary gave a single slow nod. "Gaia."

Gaia leaned in close. "Yeah."

"I was so worried about you," said Mary. Then her eyes slid back, and a final shiver ran through her body.

Gaia threw back her head and screamed into the falling snow.

CRIMSON HALO

Loki stood back among the trees and watched as Gaia knelt over the fallen girl. He felt a moment of fear when he realized that the Moss girl was still alive, but then he saw the final shudder rack her body and knew that the threat was finally over.

"Where are you!" Gaia screamed at the night. "Where are you, you bastard!"

Loki didn't move. He didn't dare move. There were sharp pains in his hip and chest. He was quite certain that at least one of his ribs was broken. If Gaia found him, he had no doubt the girl would leave him as dead as he had left Mary Moss.

For an uncomfortable moment it seemed like Gaia was peering straight at Loki's hiding place. Then she turned and ran back toward the people at the center of the park.

Loki waited until Gaia was out of sight, then he went back to Mary. He took two glassine envelopes of cocaine from his pocket and slipped them into the dead girl's coat. Then he opened a third envelope and poured a bit of the powder across her frozen face.

He took one last look to satisfy himself that everything was as it should be, then he started out of the park. For the police everything would be neat and easy. Junkie girl dies. Drugs on the body. Even if they never found someone to blame, they would never look very hard for an answer.

As Loki reached the sedan and climbed inside, he wondered how Gaia would react. The situation of the death—the death, the gunshot, the blood—it was bound to conjure images of her mother. Its effect on Gaia should be interesting.

Loki pressed the speakerphone button on the car's dash. "The task is completed," he said. He reached for the button to hang up the phone, then paused. "Have someone standing by to clean up the car," he said. "There's blood on my upholstery."

He hung up the phone and drove away.

BLOOD

To Matthew Weiss

GAIA

Mary's dead. Maybe if I say it over and over a thousand times, it'll sink in. *Mary's dead.*

I've been sitting in this tub for more than an hour now. I'm shivering and the water's cold, but I can't seem to move. I keep seeing Mary's face. Keep feeling her hair in my hands. There was blood on her teeth.

Mary's dead. I held her tonight as her eyes closed. Her life flowed out onto the cobblestone pavement of Washington Square Park. I saw who did it. I even fought him. Mary's old dealer, Skizz, hired that guy to kill Mary. Which he did, tonight.

Oh God, Mary's really dead. She won't call me tomorrow. I'm shaking and sore and Mary's blood washed off into this bathwater when I stepped in. She won't ever make me wear ridiculous clothes again. Make me go dancing with her. Tell me her secrets. Listen when I tell her mine.

What do I do now? Everything I touch gets destroyed. What does that mean for Ed? I can't seem to get out of this tub. I'm curled up. The porcelain is hard and cold under my head. I'm shaking. I don't want to cry, can't cry, can't make noise. Don't want Ella to come up here.

Oh God, Mary's dead. Is it too much for me to have a friend? Is it too much for me to trust someone? Is it too much for me to be close to someone?

I need to think. Think this through. Thinking is better than screaming. Better than crying. Better than feeling all this *pain.* I can't stand this pain. I don't want to feel this. I've got to stop this.

Breathe, breathe, breathe.

Okay.

No more.

I have to find a way to never feel like this again. Not because of my mom, or my dad, or Mary, or anyone. I've got to make sure I never, never feel this pain again.

And I've got to make Skizz pay.

TOO YOUNG TO DIE

"WAS THIS ALL LIFE WAS ABOUT?
THE STRONGER PICKING ON THE WEAKER?
SURVIVAL OF THE FITTEST?"

YOU MIGHT GET EATEN

Damn. He always forgot about that chunk of broken pavement. Ed Fargo swore under his breath and gave a sharp jerk to his wheels. He pulled himself out of the rut, then rolled around the corner of Perry Street toward Gaia's brownstone. His breath puffed out in the frigid air. January in New York was as dismal as things get.

Ed took in the scene around him. The ugly stamp of humanity's feet had already taken its toll on the winter streets. Pristine white snow was now sullen brown slush. Plowed drifts covered corners and curbs, creating treacherous mounds of filthy, spit-upon, dog-pissed-upon ice. Try getting a wheelchair through it.

"Gotta get snow tires," Ed muttered. As he made his way up Perry Street, a memory suddenly clamped over his heart, making him clench his wheels tighter, blow harder as he breathed. For a few moments he'd been distracted from the memory by other things. For a few moments he'd forgotten about Mary.

Mary was dead.

Part of him still couldn't quite take it in. Didn't want to. For the past month he and Mary and Gaia had been a real threesome. They had hung out, partied, talked. . . . It was the only time Ed had been with people he considered friends since, well, since the accident. *True* friends.

Sure, separate, Mary and Gaia had both been pretty intense. Together the two of them had been compelling, exciting . . . and infuriating. Like when Mary had dared Gaia to make out with Ed just a few nights ago. Given Ed's deeply felt but hidden lust for Gaia, that had been pretty wild. Weird, but wild.

Ed paused and rubbed his chin in the twenty-five-degree air. He realized he'd been smiling. Again he'd forgotten.

Mary was dead, killed the night before last in the park. To Ed, it looked like a years-long major coke addiction had finally caught up to her. She'd died with drugs in her possession. Gaia had been there, speaking to the cops, when Ed had arrived. Too late. He was always too late.

Oh, Mary.

True, once or twice Ed had resented how close Mary and Gaia were becoming. But Mary had been Ed's friend, too. She'd been fun, beautiful, full of enthusiasm and life and humor and outrageousness. She'd been too young to die.

Ed rolled to a stop before Gaia's brownstone. He swallowed, hard. It was freezing out *here.* What would he find in *there*? He reached toward the doorbell, thought better of it, and pulled back his hand to fiddle with the armrest of his chair, his heart pounding.

Why was this so hard?

During this last month Ed had seen Gaia unbend more, smile more, laugh more, show her soft side more than in the whole time he'd known her. It had been due to Mary. Now Mary was wearing a toe tag. How was Gaia going to react? What's more, how was Ed going to make it easier for her to deal? Gaia had refused to come to the door or talk on the phone all day yesterday. Who was to say she would even let Ed say two words to her today?

Ed's watch said eight-twelve. The Village School was opening its battered wood-and-metal doors right now. Thanks to a bunch of snow days, they'd been gypped on winter vacation and had to go back to school early. But there was no doubt Gaia would skip today. Maybe George or Ella had already called her in sick.

The thought of Gaia spending yesterday with just her clueless foster father or bitchy foster mother to console her literally made Ed's stomach turn. Today he wanted to be the one who was there for her, to hold her as she cried, to comfort her as well as he could. Now he would have a chance to protect her, just like she'd always protected him. Maybe it would even be a chance for Gaia and Ed to get closer. Maybe he would be able to tell her he loved her. That he wanted to be with her. Yeah, in *that* way.

Ed took a deep breath and tried to clear his head. Just as his gloved index finger reached out to the bell, the heavy front door opened. Gaia came out.

In a frozen moment Ed searched her face. Gaia looked pale but otherwise . . . fine. Calm. Kind of . . . *normal.* No tearstained cheeks, no swollen eyes, no pain etched on her face. She was dressed for school in an ancient pair of jeans that looked like they had been rescued from a tribe of renegade dust bunnies hiding under her bed. A pale blue, stretched-out turtleneck collar showed at the opening of a worn, electric blue, puffy down ski jacket. The jacket had a hole in it, and feathers were leaking out. Her glorious blond hair hung in wet, ratlike clumps around her head. Ed knew it would be frozen solid before she reached the end of the block. Same old Gaia.

"Hey," Gaia said calmly, tucking some wet hair behind one ear. She hitched her messenger bag higher on her shoulder, strode past Ed, and headed down the block.

For a moment Ed was too confused to do anything but stare after her. Mary was dead, right? He hadn't just dreamed it. His wheels spun as he caught up to her. "You're going to school?" he asked, hating how his voice sounded—flabbergasted, childish.

Gaia glanced down at him blankly. "It *is* a school day," she pointed out. "Is there some holiday I don't know about?"

"But—" Ed bumped over a curb that the universal handicapped accessibility codes hadn't caught up with yet.

"But what?" Gaia asked. They swung around a corner as Ed struggled to organize his thoughts into some kind of a coherent sentence.

"I thought you might stay home today," he said carefully

as he caught up to her. *Great. Great sentence. You're a genius, Ed.* "I thought you might be upset."

Gaia sniffed and wiped the back of her hand across her nose as he stared up at her expectantly. "What is it with cold air and *snot?*" she asked, just as the light turned green. Ed stopped dead in his tracks. He had to say something, *anything* that would help him connect with her. He braced himself, waiting for Gaia to realize he'd stopped and turn around.

But Gaia *didn't* stop. She crossed the street and just kept going, never once looking back. Ed's mouth worked open and closed, but nothing came out.

In a matter of seconds she was out of sight.

Ed just stared after her.

I AM PIGBOY

"Shit."

Gaia Moore stared blankly into her locker, wondering what books she should grab before rushing off to class. She was going to be on time today. If she could just figure out what freaking books she needed.

"Shit, shit, shit."

Gaia's locker was inexplicably grouped with a bunch of freshmen's. Bad luck—freshmen were even worse than seniors. New kids always get stuck with the crappy lockers, Gaia thought angrily as she shuffled a pile of cascading papers, although she guessed she wasn't all that new anymore.

Hard to believe she had lasted since September. Usually the educational system gave up on her after only a month or two. Schools in Manhattan must be a little more hard-edged than any of the other places she had been, Gaia mused.

Hello. Think, Gaia. What classes did she have this morning? She had no idea. Then it dawned on her. Chem lab. She grabbed a thick notebook and two of the less hefty textbooks out of her locker and slammed the door.

The metallic clang of her locker echoed emptily in the hallway. *Damn.* The hallways were already clear, the classroom doors closed, and the huge industrial wall clock ticked loudly above her thawing head. Gaia squeezed a little of the moisture out of her hair, tucked her books under one arm, and strode purposefully down the hall.

Usually Ed would have been here to keep her in check, to make sure she went to class in the first place. But Gaia hadn't seen him since she'd left him at the corner of Perry, looking completely aghast. Had he made it in okay?

Gaia dismissed the thought almost as quickly as it had come. Ed could take care of himself. And besides, she was done worrying. Gaia Moore had officially made a pact with herself—she was no longer a baby-sitter.

As she loped around the corner, Gaia almost collided with a small knot of seething testosterone clumped against the wall. She stopped short, blue eyes rapidly assessing the scene.

Several large, dumb bozos appeared to be picking on a smaller nerd type. One of the hulks, whose neck measurement probably exceeded his IQ, turned and trained small, piglike eyes on Gaia. She felt his animal glance sweep her from dripping hair to battered Sears construction-worker boots, lingering on her breasts, her long legs. Jerk.

"Gay-uh? That's your name, right?"

Gaia stood rooted to the spot, her eyes narrowed.

"Take a hike, Gay-uh," Pigboy muttered. "This doesn't concern you." He leaned forward, gripping the soft flannel shirt of a kid Gaia didn't recognize. The kid's brown eyes, wide behind glasses, flashed both angry humiliation and mute appeal.

Gaia frowned with irritation and impatience. Was this all life was about? The stronger picking on the weaker? Survival of the fittest?

And if that was the case, wouldn't that put Gaia at the top of the food chain?

"It's Guy-uh," she said. "Let him go."

The biggest guy snorted. "He's not going anywhere, *Guy-uh.* We've got unfinished business with Zack here."

Gaia felt her jaw clench. "Oh, your business is finished."

Pigboy laughed. "Not hardly."

Gaia moved fast, lunging forward and grabbing his left arm with one hand. She pulled it back and to the side, felt the ligaments stretching taut beneath his skin. Pigboy let out a sharp, surprised groan and went on tiptoes to relieve the pressure on his arm. It was useless. Pain and shock contorted his face into true ugliness.

"You don't even know what pain is yet," Gaia whispered close to his ear. She hated people like him. Bullies.

Bracing her feet, Gaia bent and drove her shoulder into Pigboy's back, flipping him. He landed with a heavy, sickening thud and lay motionless, staring stupidly at the ceiling, silently trying to draw air into his flattened lungs.

"Who's next?" Gaia asked, straightening and pushing her hair over her shoulder. Her nostrils flared, and her fists curled and uncurled at her sides. A thin thread of excitement snaked through her veins. She was aware that her breath was coming faster, that everything around her had snapped into vivid focus.

One of the guys stepped forward, a cocky grin on his face. How pathetic. Gaia could smell his aftershave. Was it Old Spice?

She took a step to meet him, but ducked back when he suddenly jerked forward under the weight of something, *someone*, that had just landed on his back. Confused, Gaia took another step back and watched the scene with surprise. But surprise quickly turned into awe. The kid, Zack, was clinging for dear life to Jock Two's back, his arms wrapped around his neck, his legs kicking crazily. The scene was so comical that Gaia almost laughed. The jock stumbled back and forth, trying to regain his footing, but Zack now had a firm grip around his collarbone with his left arm, and his right hand had already grabbed a fist full of the guy's hair.

In one huge, powerful movement, the jock reached over the back of his head, grabbed Zack's shirt collar and flipped him onto the ground, grunting as tufts of his hair were pulled out in the process. Gaia didn't hesitate. As the jock straightened up, she moved forward and kicked sideways sharply, her foot angled up. She watched his mouth open in a yelp as her foot connected and popped his kneecap out of the socket. He crumpled to the ground next to Zack, gasping and clutching his leg. The expression on his face took a few moments to translate into nauseating pain. Then he started to moan.

Almost immediately the third jerk leaped into action, trying to tackle Gaia from behind. She ducked instinctively, planted her feet, and felt him land on her back. With one deft movement she uncoiled his hands from around her neck and gave a little shove to send him flying over her. He crashed upside down against the bank of metal lockers. Bright red blood flowed from his nose. Gaia stared at it, transfixed. Why was it that blood was so surprisingly bright, cheerful, shiny? Like Mary's blood. Like her mom's.

She sensed movement behind her and turned to face Pigboy again, who was now struggling to stand up. She lifted a foot, ready to attack, but out of the corner of her eye she saw that Zack had struggled to a standing position and now he limped to Gaia's side. Gaia stared at him in surprise as he raised his fists and glared at Pigboy, his glasses glinting in the fluorescent light of the hallway. Gaia followed his gaze back to Pigboy. He grinned at Zack, mockery written across his face, but when he noticed Gaia balling her fists, he raised his hands in defeat and stumbled backward. Then he did a one-eighty and fled down the hall.

Gaia's breathing slowed as she took in the scene around her. In a moment she had assessed that this scene was pretty much over. She picked up her books, feeling the tension already starting to fade away. *Breathe in, breathe out. Don't look at the blood.*

Zack leaned against the wall, panting. Gaia's gaze swept him and determined he had suffered no serious physical damage.

It was over. Gaia hoped the guys would be gone before a teacher or another student found them lying in the hall. But even if they were discovered in their current, pitiful condition, she doubted they would ever point the finger at her. She was, to these assholes at least, just a skinny, blond *girl*.

"Wow. That was, uh, incredible. We were . . . incredible, huh? You're . . . Wow . . . Thanks for . . ."

Gaia shifted her attention back to Zack. "Uh-huh," she said, turning her back and striding down the hall toward chem lab. She at least wanted to make it to her desk before her legs gave out.

Even though this always happened, still Gaia never got used to it and always hated it. During a confrontation, a fight, she was unstoppable—iron and poetry in one freakish, muscle-bound body. But afterward, when danger had passed, her body took a little breather, and she literally couldn't stand up.

Gaia hurriedly ducked into class with a murmured apology to her teacher, Mr. Fowler. A wish flashed through her mind as she sank into her seat—that she could have protected Mary in the same way. She wouldn't make the same mistake again. Skizz had succeeded in killing Mary because Gaia hadn't taken care of him when she should have. She had beaten him almost to death just days ago. But sentimentality, some warped sense of right and wrong, had prevented her from finishing what she'd started. And Skizz had retaliated, but by going after Mary, not Gaia.

Now Gaia would have to go after *him*.

TIME TO BLOW SAM'S MIND

Heather Gannis expertly slid her long, silky, shiny dark hair over her shoulder and shifted her weight in her seat. In the desk next to her Melanie was picking at her split ends behind her textbook. Typical chem lab activity.

"Okay, class, what happens if I take the potassium nitrate and add it to its inverse?" Mr. Fowler asked from the front of the classroom.

"You pass out from the fumes and we get out of class early?" Melanie whispered. Heather grinned with a careful mixture of amusement and detached boredom.

The classroom door opened, and Gaia Moore slunk into her seat, two rows over and one back from Heather. Involuntarily Heather's stomach clenched, her knuckles slowly turning white on her ballpoint pen.

Melanie's brown eyes focused on Gaia. "What is she doing here today?" she whispered.

"I know." Heather nodded. "Mary Moss was killed two days ago," she said softly. "You'd think that Xena, Warrior Bitchtress, would miss a few days of school."

Melanie smiled appreciatively. "You'd think," she agreed.

But no, Heather thought bitterly, *here she is. Looking as usual as if she slept in her Goodwill clothes.*

A loud thump suddenly echoed from behind the two

girls, and they both turned to see where it had come from. Gaia's head was now slumped down on her desk. How rude.

Melanie swallowed a delicate snort.

Heather smiled again. Thank God for people like Melanie. People who adored her. People who agreed that Gaia was a complete loser.

Ducking her head so Mr. Fowler couldn't see her lips moving, Melanie went on. "You know, I can't believe that anyone could like her, anyway. But Mary seemed to. Now Mary's dead, and Gaia doesn't even look upset. What a bitch."

Heather nodded quietly. She completely agreed with Melanie, but right now she wasn't in the mood for gossip. She settled back, letting a studious look come over her face. Gaia Moore, girl loser. Ever since Gaia had shown up last September, Heather's life had taken a decided turn for the worse. In fact, until last September just about the only really awful thing that had ever happened to Heather had been her boyfriend Ed's accident, leaving him wheelchair bound. Heather shook her head. That was past history. A rough time. She was just thankful that she and Ed, after all this time, could still be friends. But why was a great guy like Ed also friends with that bitch? It didn't make sense.

Since Gaia had come here, Heather, the most popular girl in school, had been stabbed and almost died, had lost a good friend, had been burned with hot coffee, had been picked on and teased, and had practically broken up with Sam.

Oh God. Sam Moon. A photo montage, complete with corny, tinkly French music, began to play in Heather's brain. Sam, sitting at an outdoor table at Dojo's, eating a huge plate of french fries. The day he had bought her a Celtic love knot pin from a street stand in Soho. Sam, unbuttoning her shirt, breathing soft against her cheek. Heather's eyes drifted closed as Mr. Fowler droned on about the false distinction between organic and inorganic substances, blah, blah, blah.

Heather and Sam had been going out for nine months now, and the last four months had been really iffy. They had been filled with anger, jealousy, hurt, infidelity. But mostly they had been filled with Gaia Moore. Gaia talking with Sam, Gaia appearing in Sam's dorm room, Gaia distracting Sam, invading their lives. But Heather wasn't the type to lose without a fight. It was time for her and Sam to get back on track. Time for Heather to reclaim her hold on him and put Gaia out of his thoughts forever. After all, she was Heather Gannis. If she couldn't hold on to a boyfriend, who could? Yes, it was time to unsheathe her claws. Time to blow Sam's mind. Heather smiled.

"What?" Melanie whispered.

Heather snapped her mind back to chem lab and noticed her friend looking at her expectantly. The same way *most* of her friends looked at her *most* of the time.

"Oh, nothing," she said.

GAIA

So I've been trying to come up with a snappy reply to all the "I'm so sorrys" I've been getting about Mary. Today at school was pretty lame. Most of those ass-holes didn't even know Mary, except from seeing her at parties. They didn't know her favorite band (Fearless), her favorite color (fuschia), her favorite food (sate). Most of them don't know me either, except by my reputation as a social outcast. So why are they all of a sudden acting like I matter? Why do they even care? All day, during class, after class, I felt their eyes boring holes into me.

When they don't know anything *about* me.

You know, I never even told Mary I was proud of her

for kicking coke. I never told her how being her friend changed my life. Now I can't.

I can't tell her that she taught me how to have fun. I can't tell her how she taught me to actually *be* a friend.

Not that it matters now. I'm through with that. The Mary thing. And the friend thing. Ed doesn't get it yet. But he will. He'll have to. It's not that I don't want to be there for him. But I can't. I've got to start looking out for me. Just me.

There are a few things I need to take care of first. One in particular. But once that's done, it's all about Gaia.

Sounds selfish, right?

Well, I *am* my father's daughter.

NO REAL GAIA

GAIA ALONE WAS PERFECT. GAIA ALONE WAS WORTHY—
WORTHY OF HER BACKGROUND, HER TRAINING,
HER SURVEILLANCE. WORTHY OF HIS ATTENTION.

WHAT A RETARD

Slither. Cross. Slither. Ella loved the sound her thigh-high stockings made when she crossed and uncrossed her legs. Sort of slippery and grippy all at the same time.

"Really?" Loki turned to face her, his back characteristically against the anonymous white wall of this apartment. At first Ella had been surprised that Loki had chosen a doorman building for this month's pied-à-terre. Then she realized that the heavy-jowled gorilla in the cheesy maroon uniform downstairs was no doubt on Loki's payroll.

Ella shrugged, crossed her legs again, and felt a frisson of pleasure and irritation tingling at the base of her spine. "What can I tell you? You offed her friend, right in front of her. But she hasn't been crying, hasn't been doing anything. As a matter of fact," Ella said thoughtfully, examining one inch-long spiky fingernail, "she's been slightly less awful, actually. At least she's coming home for meals. So old George isn't quite as twitchy about her as he usually is."

The force of Loki's intense look made Ella's cheeks heat. Damn him. Even after years he could do this to her. Blurred images flitted through her mind of Loki in bed with her, Loki sliding next to her, the cords in his neck tightening as he moved. Ella warmed at the memory of his surgical precision, his superhuman control. His skin was smooth, his hair like heavy silk. There had been a painful exhilaration on Ella's part when they had first become lovers—the young, stupid, beautiful Ella she had been then. Loki was so dangerous, so frightening, so powerful. Yet he had chosen her. Giving in to him had been as strong and as addicting as jumping off a cliff. Now of course she realized that Loki choosing her to be his lover was like Loki choosing Puffs to be his tissue brand of choice. Her stomach tightened. The older, wiser, still beautiful Ella she was today awaited his next question.

"Has she been with her other friends?" came his soft voice. "The wheelchair guy? Ed? Anyone from school? Anyone . . . else?"

Like Sam Moon, you mean? Ella thought sarcastically. She had to gulp hard to keep a jackal's grin off her face. Sam Moon had been *delicious.* Not only had he been fabulous in bed—strong, uncomplicated, and enthusiastic, with the stamina of a Mack truck—but there had been an added layer of pleasure in knowing that Ella was sleeping with the object of Gaia's affection. She almost laughed out loud right now, just thinking about it. Gaia had been eating her guts out over Sam Moon for months. And Ella had bagged him first. It was almost faith restoring.

On the surface Ella shook her head no, trying to look attentive and professional.

"No. She just doesn't seem interested. The only time I've seen her evince the slightest bit of excitement was when she beat up those kids at her school. Gaia has the emotional capacity of a hyena," Ella said.

Loki regarded Ella coldly. "She's a survivor. Like a hyena, you could put her down almost anywhere, and she would survive. She would adapt. She is very strong, our Gaia."

A tiny muscle twitched in Ella's smoothly made-up cheek. God, she hated that bitch. To hear Loki salivating over her was perfectly nauseating.

"Uh-huh," Ella said, trying to keep the sullenness out of her voice. Jesus, how long was this going to go on? How long was she going to be stuck here, playing baby-sitter to her foster daughter? Daughter. When the very name Gaia made a taste like cigarette ashes rise into Ella's mouth. She swallowed, making a face.

WORTHY

Loki turned his back to Ella and strode over to the windows. It was already dark at four thirty. From these windows he could see the big X formed by Broadway and Seventh Avenue as they crossed and reversed positions. He sighed. Ella was rapidly reaching the limits of her usefulness. The open hatred on her face when she spoke of Gaia was more than annoying. Still, he knew Ella was under control. She wouldn't dare touch a golden hair on that beautiful head.

Loki sighed again, this time with pleasure. In the window's reflection he could see Ella behind him, no longer even bothering to pretend to pay attention to him. The woman looked at her nails, crossed and uncrossed her legs, yawned, gazed at the ceiling. The fact that she failed to be inspired by Gaia was proof of her own inadequacy.

Gaia alone was perfect. Gaia alone was worthy—worthy of her background, her training, her surveillance. Worthy of his attention. Worthy of something more than attention. The fact that Gaia had witnessed the death of one of the pathetic props in her difficult life—had witnessed it and not crumpled, had watched her friend die and yet shown no signs of weakness or trivial human emotion in the days following—well, that just proved how very special his beloved niece was.

A thrill of excitement made his breath come a fraction of a second faster. Gaia was more to him than just a niece. As his identical twin's daughter, she shared his DNA. She was made out of the very same stuff as he was. It was one more reason to believe her potential was limitless.

Loki had been observing Gaia for quite a while. He had

been patient, though sometimes a little cruel. In that time, and especially during the last few months, he had been disappointed by Gaia's obvious similarities to her father: her sentimentality, her sensitivity. It undermined her strength, her ability to dominate those around her.

But maybe the time had finally come. Maybe Gaia had finally left that childishness behind with the death of her friend. It certainly looked that way.

Soon the chrysalis would split apart. Soon the beautiful butterfly would emerge. Soon Gaia would come and sit by his right hand as his successor—and his equal.

WHY IS IT MADE OUT OF MEAT?

"What is chicken potpie, anyway?" Ed asked, shoveling a small forkful of it into his mouth. He glanced across the school cafeteria table at Gaia. Day three after Mary's death and the silence was nerve-racking. Gaia was still showing no signs of weakening or needing comfort. She must really be keeping it bottled up inside.

"What's a chicken pot? Like a pot just to make chicken in? Where do they get these names?"

Gaia looked up at him and almost smiled. That is, her lips pressed together in a flat line for a moment. Which was the most he'd gotten out of her, besides her snot comment, in three days.

She shrugged. "You didn't have to make it, you don't have to clean it up, so what are you crying about?" She took a bite of her own lunch.

Ed opened his mouth to protest, his temper flaring. What was Gaia's problem? Did she think she was the only one who'd lost Mary? He laid his hands flat on the table, but the thought of Mary took the wind out of his sails. He hung his head and stared down at his lunch, defeated.

Ed and Gaia usually had lunch together, though not in the school cafeteria. They were both big believers in searching for lunch cuisine elsewhere, off campus. They had so many places to choose from. So there was no reason to be sitting here in the cafeteria eating chicken pot . . . whatever . . . when Ed didn't believe for a second that an actual chicken had gotten anywhere near the school kitchen.

Except that Gaia had shrugged when he suggested different dining options. Now Ed stared at her, gathering the strength to give talking another try. He was that kind of guy.

"You know, I'm glad you're not a vegetarian," he said, trying to sound cheery and casual and failing miserably. "I don't get the whole vegetarian thing. I mean, if we're not supposed to eat animals, why are they made out of meat?"

Not one of his most original lines, and Ed had forgotten what comedian had said it first. Still, even though it was the Ed Fargo entertainment hour, he wasn't getting any reaction.

"So, got any plans later?" Ed tried again. "Want to come over tonight and watch a movie or something?"

True, Gaia had only been to Ed's house once before, despite four months of being friends. Just thinking about Gaia seeing his folks again made Ed wish he had kept his mouth shut. His parents, the lovely and charming Mr. and Mrs. Fargo. The ones who were gearing up for his older sister's engagement party. The ones who were pulling out all the stops for her. The ones who couldn't help wincing every time his wheelchair bumped a piece of furniture.

He started to say forget about it, but then Gaia met his eyes. Clear blue eyes, as untroubled as a spring morning in Maine. "No, thanks," she said. "I've got some stuff to do at home."

Ed hated the way her focus slid past him, as if he wasn't even there. This really had to stop. "Look, Gaia. I know how upset you are about Mary," he said, just jumping right in. "And I miss her, too," he continued, watching Gaia's jaw tighten. "Mary was terrific; she was a good friend. It's really horrible what happened to her."

Gaia swallowed and put down her fork. "I don't want to talk about it," she said stiffly.

"I know," Ed said, really gearing up now. "In three days you haven't mentioned her name. I mean, *I'm* all torn up about it. She was a good friend of mine. You guys were even closer." He lowered his voice and leaned across the Formica-topped table. "Mary's gone, and it sucks. We've lost a good friend. Can't we talk about it?" Ed felt upset and uncomfortable, and he was aware that he was walking a fine line with Gaia.

Gaia slowly shook her head, her eyes large and solemn. Her face looked stony and pale, and Ed hated making her feel this way by forcing the issue. But didn't she know that if she kept it all bottled up, one day she would just explode?

He tried again. "Gaia—I know it's not the same thing. But after my accident, I was a mess. I was going through every kind of therapy, and I just wanted to die." It seemed wretched and stupid to be confiding in her this way right in the middle of the school cafeteria. But he had to get through to her. "I was keeping everything inside, too—didn't want to upset my folks any more than they already were. And I figured I wasn't going to stick around long enough to worry about having a healthy mental attitude."

Across the table Gaia remained silent. These were things he'd never told anyone, and he felt like he was burdening her. "Anyway," he pressed on, "finally I decided to get over myself. Do the best I could. Part of that was just talking about things. Getting it out. The only person *I* had to talk to was the shrink my parents forced on me. But even he was better than nothing. And you have someone—you have *me*. I just—I don't know. I just wish you would talk to me about Mary. I mean, you—it's like Mary never existed or something."

Quietly Gaia sat there, her breathing shallow, her eyes wide and unreadable as she scanned the room, not looking at him. Ed felt his fists clench in frustration.

How freaking typical. In the four months he had known Gaia, he had seen her furious, violent, shy, antisocial, rude, sensitive, generous, forgiving, and reckless. He didn't think he had ever seen her truly happy, and he knew he had never seen her weak. Why was he expecting something different now, just because her other best friend had been murdered in front of her only three days ago?

Abruptly Ed pushed his lunch tray away. What was this stuff-to-do-at-home shit? Gaia didn't consider the Nivens' house her *home*. She'd never referred to it that way before. Also, if memory served, and Ed thought it did, then Gaia was usually desperate to get out of the Nivens', and stay out, for as many hours of the day as possible.

Light dawned, and Ed suddenly softened. He leaned across the table, his eyes narrowing. "Who are you, and what have you done with the real Gaia?"

It was an old joke, an ancient joke, but still chuckle worthy, in Ed's opinion.

Instead Gaia looked suddenly, inexpressibly sad. It was only for a moment, but sadness washed over Gaia's face as if she had stepped in front of a tall building that blocked her face from the sun. Then it was gone. Her face twitched back into its beautiful, expressionless mask. "There is no real Gaia," she said softly.

IT'S ALMOST FUNNY

Gaia stepped off the number six local on Eighty-sixth Street and started walking west. The January cold whistled down the wind tunnels made by buildings on either side of her. It whipped her hair around beneath the sweatshirt hood that stuck up from beneath her ski jacket.

It hadn't been easy, ditching Ed. First he'd asked her to come over to his place. Then he had suggested eating together, or catching a movie, or going for coffee. Was he ever going to get off her back?

Now, reaching Fifth Avenue, Gaia turned left, then crossed the wide street, heading for the huge columns of the Metropolitan Museum of Art. Here was the plan: first, an hour of culture, then a bowl of potato-leek soup from the soup Nazi, then a couple of hours downtown in and around Washington Square Park and Tompkins Square Park, enjoying the lovely January weather and looking for her good old pal Skizz under cover of darkness.

Gaia shivered in anticipation. Never once had she considered using her unique strengths to take another person's life. Now she could think of nothing else.

A mental movie had been running through Gaia's head constantly since the day after Mary's death. The scenes often changed, but the theme was always the same—Skizz lying at her feet; Skizz dangling limp and silent as her hands clasped his neck; Skizz dead, done, gone forever.

Gaia now rubbed her eyes to clear the image as she climbed the steps to the Met. She knew part of her, a huge part of her, didn't want to kill Skizz at all. Somewhere deep down, a voice raged at the pure *wrongness* of it. How could she take a life? What would her father think? But then, she reminded herself, what did she care about what he thought?

But Skizz needed to die. And Gaia was *past* caring about right or wrong. Was it right that Mary would be lying underground in a matter of days?

No. It was time that Gaia forgot about her silly ideals.

The plan was simple—kill Skizz, get the hell out of here, and begin a new life somewhere. Somewhere where no one would know her.

When Gaia walked through the huge, heavy bronze doors of the museum, a strong, heated blast of air whooshed down on her. It instantly dried the snowflakes clinging to her hair. Inside, it was stuffy, overheated, and dry. Gaia shrugged out of the puffy ski jacket and tied its floppy arms around her waist. She snagged a map from the info desk and made her way to a bank of elevators.

An elevator, a couple of long halls, and a wide stairway later, she found herself in a series of rooms devoted to German expressionists. As Gaia wandered over in front of a Nolde painting, she had a flashback of her mother, Katia. Katia had taught Gaia how to look at art, how to love it, how to let it get inside her. She sank down on a bare wooden bench.

This painting was called *Three Russians*, and it showed two men and a woman all bundled up, as if perhaps they had just strolled down a New York street in the middle of January. The brush strokes were coarse and broad; the paint clung thickly, stickily to the canvas in crusty swaths. Three Russians. All dressed in fur. They had long, thin noses, high cheekbones . . .

Katia Moore had been Russian. She had spoken with rolling *r*s and worn clothes she had brought from Europe. She had often had long conversations with Gaia in her native tongue, and for years Gaia had thought of it as their own secret language. Katia had been so unlike other kids' mothers. Gaia's whole family had been so unlike everyone else's. Which was why she was here now, seventeen years old, a genetic freak made much worse by her father's intensive, relentless training. Training that had ended as abruptly as her mother's life, and on the same night. Five years ago.

Gaia's breath lightly left her lungs as she felt herself sink onto the hard bench. It was so hot in here, so dry.

I'm a freak, thought Gaia. *Genetically incapable of feeling fear. Why?* she screamed silently. Why had she been made like this? As a child, when she realized, she *knew* that she simply never felt fear, it hadn't been a big deal. Lots of kids had seemed reckless and fearless—like that day she and four of her friends climbed up to the roof of the Rosenblitts' shed, jumped from there to the roof of the Stapletons' garage, then crossed over to the other side and leaped seven feet down into a pile of compost. Paratroopers! Okay, it had been disgusting, landing in all the fruit rinds and eggshells, but it hadn't been scary. Not for any of them. It had been fun.

But now, at seventeen, never feeling fear had become a weight around her neck. It had made her friends a target on more than one occasion. It had gotten Mary killed. But it would also make it possible for her to kill Mary's killer, with nothing to hold her back.

Standing up, Gaia realized she was hungry. Maybe it

was time to hit the soup wagon. She took one last quick look around the German expressionists. Gotta hand it to them—they were masters at depicting all the agonies of the human condition. Thwarted love, psychic torture, the sheer pain of existence all laid out for the viewer in bright, jewel-like colors. All these paintings of anguish. It was almost funny. Gaia hiked up her messenger bag, turned, and left the *Three Russians* behind.

NOTHING OF KATIA

Tom Moore stood in the shadows near the door of the Metropolitan Museum of Art. George was right. In the past five years Tom had seen Gaia only a handful of times, and always at a distance. It was simply too dangerous for them to meet face-to-face. It had always seemed like the best thing to do, for Gaia's safety. Now Tom was wondering if he had inadvertently destroyed Gaia in a way that was more devastating than just a physical death. He was wondering if he had destroyed her soul.

The night Katia had died, Tom's only thought was to save his and Katia's child. So he had left, and used his CIA connections to arrange for Gaia to be sent away, to keep changing addresses, to keep on the move. He'd thought he was protecting her. Now it looked like he was setting her up to become emotionally warped, unable to respond to another human being. Stunted. For all of her many and amazing talents, strengths, and resources, his beautiful daughter seemed unable to honestly grieve over the death of her closest girlfriend. She seemed unable to reach out to others for help. She seemed unable to express any kind of emotion at all.

It was appalling, what Gaia was becoming. A month ago Tom had been filled with hope. To the best of his knowledge, Gaia had made some friends, was seeing them, talking, laughing. Now one friend was dead, and Gaia was cutting the other friend out as if he were a tumor. She hadn't shed one tear.

Something had to be going on inside Gaia—that much was clear. It just didn't appear to be the *right* something. In this new, automaton like Gaia, Tom could see nothing of Katia's passion, her fire, her will to live. What he could see was coldness, detachment, anger. And what else? Mercilessness. Where was Katia's gentleness, her generosity, her warmth and affection?

Maybe Tom didn't know his daughter at all. He certainly didn't understand her. A chilling determination was written all over her face—in the set of her jaw, in the distance in her eyes. It reminded him of someone—and in a chilling flash Tom realized that that someone was Loki.

What was Gaia capable of?

Tom's head swirled with indecision—he, who was famous for being able to evaluate a complex situation instantly and unerringly make the correct, the only decision, felt at a loss. He had no idea what to do. It was dangerous for him to appear in her life, to intervene in the situation he had created for her. It would be dangerous for both of them and for his country. But at this moment Tom felt he would risk everything just to be able to approach his daughter, give her a hug, offer her a shoulder to lean on. Steer her away from whatever it was she was planning to do. But how could he, when the very act of contacting her might be enough to get a bullet put through her head?

Just like Katia.

LOKI

How can I express my feelings toward my only brother, my identical twin? I can tell you that I hate him, but the word *hate* doesn't really begin to cover the depth of the feeling I have for him. He is light; I am darkness. He is a plodding government worker—I am exquisitely subtle in my work. I have raised what I do to the level of an art. He cannot approach my greatness. Every day that he lives, he taints my own existence. It is clear that he must be destroyed. Only by standing alone can I attain my final destiny.

I have tried to take his life. It proved to be a mistake that put parts of my life beyond repair. For now, trying again is not an option. But there are other ways to destroy a man besides death.

Gaia. Katia's child. She is the perfect revenge. She is the child that should have been mine, would have been mine—will someday be mine. Gaia is poised on the brink of greatness. I can see that now. Before, I thought she had potential. Now, seeing her reactions to this latest test, the death of the girl Mary, I am convinced Gaia is almost ready to break free from her father's influence. She is showing strength beyond measure. She is unclouded by emotion. She is free of sentimentality. She is ready to be a killer. Gaia will belong to me.

And when she does, I will twist the knowledge of her betrayal in Tom Moore's heart like a knife.

GAIA

Skizz is lying low. I froze my ass off last night going back and forth between Tompkins Square Park and Washington Square Park, looking for him, but after five hours he still hadn't shown his ugly face. But I'll get him. For Mary's sake.

Okay, I know it wasn't actually Skizz who physically killed Mary. The guy I fought in the park that night was someone completely different: someone strong, trained, and lethal. Skizz is a fat, sloppy joke. But I know Skizz hired the guy. I'm not stupid. That guy was probably one of Skizz's clients who owed him, big time. Mary was his way of repaying his debt. The way I figure, Skizz now owes me his life. God knows the police aren't going to do anything to make him pay. To them Mary is just another drug addict who got what she deserved.

After I got back to George's last night, I couldn't sleep. I thought about all the ways I could take Skizz apart. Facing him, sideways, from the back. In my mind I heard his shoulder snap as I bent it. I heard the choked scream of pain rip from his throat as I broke his fingers.

I also thought about Ed. I thought about how I never want to see him again once this thing is over. I don't want to see the look in his eyes when he realizes that I've killed someone. As for me, I'll probably never look in the mirror again after it's done and Skizz is dead. But I don't know what else to do. I don't know how else to make it up to Mary.

RESOLUTIONS

HE WAS A MAN. A MAN HAD BALLS. HE WOULD FIND THE BALLS TO BREAK UP WITH HEATHER.

THE NONEXCITED STATE

Now, why doesn't Starbucks have a concession right here? Sam Moon wondered. He stretched and yawned, his heavyweight rugby shirt riding up to expose smooth skin. The life of the premed student. All work and no play. Actually, last semester Sam's life had consisted of too much play, too much obsessing about Gaia, and not enough work. Which his grades had demonstrated. Which had prompted a heartfelt man-to-man with Dad. Which had prompted Sam's starting this semester by working his butt off.

He looked around the study room he was in. A wide wall of glass closed the room off from the central lobby. The NYU library was ten stories tall, with a huge open vertical space in the middle and floor after floor of books encircling it like a vise. It always made him feel nauseated just looking at it.

Sam shifted again. How long had he been sitting here, wading through the text and class notes for his human sexuality class? At least three hours. He needed coffee. He needed a Danish. At the beginning of the year someone had turned him on to onion bagels with scallion cream cheese. He'd thought they were incredible. Until the night he'd thrown one up after doing seven tequila shots in Josh Seidman's dorm room.

Once you throw something up after seven tequila shots, you never want to eat it again. Fact of life.

Human sexuality. What a laugh. The course was required for premeds, and he and his pals thought it would be a hoot. Instead it somehow managed to suck every last bit of humor from the subject and turn it into something so dry that sometimes Sam wondered if the team who wrote the textbook had ever, ever gotten it on *once* in their whole dreary academic lives.

Thinking about sex made Sam think about Heather. Heather was gorgeous. Heather was willing. Heather was sexy. All his friends envied him. But Sam couldn't help it: He wanted Gaia. Tall, beautiful Gaia, who didn't have as much fashion sense in her whole body as Heather had in her pinky. But it didn't matter. His entire being cried out for Gaia.

"Moon Man." One of his suitemates, Mike Suarez, whacked him on the shoulder with a dog-eared copy of *Time* magazine.

Sam jumped. "Hey," he said. "What's up?"

Mike sank down into the chair across from Sam's. He kept his voice down. "You gonna use your meal card tonight?"

The question was so random that Sam couldn't even wrap his mind around it. "Uh . . ."

"I'm broke, lost my card, thought if you had other plans for dinner, I could use your meal card tonight."

Sam fished out his wallet and threw the meal card to Mike. "Take it."

"Whoa, thanks, man. I'm gettin' a new card soon." Mike shuffled to his feet, huge, battered sneakers flapping as he left. He needed to replace the duct tape holding them together. All the snow was making it unravel.

"Yeah, whatever," Sam said. He stood up, stretched again. God, what day was it? Wednesday? Thursday? Had it been only Sunday night, New Year's Eve, that he'd finally had a chance with the object of his obsession? And he had run out on her. He had taken one look at her stepmother and realized she was the same woman he'd slept with the night before.

New Year's Eve. The new year. Resolutions. He had resolved to get better grades this semester. Had resolved never to eat onion bagels with scallion cream cheese. For that matter, he had resolved never to drink tequila shots with Josh again. Maybe he needed to make some resolutions about his warped love life.

For one thing, he should break it off with Heather once and for all. They had little fights, they both cooled down, they drifted back together and back into bed again. Then it would start over.

If he didn't get the balls to really break up with her soon, she probably never would, either. He wasn't blind. He knew it was a big prestige thing for her to have a college boyfriend. And she probably cared for him. If he didn't break up with her, they would just drift along in this lame-ass way, neither of them happy, until finally *boom.* They'd be standing at the altar, pledging to go through with this sitcom for life. He couldn't let that happen. He was a man. A man had balls. He would find the balls to break up with Heather.

Then maybe he could pursue Gaia the way he wanted to: urgently, relentlessly, determinedly. He could wear her down. He knew it. He would overwhelm her with his love. She would soften toward him. Forget his past mistakes. Fall in love with him. And they would be together and stay together. Sam smiled at this image.

Mindlessly his gaze drifted down to the text page before him. It was almost a full-page, head-on photo titled "A Male's Reproductive Organs (the Nonexcited State)." Sam stared at it blankly. *Oh, right,* he thought. *Balls.*

ED BANGS HIS HEAD AGAINST THE WALL

"I'll go with you."

Gaia's eyes narrowed as she looked at Ed. She leaned back enough to shut her locker door, then dropped her bag to the floor so she could put on her ski jacket. A few limp, grayish feathers leaked out through its hole and fluttered to the ground.

"No, thanks," she said, trying not to sound like a complete bitch and not quite succeeding. "I think I'll just go do it. Mr. MacGregor's on my back about this paper, and I need to knock it out. I can't study on Perry Street—that woman is always on my case about something. A couple of hours at the NYU library ought to do it." Picking up her bag, she slung it over one shoulder and jerked her hair out from beneath the strap.

Ed's wheelchair blocked her way. "What is *with* you?"

Forcing her face to remain calm, Gaia said, "What?" She could see the frustration and uncertainty on his face, and she wished it weren't there. But what could she say to him? *I'm sorry, Ed, but I don't want you to come with me because I will probably get you killed and because I'm going to swing by the park first and if I see Skizz, I plan to kill him, and I don't want you to know that about me?*

"The way you're acting." Ed's arms made choppy movements in the air as he struggled to express himself. "I mean, I need to talk to you, you know? We lost a good friend. I feel like I need some help here, and I want to help you, too. Last night I reached for the phone twice to call Mary to see what was up, then I realized . . . Look, this is a hard time for you—for me, too. But you just keep acting like I should go screw myself."

"I know this is a hard tune," Gaia said. "And I'm not telling you to go screw yourself. But I have this paper due. I'm tired of all the teachers getting on my case. I just want to do some stuff, get them off my back. I'm sorry if that's inconveniencing you."

Dark brown eyes bored into her blue ones. "Gaia . . ."

"Gotta go," Gaia said briskly. "Bye." She made a quick pivot around his wheelchair and strode toward the east side entrance of their high school. The one with stairs. The one Ed couldn't follow her out of. She could feel him watching her. It didn't matter. It didn't matter. It didn't matter.

GIRL, 17, SLAIN IN PARK

"Moon Man. Come on." Keon Walters gestured toward the tiny black-and-white TV perched on Mike's footlocker. "We're talking national play-offs here."

By squinting, Sam could just make out minuscule football

players moving toward each other through the thick snow on the screen. A bent wire coat hanger was stuck into the antenna outlet, and Mike was standing behind it, maneuvering it in tiny increments to get a better picture.

"There! Right there, man," said Keon.

"I can't, guys," Sam said. "I've got to review some of this comparative anatomy stuff."

"Oh, is Heather coming over?" Mike asked innocently. Keon snorted.

"Ooh, Heather, baby," Keon said, scrunching up his lips to make a kissy face.

"Yeah, yeah," said Sam, heading out the door.

He was near the staircase at the end of the hall when a door opened and Sherri Banks stepped out, holding a stack of newspapers. "Oh, hey, Sam. Where you headed?"

"To the library. What about you?" Sam asked, pulling on his jacket.

"I was just running down to the recycling bin. Actually, since it's on your way, would you mind taking these down for me?" Sherri asked, holding out the newspapers.

"Yeah, sure," said Sam, taking them.

"Thanks!" Sherri disappeared behind her door, muffling the sounds of Smash Mouth that had been drifting out behind her.

Sam trotted down the four flights of stairs, then headed to the big recycling bins in a small room off the dorm lobby.

He threw Sherri's newspapers into the paper bin. A headline on the top sheet caught his eye.

Girl, 17, Slain in Park

Instinctively Sam grabbed the paper and scanned it rapidly. *Oh my God.* Goose bumps tightened the skin on his arms, legs, the back of his neck. "Mary Catherine Moss, age seventeen, was killed on New Year's Eve in Washington Square Park in what was an apparent drug hit," the article read. Sam devoured the details. No suspect as yet; police following leads. Young girl—only witness, tall, blond hair, wishes to remain anonymous—questioned at the scene.

Mary. Gaia. Sam was supposed to go out with them on New Year's. Then he'd shown up at Gaia's, seen Ella Niven, and totally lost it. He'd fled the scene like a frightened rabbit. So Gaia and Mary had gone out without him. And Mary had gotten killed. And Gaia had been there.

Sam reread the article, leaning against the cinder-block wall. *Oh my God.* Mary was dead. Mary had been one of Gaia's best friends, along with Ed Fargo, Heather's ex. Gaia had seen her best friend killed right in front of her! And it was Sam's fault. If he had been with them—if he hadn't stood Gaia up—they might not have been in Washington Square. Or the killer might have seen Sam and left them alone.

He had to talk to Gaia right away.

MUGGING IS A BIG NO-NO

"Umph." Gaia couldn't restrain the involuntary grunt of pleasure as she bit into her hot German sausage. Only one street cart she knew sold real German sausages, and man, they were killer. Well worth a detour anytime, even though it meant getting a bit of a late start on her *Faerie Queene* paper for Mr. MacGregor's Brit lit class.

It was dark now, or as dark as it got in Manhattan, what with streetlights, traffic lights, building lights. Gaia was taking a shortcut down Great Jones Street, heading for the NYU library. The street was cobbled, the sidewalks accessorized by shiny black piles of garbage bags. One really good thing about winter, Gaia mused as she chomped, was that the trash froze, eliminating a lot of the smell.

Taking another bite, Gaia remembered how Mary had introduced her to knishes a few weeks ago. Mary had grown up in Manhattan and was on intimate terms with every street-food vendor around. When Gaia had taken her first bite of a knish smeared with yellow mustard, Mary had laughed at the wondrous expression on her face.

Suddenly Gaia had an instantaneous prickle of awareness. Without even thinking, she quickly stepped away from the curb. The next moment she heard the distinct whir of a bicycle's wheels. Then she felt someone grab her bag and yank, hard. If her preternaturally acute senses hadn't told her to sidestep, this jerk would have knocked her down with his bike. As it was, he was almost pulled off balance as he pulled on her strap.

In an instant all her reflexes were on full alert, her muscles pumped and ready for action. Her right hand clamped around the strap of her bag, hoping it would hold. She gave a sharp pull, and the biker swung in a large, wobbly arc around her, trying to steer, pedal, and pull her bag away at the same time.

Gaia chewed quickly, swallowing bits of sausage.

"Let go!" the biker shouted. "I'll kill you!"

"You idiot," Gaia muttered. Using both hands, she swung her pack out and around, forcing the biker's front wheel to smash against the high stone curb.

He let out a confused yelp, pitching headfirst over the handlebars and onto the sidewalk. Amazingly, he hadn't let go of the bag. Gaia was bent over, the strap pulling heavily through her jacket. She took a big step forward and stomped on the biker's hand, pinning it to the sidewalk.

"This . . . doesn't . . . belong . . . to . . . you," Gaia said slowly and carefully, punctuating her words by leaning on his hand. The biker's face was contorted with pain, and his other hand scrabbled at her ankle, gripping her pants with his fingers.

Bending down, Gaia gave him a swift upper cut to the

nose, putting enough power in it to snap back his head and make his hand finally release her pack. Stepping back quickly, Gaia straightened and pulled the bag onto her shoulder with both straps. Her breathing had scarcely altered, but her senses were humming: She could smell his stale sweat through his cheap jacket, smell the tangy, coppery scent of the blood trickling from his nose. Bright red blood. The night air felt cold and crisp and seemed to sharpen her vision.

The biker scrambled back to his bike just as Gaia reached it. She anchored her body weight, then spun in a quick, smooth roundhouse kick that knocked him backward onto the sidewalk. He lay there awkwardly for a moment, like an upended turtle. By the time he'd crawled to his feet, Gaia had kicked out several spokes on his front wheel.

"You bitch!" he screamed, coming at her again. Almost effortlessly she grabbed his hand and twisted it back, forcing him to his knees.

"Mugging is bad." Gaia's voice, unnaturally steely, cut through the mugger's cries. "People don't like being mugged. You got it?"

The biker whimpered as she slowly pulled back on his arm. "Got it!" he finally screeched.

Suddenly she let him go. He crumpled to the sidewalk. "You bitch," he croaked.

"You started it," Gaia snapped childishly. She headed down the sidewalk, leaving the mugger behind as she had left

Ed behind several hours earlier. She walked quickly, wanting to put as much distance between her and the biker before the familiar lethargy hit her. With great luck, she was almost two blocks away and right in front of a lighted bus stop with a bench when the weakness overwhelmed her, making her knees give out. She sank down on the bench next to an older, bundled-up black woman who gave her a disgusted look. Maybe she thought Gaia was on drugs.

Gaia leaned against the clear Plexiglas bus shelter, feeling all sensation pool in her feet like they weighed a thousand pounds each. A few moments later the bus pulled up and the woman got on, shooting Gaia another angry look. Gaia almost laughed.

After a few minutes Gaia felt the return of nerves, of muscle strength. She mentally checked herself out: All systems were go. The NYU library was just another two blocks to the west, on West Fourth Street, facing Washington Square. Gaia decided to find a library seat where she would have a view of the park through a picture window. Who knew? Maybe she would see Skizz slinking into the park.

Every time she thought of Skizz, an odd trickle of sensation crept up her spine. In her short life she had beaten some losers senseless. She had sometimes even enjoyed the physical and mental challenge that a closely matched fight presented. But this was different. There was no turning back from murder.

Gaia's thoughts turned to the guy who had killed Mary. The one who had actually pulled the trigger. Now, *there* had been a closely matched fight. He had been unusual, Gaia thought as the NYU library loomed ahead of her. Most people she fought were pathetic, unschooled, unskilled—sitting ducks compared to her, with her finely honed reflexes, supernatural strength, years of training, and lightning-fast reaction times. But that guy—he had been different. He had been as good as she was. Maybe better. It was the first time she had met someone like that. Besides her father, that was.

Inside the library Gaia flashed her Village School ID. The guard nodded, bored, and let her through the turnstile. There was a bank of computers in the right-hand reading room. Gaia headed there. The computers had access to both the Internet and the library's card catalog. It would be a good place to start. And the reading room had a view of the park.

In the room, bright fluorescent lights made everything look sort of washed out and off register, made the students look even more pasty faced and hollow eyed.

Now Gaia needed a chair that faced the doorway. It was a habit she'd picked up from her father. There was an easy chair with a view of the window, but it was mostly hidden behind a scratched Formica end table with a depressed-looking philodendron on it. Gaia headed toward it, automatically checking out the scene for weird vibes, possible sources of danger, likely escape routes. It was something she did without thinking, almost without being aware of it. Even in an innocuous place like a library.

As she glanced around, she became aware of someone watching her—and a moment later she found herself staring into a pair of beautiful, startled hazel eyes. It took her brain less than a thousandth of a second to register why those eyes looked familiar. They belonged to Sam Moon.

THIS IS MRS. MOSS

"I'll get it, darling," George Niven called. There was a muffled reply from Ella as George headed into the study to grab the phone.

"Hello?"

"Hello. This is Patricia Moss," said an unfamiliar voice. "Mary's mother."

George had a sinking feeling. He'd seen the article in the newspaper. He'd only noticed it because of the headline, GIRL, 17, SLAIN IN PARK. Then he'd scanned the paragraph and recognized Mary's name. It was more than strange that Gaia hadn't mentioned anything to him or Ella. His knuckles tightened on the phone. "This is George Niven," he responded. "Gaia's guardian. Let me say that I'm so very sorry about your loss."

A hesitation. "Thank you. This is a very difficult time for us." Her voice broke. "I know Gaia must be extremely upset. I wanted to tell her that if she would like to come be with our family during this time, she's more than welcome."

"Thank you," said George. "I'll be sure to tell her."

"I also have a favor to ask her," continued Mary's mother. "But I'll wait until I speak to her. If you could ask Gaia to call me."

"Of course," said George. "I'll see that she does. Take care, and please let us know if there's anything my wife and I can do to help."

"Thank you," Patricia Moss whispered hoarsely, then hung up.

George replaced the receiver and rubbed his chin thoughtfully. He hadn't seen Gaia much lately. He'd promised Tom to keep closer tabs on her, but agency work kept him away most of the time. When he *had* seen Gaia, he hadn't noticed any signs of grief. Mrs. Moss had assumed he knew about Mary's death, and he had, but not because of anything Gaia had said. This whole thing was getting so much more complicated than he had expected. He loved Tom Moore like a brother and would do anything for him. He'd jumped at the chance to take Gaia in, shepherd her through her last years of high school. But it was all getting so complex.

The study door swung open, and Ella came in, holding out a cut-glass tumbler full of scotch and water.

"Thank you, darling," said George.

"What's wrong, honey?" Ella asked. She smoothed her fluffy, chartreuse wool sweater down over her full breasts and tugged it down on her waist. Then she curled up on the leather sofa, one leopard-print leg coiled beneath her.

"That was the mother of a friend of Gaia's," said George, taking a sip of his drink. He hid his recoil at its bitter taste. Everything tasted bitter to him these days. Ella, considerable though her charms were, had never been a cook. Last night she had made a risotto that had tasted so awful, she herself hadn't been able to eat it. Still, she'd looked pleased when he'd managed to choke down half a plateful.

"Is everything all right?" Ella's remarkable green eyes opened wide in concern.

"You know that article I showed you in the paper earlier? About Gaia's friend, Mary Moss, being killed on Sunday night?" said George. "Mary's mother wants to talk to Gaia. She knows she must be pretty upset." He looked at his wife to confirm the unstated question.

Carefully arched auburn brows drew delicately together. "Upset?" Ella said musingly. "I haven't really seen it. You know what Gaia's like. But since Sunday—no, I have to say she hasn't seemed upset. Are you sure she knows? Maybe she thinks her friend's just out sick or something."

"Mary's mother seems certain Gaia knows," George said, frowning in concern. "Poor Gaia. She must be keeping it all bottled up inside."

Ella made a *tsk, tsk* sound. "That's dreadful. I feel so sorry for Mrs. Moss. And poor Gaia. No wonder she's been so . . . *difficult* lately."

George nodded. Ella pushed her mane of tangled red curls over her shoulders. She gave him an inviting smile. George felt the quickening of his body. His wife lay back against the leather couch, her hair floating out behind her like sea coral. She held out one slim white hand. He moved toward her.

HEATHER

I am not the type of girl who has to wait around, hoping for the phone to ring. I mean, I never have been. Ever since I was thirteen, guys have been asking me out, and it's always been easy come, easy go. Except for Ed. I really did love him. He was like my soul mate. Until the accident.

The accident changed both of us so much, split us apart. It wasn't like I dumped him just because he couldn't walk anymore. It was so much bigger than that. I mean, I was almost sixteen—I had the whole rest of my life ahead of me. And Ed hated what had happened. He hated himself—the new postaccident self, that is. And it got so he hated me, too.

Which is why I'm psyched about us maybe being friends again now. We went bowling not long ago, and it was so fun. Being with him is easy, uncomplicated, light. Not like being with Sam.

Yeah, Ed's still in a wheelchair. And I can't say he's the same old guy. He's harder now, not as sweet or eager to please me. And there's something else, too, some other layer to him. He's not just good-time Shred anymore. He's a little more than that now. I don't know how to explain it.

Maybe he's just older.

NOT LONGING. NOT LOVE.

HE WOULD BE LYING THERE, FLATTER THAN A PANCAKE BUT STILL SOMEHOW LOOKING GOOD.

Okay, I'm a modern woman, Heather thought. *I can express my needs. Right now I need a boyfriend who adores me.*

Heather picked up the receiver and punched in memory dial #1. On the other end the phone in Sam's dorm suite rang and rang. "Pick it up," Heather said softly. "Pick it up. Be there."

Things with Sam had been weird for too long. If she left it up to him, they would just drift along like this forever. It was time to put her Reclaim Sam plan into action.

Last summer things had been so great. She and Sam had had such a good time. They had gone to movies, gone dancing, hung out with friends. They'd slept in the same bed a few times but hadn't had sex. She hadn't been ready then.

Now she was ready. Because when she and Sam were making love, she could forget about everything else for a while. Forget about Gaia, forget about Ed, forget about her family.

"Hello?" a voice answered at the other end of the line.

Heather instantly assessed it as a non-Sam voice.

"Hi. This is Heather," she said.

"Hey, Heather. It's Mike."

"Hi, Mike. Listen, is Sam there?"

"Nope, sorry," said Mike. "He's wearing out the study

chairs over at the library. His dad had his hide over Christmas because of his grades."

"Yeah, I know," said Heather. "So he's at the library?"

"Yep. I'll tell him you called, okay?"

"Okay." Heather hung up the phone. So Sam was studying at the library. He wasn't somewhere with someone else. Like Gaia. As soon as the thought intruded, Heather quickly shut it out. God, if only Gaia would disappear. Heather's life would be almost bearable again. For Heather, Gaia's existence was like getting clubbed on the head constantly and still trying to go around and live a normal life.

Hmmm. With Sam unavailable, Heather had to move to plan B: be busy, be popular. Then when Sam called, *she* would be out. Everyone knew that guys always liked girls who seemed a tiny bit out of reach.

Heather scrambled off her bed. Though NYU students were already back at school, her sister Phoebe wasn't due back at SUNY Binghamton for another ten days. It was fun having Phoebe around. She was the coolest, even though she and Heather had had their differences in the past. But Phoebe had been really happy lately and really sweet to Heather. Maybe she'd be into catching an early movie at the Angelika or something. A sisterly thing.

A bathroom connected Heather and Phoebe's bedrooms, and Heather heard the shower water shut off. She gave the door a brief tap and opened it.

"Hey, Feeb, I have a great idea," Heather began.

Phoebe had just stepped out of the shower and was reaching for a fluffy gold towel. It took only moments for Heather's gaze to sweep her sister's body. She blinked as Phoebe quickly wrapped herself in the towel, brushing long, wet strands of hair out of the way.

"Whoa," Heather said without thinking. "You're . . . really skinny."

"Really skinny" didn't begin to describe what Heather had caught a glimpse of. She knew Phoebe had been dieting a lot—an attempt to get rid of the freshman fifteen she'd put on last semester. But until now she'd simply thought Phoebe looked fabulous, model slim in her bulky winter clothes. Naked, Phoebe looked like something else. Heather could see Phoebe's ribs, her hipbones. Phoebe was much too thin.

Phoebe briskly started toweling her hair. "Thanks," she said.

Heather looked closely. Her sister's skin seemed stretched over her facial bones. Her eyes looked deep set, her cheekbones carved and prominent.

Without makeup her sister looked pale, anemic, underfed. With makeup, Heather knew, Phoebe looked stunning.

Bending over, Phoebe combed her hair out with her fingers, then expertly wrapped a towel around her head. One, two, three . . . Heather counted the knobby vertebrae on Phoebe's back.

"Um, do you think maybe you're a tiny bit *too* thin?" Heather asked.

Phoebe stood up and tucked in the towel ends. She smiled at Heather.

"Heath-er," Phoebe said in an older-sister singsong. "I'm not dieting anymore. I'm just watching my weight. Trying not to go overboard. You wouldn't believe how awful it was when I put on all that weight at school. It was like, I couldn't button anything. I was practically a size nine! I'm never going there again, let me tell you."

Phoebe turned away from Heather and went into her own room but didn't start getting dressed. *She's waiting for me to leave her alone,* Heather thought.

"No kidding, Feeb," Heather said, moving into Phoebe's room. "Maybe you don't want to be a size nine. But you don't want to be a size zero, either. I think you could lighten up on the diet, maybe even put on a few pounds."

"Oh, no way," said Phoebe, sounding irritated. "My body is finally the way I want it. No way am I going to sabotage it now." Her eyebrows came together, and she looked at Heather with narrowed eyes. "You know, maybe you're just jealous because I'm where you want to be." Phoebe turned her back on Heather and opened her closet door. "Okay, clear out. I have to get dressed."

It was a dismissal, and Heather cleared out.

GLORIOUS, LIVING COLOR

Sam's first thought on seeing Gaia was that his sheer longing to see her had somehow made her materialize in front of him. He'd tried to call her from the dorm lobby, but Ella had answered, and he'd hung up. He'd decided to head to the library, keep trying to call, and maybe later go over to her house and—this was where the plan got fuzzy. Throw rocks at her window? Lie in wait for her all night? Now here she was, right in front of him, in glorious, living color.

Looking at her, at her beautiful, solemn face, he felt like all of his fantasies had been fulfilled. In that one split second he imagined that yes, Gaia loved him, yes, Gaia had come to find him, yes, they were going to be together forever, just the two of them. . . .

Then he saw the cold, forbidding look in her eyes, mingled with a flash of surprise and something else? Not longing. Not love. What? He couldn't tell.

As she stood there, seemingly frozen, her deep, ocean blue eyes locked on to his, Sam got up slowly from his chair.

He walked toward her. He didn't think about the boyfriend Ella had told him Gaia had. He didn't remember that Gaia had never acknowledged the gift he had given her—a finely carved wooden chess set in a small red box. He didn't remember that he had sent her e-mails that she never answered.

All he knew was that her best friend had died, that he had let her down, that she must be hurting. That possibly she hated him.

Sam swallowed dryly, forcing himself to remain calm. As he approached her, Gaia turned and headed to a chair over by the window. She set down her black nylon bag. His gaze focused on her strong, beautifully shaped hands. Her knuckles were scraped, and the blood looked fresh.

Sam felt hyperaware, like he and Gaia were suspended together in a time warp. He could hear her unzip her bag. Hear the chair cushion rustle as she sat down. Hear her click open her pen.

He took a couple of deep, calming breaths. "Gaia," he said, his voice sounding unnaturally loud in the library's silence.

She froze again, then slowly, deliberately turned her head to gaze up at him.

He steeled himself against the coolness in her expression. "I just found out about Mary," he said in a blunt whisper.

Her delicate brows drew together, and her eyes widened. He saw her swallow, then glance away from him.

"I'm so sorry," he said softly, sinking to a crouch next to her chair. "I didn't know until an hour ago." He shook his head. "I can't even imagine what you're going through. I wish I'd known. I wish I'd been there."

Now she was actively glaring at him.

Sam floundered, not knowing what else to say. *I love you? I'm sorry? I made a huge mistake?*

"Did you . . . was there a service for her?" he asked.

If he didn't know better, he would swear that Gaia had just flinched. But she wasn't a flinchy sort of girl.

"I don't want to talk about it," Gaia said.

Sam held up his hands. "I understand. I know you must be . . . Well, it's a tragic thing to happen. I just can't believe it. And you guys seemed like really good friends."

Gaia's jaw clenched, and Sam felt like he was drowning. If she burst into tears right now, he would sort of know how to deal with it. Hold her close, pat her back, stroke her hair, murmur soothing words. But she was just looking at him steadily, as if he were a microbe. An interesting microbe, perhaps, but a microbe.

Sam took a deep breath and surged forward. "When I first read about Mary in the newspaper and realized what night it was, I was just so shocked," he blathered on. "I feel like it's my fault because I wasn't . . . wasn't there. I've been wanting to talk to you about that, about that night, why I left—I just—I um . . ."

"You think it was *your* fault?" Gaia said. He picked up on the anger in her voice.

"Well, because I was supposed to be with you guys on New Year's," Sam said. "And . . . I'm so sorry I wasn't. I shouldn't have left. Maybe if I hadn't, Mary wouldn't have . . . died."

"So *you* could have stopped it," Gaia said sarcastically. She was keeping her voice down, but people still turned their heads to look at them. "The mighty Sam," Gaia continued. "The wonderful Sam. Everything revolves around Sam."

"I didn't say that," Sam said, feeling defensive. "I just meant—"

"You know, Sam," Gaia interrupted coldly, "I hate to tell you this, but this isn't about *you*. This isn't about how *you're* sorry. How *you* could have prevented it. How everything would be perfect if only *you* were there. The fact is, you *weren't* there. I don't care why. But you weren't, and as far as I'm concerned, it doesn't matter if you're ever there *again*. Now, if you don't mind, I came here to *study*!" She leaned forward and hissed the last word. It felt like a slap in the face, and Sam recoiled.

He started to speak again, but she fixed him with a glare so fierce, his face felt sunburned. Feeling like a total and complete ass, he rose to his feet, backed away from her, and slumped back in his own chair.

That had gone well. He reviewed what he had said, and it seemed not too bad. Gaia had deliberately twisted his words. Okay, she was angry at him. That much was clear. She must be superupset about Mary. Too upset to let him comfort her. Too upset to forgive him for letting her down.

Sam sat, smoldering, in his library chair. Having Gaia ignore him so steadily was like having a weight on his chest.

But he wouldn't give her an easy out. He was going to sit right here until he had reviewed his comp anat notes, and if that made her uncomfortable, it was too bad. Maybe she would even relent. Maybe he might possibly get another chance.

Did she remember that one amazing night when he had come home to his dorm room to find her asleep in his bed, wearing only his tank top and a pair of his boxers? Every detail of that night was burned into his memory.

Sam shifted uncomfortably in his library chair. *Don't go there,* he warned himself. But it was too late. His lips tingled as he remembered what it had felt like to finally kiss Gaia, hold her tightly, tell her he loved her.

Sam stared blankly at his notebook. Minutes passed. Minutes during which Sam wondered if it was possible to redeem himself in Gaia's eyes. Make her care about him. Make her see how much he cared about her.

In a wild fantasy he thought about running upstairs to the tenth floor of the library and flinging himself through the glass partition. *That* would get her attention. He would plummet down, down, down and land with a satisfying, final splat on the marble tumbling-block pattern of the library floor. He would be lying there, flatter than a pancake but still somehow looking good. Gaia, realizing that nothing mattered but their love, would rush over and kneel by him, holding his hand to her breast while tears slowly seeped out of her beautiful eyes.

"I'm sorry," he would whisper with his last breath. "I'm a dumb-ass, but I love you." No, scratch the dumb-ass part. He would come up with something better. "I didn't mean to be an asshole," or something like that. She would forgive him. She would lean over him, her soft breath fanning his face. Her soft, full lips would gently, so gently touch his. . . .

Sam realized he was breathing quickly. His hazel eyes pulled into focus. *Get a grip.* He licked his lips, glad that his face, which felt hot, was looking downward. Okay, he would let Gaia be furious with him for now. But soon he would get her to forgive him. Right after he broke up with Heather.

COME ON, COME ON

Wheeling up to Gaia's front door, Ed felt his pulse quicken. *Come on, come on,* he urged silently. *Please be home, Gaia. Let me in.* He pressed the doorbell.

It was almost ten. Which was no guarantee that Gaia would be home from the library, if that's where she had really gone. If her guardians, her foster parents, cared where she was and when, Gaia sure didn't let it hamper her. But Ed had thought he would give it one more Boy Scout try. He just had to talk to her, had to get through to her somehow. He knew she was hurting. He was hurting, too. And the only person he really wanted to talk to about it was Gaia. Obviously they should be taking care of each other during this nightmare. So why was Gaia making him do this alone? Why wasn't she coming to him so they could help each other? He had to make her see that she could lean on him. Even if she had to bend down to do it.

George Niven opened the door. "Hello—Ed, is it? What can I do for you? It's kind of late for a school night, isn't it?"

"Yes, I'm sorry about that," said Ed, using his best speaking-to-parents voice. The one that had always worked on the Gannises. "I hope I didn't disturb you." He noted that Mr. Niven was wearing his bathrobe.

"Oh, no, it's okay," said Mr. Niven.

"Is Gaia home?" Ed asked.

A pained expression crossed Mr. Niven's face. "No, Ed, I'm sorry. She hasn't been here since this morning. My wife says she mentioned going to the library, but I'm afraid that Gaia doesn't always leave an itinerary with us." He looked embarrassed, as if he should be doing a better job of keeping tabs on her. *Good luck,* Ed thought cynically.

"Oh, well," he said. Another wasted trip in the freezing night air.

"Listen, Ed," said Mr. Niven. Ed looked up. "Did you know Gaia's friend who was killed? Mary Moss?"

Ed felt a fresh stab of pain. "Yeah. We were good friends."

"I'm sorry. It's a terrible thing," said Mr. Niven. "Is Gaia . . . Does she seem very upset about it?" He looked concerned.

For a moment Ed thought about how Gaia had been ever since Sunday night. "Oh, who knows?" he answered disgustedly. "Sorry to bother you. Good night." He spun on his wheels and headed down the block quickly.

He'd come all this way for nothing. His mom had asked him to run out to the bodega and get a quart of milk and a newspaper. He'd used the opportunity to come way over here to the West Village. The plan was to tell his mom that the store had been out, and he'd had to go up practically to Twelfth Street.

Gaia, where are you? he wailed silently as he headed east on Bleecker Street. *Don't you need a friend? Don't you need me? Aren't I the only friend you have?* Rhythmically Ed's hands slapped against the wheels, keeping him moving forward.

Making a split decision, Ed turned at the next corner and began the long, zigzagging route over to West Fourth Street. That would take him to Washington Square Park. He could pass through the park quickly on his way home. He could peek into the library. Maybe Gaia was even *in* the park, having a freezing-cold late night game of chess with Zolov.

Ed was breathing hard when he got to the park. His lungs

were burning from pulling in the cold night air again and again. His shoulders were tired, and his hands felt like they were frozen into claws. If his parents knew he was here alone at this time of night, they would kill him. Twice.

Suddenly something ahead of him made Ed stop dead in his tracks. His stomach lurched as his wheelchair jerked forward.

Oh.

The scene was no longer marked by crime scene tape, and the chalk outline where Mary's body had fallen had been erased by people's feet and snow. But on the cobbled pavers, Ed could detect a faint dark stain. Mary's blood.

Ed's breathing quickened as he stared at the mark. Was this all Mary's life amounted to now? A stain on the pavement? His chest constricted at the thought.

Almost simultaneously a light-colored flash caught the corner of his eye. Startled, Ed peered into the darkness of the shadows beneath the trees. There it was again. Moving away from him. A million women in the world had blond hair, but somehow Ed knew instantly who that particular blond head belonged to.

He spun to the right, whipping down the path, and managed to intersect with Gaia just as she was emerging from the trees' shadows onto the path again. They almost collided as Ed yanked his chair to a stop in front of her.

"Hey!" She backed up, startled. "Ed!"

"Gaia, what are you doing here?" Ed demanded stupidly, momentarily forgetting that he had *expected* to find Gaia here. "I just stopped by your house—they said you were at the library. . . ." His voice trailed off as he took in the conflicting emotions crossing her face. Four months ago he would have said Gaia's two main emotions were impatience and irritation, but he knew her slightly better now. He was seeing confusion and almost—could it be?—embarrassment. Discomfort. She looked away from him, as if thinking of a story to tell him.

"Gaia," Ed said again, this time more deliberately, suspiciously. "What are you really doing out here?"

She faced him defiantly. "I *was* at the library. It's right over there, remember? What are *you* doing here?"

"I went out to get milk for my mom," Ed said. "I went over to your house. I've been worried about you. I've wanted to talk to you. I was almost home," he recited, when I just found myself coming here." He shrugged. "This is where it happened." For a split second Gaia appeared to soften a little.

"I had no idea seeing this would make me feel this way. I don't know." Ed looked at her, his dark brown eyes meeting her blue ones. "Maybe I somehow *meant* to see it. You know, to help me deal with things. But that's not what *you're* doing here, is it?"

"Why not?" Gaia said.

"Because you look weird," Ed said flatly. "Because you've been *acting* weird."

"Thanks," Gaia said snidely. "I already said I was at the library. I decided to hang out here for a while and get some fresh air on my way back to Perry Street."

Ed's brain started humming. Obviously Washington Square Park was on the way between the NYU library and Gaia's brownstone. But he knew she was lying. During the time he had known her, she had *always* been evasive and tight-lipped. But as far as he knew, she had never lied to him before. This was a first.

Gaia shifted her weight from foot to foot as she stood in front of him. She grew visibly impatient. "Well, gotta go," she said, turning.

"Wait!" Ed's voice came out louder than he intended. "I know what you're doing here."

She turned as gracefully as a gazelle wearing construction boots. "Oh, really?"

"You're looking for Skizz." Ed's skin felt tight as he said it. The thought had just popped into his brain, and he wasn't sure where it had come from. But as soon as it left his lips, he knew it was true. He could tell by the wild, wary look that flashed in Gaia's eyes, the sudden tightening of the line of her body. The way her hand tensed on the strap of her bag. Her knuckles, he noticed, were grazed and raw.

Then Gaia relaxed. Her face became a careful mask. "I wanted to ask him some questions."

Another lie. Ed saw it as clearly as if a neon sign had lit

up over her head. Was this Gaia, the person who had been his closest friend for the last four months? Was this the same girl he longed for with an almost frightening intensity?

Yes. It was.

"That's not true," Ed said evenly, looking into Gaia's eyes. "You're looking for Skizz, and it isn't to ask him some questions."

"Well, don't worry about it," Gaia said. She looked around with studied casualness. She shifted her feet. Obviously she wanted him gone.

Ed suddenly felt afraid. Afraid for Gaia, afraid *of* Gaia.

"Look, let's go get a cup of coffee," he said. "Let's get out of here."

Gaia looked at the ground, scuffing her boots against the cobblestones.

"Gaia, come on," Ed said. "You don't want to be here."

"You don't know anything about what I want."

When he looked into her face, he didn't recognize her. "Please, Gaia. Come on. Don't do this." Whatever "this" was.

"Just leave me alone!" she snapped, and she whirled and disappeared into the darkness without a sound.

A cold feeling of dread settled over Ed's heart as he stared blankly at the spot where she had stood moments before.

GAIA

Last night I did the strangest thing. It was after Ed found me in Washington Square Park. I was freaking and didn't know what to do. So I headed up St. Mark's Place and ducked into a thrift shop for a few minutes, trying to get my act together. Then I looked out the plate glass window, and right across the street was this old, crumbly, odd-looking church.

I crossed the street and read its sign. It was a Russian Orthodox church. Is that bizarre or what? Only in New York.

Anyway, I went up the steps and tried one of the heavy wooden doors. There was graffiti sprayed onto the front of the building. Gang signs. But the door opened. Inside, it was cool and dim and smelled heavily of incense. I haven't been inside many churches in my life, but here I was, just a few minutes after I had been in the park planning to murder someone. I felt like I was in an episode of *The X-Files.*

There were people up by the altar, polishing brass candlesticks, and someone running a vacuum on the worn red carpet. There were no pews, so I leaned against a cool stone column for a while. It was strange, being inside that church, so late at night. So quiet, so peaceful. So different from the things going on inside my head.

Don't get me wrong, I'm not much of a believer. But right then and there, for some reason, I said a prayer for forgiveness.

KIND OF AN ASSHOLE

HE WAS STILL SHOCKED WHEN THE FIRST
THIN THREADS OF PAIN REGISTERED IN HIS BRAIN . . .

ED'S GOING DOWN

Note to Myself: Scratch being an undercover agent as a possible career. Not only is a guy in a wheelchair kind of hard to disguise, but he's also so freaking slow!

Ed paused at the corner of Broadway and Waverly Place, his hot go-cup of latte perched in the screw-on armrest cup holder his aunt had given him for Christmas. Where had she gotten it? he wondered. Wheelchairs R Us ? He had to admit it came in handy.

When the light turned green, Ed spun his wheels, moving aggressively through the crowd. He knew people usually didn't mind being bumped by a cripple in a chair. They would turn around, ready to glare, ready to curse him out, then catch sight of him. Seeing a young man in a wheelchair usually calmed them right down.

Gaia had managed to completely give him the slip again after school. They had eaten lunch together like two chewing statues. She hadn't even bothered making an excuse as to why she'd split on him last night or why they couldn't get together tonight, a Friday night.

Now, as Ed bumped up the handicapped-accessible sidewalk ramp, he remembered how tired Gaia had looked. Her nose had been running, and she'd wiped it on her sleeve. He knew without a doubt that she had been out late, in the cold, hunting Skizz, but somehow the crowded cafeteria of the Village School hadn't seemed like the best place to confront her.

Ed was pretty much at the end of his rope with Gaia. It had been five long days since Mary's death, and Gaia had hardly said more than three sentences to him. Then last night had been so weird. What was she thinking? What was she planning? He had to know. Which was why he had already checked the Starbucks on Astor Place and made a complete circuit of Washington Square Park. No Gaia. His arms and shoulders were going to look like Hulk Hogan's if he kept getting these kinds of workouts.

Now he was going to hit Tompkins Square Park. The whole idea of Gaia lying in wait for Skizz made his blood run cold. She'd already beaten the crap out of Skizz once. What else could she do?

Ed was tired. He was three blocks from the park. He took a sip of his coffee, enjoying the way the warmth seeped down through his esophagus and pooled in his stomach.

"Hey!" he cried angrily as a hand sharply knocked his coffee away. Instinctively he grabbed his wheels, only to be stopped by a long, wavy knife blade shoved under his nose. He could feel the sharp edge, cold against his skin.

"Don't move."

Oh shit.

His attacker wasn't that big, just a young street kid of indeterminate age and race, his hair wrapped up in a bandanna.

There was a small, homemade-looking tattoo of a sun right in the middle of his forehead. His upper lip had dark, downy fuzz, and small, unevenly mowed tufts of stubble blotched his chin.

"Gimme your money." The command was quiet but had an underlying thread of desperation.

Without warning, Ed was flooded with an adrenaline-soaked rage. He knew that before his accident, he would have been five inches taller than this jerk and outweighed him by forty pounds. This guy never would have picked him as a mark. But here he was, Mr. Victim in a Wheelchair. His stomach roiled, and a bitter taste rose in the back of his throat. This sucked.

"Give it!" the mugger said, and quickly flicked his knifepoint across Ed's cheek.

Since knowing Gaia, Ed had been witness to more acts of violence than he had in his whole previous Gaia-less existence. And yet he was still shocked when the first thin threads of pain registered in his brain and still scared by the unnaturally hot flow of blood down his cheek.

Hating himself, hating the way his hand was shaking, Ed reached into the inner pocket of his jacket and pulled out his wallet. He remembered with grim, futile satisfaction that he had just spent his last five dollars at Starbucks, and only that morning his mom had asked for her Visa card back because she was getting a new one.

But the mugger wasn't going to check it out here. He took the wallet, sheathed the knife, and spun. He was gone, out of sight, before Ed could count to seven.

Well, shit. His heart was pounding loud in his ears; his hands were trembling. He reached up to touch his burning cheek and saw his leather glove shiny and dark with blood. A thought hit him like a hammer: Ed was desperate for Gaia's presence. If she had been here, this never would have happened. She would have kicked that guy's ass from here till Tuesday. Ed would have been avenged.

The realization was like being punched in the chest, and for a moment Ed literally couldn't breathe. A short time ago he'd been tall for his age, starting to get his adult weight, his grown-man muscle. He'd been the biggest, baddest daredevil on a board this side of America. Now what was he?

When he reached First Avenue, he turned for home. Forget the park right now. Forget Gaia. People glanced at him in alarm, then quickly turned away. He probably looked like some whacked-out Desert Storm vet, rolling along with a murderous expression and a bloody cheek. He ignored them. He'd learned how to ignore a lot of stares in the last couple of years.

At his apartment building Ed wheeled through the automatic doors. He crossed the lobby and rolled inside the elevator, pushing hard to get over the little gap in the floor. Automatically he punched his button. His cheek felt thick and sticky. There was a knot in his throat he couldn't swallow.

Once Ed had been tough, strong. When he and Heather were together, she had relied on *him*. And other guys had steered clear of his territory. He was cool. He was Shred. He had probably been kind of an asshole, if you wanted to know the truth. But at least he hadn't been pathetic.

DINNER WITH THE GANNISES

"Please pass the salt stuff," Mr. Gannis said, motioning to the middle of the table.

"The substitute?" Heather's mother asked.

"Yes," said Mr. Gannis.

Heather sat quietly, cutting her chicken breast into little squares, scooping up bits of scalloped potatoes. Since her father's heart attack two years ago, he'd been on a low-salt diet. Her mother couldn't eat shellfish. Now Phoebe was practically starving herself. Did everyone in her family have bizarro eating issues except her?

Heather glanced across the table at her other sister,

Lauren. Lauren was twenty and finishing her undergrad degree at Parsons. She was shoveling in her dinner with enthusiasm. A few days ago Heather would have been disgusted by her sister's huge appetite. Now she was grateful that at least one family member appeared to have *some* sanity.

Why didn't anyone seem to notice that Phoebe had eaten only half a salad so far, with no dressing? That she was just pushing the chicken around on her plate? Now that Heather was hyperaware of Phoebe's eating habits, it stunned her that she hadn't noticed them before. It left her feeling helpless and angry.

Who could she talk to about this? Sam? Maybe—except the next time she saw him, she wanted him to focus on her, not Phoebe. Her mother? No, her mom believed that you could never be too rich or too thin. Her father would simply refer Heather to her mother. Lauren would be no help at all. What about Heather's friends? Instinctively Heather shrank from the thought of confiding in any of them. She still hadn't let on to anyone about her family's finances, or lack thereof, and she knew that Phoebe's eating disorder would simply become a hot gossip topic. It wasn't any of their business.

What Heather needed was a *real* friend. Just one good friend.

GAIA

You know, Mary, when you were alive, I was starting to feel like I was sort of almost normal. I mean, I had friends (you and Ed), I was going to school, I was in love with someone (Sam), I was doing normal teenagery things. Now you're gone, and I'm like the poster girl for dysfunction. I can't deal with school. I can't deal with Ed. I saw Sam yesterday, and it was awful. Everything out of my mouth was the opposite of what I wanted to say.

Why is my life such an unending horror show? What do I have to do to make it bearable?

I am tottering on the brink. I'm almost afraid of *myself.*

TOM MOORE

I've seen the look in her eyes. I know that look because I've seen it too many times to name. I've seen it in the heartless gazes of trained assassins. Sometimes I've seen it when I've looked in the mirror. I know all too well what it means.

Gaia is after her friend's murderer. She wants to kill him. She wants to make him pay for what he did. Understandable under the circumstances. Who wouldn't fantasize about doing the same if someone they loved were brutally murdered?

Believe me, Gaia, I understand.

But Gaia can't afford to do as others do. She can't afford to have fantasies of revenge. Because unlike most people, Gaia is capable of following those fantasies through.

And once she does, once she has a taste for blood, I don't know if she can ever go back. Not someone like her—born to fight, physically and mentally built to destroy anything that gets in her way. Built to kill.

I'm watching you, Gaia. I'm waiting for you to make your move. But I can't protect you from yourself. You've got to do that.

I believe in you.

Do you believe in me?

DADDY'S LITTLE GIRL

THEN WITHOUT A CONSCIOUS THOUGHT SHE WAS MOVING, SPRINTING DOWN THE COBBLED WALK WITH HER HAIR FLYING IN BACK OF HER . . .

RED AND GREEN M&M'S

It's a universal law that if you drop anything on the floor within a ten-foot radius of a bed, that object will slowly and surely be sucked underneath the bed by some unseen magnetic force.

Or at least that's the theory Gaia came up with on Saturday morning when she was searching desperately for her only working pen. It had mysteriously disappeared when she took a bathroom break. Now she was on her hands and knees, swatting aside dust bunnies and pushing aside her ancient, faded quilt.

Eureka. There it was. With a large sweeping gesture Gaia fished the pen out from under her bed, her arm coming out covered with large clumps of dust and quite a few long blond hairs.

A thin, stiff piece of paper was stuck to her sleeve, and Gaia pulled it off, then froze. It was a note. Little red and green stains had smudged some of the words, but Gaia knew instantly what the note said.

Sinking back on her haunches, Gaia read the apology letter she held in her hand, a fresh wave of pain washing over her. It was from Mary. From when Mary had kicked coke and asked Gaia to be her friend again.

Gaia rubbed her finger along the page, stained with the

colors of the M&M's Mary had included with the note. How could these words still be here when Mary was gone? She continued to feel the texture where the pen had scratched the paper. Maybe by touching the grooves, the indents, she could touch the person who had left them there. If only . . .

"Gaia! Telephone!" Ella's strident voice ripped through Gaia's thoughts like a knife. Gaia winced and stood up, almost tripping on a moldering pile of laundry. She scooped it up in one arm and went downstairs, trying to make her mind blank. She needed to have her guard up to deal with Ella.

Still holding the laundry, Gaia entered the first-floor kitchen and wordlessly took the phone from Ella. Her foster mother's fingernails were long and blood-red, as though she had just plucked out the heart of a victim and hadn't rinsed off yet.

Gaia cradled the phone between her shoulder and ear, trying not to drop her laundry.

"Hello?" she said, already knowing it was Ed. No one else ever called her. Not Sam. Certainly not her father, wherever the hell he was.

"Gaia?" said a woman's husky, unfamiliar voice.

Gaia's neck prickled. Alarm bells went off. "Yes?" she said tightly.

"This is Patricia Moss. Mary's mother."

Oh, crap. Double crap.

"How are you, dear?"

"Um . . ."

"I know. We all feel that way," said Mrs. Moss. "I've been worried about you. Did Mr. Niven tell you I phoned?"

Yep. She had found his note, taped to her bedroom door.

"Yes, he did," Gaia said.

"Well, do come see us, dear, if you feel up to it," Mrs. Moss went on quietly. "Now, I wanted to tell you—Mary's . . . funeral is next Wednesday, at eleven o'clock, at the Riverside Chapel. We were thinking . . . it would mean a lot to us—to all of us—if you would agree to speak."

"What?" Gaia's voice sounded like it had been planed down to a thin rasp.

"If you would say a few words at Mary's funeral," continued Mrs. Moss. "I know you weren't friends for very long, but we feel that in some ways, you were her only true friend."

Why? Because I got her killed? Because I went too far with her drug dealer, and he paid someone to shoot your daughter in retaliation? Gaia felt something like hysteria rising in her throat.

"Because you were the one who made her face—made all of us face—her problems," said Mrs. Moss. "Please—it would mean a lot to us."

This was too horrible, too awful to contemplate. "I'm sorry, I can't," Gaia said curtly. She hung up the phone before Mrs. Moss could say any more, then whirled to see Ella, leaning against the wall, smoking a cigarette. Was that the hint of a smile? Gaia suddenly had the sensation that Ella was a cat and that she, Gaia, was a slab of tuna.

"Dear, dear," Ella crooned in honeyed tones. "Was that poor Mrs. Moss? That poor woman. To lose your daughter that way . . ."

Gaia frowned. To have Ella even mention Mary's name was more repulsive than she could stomach. She remembered when Ella had finally goaded Gaia into punching her, about a month ago. If Ella didn't watch it, they were going there again.

"What do you know about it?" Gaia said coldly. She knew she hadn't mentioned Mary's death to the Nivens.

Ella produced a newspaper from behind her back. "Only what I read," she answered smoothly. "What a shame. That innocent girl—they say it looked like a drug hit. No doubt some awful dealer got her hooked. Maybe she owed him money or something."

Gaia felt her blood starting to pound in her ears.

"And they didn't even catch him," Ella went on. "That monster is still out there, preying on other innocent girls."

Her words spiked into Gaia's chest as if they were barbecue skewers. A dull pain roared in Gaia's head. Today. Gaia had to find Skizz today. Blindly she stumbled over to the laundry room and threw her clothes into the washing machine. She measured out a cup of detergent and closed the lid. If only she could rid the world of Ella *and* Skizz in one fell swoop. The machine started to chug, and Gaia leaned against it, her knuckles white as they gripped the sides.

Okay, calm down. You have a plan. Ironically, her father's words came back to her. *Don't let emotion—not anger, not pain, not love—cloud your actions. That will get you killed.*

Gaia paused. Scratch that last bit. She wasn't daddy's little girl anymore. She didn't need his advice.

Screw him.

GET SOME FRESH AIR

"Um, Gaia?" George said, tapping on her open door.

"Yeah?" Gaia looked up from her bed, where she was putting on socks still warm from the dryer. Ecstasy.

"Ella and I thought it would be nice to take a drive out into the country. You know, get out of the city, get some fresh air. Maybe stop at a little restaurant and have dinner. We'd like for you to come with us."

It was actually tempting. Gaia longed to be somewhere out of the city, somewhere where snow was really snow. But two things held her back: Gaia was about to head out to hunt for Skizz, and there was no way she would be cooped up in a car with Ella for more than, say, ten seconds.

Gaia sighed regretfully. "I'm sorry, George. It does sound kind of . . . *neat*, but I better get to the library and work on my paper."

George shrugged. "Oh, well, maybe some other time. Don't work too hard, now. Will you be okay for dinner? We might not get back till late."

"I'll be fine," Gaia said. "You guys have fun." After George left, Gaia shook her head and took a deep breath. George was another person who would be horrified and disappointed in her if he knew her plans for Skizz. For an instant she pictured herself in prison, in handcuffs, looking out through a cell's bars at Ed and George. And Mary. Shivering, Gaia blinked and erased the image from her mind.

Twenty minutes later, after she was sure George and Cruella had left, Gaia put on her leaking down jacket and headed downstairs, leaving bits of ragged feathers every third step. Her stomach was tight, and she felt unbearably tense. Was this really her, planning to murder someone?

Yes. It was. She was going to do it.

Just as Gaia was reaching for the front door, a thought hit her: gloves. Her hands were already dry and chapped. Maybe the Nivens had some spares.

In the hall closet Gaia found a pair of white mohair gloves

edged with fake leopard skin. So practical. Gaia pushed behind the coats to the wall shelves. Bingo. Next to a small red box shoved into the corner was a pair of George's leather gloves, lined with Thinsulate. Ah. They were only a tiny bit too big, thanks to her huge, gorilla-like paws. Perfect. She arranged the other gloves neatly on the shelf, then backed out of the closet.

As she was about to close the door, the red box caught her attention. Shiny wrapping paper. It looked like it could be a leftover Christmas present, but that didn't compute. Ella wasn't the kind of woman to leave any kind of present unopened for very long.

Gaia picked up the box, shook it a few times. She could hear all the pieces jiggling around inside. Curiosity almost prompted her to open it. Almost.

She shrugged and stuffed the box back up on the shelf. It was probably some cheap costume jewelry from one of Ella's secret admirers. How lame. The idea made Gaia's stomach turn. Or had it been turning already?

Outside, the sun was just setting. The air was cold, but not as damp as it had been. Maybe no more snow tonight. Almost instantly, as Gaia headed down Perry Street, her nose started running. This time she was prepared, though, and she pulled a wad of toilet paper from her pocket and mopped up the worst of it.

If she walked fast, she could make Washington Square

Park in fifteen minutes. If she stopped for a chickpea roti at one of the many little delis on the way, she could add two minutes to that time. Her stomach felt kind of upset, but maybe she should eat, anyway. Low blood sugar would make her feel shakier than she already did. Today was the day. She could feel it.

It was weird about Skizz. The last time Gaia had seen him, he had looked like something the dog had brought in. Gaia had definitely gone overboard. The truth was, she had practically beaten him to death. Now, not even two weeks later, he should still be in pretty bad shape. And he *had* been in bad shape when Gaia had last seen him. He'd been a mess. But apparently not too much of a mess to hire some sleazeball to do his dirty work for him.

Gaia strode along, walking fast to keep warm, licking spicy curried chickpeas off her gloves.

The West Fourth Street entrance to the park was right on the corner, and Gaia headed in. It was dark in this corner, the overhead lamps burned out. Hands by her sides, she moved forward toward the center of the park. First a quick check by the chess tables, out of habit, then a circuit around the park perimeter.

"Smoke, smoke, smoke," offered a tall, thin guy in a rasta hat.

"No, thanks," Gaia said, and kept moving.

At the chess tables Zolov sat before an empty seat. Gaia

wished she had twenty minutes and twenty bucks. A couple of other regulars were packing up their pieces, getting ready to head in out of the cold and dark. On a January night the only people still offering a game were players who were so chess obsessed they didn't feel the cold or so desperate they didn't have anyplace else to go.

Of course, Sam wasn't there. He was probably safe and warm in his dorm room. Probably with Heather. She was probably rubbing his shoulders.

Oh, stop it!

No sign of Skizz so for. Was he lying low after the murder? It seemed uncharacteristically sensible of him.

Not that the park was devoid of weirdos and various lowlifes. She'd barely made one circuit of the perimeter and had already been approached about eight times. Why was it that pond scum guys always seemed to think they had a chance just because she was alone, just because she was female? A while ago Gaia would have been happy to provide a graphic demonstration of just how wrong they were. Tonight she didn't have time.

As Gaia was heading out the park's Waverly Street entrance, planning to circle the block, she caught a glimpse of a figure about sixty yards ahead. It was night, but the guy moved under a lamppost. . . . His dark, shapeless coat was bulky, a black knitted cap pulled low on his Neanderthal brow. One arm was in a sling. The other hand—yes. It was taped.

Skizz.

Gaia froze less than a second. Then without a conscious thought she was moving, sprinting down the cobbled walk with her hair flying in back of her, the wind streaming icily over her taut face.

She was going to do it. She wasn't sure how, but she was sure of the outcome. She was going to kill Skizz.

Raw power pumped through her veins. Her arms were already coiled, iron hard, ready to crush his skull. Her eyes lasered in on him, pinning him to one spot as she flashed forward. *Time to die.*

Gaia sensed the car before she actually saw it.

A dark, beat-up sedan screeched to a halt by Skizz, the back door already popped open.

No.

No, no, no. There was no way.

As Skizz moved toward the car, Gaia poured on the power. She was almost to him. Thirty more feet, twenty. Her boots sounded like muffled thunder on the sidewalk. She just needed to . . .

Skizz stepped into the sedan, slamming the door behind him. The car lurched into traffic, moving away from her.

Oh God! No! Get back here, you son of a hitch! You killed Mary! I have to do this now! For a moment Gaia was desolate, panting and gasping for breath. Then grim purpose hardened her face, and she raced into the street. She could catch that car. She could do it. She was faster than anyone. She would catch the car, yank open the door, and rip Skizz from its interior. With any luck his legs would be crushed beneath the car wheels.

Gaia raced after the dark car, the hard street shocking her joints as she ran. Her fury made her feel like an arrow, streaking through the cold air. When she caught the car, she would jump onto the trunk and hang on. Then when it stopped, she could—

The next thing Gaia knew, she was taking a dive into the curb. Several things registered all at once: screeching brakes, honking horns, traffic lights flashing crazily above her, and another person tumbling down on top of her.

Moaning, Gaia tried to curl into a ball, her shaky hands struggling to push her way out from under this other human being.

"Are you crazy?" a voice demanded roughly. "Were you trying to kill yourself? You ran right into me!"

A man's face, concerned and angry and scared, floated over her as he stood up shakily.

"Unh," Gaia managed, gasping for breath. Her heart still pounded. She knew Skizz was gone. If she were the kind of girl who cried, she would have wept with frustration and rage. She'd been stalking him for days, and this was the first sighting she'd had. Now he was gone. Dammit!

"Look, I'm calling an ambulance," said the guy. He pulled

a cell phone out of his suit pocket and started to punch in numbers. "You look pretty scratched up." He glanced down at his own, unharmed body, then at Gaia. "I guess you broke my fall. What the hell were you running for, anyway?" People kept walking by as Gaia gingerly rubbed the side of her leg that had hit the curb hardest. At that moment she was glad of the typical New Yorker's aversion to getting involved.

"I'm all right," Gaia managed. She tried to sit up, but a fresh wave of pain made her sag. "Don't call an ambulance."

The man hesitated. "I better," he decided. "Something could be broken. You were going pretty fast."

Shaking her head, Gaia said, "No. Nothing's broken." She wiggled her foot to show him, even though it hurt so much, she sucked in air with a whoosh. "I'm fine," she choked out.

"Can you stand?"

"Uh-huh," she said, not knowing if she could or not. Knowing she had to. The guy gave her his hand, and Gaia, gritting her teeth at both the pain and the fact that she had to allow a stranger to help her, raggedly rose to her feet. As long as she didn't put weight on her right side, she was fine. God, how fast had she been running to hit the curb that hard? Sweat beaded on her forehead. She felt dizzy and sick. Her hip really, really hurt.

"Where do you live?" asked the guy.

"Perry Street. Not far." What did it matter if he knew? What did it matter? So what if he were a random psycho in a chalk-stripe suit? So what if he was about to kidnap her and kill her? No big deal. Gaia tried to control her breathing, started the mental exercises that would allow her to negate the pain. She touched her right foot to the sidewalk. Her leg didn't buckle, though a bolt of white-hot pain shot up her leg and almost made her moan. Nothing was broken.

"Why don't I flag you a cab?" The man seemed uncertain, as if she might sue him for walking in the wrong place at the wrong time. The whole experience of living with New York paranoia suddenly struck Gaia as ridiculous, horrible, and funny. It would also have been a little bit scary if Gaia could feel fear.

Gaia nodded. "Maybe that would be best."

Back at the brownstone, she opened the door, then locked it behind her without looking back. Her forehead felt cold and clammy with sweat. Leaning against the wall, she limped slowly down the hallway to the little powder room tucked under the stairs. Silently Gaia gave thanks that George and Cruella were still out. Then she opened the toilet lid, leaned over, and barfed.

ED

Okay, I've decided to give Gaia a call. I know, I know. I'm a glutton for punishment. After the way she's treated me—okay—stomped all over my heart, I should just let her stay on her polar ice cap and blow her off forever. That's what she said she wants.

But I've been thinking, and there have been times in the last four months when I felt like I caught a glimpse of the Gaia beneath the mask. Just a glimpse, when she let her guard slip, let her real self shine through. When that happened, I saw not a superwoman, not a Norse goddess, but just a girl. Just a girl with no parents and no other friends but me. And maybe that girl needs my help. Even if she doesn't realize it yet.

A PERMANENT TWILIGHT

GAIA WANTED TO GO BELOW THE BELT?

FINE.

LIMITED USEFULNESS

"How badly is she hurt?" Loki subdued the acidic thread of anger in his voice as he buttoned up his shirt. Ella was still sitting on the bed, one foot dangling lazily over the edge. Loki's hands clenched and unclenched by his sides. He turned toward the window, furious that Ella hadn't told him of this development as soon as she had arrived at his apartment.

In the reflection of the window he saw Ella shrug.

He waited.

"Nothing's broken," Ella said finally. "She must have a bad bruise, but I haven't seen it. Unless you want to add peeping at her in her bath to my list of duties."

Loki's stomach tightened. This foolish, shortsighted woman. If she had two brain cells left to rub together, she would be anxiously *trying* to add duties to her list. Obviously she had no idea of her increasingly limited usefulness to him. In and *out* of bed. Had she not thought ahead as to what her future would be when she could no longer serve him? Did she assume he would simply wave good-bye and let her go live somewhere happily ever after? Did she assume Loki would trust her to keep all his secrets? Did she assume he would keep her on as his lover?

Smoothly he turned to her. Soon it would be time for her

distressingly inadequate service to end. In the meantime she did provide a conduit of information that would be hard to duplicate.

"No," he said evenly. "But you might keep an eye on her. If she needs medical attention, see to it."

"She won't need medical attention," Ella said, fishing out a cigarette and tapping it against her wrist. She started to light it but was stopped by Loki's glacial gaze. "She's indestructible." She sounded bitter about it. Loki suppressed a smile.

"Luckily for you," he said, keeping his voice hard.

"I can't keep her locked in her room," Ella protested.

"No. But you can do your job," Loki said. "Do try, will you?"

"Yes," Ella said.

"You are dismissed." Loki turned away again.

After Ella had resentfully slunk out of the apartment, Loki permitted himself the pleasure of ruminating on Gaia. It was almost time. Despite his anger at Ella for not eliminating the dealer yet, still, Loki was pleased. According to his report, Gaia had been absolutely hell-bent on the kill. Would she do it? Would she cross the line? It was a tantalizing notion. If she did, he could finally make his move.

WORTH A SHOT

"Gaia? Hey."

Hesitation. "Hey." She sounded distant. Like that was new. Ed shifted in his bed, switching the phone to his other ear and punching his pillow a couple of times. His thin legs barely made ridges beneath his down comforter.

"Listen, I'm going to give you another chance." Silence at the other end. "How are you doing?"

"I'm doing fine," Gaia replied, already sounding testy.

"Well, can we get together? I have a whole list of new complaints about my parents and no one to listen to me."

Silence while he imagined Gaia smiling.

"Ed, listen," she said haltingly.

Ed the basset hound pricked up his ears. Was she giving in? He couldn't wait for her to see his face, with its knife cut going across his cheek. Then she would be sorry. Then she would be all concerned about him, full of anger at his mugging. It would be great.

"I'm not interested. Okay?" Gaia continued.

Ouch. Ed almost slammed down the receiver, but some perverse impulse made him pull it back to his ear. Gaia wanted to go below the belt? Fine.

"Interested in what, Gaia? Looking for Skizz? Or have you found him yet? I didn't read about any bodies being found in the East River. Or maybe you were planning to dispose of him in the Hudson. I'm out of the loop with what all the young murderers are doing with their prey these days."

"Very amusing," Gaia said, her voice sounding muffled. Her tone had dropped from chilly to below freezing.

Now what? He'd blown this sky-high one minute into the conversation.

"Gaia, just talk to me," he said.

He was such a pathetic sucker.

"Ed, I don't want to talk."

No shit. Ed's jaw set as he tried to keep himself from blurting out, "I got mugged!" He wouldn't stoop that low. He wouldn't use his near-death experience to get Gaia to show some sympathy and interest.

Ed willed a snappy comeback to pop into his mind. He'd already used "whatever" the last time he'd hung up on her. Maybe he should come up with a list and keep it by the phone. How to hang up on Gaia: fifty different ways. He was sure it would come in handy.

After racking his brain for a cool, disinterested, sarcastic line for a full twelve seconds, Ed found himself saying the one thing he hadn't planned on.

"You're going to realize you need me," he said in a low, harsh voice. "When you do, you'll be lucky if I'm still here."

There. That was it. The perfect last word. What could she possibly say to that?

"Ed. I don't need you. I don't want you. I'm sorry but I don't see how you—a neurotic guy in a wheelchair—could actually help *me.*"

Ed was too stunned to breathe.

"It's not that I don't want to talk now, or tomorrow, or next week, or whatever. I don't want to talk ever. I don't want you in my life," Gaia hissed. Ed swallowed. "Get the hell out of my life."

The phone went dead. Before he could really comprehend what had just happened, Ed felt the tears coursing down his cheeks.

LATER

"Ed?" Mrs. Fargo called from outside the door.

Ed was still clutching the cordless phone as he lay back against three huge, puffy pillows. From his bed he could see the hazy January sky trying to convince him it was truly daytime and not a permanent bleak twilight.

"Yeah?"

The door opened, and his mother came in, dressed for success in camel flannel slacks, a matching cashmere twin-set, and a discreet pearl choker at her throat. Ed was sure his sister's fiancé's parents would be suitably impressed. Today the two sets of parents were meeting at the Russian Tea Room to discuss wedding plans. Ed hadn't been invited, thank God.

"Honey, it's almost eleven o'clock," his mother said. "Shouldn't you get up and get dressed?"

This was obviously a rhetorical question.

"Yeah, okay," said Ed.

"Have you done your exercises?" Mrs. Fargo asked, automatically picking up clothes and folding them over the back of a chair.

"Not yet."

His mother's eyes met his, and Ed waited. She was obviously warring with herself, trying to determine how much to nag him. Ed breathed a sigh of relief when he saw she'd decided against it for today.

"Your father and I will probably be gone until about three. There's food in the kitchen. Do you need anything?" She paused in the doorway.

"No, I'm fine," said Ed.

"Okay, then. See you later." The door shut silently.

As Ed began to do the repetitive stretching movements that kept his leg muscles from atrophying further, he realized that his mother was making progress. For almost six months after the accident she had refused to leave him alone in the house in case he fell or needed something. In case he would commit suicide while they were out.

For her to leave with such a show of casualness was a big step forward. Ed grunted as he gripped his left ankle and flexed it. It didn't hurt, of course, but he could feel his back muscles pulling. Forty minutes of this, then half an hour of free weights for upper-body strength. Months ago, when Ed had decided that he would go on living even in this form, he had realized there were things he could do that would marginally improve his existence. Trying to keep what was left of his body in shape was one of them. Making friends, keeping connected to other people, was another. Trying to date, to think of himself and others in a romantic, sexual way, was a third.

It seemed like he was down to one out of three. He knew he needed somebody—a friend, a lover. He had been hoping Gaia was that person. But maybe he needed to reexamine his options.

MAKING SAM HEEL

"Look at this pile of crap," Heather said in disgust. Phoebe glanced up from her magazine, looked around the room, and nodded. Piles of clothes were on every spare surface of Heather's bedroom. They almost swamped Phoebe on the bed and covered the small rocker in the corner and most of the floor.

"This is a humongous pile of crap," Heather said again. "All this stuff and I can't find one cute outfit."

"I know what you mean," said Phoebe. "All of my stuff is horrible—totally last year. And it doesn't fit. I just want to go shopping all day long and get some stuff that's decent."

Heather sagged against her bed. "Me too."

In the past day or two Heather had been trying to think of what to do about Phoebe's condition. She couldn't tell her friends, and she hadn't seen Sam in days. Who else was there? She just had to shut up about it and try to enjoy hanging out with Phoebe without talking about anything controversial. Like food. Or weight. Or bodies.

Before all this happened, Heather wouldn't have believed how often and in how many different situations a person could mention one of those topics. Staying off these subjects reduced her conversation by about eighty percent. She thought about all the times she had moaned about her weight or her size or her waistline. Now she wished she hadn't wasted her breath.

"Feeb—what's going to happen?" Heather asked.

Phoebe looked up, her face closing.

"I mean about Dad, and the money and all," Heather clarified. "I mean, how long am I supposed to wear these clothes?" Of course, the question was bigger than that, and both sisters knew it.

Taking a deep breath, Phoebe said, "I don't know. Mom said something once about Grandma Nancy helping out, but I don't know what that means."

"Do you think Mom is going back to work?" Heather asked.

"Get real," Phoebe scoffed. "What would all her friends think? No, I think Mom and Dad are just going to keep doing what they're doing and hope it all turns out okay."

"But—"

"Listen, try not to worry about it," Phoebe advised, rolling off Heather's bed and standing up. In her black leggings and wide-wale corduroy shirt she looked model thin and chic. Except that her leggings were baggy. Heather didn't know Lycra could *be* baggy. "Everything will be okay. I've got to get over to Sasha's house. See you later."

"Later," said Heather.

For three minutes Heather lay among the pile of clothes on her bed, wallowing in self-pity. Then she remembered that she was Heather Gannis, dammit, and she deserved better than this. Even from herself.

She picked up the phone and hit memory dial #1. Sam himself actually answered. Miracle of miracles.

"Hi, Sam. It's me," Heather said, feeling the warm fuzzies starting to come over her.

"Hi," Sam replied. His voice was so adorable, so husky, sexy. "I feel like it's been ages since I saw you. We really need to get together."

"Yeah, we do," Heather agreed happily. "I really miss you. How's the studying going?"

Sam groaned. "I feel like I live at the library. I only came home to shower."

"But the semester just started," Heather felt compelled to point out.

"I know. I'm just trying to get off on the right foot. I've got four bitch classes this semester, and I've got to finish that incomplete in comparative anatomy from last semester."

The warm fuzzies were being slowly, surely replaced by a feeling of resentment. "Sam," Heather began, trying to keep her voice reasonable. "We're supposed to be going out. Supposed to be boyfriend and girlfriend. But we never see each other anymore. I mean, I spent New Year's with my *girlfriends!*"

A sigh on the other end.

"You're right," came Sam's unbelievable answer.

Hope bloomed once more.

"I'm sorry," he continued. "Dad gave me such a hard time over Christmas that I kind of freaked out about my grades. But you're right—I can't study twenty-four hours a day. And we *do* need to talk."

"Not just talk," Heather said suggestively. She was smiling and twirling the phone cord around her wrist. Finally Sam was saying some things she actually felt like hearing. There was a chance he just might come through for her after all. She could even tell him about Phoebe. After all, he was premed. He might have some idea what Heather could do.

"Yeah. Listen, what about tomorrow?" Sam suggested. "After classes I'll take the day off from studying. Unless . . . are you busy after school?"

"Nope," Heather said happily. "I could come over to your place. We could hang out for a while, maybe get something to eat over on MacDougal. I just want to see you."

"Yeah, okay," Sam said. "See you tomorrow."

"Bye, Sam," Heather said. "Can't wait to see you."

He'd already hung up.

NEVER SHOW WEAKNESS

THEY MIGHT PLAY THIS GAME OUT FOR ANOTHER HOUR, BUT THE END WAS NOW CERTAIN. GAIA WOULD WIN.

NO MATTER HOW COLD

Try as he might, Ed couldn't think of a single thing worse than a freezing, wet Monday morning in January when he had to go to school, when Gaia had completely ripped out his heart and was probably doing reckless, dangerous, or stupid things or all three, when he had just lost one of his good friends, and when he had a very visible cut on his cheek from getting mugged over the weekend. Was there anything that could be worse? He thought about it for a second.

Ed's locker was on the lower tier, of course, since he'd lost almost three feet in height since junior year. Wheeling up to it, he flipped open its combination lock and started to rummage through the unorganized mess inside, looking for something resembling this morning's books.

Okay, here's a thought: Ed wakes up; there's nothing for breakfast except Fiber One cereal. Over breakfast his folks tell him they're getting divorced because his dad has decided he was meant to be a woman and is having a sex change. Right after that announcement their house catches on fire and burns to the ground, and Ed is carried out of the burning building in nothing but his boxers. Outside in the freezing weather in his boxers, with his scrawny white legs showing, every hot girl he's ever wanted shows up and sees him. Well, okay, that might be worse than the way he felt this morning.

Clawing through the wreckage in his locker, Ed pulled out some notebooks and a couple of possibly appropriate textbooks and dropped them into one of the side bags attached to his wheelchair. Side bags, cup holders—what was next? Maybe some kind of James Bond rocket engines strapped to the back so Ed could shoot down school corridors at Mach 1.

Ed laughed hollowly at this scenario as the school bell rang and the halls suddenly emptied. Like rats, students scurried into classes, books tucked under their arms. Ed slammed his locker shut and started to wheel off to his first class. Then he saw a tall, slim, wild-haired goddess stride around the corner and fling open her locker. As usual, Gaia had avoided being on time. Her mouth pressed into a thin line, she stooped to drop her bag on the ground, then straightened slowly to rifle through her locker contents. Ed saw her find a forgotten, half-smushed Ding Dongs package, which she tucked into her bag with satisfaction.

Every time he saw Gaia, Ed's heart sped up, his breathing quickened, his pupils dilated. For some reason—okay, a million reasons—Gaia was very special to him. But today things were going to be different. She had stepped over the line. He knew she hadn't meant what she said. Couldn't have meant it. But that didn't make it any less hurtful.

Slowly Ed rolled down the hall. He had to pass her to get to his first class, just as she had to pass him to get to her chem lab. In an instant a dozen different scenarios raced through his head as he considered his approach. How should he be? Reproachful, normal, angry, mean, sad? He decided to just ignore her.

As usual, Gaia took the initiative away from him. As he was formulating the perfect greeting, she looked up, glanced at his face, and frowned.

"What happened to you? Cut yourself shaving?"

For one awful second Ed had a flashback to Friday night, being mugged in the dark by some scumbag with a knife. He could have been killed. As it was, his wallet and his pride had been ripped away from him, leaving him wanting to crawl into a dark hole and disappear. And this is the concern he got? A frown and a snappy remark? Besides, he thought Gaia didn't want to talk to him. Wasn't that what she had said?

Suddenly Ed was very tired. Tired of not getting what he needed from someone he'd thought was his best friend. Tired of playing games to get Gaia to notice him, to take him seriously, to feel for him what he felt for her. He was exhausted—too exhausted to play anymore.

"Mugged by asshole with knife," Ed said shortly, continuing on past Gaia.

A strong hand reached out and yanked his wheelchair to a halt. Blue eyes bored into his, then flicked across his cut cheek, assessing the damage. In that moment Ed saw concern, anger, sympathy, and some unnamable emotion in

Gaia's eyes. In the next moment her eyes went blank, as if she had pulled down a shade over her mind.

Gaia straightened. "Any other damage?" she asked, making it sound casual.

His lips tightened. "No. No other damage."

Turning back to her locker, Gaia stuffed in her puffy ski jacket, holding it in place with one hand while strategically slamming the locker shut with the other. Bedraggled feathers whisked into the air and swirled crazily before floating downward.

That was it, Ed realized. That would be the sum of her response to his almost getting killed. Some friend she was. Anger rushed through his veins, making him feel flushed and reckless and mean.

"Going to Mary's funeral on Wednesday?"

For a split second Gaia froze. If Ed had blinked, he would have missed it. It wasn't quite the gratifying response he had hoped for.

"God, no," came Gaia's reply. Then she tied her avocado green wool sweater around her waist and hitched up her books.

Angrily Ed pushed against her jean-clad hip. "Get out of my way," he snapped, then looked up in surprise at Gaia's sharply indrawn breath. She pulled back away from him, breathing tightly.

"I'm not in your way," she said. She turned and walked

in the other direction, moving slowly and deliberately, not looking back.

Ed spun away, rolling down the hall fast. This day had, in fact, just gotten worse.

SHE HAD A LOVER

"Heather, it'll be great," Megan said. She leaned forward to get closer to the industrial mirror attached to the school's second-floor bathroom wall. At the row of five white, matching sinks, she occupied the last one. An open makeup bag was propped by the pitted silver cold-water handle.

"Look, first dinner at Dojo's," Megan went on. "Then we could hit Melody's and see who's playing. Come on. Don't stand us up for Phoebe again."

Heather peered at herself in her own mirror. She took a tiny dab of gloss and smoothed it over her sable brown eyebrows, making them shiny and perfectly shaped.

"Sorry, no can do," she said.

Megan paused and regarded her friend. "Heather, you hardly come out with us anymore," she complained.

Yeah, and you probably spent close to two hundred bucks last weekend, thought Heather. *Sorry, but I don't think my allowance will really cover that.* She smeared a dab of olive shadow in the crease of her lid, then redid her raisin-colored lip stain.

"So what are you doing today that you can't come with us?" Megan asked, her jaw set. She turned and crossed her arms over her chest.

Heather looked at her. She and Megan had been friends for six years, ever since junior high at Brearly. They used to be able to tell each other practically anything. Heather remembered long, sleepless nights spent at Heather's family's summer house, where the girls would stay up, eating, talking, and laughing until the sun came up.

But now everything was different. Megan's life had continued on normally. Her parents had gotten divorced, but that was no biggie. Practically everyone's parents did, sooner or later. Her mom had gotten remarried. Her father had moved to France. All that meant was that now Megan had fabulous summers in Europe while Heather sweltered in the city.

"I went with you to Ozzie's on Friday," Heather pointed out.

Megan rolled her eyes. "That was *Friday.* Now, why can't you come tonight?"

"As it so happens, I'm seeing Sam," said Heather, unable

to keep the triumph out of her voice. Sam was the one big status symbol she still had, that she could still flaunt.

Sure enough, Megan looked impressed. "I thought you guys were doing the on-again, off-again thing."

"We're on again," Heather said with a shrug. "I'm going over there now to hang out, and maybe we'll grab a pizza."

"Well, good," said Megan. "I'm glad he's decided to surface."

Heather nodded. "He's been studying like crazy." She tucked in her shirt and smoothed it down over her hips. Then she rubbed the tops of her black loafers on the backs of her chinos to shine up the tops. "But I finally said, 'Sam, you have to make time for us, too, you know.'"

"What did he say?" Megan asked.

"He apologized," Heather said, a coy smile playing around her lips. "He said I was right. And he blew off a bunch of stuff so we could be together today."

"Cool."

There it was. The envious tone was back in Megan's voice. God, that sounded so good. Heather felt very cheerful and generous. She put a hand on Megan's shoulder and gave her a warm smile. "Don't give up on me, okay?" she said lightly. "I definitely want to hang with you guys. It's just I need to see Sam, too."

"Oh, sure, of course," said Megan, all her irritation gone. She smiled slyly. "You need to keep him happy."

Heather laughed, feeling cool and sophisticated: She had a lover. A college guy lover. She was *Heather Gannis*, and for a few moments she could forget about everything: Phoebe, her parents, and even Sam's frustrating flakiness. Right at this moment everything was perfect.

BLITZ

Wordlessly Gaia moved her rook to bishop's seven, then glanced up into Zolov's face. Zolov looked older than dirt today; a week's worth of straggly white whiskers blurred the edges of his face, and his threadbare trench coat was streaked with something that looked like motor oil. His eyes were deeply sunken, his wrinkles more sharply defined. The cold air had chapped his skin and lips and now whipped through the sparse, whitish gray hair on his hatless head. Last week he'd had a maroon polyester knit cap. Gaia wondered what had happened to it.

Zolov considered the board for long minutes. One hand in a fingerless glove stroked his rough chin as he pondered.

In the months Gaia had been hanging out among the chess junkies in Washington Square Park, Zolov was the closest thing to an international grand master that she'd seen. Despite being homeless, despite his ragged clothes, unkempt hair, and sour, permeating body smell, still, he was a truly brilliant player, and Gaia had learned some interesting middle game forms from him.

She waited impatiently for him to make his move. It was twilight in the park, that strange half hour between day and night when it was difficult to see clearly. The overhead lamps had just flickered on, casting their sickly yellow-gray glow over the snow-flecked asphalt and the concrete benches where they sat. After school Gaia had gone first to Tompkins Square Park, then here, trolling every path, making perimeter checks, until she was sure Skizz wasn't around. Today the plan was to simply hang here until she couldn't stay awake any longer. She had spotted Skizz on Saturday and had dragged herself back to the park yesterday only to strike out again. It was enough to make her scream. If she *wasn't* looking for Skizz, he'd probably be in her face every twenty minutes for some reason or another. Now she was sitting on this frozen bench, killing time by playing Zolov. Her leg and hip were aching with a deep, painful throb that made her whole being coil with tension. Okay, she would stay here till midnight, then go back to the Nivens' and soak in a hot bath. Just the thought of sinking into the steamy water was enough to make her almost moan.

Zolov reached out with one gnarled hand and carefully moved his king to king's three. On the sidelines his red Power Ranger stood steadfast. The Power Ranger was Zolov's talisman—something he was never without, something he guarded fiercely. Gaia had seen Zolov asleep on a park bench, with the tiny feet of the plastic Power Ranger tucked into the ratty scarf looped around his neck.

Sitting back, Zolov hacked a couple of times, a hollow, rattling sound coming from his concave chest. As she examined the board, Gaia wondered if Zolov had pneumonia.

Then, like a computer, Gaia's mind raced forward, seeing all the different possibilities, the different permutations of play. Her blue eyes widened as she saw Zolov's fatal flaw. It couldn't be. He had goofed. With that one move he had sentenced himself to a sure loss. They might play this game out for another hour, but the end was now certain. Gaia would win. It was amazing.

For five minutes Gaia reran the possibilities in her mind. She came to the same conclusion. It was mate for Zolov, all the way around. Calmly she sat there, frozen and sore, and waited for Zolov to see it too.

It took him another minute. Then his wild, inch-long silver brows wrinkled and came together. His dark eyes stared at the board. He hacked a couple of times. Still Gaia sat.

When she was sure Zolov knew the outcome, she reached out a hand still clad in one of George's leather gloves and gently knocked over his king.

Zolov stared at her. Then slowly he reached into the tattered pocket of his filthy coat. He withdrew a twenty-dollar bill and pushed it across the table as if it caused him physical pain to do so. Gaia wouldn't insult him by refusing to take it.

She stood up, stretched, and pocketed the twenty. "Later, Zolov," she said, trying not to groan as her injured hip screamed in protest at her movement. "Good game."

Zolov nodded, looking confused, and quickly righted his king. Behind Gaia a guy in a plaid shirt and shiny satin baseball jacket moved forward to take her place.

Gaia moved away, forcing herself not to feel pain, forcing her walk to be smooth and fluid. Forcing herself not to worry about Zolov. Never show weakness. Never show fear. Gaia knew she couldn't show fear if she tried. When she was younger, she had spent long hours in front of a mirror, trying to form her face into a mask of fear. Eyes wide, mouth opened in an O, the most she had managed was sort of a look of surprise. Even dismay, perhaps. But the blue eyes staring back at her from the mirror had never managed to register fear. And never would.

On the corner of Waverly and University Place there was a hot dog vendor, and Gaia bought herself some dinner: one large dog with the works, one Coke. Mary had always gotten a hot dog with just mustard and relish. She'd loved yellow mustard, insisting it was one of the four food groups. She had drunk diet Coke. She had also introduced Gaia to Pellegrino. Mary had been full of contradictions.

Gaia walked down Waverly on the outside of the park, eating her hot dog. *Come on, Skizz. Why don't you show soon? I need this to be over. I need to have this behind me. I can't keep thinking about this thing I'm going to do. Once you're dead, I can move on.*

An uncomfortable thought came to Gaia as she tossed her hot dog wrapper in a trash can. Move on to what? What waited for her on the other side of Skizz's death? What did she have to look forward to? What purpose would her life have afterward?

Just don't think about it.

GAIA

I know Ed thinks I'm being a total jerk. But there's nothing I can do about that. He thinks I don't care about him. But I simply can't *allow* myself to care about him.

Take today, for instance: If I had time, I'd be really upset about his getting mugged at knifepoint. I'd want to hear details. I might even want to try to track the guy down and take him apart for hurting my friend. If I had time, the thought of his being alone and scared while he was being mugged would really hurt me inside. And now, when he's obviously angry at me, I'd want to try to work it out with him.

Not only that, but I might even mention that I sort of got hit by a curb on Saturday and have a humongous, black bruise from my waist practically down to my knee, and every time I take a step, I feel like the bone is going to snap in two. Then he would fuss over me and be all concerned.

But I can't do that right now. I just have to get through the next few days and look for Skizz. That's the total agenda.

Then I'm gone.

A USEFUL SKILL

WITH AN ODD, TORTURED EXPRESSION ON HIS FACE SAM HESITATED, THEN BENT HIS HEAD AND MET HER LIPS.

A HARD GAME

Tom watched Gaia disappear around the corner of Waverly and MacDougal. Her hands were stuffed into the pockets of that ugly jacket, and she was leaving a wispy trail of gray feathers behind her, as if she carried within her a personal snowstorm that occasionally burst free.

The overwhelming impulse to follow her tightened Tom Moore's gut. Cupping his hands, Tom held them to his mouth and blew on them, trying to warm them. He checked his watch, which could give him the current local times of any of a dozen countries. Here in New York, it was almost precisely five thirty. Time to meet his contact.

Across the street from Washington Square Park was a long row of brick town houses that dated back to the mid-1800s. Most of them now belonged to NYU and housed various offices and student resources. Tom tightened the belt of his midnight blue trench coat, grateful for its cashmere lining, and crossed the street, dodging between two taxis. At five thirty on the dot, he was quickly mounting the worn and cracked marble steps of number twelve. The brass plaque to the right of the heavy glass door said French Students Union. Tom pushed open the door and went in.

Inside, threadbare maroon carpeting dulled the sound of his footsteps as he headed up the uneven staircase. On the fourth floor was a series of doors. Tom walked unerringly to the last one on the left, then turned to check the hall for visitors. It was quiet and deserted. He knocked four times, then twice, then once. A buzzer opened the electronic lock, and Tom pushed open the door.

"Hello, Tom," said George. "Right on time."

"George," said Tom, extending his hand. He loosened his coat and sat in the leather armchair across from his old friend. He rubbed one cold hand across his face, then took a deep breath. "I just saw her," he said, his face looking older than its forty-two years.

George nodded, gave a smile that didn't reach his eyes. "You probably see her more than I do," he said without humor.

"I'm worried about her," Tom said unnecessarily.

"We all are," George replied. "But you trained her too well, my friend. She's hard to keep up with."

Tom couldn't stop the look of paternal pride on his face.

George pushed a manila folder across the table. "We've received intelligence that Loki's interest in our girl has taken on a new twist. There's reason to believe that he wants her—for himself."

Tom's blue eyes, a darker, more clouded color than his daughter's, glanced up sharply. "But why?"

George looked uncomfortable. "You probably know Loki better than almost anyone, Tom. What does your instinct tell you? Why would he want her?"

A small muscle in Tom's jaw twitched, and a slow-burning fire seemed to fill his gaze. "I'll kill him first."

"Take a number," George said dryly. "Lots of people want Loki dead."

Tom paused and stared intently at his friend. "I have another favor to ask, George. This friend of Gaia's that was killed. Mary Moss. The papers said it was some kind of drug hit. Is that true?"

"It looks like the reports are legit," George replied, his body slackening against the chair. "The poor girl was apparently a recovering coke addict. They found drugs on the body."

"I'm worried about Gaia," Tom continued. "I'm worried she might try to go after the dealer. Can you find out some information on him for me? Anything I can use to track him down?"

"Of course," George said, nodding, "I'll do what I can."

"When's our next meeting scheduled?" For Tom and probably George, too, work was a sure refuge. By focusing on details, protocols, expected outcomes, and failure rates, he could avoid talking or sometimes even thinking about pain, loss, betrayal, or loneliness. It was a useful skill.

WHAT A HOTTIE

"You want some tea or something?" Sam gestured at the small electric kettle perched on a white plastic milk crate. "I've got some hot chocolate here somewhere."

Heather laughed, wrinkling her nose. "Sam. I'm not a child," she said, giving him a look that said he of all people should know better.

He laughed, too, and ran a hand through his wonderful goldish brownish reddish hair. Heather felt a pang. Why were they still so bizarrely uncomfortable with each other? They had been going out for nine months! But they were still unsure and awkward around each other, as if they had just met.

"You want a beer, then? There's some in Mike's fridge. Or water?"

"Sam." Heather bunched up Sam's pillows against the cinder-block wall. She edged back on his bed so she was half reclining. "I'm fine. I don't need anything. Except you. Now, come here." She patted the rough wool army blanket that covered Sam's narrow bed.

In this small room Heather almost felt that she and Sam could make a connection. This was where they spent their alone time, this was where they made love.

Sam looked uncomfortable as he came and perched on

the side of the bed. "Heather, I—we need to talk," he said.

"Can we talk later?" she asked, sliding her hand up the rumpled sleeve of his shirt.

"Um," Sam said, not looking at her. "It's just that I've been thinking, and . . . well, I was wondering where we were going with this, and—"

Heather put one finger against his mouth. "Shhh," she whispered. "Later." Then she leaned forward and gently put her mouth over his. He was unyielding for a moment, hesitant. But she put her arms around him and pressed herself close. His hands on her arms held her in place, and he moved his mouth away.

"Heather, wait—there's something I wanted to say to you."

"Oh, Sam," she whispered. "Can't it wait?" She looked deep into his eyes. "I haven't seen you in ages. I *need* you." He smelled so good—he always did. Like laundry detergent and snow and himself.

She leaned close again. "Kiss me," she asked softly. "Kiss me, Sam."

With an odd, tortured expression on his face Sam hesitated, then bent his head and met her lips. She curled her arms around him and leaned backward, pulling him down with her.

Sam's arm came around her waist, and Heather felt the familiar, thrilling tingle that being close to Sam always produced. They'd had a lot of ups and downs—she'd been unfaithful to him with Charlie Salita; he'd admitted that he was obsessed with Gaia Moore. But here they were, together and alone, and Heather desperately wanted to love him and have him love her. If she could have just one thing in her life that was certain, strong, constant . . . it would make everything else all right. She curled her left hand around his neck and pressed closer to him.

God, she loved kissing. Not that she had kissed that many people. Ever since eighth grade Heather had been so popular that she could afford to be picky and, in fact, had an obligation to be picky, to be hard to get. There were standards to set.

She hadn't even gone to third base until her first real serious boyfriend, Ed Fargo. And since Ed there had been only Sam. Heather was working hard on forgetting that Charlie Salita had ever happened. Thank God, Sam had never found out about that disastrous mistake. She had been completely falling-down drunk, she had been angry at Sam, she had been furious with Gaia, and she had ended up going into a bedroom with a gorgeous hunk from her school. She still didn't know if she had agreed to have sex with Charlie or whether he had raped her. The whole thing was so horrible, she just couldn't think about it. *Focus on Sam.*

"Mmm," she hummed under her breath as he pressed

closer. They were kissing slowly, without urgency, more cuddling and smooching than getting hot and heavy. It was really nice, just what she needed. She slipped her hand under his shirt in back, gliding up over the smooth skin. She didn't even remember Charlie, didn't remember anything but kissing him. She had no idea how he had felt or if she had liked it or hated it. Which was good. The less she remembered the better, right? The easier it should be to block it out.

"Heather," Sam said, pulling back a bit.

She smiled up at him and shifted so she could pull her shirt out from her waistband. Sam was always so gentle, so loving. He always cared about her feelings, never made her feel like it was just physical. She took his hand and pushed it under her shirt in back. She pressed against him, her breasts flattening against his chest. She wriggled a little against him.

He drew in a shaky breath.

He was nothing like Ed. When she and Ed had lost their virginity together, well, the first time had been so amazing. They knew what they were supposed to do but didn't realize it might be physically difficult, especially on a sandy beach. It had been pretty uncomfortable for her, and she had cried while he held her. Once she had gotten used to it, it had still been so awkward and weird and new that they had both been amazed, awestruck. She had been almost crazy with love for him, this reckless skate rat who was so different from her other friends.

After that very first time they had been wild for each other, sneaking chances to be together whenever they could. It had been summertime, and their skins would be sweaty and slick and smooth as they moved together, delight written on their faces. Ed had been strong, inventive, funny, and intense in bed, and sometimes, when he was looking deep into her eyes and she could feel him against her, their connection had been so mind-blowing that tears had come to her eyes. *This is it,* she had thought. *This is what I want for the rest of my life.*

Then there had been the horrible accident that left Ed paralyzed from the waist down. Heather and Ed had gone from the highest high to the lowest low in about twenty seconds, and they had never recovered.

Months after they had broken up, Heather had met Sam. Sam had practically saved her life; he'd made her happy again. All her friends went from feeling sorry for her to envying her. It had been great.

Heather stroked her fingers through Sam's soft, wavy hair as he lowered his head and began to unbutton her shirt. He kissed her neck, under her chin, then began to trail a line of kisses down her throat as he undid buttons one by one. Ed's hair had been thick and straight, dark as coffee. It had brushed against her stomach as he . . . oh, Ed.

Sam raised his head. "What?" he asked.

She stared at him dumbly. "Huh?"

"Did you say something?" Sam's hazel eyes were heavy lidded, his mouth smooth and kissable.

Heather shook her head. "Uh . . ."

Waiting, Sam hovered over her chest, his hands holding the two edges of her shirt. Suddenly, with no warning, Heather felt yucky. As if Sam had just turned into Charlie Salita. What a bizarre thought. She must be losing her mind. All she knew was that she suddenly just wanted to go home.

"You okay?" Sam smiled softly, stroking her.

"Oh, jeez, Sam, I forgot!" Heather said inanely. She sat up and buttoned her shirt as quickly as she could with trembling fingers.

"What? Forgot what?"

"I'm supposed to go home for dinner tonight!" Heather blurted out. She stood up shakily, wondering where she'd put her shoes. "I'm sorry, Sam. I told Mom I had a date with you, but . . . ," she blathered on, conscious of Sam's uncomprehending stare as she shoved her feet into her shoes, grabbed her purse and her bag, and tore out of Sam's room like it was on fire.

HIS TORTURED SEX LIFE

Sam sat on his bed, looking at his half-open door for who knew how long after Heather had left. He was a . . . what was the word? A dog? All the things that described him seemed so old-fashioned, like they were from a forties movie. A cad, a rotter, a heel. The only modern word he could think of was *dog*, and that seemed so . . . harsh somehow. Better just to call him a loser.

How else to describe a guy who was making out with his girlfriend, the girlfriend he was determined to break up with, while fantasizing about another girl, a girl who hated him, a girl who had totally shot him down the last time he saw her? Instead of Heather's rich, dark hair Sam had seen a blond, tangled sprawl across his pillow. Instead of Heather's neat, curvy little body Sam had felt long legs, a firm, flat belly, strong arms holding him tightly to her.

"Yo! Moon Man!" Mike Suarez barged in through the open door. "You eaten yet?"

Sam wordlessly shook his head.

"Come on! It's Italian night over at Weinstein!" Mike pounded the door with a closed fist, sign of an excess of testosterone. Sam leaned over and methodically put on his hiking boots. Their dorm didn't have its own dining room—to eat, they had to go to Rubin or Weinstein dorms or to Loeb center. A bitch when it was cold and snowing and when you had just sunk to a new low.

Mike and Sam headed out and started trotting down the four flights of stairs to the lobby. It was official: Sam was an asshole. Once Heather started kissing him and moving against him, he'd lost the will to break up with her. His mind knew what he had to do, but his body had refused to listen. How weak was that? Compared with his tortured and convoluted sex life, his premed classes were a walk in the park.

ED 'N' HEATHER

"I'm borrrred." Ed tried to put as much anguished whining into his voice as possible. On the other end of the phone Heather giggled, then stopped and cleared her throat.

"Ed, it's a Monday night," she said briskly. "Go do your homework."

"Done." He waited. Why had he called Heather? Well, who else did he have to call? It's not like he had a best friend or anything. It's not like anyone else was calling *him.* Given a choice between phoning his ex-girlfriend, whom he was now sort of friends with again, and sitting around at home in a vegetative state, wondering what the hell Gaia was up to, he had chosen calling his ex.

"Watch TV," was Heather's next suggestion.

"TV rots your mind," was Ed's opinion. "What are you doing?"

"Oh, well, you know . . . the usual." That sounded pretty lame.

"Have you eaten yet?"

"Actually, no. I just got in. I'm starving."

Ed's spirits brightened. "Me too. Look, why don't I stop at Ray's, pick up a pizza, and bring it over? We'll hang out, we'll eat . . ."

"I shouldn't admit this," Heather said dryly, "but that's the best offer I've had all day."

Ed didn't give her a chance to change her mind. "See you in a few."

THE GANNIS HOMESTEAD

It had been a long time since Heather had seen Ed eating in her kitchen. He still ate with gusto. She watched him demolish his third piece of pizza while she toyed with the crust of her first.

Ed's dark eyes focused on her plate. "Don't tell me you're dieting," he said warningly.

"No, no," Heather said, cutting herself another half slice. She took a bite.

"Good, because I hate that crap," said Ed. "If you went on a diet, you'd shrivel up and blow away. And you look good the way you are."

Silently Heather hoped Phoebe wasn't anywhere near the kitchen. Her cheeks warmed at Ed's compliment. It had been ages since she'd thought of him in *that* way. Well, it *had* been ages, until this afternoon, when she had been with Sam. Now she looked at Ed across the table, the way his dark hair fell across his forehead, his broad shoulders, broader and heavier now with muscle, his arms and strong, lean hands. Even that big cut across his cheek didn't detract from his good looks.

"Ed, how sexist of you," she said sweetly. "Next you'll start talking about big boobs and wide, child-bearing hips."

Across the table Ed grinned evilly at her. "More cush to the push."

Her eyes widened in outrage, and she threw a piece of crust at him. "What a pig! No wonder you don't have a girlfriend!"

Deflecting the crust, Ed snickered. "You think that's it?"

"Hello, Ed!" said Mr. Gannis with forced heartiness. He came into the kitchen and opened the fridge. "You're looking well."

"Thanks. You too," Ed said easily. Heather grimaced to herself.

"What are you kids doing tonight?" Mr. Gannis asked cheerfully, popping the top of a beer bottle. He slowly poured it into a pint glass. Ed watched the foam build.

Shrugging, Heather said, "Watching a movie?"

"Well, honey, you know tonight's the State of the Union Address," Mr. Gannis said. "Your mother and I were planning to watch it. Maybe you kids could hang out in your room so we won't disturb you."

"Sure, whatever," said Heather. "Come on, Shred. Unless you want to watch the State of the Union report with Dad."

"Oh, no, thanks," Ed said.

Heather hid a smirk as she watched Ed expertly push back from the table and head down the hall to her room. Of course he still remembered where it was.

Inside her room, he looked around, assessing changes.

"Different posters," he said.

"Yeah," she said, flopping sideways on her bed. Ed's face

looked very still—no longer lighthearted and open, the way it had been earlier.

"What's wrong?" Heather asked. "I know that look."

Surprise crossed his face, then he shook his head. "I'm just . . . It's just insulting, that's all."

"What is?" Frowning, Heather ran through everything she had said in the last twenty minutes. Had she hurt his feelings somehow?

"Look, if I wasn't in a wheelchair, there's no way your dad would have suggested we come hang out in here," Ed burst out. "Before, I'd have had to crawl over his dead body to get into your room. Now it's like, sure, go in, you . . . eunuch!"

Heather felt shocked, and she realized he was right. It was as if her dad considered Ed absolutely no threat to her virtue, like he was one of her girlfriends. It *was* insulting. Why, Ed had been more threat to her virtue than anyone she'd ever met!

"Eunuch," Heather said admiringly. "Someone's been doing his English homework. That's a mighty fancy word."

She saw Ed's hands clench on his wheel rims as he stared at her in angry disbelief. Quickly she scooted to the edge of her bed and leaned toward Ed.

"Let Daddy think what he wants," she said softly. "I like having you in here."

Interesting, she thought as she watched Ed's pupils dilate.

GAIA

This situation is starting to prey on my brain. I didn't see Skizz again last night. I'm going to end up with pneumonia if I keep freezing my butt off like this.

On top of that, when I got home, the Wicked Witch of the West Village was waiting for me, chain smoking and knocking back gin and tonics. The alcohol fumes almost knocked me down when I opened the front door.

The weird thing was, she didn't say a word. Just stared at me with those acidic green eyes as smoke coiled around her flame red hair. I waited for her to start in on me, but she just bored holes in me with her eyes as I trudged up the stairs. I didn't see George—I hope I don't find him buried in the backyard soon.

You know what? I feel very tired. Last night I wanted to just lie down in the snow and fall asleep. I'm tired of looking for Skizz, though I won't stop. I'm tired of tensing up every time I have to go back to Perry Street. My hip is still killing me. My whole thigh is mottled black and purple and deep blue, with tinges of green and yellow around the edges. Very artistic.

Okay, here's my fantasy. Some night soon I find Skizz. Quickly, without thinking about it, I finish what I've decided to do. Then I go home, stopping for a box of chocolate Krispy Kreme doughnuts on the way. I take the doughnuts into the bathroom and run a deep tub of water as hot as I can stand it. I set a fluffy white towel, two cans of Coke, and a bottle of Advil on a little table. I sink into the water. I take four Advil pills and drink a Coke. I eat three doughnuts. I drink another Coke. I fall asleep.

No one calls me, no one comes in, no one needs the bathroom. When I finally get out of the tub, glowing pinkly and shriveled like a prune, Ella tells me I've been kicked out of the Village School and am being transferred to another foster home in, say, France. I never have to see anything that reminds me of Mary again.

I never see Ed again, never have to explain anything to him. And best of all, someone else is planning it all for me.

I eat another doughnut as I pack.

That would be the perfect day for me.

It's not too much for a girl to ask, is it?

PERFECT DAY

EVERY TWENTY MINUTES SOMEONE WAS HAVING SEX,

AND IT WASN'T GAIA.

WELL, SHIT

The only good thing about Tuesdays, in Gaia's opinion, was that they weren't Mondays. Mondays were so awful, it was like a blow to the head. Tuesdays were more of a dull, achy pounding.

As Gaia determinedly pushed her stack of textbooks back in her locker, she caught sight of Ed turning the corner at the end of the hall. Probably she should say hello to him. She'd been a little harsh, although she'd meant what she said. But she could at least be civil. It was just—in her mind, she had already crossed a line. She had left him behind as surely as if she'd already skipped town. There was no explaining it or justifying it to him. And it was too late to change her mind.

But today she wanted to at least be nice to him. Try to make him see that she didn't hate him, no matter what it looked like. Say a simple *hello*, and keep on moving. Maybe one day he would understand that it was for his own good.

Before Gaia could take a step in Ed's direction, her archenemy, Heather Gannis, stepped into view. Strangely, Heather slithered up to Ed and squeezed his shoulder. One side of her mouth quirked. Gaia moved forward, waiting for Ed to push Heather's hand away and roll past her.

But no. Ed smiled boyishly, suddenly looking younger and charming. Even adorable. Gaia stopped as if she had been poleaxed.

"I had such a good time last night," Heather said.

Her stomach clenching, Gaia leaned against the bank of lockers. Had she woken up to an alternate universe? She knew that Ed and Heather had been involved once, though she hated to think about it. And she knew they were civil to each other now, though the reasoning escaped her. But what the hell was *this* about?

"Me too," said Ed, grinning. His dark eyes looked up into Heather's, and something unnamable passed between them. Then the bell rang, and Ed continued down the hall. Gaia pasted a sardonic look on her face and loped forward, already formulating the kind of crap she would give Ed about his recent lapse in good taste.

Before she could open her mouth, Ed calmly said, "Hey, Gaia." Then he rolled right past her without looking back, leaving her gaping at him like a goldfish on a sidewalk. For a moment Gaia closed her eyes and rubbed one hand over her lids. She definitely needed more sleep, more Advil, more coffee. She would need all the help she could get to deal with this bizarre and disturbing development.

LAH-DE-DAH

In chem lab Heather pushed her goofy safety glasses up onto her shining dark hair, managing to look both chic and careless. She caught sight of her reflection in one of the glass-fronted cupboards that lined the back of the room and smiled at herself.

As she and her lab partner, Megan, set up their Bunsen burners and their stupid little asbestos pads and their beakers that would have been so much more appealing if they had held frozen margaritas (no salt), Heather couldn't remember the last time she had felt so happy.

"Well, *you're* glowing," Megan said accusingly under her breath. In the front of the room Mr. Fowler droned on about chemical reaction this and mechanical reaction that, but he was easy to tune out. Gaia Moore, however, was not. She came into the room looking like an oversized refugee, as usual, and took her place two desks away.

"You and Sam must have gotten along well," said Megan knowingly. "*Really* well."

Seeing Gaia's back stiffen almost imperceptibly, Heather wanted to burst into song.

"It was really nice," Heather said demurely. "Sometimes just being alone with him is all I need."

Megan snorted in an unladylike way. "Were you there late?"

For once Heather appreciated Megan's usually annoying habit of speaking a tiny bit too loud. Obviously Gaia was overhearing every word. It was *delicious.* What better way to celebrate Heather's happiness than by twisting a knife right in Gaia's guts? Call her sentimental.

Heather shook her head. "No—I got home pretty early. Then Ed came over, and we hung out in my room."

Megan gaped at her. From the corner of Heather's eye she saw Gaia's head turning toward her, as if someone were pulling a string.

"Ed Fargo?" Megan squealed. She took off her safety glasses to stare at Heather.

"Ed and I are good friends," Heather said calmly, lighting their Bunsen burner. "Really good friends."

"You hung out in your room? Your dad let him into your room?"

Stifling a giggle, Heather nodded. "What Dad doesn't know won't hurt him," she said mischievously.

"You and Ed . . ." Megan seemed at a loss for words. "And Sam?"

"I had a very full day yesterday," Heather allowed. Then she turned right toward Viking Girl and smiled big, catching Gaia by surprise.

"I had forgotten how *great* Ed is," Heather said breathily. She actually winked at Gaia, even though she didn't think she had ever winked at anyone in her life. The response was intensely satisfying: Gaia looked startled, repulsed, confused, and angry all at once. Heather wrinkled her nose at Gaia in a girlish way, then turned back and busily started her experiment. Life was good when you were Heather Gannis.

BOINKING LIKE WEASELS

By the time trig class was half over, Gaia still hadn't recovered from the sharp nosedive her world had taken in the last two hours. For some reason, dealing with the gross unfairness of losing both her parents early in her life was one thing: She could somehow wrap her mind around it and try to function. But the idea of wretched, horrible, fakey bitch Heather Gannis having both Sam Moon and Ed Fargo drooling over her was more than Gaia could stand.

Sure, Heather was gorgeous. The glossy dark hair, the uptilted hazel green eyes, the peaches 'n' cream skin. And she was a normal height, and she had girlie curves. Her sweaters actually had stuff to cling to. She wasn't gargantuan, muscled like a truck driver, awkward, and mannish. But so what? Did that make it fair?

In all of Gaia's seventeen years she had only ever desired one person, and *Heather* was having sex with him on a regular basis. In the last five years she had been friends with only two people. One was dead, and Heather was friends with, and possibly having sex with, the other one. How unfair was that?

And what was this, with all these people boinking like weasels all the time? Every twenty minutes someone was having sex, and it wasn't Gaia. In her whole life she had been kissed romantically exactly *four times*, and one she wasn't sure about, one was Charlie Salita because she was luring him into a trap, and the last one was with Ed on a freaking *dare*! Only one time had actually been fun, and that had been with a random guy in a club. This was just so lame. Mary had been right. Gaia was clearly a case of arrested development. In the romance department. Not in the martial arts/muscles/nerves-of-steel departments.

Gaia suddenly felt unbearably hurt. And she hadn't thought it was possible to hurt any more than she already did. Usually, no matter what happened, she just kept on moving. Kept her head up. This time last year it didn't matter that she was alone, that she had no friends, that she had only herself to depend on. Why should it matter now?

Gaia shook her head, keeping her eyes cast down on the meaningless trig equations in front of her. She was lost and spinning and didn't know what to do with herself. If she could have felt fear, this would be a good time. Because she couldn't, all she could feel was a sort of nausea.

SLOW BURN

Today's Menu: Corned Beef Hash (no doubt Alpo brand), creamed corn, steamed spinach, and a square of spice cake. Groaning, Ed decided to grab some falafel at Falafel King, only a block and a half away. Yes, it was cold outside. Yes, he would have to negotiate snowdrifts and piles of garbage. But he couldn't eat this swill, and a lad had to keep up his strength.

As he swiveled and headed out the cafeteria, he saw Gaia standing in line. Her eyes caught his, and she looked away. He smiled to himself as he remembered the scene in the hallway this morning. That had been fun. Gaia had looked so pissed. Now he kept his eyes on her as she looked away. Was he mistaken, or was she doing a slow burn? Did she want him now that she probably thought Heather did? Not that Heather really did, of course: Despite hanging out with Ed last night, she was still together with Sam, as far as Ed knew.

So in reality Ed was still girlfriendless, loverless. But he knew it looked to Gaia like that might have changed, with Heather. Hee hee.

He stopped in front of Gaia. As usual, despite the scowl on her face, she looked beautiful. She and Heather were so different: Heather was groomed, sophisticated, and sexy in this confident, self-aware way. Gaia was always a mess, completely unsophisticated, and sexy in a way that was all the more devastating because she seemed so unaware of it. Heather looked like she was ready to be led to bed. Gaia looked like she had just gotten out of it. It was enough to make a guy postal.

"Hey," Ed said.

"Hey," Gaia responded without looking at him.

It was ridiculous, but Ed felt so confident, he felt like it wouldn't kill him to forgive her—to make one last try.

"Want to go grab some falafel at Falafel King?"

A nanosecond of indecision crossed Gaia's perfect face.

She shook her head. "No, thanks."

This was so stupid. "Gaia—"

"What?" she said, looking at him finally. Irritation had bloomed in her voice. Her blue eyes were cold.

You know what? He didn't need this. Shaking his head abruptly, Ed wheeled away.

GAIA

Okay. Here's my new fantasy. I still kill Skizz. I still get the doughnuts. But on my way home to the hot bath, I see Heather, Sam, and Ed all get hit by a bus. Only Ed makes it. And it isn't so bad for him because he's *already* in a wheelchair. He begs my forgiveness for five years. I'm not sure if I ever give in.

SKIZZ

So some guy calls—my private cell, no less. Says a friend of a friend told him I got the shit. You a cop? I said. He laughed. Named some names no cop knows. So I know he's legit—just some asshole with a hungry nose. I say meet me at midnight. He begs. Big party, boring people, really needs it sooner. I've heard that story a million times. Anyway, he begs and promises. So I haul my sorry ass out of bed, do a couple of lines like a quality control check. Take some of them pain pills the hospital gave me. Ready to roll. So I'm heading to the corner of frigging Waverly and MacDougal, and it's light out, and I'm gonna be a frigging sitting duck. Asshole better not let me down.

POSITIVELY INSANE

THE FAMILIAR, HEADY RUSH OF ADRENALINE POURED LIKE WHISKEY THROUGH HER VEINS.

OUT OF HER MISERY

"I'm telling you, you've got to get me out of there." Ella's voice was brittle. She lifted her heavy crystal tumbler of gin and tonic and took a healthy, if unladylike, swig.

"Your job is unfinished." Loki sounded completely unconcerned with her mental state. He sat behind a smooth black desk, its top bare except for the heavy manila file he was leafing through. The room was silent except for the ice tinkling in Ella's glass and the occasional muted turning of papers.

"Forget the job," Ella said rashly, and was rewarded with Loki's icy stare. She took a breath and forced herself to calm down. "Look, I've been doing it for a long time," she reminded him. "I can't take living with that—that horrible sack of *laundry* another day. You've no idea what it's like. I can't bear it." She ached for a cigarette with a palpable longing. With one red-clawed fingertip she smeared the trace of lipstick left on her glass.

"You'll bear it because I say you have to," Loki said quietly, calmly.

Ella was upset and angry and fed up, but she wasn't stupid. Her danger-sensing antenna prickled, and once again she told herself to calm down.

"It's just very frustrating," she said more reasonably.

"George is *repugnant.* If I have to let him touch me one more time—" She took a deep breath. "And that girl. I know you think she's hot stuff, but to me she's nothing but hateful, rude, and disrespectful."

Loki actually let his papers rest on his desk and looked up at her. "And that hurts your tender feelings?" he asked disbelievingly. "What does it matter how she is to you? Your *feelings* are completely immaterial in this situation. So what if old George wants a feel now and then? Lie on your back and think of England." He quoted the old saying with obvious callousness.

"You don't seem to remember," he continued softly, "that your usefulness is limited only to what information you bring me about Gaia. Your many mistakes have been overlooked, for the time being, because like it or not, you're still closer to Gaia than anyone else on our side."

Ella drained her glass and set it down, too hard, on the glass-topped coffee table. The noise it made sounded like a gunshot. Loki's face was a mask.

Silence filled the room. Once Ella had been Loki's protégée, his rising star. Now she was yesterday's socks. He had found her when she was younger than Gaia, had molded her into what she was today. But now she had the sickening feeling that he thought of her as the trial run and Gaia as the final test. But not if she could help it. She licked her lips.

"I know," she said, allowing resignation to fill her voice.

"Is she going to the Moss girl's funeral tomorrow?"

Ella shook her head. "The girl's mother called several times, asking Gaia to speak at the service. Gaia refused. She was a real bitch, in fact." She studied her nails.

Loki smiled. "What's the point of going? Gaia doesn't allow mere emotions to cloud her judgment. The girl's role in her life is over, so Gaia moves on. She's like a shark, our Gaia." As he looked out the high window, Loki's face softened almost unnoticeably. "Like a beautiful, perfectly designed shark: nature's perfect predator. . . ." His voice trailed off thoughtfully.

If Ella had to listen to any more of this, she would throw up all over the white carpeting. Instead she lurched to her feet, unsteady for a moment on her high heels. She pulled down her tight skirt and smoothed her hands over her hips. For a moment she hoped a look of sexual interest would cross Loki's carved face. When he gazed back at her impassively, she felt ashamed, angry.

Standing at the elevator bank a minute later, Ella quickly lit a cigarette, ignoring the smoke-free-building signs plastered in front of her. Her feelings felt raw. She needed some kind of balm, something that would soothe this rough, maddening itch.

Two words popped into her fevered mind. *Sam Moon.* That delicious boy. Ella inhaled her smoke deeply, drawing it down into her lungs. Already she felt her nerves unraveling, smoothing out. Okay. First she would go home and get some rest. Then she would look up her old buddy, old pal, Sam Moon.

When the elevator doors dinged open, Ella was smiling.

MRS. MOSS'S REQUEST

No one used the handicapped-only side entrance at the Village School—no one but Ed. He used to be self-conscious about it, but now he just figured, why beef about having your own private entrance and exit? It was better than being one of the lemmings.

Today Ed waited for the door to open and wheeled himself through. Cold air instantly swirled around him, insinuating itself under the collar of his coat, around the wrist cuffs of his gloves. He'd seen Gaia striding out the front doors only moments after the last bell had rung. No doubt she was keeping another one of her stupid appointments with fate. Trying to find Skizz. Ed had wondered what she would do to Skizz when she found him. Would she . . . go all the way?

She wouldn't, would she? Sure, Gaia had a warped sense of appropriate behavior, but she wasn't a killer. Was she? What was going through her head? Ed wanted to spit with frustration and anger.

He started to wheel himself down the long, sloping wooden ramp.

"Ed?" came a hesitant female voice.

Looking up in surprise, Ed saw Mary's mother standing to one side of the ramp. She looked pale, with red-rimmed eyes, and seemed about ten years older than she had over the Christmas holidays.

"Mrs. Moss," Ed said, concern creasing his forehead.

"Forgive me for tracking you down at school," Mrs. Moss said awkwardly.

"It's okay."

Having gotten his attention, Mary's mother seemed unsure how to continue. She was silent for long moments, looking uncomfortable, as Ed took in her dark green wool coat, the expensive leather gloves lined with fur. She wore no hat, and her wavy hair, once red like Mary's but now faded and streaked with white, was being tossed by the chill wind.

"Um, can I help you with something?" Ed asked gently.

"Yes," Mrs. Moss said with a rush of relief. "Yes. I hate to impose on you, but—" She twisted her hands together.

"It's okay," Ed said again. "If there's anything I can do to help . . ."

"The thing is," said Mrs. Moss, "we—my family and I—feel so strongly that Mary would have wanted Gaia to take part in her . . . services tomorrow. It was Gaia who confronted Mary about her . . . problem, and she was why Mary decided to quit."

"Uh-huh," Ed said stonily. He saw where this was going.

"I've called her several times," Mrs. Moss continued, looking almost embarrassed, "but I guess . . . . maybe she's overwhelmed with grief. As we all are."

Maybe she's overwhelmed with being an asshole, Ed thought.

"Anyway. I was hoping. The services are tomorrow. I know you were planning to come, and I thank you. But—I know you're Gaia's friend—do you think there's any way you could talk to her? Ask her, as a friend, to do this for another friend? Even if . . . even if that friend is no longer here?" Mrs. Moss ended on a cracked, hoarse whisper.

Ed felt like his guts were being churned in a washing machine. Gaia was being such a bitch! How could she say no to Mary's mother? How could she be so cold to another person's pain? *Overwhelmed with grief, my ass!*

"I'm sorry you've been having a hard time getting through to her," Ed said, a rigid cord of anger threading through his voice. "She's been taking a little vacation from being human lately."

Mary's mother misunderstood. "Oh, believe me, I know," she said, forcing a thin smile. "I think we all have. This kind of thing is just too painful to bear sometimes—it hurts too much to deal with. I don't blame her at all. It's just—I know it would mean so much to Mary. And I feel that we let her—Mary—down so badly." She looked away, her eyes haunted. "I wanted to be able to do this one last thing for her."

Ed felt that if Gaia were here, he would somehow regain enough use of his legs to personally kick her perfect ass from here till next week. Seeing Mrs. Moss, with all her raw pain on display, made something snap inside Ed. Suddenly he knew the time had come to quit being put off by Gaia's rudeness, her prickliness, her deliberate jerkiness. He was going to get through to her, he was going to get her to agree to go to Mary's funeral, or he was going to beat the shit out of her and make her cry—just as Mary's mother was crying. It didn't matter if he destroyed what was left of their friendship forever. If there was anything left at all. It didn't matter if it would totally and irrevocably ruin his chances of making her see him as a possible boyfriend. This was it.

"I understand," he told Mrs. Moss, already feeling the adrenaline racing through his veins. Despite the cold wind his skin was flushed, and he felt hot and uncomfortable. "I'll find Gaia and ask her. I'm sure she'll be there."

"Oh, Ed, do you think so?" The light of hope in her eyes was heart wrenching.

"Yes," he said, his calm voice belying the raging emotions twisting inside him. "I really do."

A WALK IN THE PARK

On her way to Washington Square Park, her home away from home, Gaia decided to spring for a cellophane-wrapped package of five churros. Churros, in her opinion, were right up there on her list of favorite fried foods. These of course were no longer hot; Gaia had no idea when the short, dark Guatemalan vendor had fried them—perhaps this morning? But anyway. Even cold and a little stale, they were greasy, doughy, sugary, and satisfying.

The sky overhead was heavy with low, sullen clouds. They couldn't possibly be about to get more snow, could they? The paper had said that this year was a record breaker in terms of number of freezing days and amount of precipitation. It was as if the weather were responding directly to Gaia's emotions. Low and, yes, she admitted it, sullen.

Ugh, what a sucky day. Ed and Heather, Sam and Heather, mind-numbing classes, an awful lunch . . . and to top it all off, the only underwear she'd been able to find was an ancient pair with too loose elastic. She'd been hitching them up all day.

Automatically Gaia swerved to go past the chess tables. Zolov was there, still hacking as he methodically decimated the opening play of an out-of-place businessman in a thick Burberry coat. Mr. Haq was walking fast toward his taxicab, his break over, and his opponent was still staring in frustration at the unfinished game on the board. Only a couple of other hard cores were there—the crappy weather having scared off all but the most dedicated.

What was she doing here? Skizz most likely wouldn't show until late tonight. She should go home, do her homework, rest a little, then head out again and hit Tompkins Square Park as well. Okay, maybe just a quick perimeter check. Through the park to the replica of the Arc de Triomphe, take a left on Waverly, another left on MacDougal, etc., etc., etc.

THE ANGEL OF DEATH

Was she hallucinating? Had her hunger to get Skizz, to make him pay for hiring Mary's hit, finally caused her mind to snap? Because it looked like the object of her quest was standing in broad daylight on the corner in front of her, down at the end of the block.

Gaia quickened her pace, her trained eyes sweeping the area for anything that might mistakenly interfere in her final meting out of justice. No mistakes this time.

Amazingly she got closer and closer, and none of her alarm antennae went off. Her boots crunched on salt chunks as she rushed down the sidewalk. Her heart sped up, her lungs began to suck in air. The familiar, heady rush of adrenaline poured like whiskey through her veins. At last she would get her hands on Skizz. She would see his skin split under her blows, feel his bones shatter. She would finish the job that Mary had stopped her from finishing almost two weeks before.

Skizz was glancing around, looking nervous and pissed. He hadn't seen her yet. What luck, what luck, what luck . . . Hands clenched inside leather gloves, injured hip seeming strong and whole, mouth already dry, Gaia moved forward: the triumphant angel of death.

Time was moving slowly, so slowly as Gaia sorted plans, actions, approaches, and filed them into her hyperexcited brain. This was it, the goal that had defined her life, had become her life, ever since Mary died on New Year's Eve. She actually smiled.

There was no going back now. Her life would never be the same.

Gaia broke into a run. She didn't want to blow it this time. She could already feel Skizz's bones breaking. She could already see the blood. She could smell it. She was glad she didn't have a gun. Using her bare hands would be so much more satisfying.

Visions flashed through Gaia's mind in time with her steps as they pounded against the pavement. Mary, her teeth stained with blood. Skizz, lying dead on the sidewalk. Her father.

Halfway across the park Gaia suddenly became aware of two things: One was that Ed was heading toward her across one of the streets that lined the park. He was moving fast, and he looked furious. How weird. The other was that a nondescript tan sedan had pulled over to the curb, and Skizz was stepping forward to meet it.

No, Gaia screamed to herself, remembering how Skizz had escaped before.

No, no, no. It felt like a recurring nightmare.

Gaia's feet pounded the sidewalk as she raced toward Skizz. As soon as she was close enough, she could bring him down in a flying tackle. . . .

But Skizz didn't get in the car. As she raced toward him, Gaia watched events unfolding one frame at a time, almost in slow motion: The darkened back window of the car rolled slowly down. The dull metal barrel of a gun peeped coyly out.

A flash of fire lit the dark interior of the car, revealing a dark shadow in silhouette. The air was filled with a deafening burst of sound. Gaia stumbled to a disbelieving halt.

Fifteen feet from her Skizz jerked oddly, his body twisted at an inhuman angle. Gaia saw a look of astonishment cross his ugly, pock-marked face. As he fell backward, he peered down at his chest, put up his hands to stem the exploding red flower blooming there. His body hit the ground like a rock. The car roared away down West Fourth Street and was gone, leaving a thin trail of foul monoxide in its wake.

Oh God, Mary. Oh God. Gaia shook herself from her stupor and sprinted toward Skizz's body. She reached him, panting, and knelt down above him.

Oh, Mary. Gaia felt every fiber of her body explode in rage. Someone had beaten her to it. Someone had taken away the only thing she'd had to hold on to. What a waste. What a senseless waste.

Wake up. Gaia found it hard to fathom that Skizz was actually dead. She desperately wanted to wake him up—she wanted his last conscious moment to be of her railing at him, avenging her friend. But his eyes were open and glassy: He'd been dead before he hit the ground.

This was it. This was the limit of what Gaia could bear. She had finally reached it. Anguish over Mary's senseless death, the pain and desolation she'd felt since then, her confusion over Ed all roiled up out of Gaia in a raw, appalling wail. Screaming with rage and despair, she balled her fists and slammed them into Skizz's chest, once, twice. Her hands came up bloody. "You bastard!" she screamed. "You bastard! You son of a bitch, you die, you hear me? You go on and die!"

A strong hand grabbed her shoulder and pulled her backward.

"Gaia, stop it!" Ed commanded her. His face looked pale and shocked.

"Get off me!" Gaia shrieked, batting his hand away. "Don't you get it? Don't you see? Skizz is dead! He killed Mary, and now he's dead! And I didn't do it! I was going to kill him, Ed," she blurted out. "I was going to kill him, and before he died, I was going to make sure he knew it was because of Mary." She drew in a choking breath. "But I didn't! I didn't do anything! Oh God! Mary, I'm sorry!"

A crowd of people had formed. From far off, Gaia heard police sirens. Her head was about to explode. Her chest felt like an ax had been buried in it. If she didn't get out of here right now, she would turn into even more of a shrieking, freaking lunatic.

Abruptly she stood up. "Dammit!" she shouted. Pulling back her right foot, she savagely kicked Skizz's dead body. "Dammit to hell!" The gathered crowd murmured in alarm.

"Gaia, for God's sake!" Ed yelled. Again he pulled roughly at her, his hand slipping on her puffy nylon jacket. "Gaia! Stop it! You're not doing anything!"

Eyes wild, hair in a yellow tangle around her tragic face, Gaia stared at him. "I know," she whispered hoarsely. Then, as the sound of police sirens grew closer, she turned, gave

Skizz one last glance, and ran off. In seconds she had disappeared.

Ed was ready to scream himself. Gaia had snapped. She had truly snapped, and why? Because she had been going through all this alone. Because she hadn't trusted him. Because she had shut him out. Feeling a renewed burst of anger, Ed popped a wheelie as he spun to head after her.

POINTLESS

What to do? Where to go? Gaia hit a jogging stride that covered ground fast. Her brain felt like it was going to burst out of her skull. Catching sight of her reflection in a store window, she cracked a startled grin. She looked positively insane. Her leather gloves were dark and sticky with blood, and she had a smear of it on her jacket. Her hair looked like it had been styled by a Weedwacker, and there was a look in her eyes that would have scared her if she could, you know . . . yeah.

Skizz was dead. Skizz was dead. He had died a pathetic,

public, drug dealer's death on a New York sidewalk, and no one would mourn his passing. He'd probably been the target of another drug dealer or maybe a client he'd screwed over one too many times. By tomorrow the ranks of lower-level dealers would have moved up seamlessly to take over his trade and accounts, and like water closing over a sinking pebble, it would soon be impossible to tell that Skizz had ever existed, had ever taken up space on earth.

But Gaia hadn't been the cause of his death, and for that she would never forgive herself. *I'm sorry, Mary. I'm sorry.*

A car horn blaring broke into Gaia's thoughts and made her stop short. With dull surprise she noticed she was at a broad intersection far away from Washington Square Park: She almost never made it up this far, to Fourteenth Street. Fourteenth Street was as different from the Village as the Upper East Side was different from the Bowery. It was a very wide, two-way street, teeming with traffic. Big, lower-end department stores selling everything from luggage to masking tape to wall clocks featuring porcelain unicorns lined both sides of the avenue. In between the stores were tiny cubbies selling perfume, electronic equipment, candy, ethnic foods. . . . It was loud and garish and gaudy. After the narrow, quaint, one-way streets of the West Village, the three-story old brick buildings, the charming little pastry shops and antiques stores, Fourteenth Street was like a big, startling slap on the back.

What was she doing here? Gaia faltered on the street corner, mesmerized by the four lanes of traffic speeding past her. How easy it would be to step out into it. It would all be over in moments, her whole, stupid, messy, pointless life. She probably wouldn't feel a thing.

The light changed, and still Gaia remained, standing on a corner next to a trash can. Behind her was a subway stop for the F and the L trains. She felt their rumble beneath her feet. She looked down. There was blood on the toe of her boot.

Oh my God, what am I going to do? Her friendship with Mary and Ed had seemed to give her life a little structure, purpose. They had cared about her. They had been teaching her how to care about them. As if she could have a normal life. Then Mary had died. In the end, Mary's seventeen years of life, from birth, through school, through family holidays, through adolescence, had been worth five hundred bucks.

Revenge against Skizz had been the only thing keeping her going for the past week. It had been the only goal she could wrap her mind around. She had hoped the pain would stop with his death. She'd never figured on someone beating her to him.

Now what was she going to do with herself? Years of her life stretched before her like some arid chasm, like thousands of miles of desert with no water, no other people in sight. Really, what was the point? Shaking her head, Gaia acknowledged that there *was* no point. There was no purpose in her going any further with this. This charade of an existence.

Yes. Just a few quick steps into the street . . .

CREAM PUFF

Ed saw Gaia standing on the street corner, looking pensive. With a last burst of energy he rolled right up into her, knocking hard against her hip. She winced and sucked in breath.

"What the hell do you think you're doing?" Ed yelled at her. His brown eyes were narrowed, his hair and face damp with sweat. Cheeks flushed, he was still blowing hard with the effort of following her for block after block, catching up with her.

Gaia turned, anger coloring her cheeks and making her blue eyes ignite. "Why do you always have to interfere?" she asked snidely.

Ed pushed his sweaty hair back off his forehead with an

impatient gesture. "Yeah, you're bummed. Skizz is dead, and you didn't get a chance to kill him. You're disappointed!" he spat. "You're disappointed you didn't get to make the stupidest mistake of your life." He saw her eyes flare open.

"You're disappointed you didn't get to destroy *yourself* along with destroying *him*. You stupid *idiot*! You would have ended up in jail, no better than any other lowlife murderer! Is that what you wanted? You stupid *bitch*!" he shouted, enraged.

Gaia stared at him in horror. "Go screw yourself," she choked out. She moved quickly to the side, obviously intending to lose him.

Quickly, without thinking, Ed spun sideways as well, making Gaia literally trip over his left wheel.

"Oof!" She sprawled gracelessly on the filthy sidewalk in front of him. "You shit," she hissed. "Get out of my way."

"Make me," he taunted. "I'll get out of your way when you promise to go to Mary's funeral. That'll show me you're not completely hopeless. That'll show me you still have some human quality in you."

"When hell freezes over!" Scrambling to her feet, Gaia backed away from Ed carefully, but he pursued her.

"If you're not getting the message, leave me alone!" Gaia snarled.

"Make me," Ed said again.

In the short course of their relationship Ed had never pushed her this far. In any dispute he was always the one to back down, the one who tried to make up, the one who placated. Those days were over.

"What is *wrong* with you?" she said, eyes narrowed. She was still backing away from him, and over her right shoulder Ed caught sight of a subway sign. So that was her plan. She knew most subways were Ed-proof. He had to accomplish his mission fast.

"No, no," Ed murmured with deadly calm, his brown eyes locked on hers. He was still breathing hard, but he ratcheted down his voice. "The question is, what's wrong with *you?* You had exactly two friends in this world, which isn't a surprise, considering what a cold, insensitive *bitch* you like to pretend you are."

Gaia's eyes flickered. He reloaded and kept firing at her.

"You had two friends," Ed continued, rolling slowly toward her as she backed away. "One of them died a stupid, tragic death. But you know what? Here's a life lesson for you. The life lesson is that even though you lose one friend, it doesn't mean you need to lose *all* your friends. It doesn't mean you can't make new friends in the future. Hasn't anyone ever told you that?"

Gaia made a cruel, mocking face. "Ed, eat shit and die," she said conversationally. "You don't know the first thing about me. You don't know what you're talking about."

Ed felt his face contort again in anger, and he jerked his wheels, making his chair surge forward. He let his metal footrests whack Gaia's shins painfully, and she shoved at him. He held his wheels in place. She whirled and sprang for the subway opening. He watched almost in amusement as she realized that she didn't have a token handy to get through the turnstile. But a train had just pulled out, and people were streaming through the swing gate to one side. Gaia darted through, edging past people: totally illegal.

Two can play at that game, Ed thought, wheeling quickly forward. Ahead of him Gaia looked back, crashing into a young gang banger as Ed pushed himself through the gate. Then Ed was on Gaia again, at the top of a cement stair that led down to the train platform. The air, only feet from the opening, was dank, chill, and smelled of urine and steam.

"You're wrong," he spat out, coming to within a foot of her. "I *do* know the first thing about you. I know you're a self-centered *asshole.* This whole thing with Skizz wasn't even about Mary! It was all about *you*! *Your* ego, *your* feelings, *your* pain. You weren't helping Mary by hunting Skizz—you were helping only yourself." His jaw was clenched so tightly, it almost hurt to talk. "You're not in charge of fixing the world, you know? You're just one person. Give it a rest!"

Gaia stared at Ed, a tiny muscle under her left eye twitching. He could practically feel the white-hot anger and hatred coming off her. It was like losing a friend all over again, and it made him unbearably sad. But not as sad as the thought of Gaia, beautiful, special Gaia, going through life so totally screwed up.

"Roll on home, loser," she said softly.

"Bite me," he offered. He shook his head. "You think you're so tough," he said. As he spoke, his voice rose in volume and intensity until he was shouting again, so loudly that veins stood out in his neck. "You are such a deluded *coward*. Tough Gaia. No one touches her. She doesn't care about anyone. She's a freaking icicle. But *I* know the truth, even if you don't. I know you're a *cream puff*! I know you're hurt about Mary and lonely without *me*. I know you're scared to go to Mary's funeral. You stupid, stupid asshole!" he yelled. "You don't even know how much you love me!"

Gaia stepped back, but Ed wasn't finished. He was more enraged than he'd ever been in his whole life. He saw Gaia force her face into a controlled mask and knew if she said another flippant remark, he'd never forgive her. Without warning his fist swept out and smacked her across the face, hard. Her head snapped sideways, and she staggered, just for a moment.

Time almost seemed to stop in the first few seconds after Ed had hit her. It was funny, Gaia thought dully, holding her hand to her cheek. She had been in more fights than most heavyweights, and this was the first time she actually had felt pain on contact. Slowly she straightened and looked across at Ed. He looked as shocked as she felt, and in his transparent, dark brown eyes she could read regret, fury, love, and a terrible sadness.

She swallowed hard. Here she'd been so proud of herself for successfully holding herself immune from friendship. Now Skizz was dead; she had no friends, no parents, no nothing. She had been sure she could control the pain, but her hip was killing her, her cheek felt like it was on fire, and her emotions felt like Ed had rolled them through broken glass and then sprayed her with water from the Dead Sea.

I simply cannot stand this, Gaia thought in the last, silent moment before she pulled back her right arm, swung it in a huge, lightning-fast arc, and gave Ed a powerful punch right across his kisser.

His eyes had just time enough to register surprise before his chair jerked backward and began to fall down the long, scarred cement steps toward the train platform. Ed's strong arms scrambled for his wheels, and for a second he managed to keep himself upright, but Gaia could see it was only a matter of moments before he tilted backward and crashed down the steps, probably breaking his neck and paralyzing the *rest* of him.

Without wasting time on thought, Gaia lunged after Ed and scrabbled for his jacket, his arm, anything. She missed, and he continued to slide backward, now on the third step, now on the fourth. His angle of descent was increasing as his chair leaned farther and farther back. The distant roar of an incoming train grew louder.

Again Gaia lunged at him, her fingers brushing against his shoe. His wide, frightened eyes locked on hers, but Gaia saw no blame in them—only fear. That odd, familiar emotion that she recognized so easily in others, yet never felt herself.

Curiously, neither of them made a sound: Ed didn't cry out for help; Gaia didn't call his name. A gust of stale air announced that the train was about to reach the station.

With a last surge Gaia plunged heedlessly down the steps, throwing herself at Ed. Her bloodied glove snatched at Ed's jacket lapel and held it in an iron grip. With one arm she gave a powerful yank and managed to haul him forward. His wheelchair, freed of its weight, bounced crazily down the remaining steps, gathering momentum. It sprang across the narrow platform and smashed into the front of an express train, steaming through the station on its way to Twenty-third Street. The chair popped up high, seemingly weightless, then crashed down again on the roof of the train's third car. The train's speed ricocheted the chair off the track, and it came to rest on the platform twenty feet away. It was mangled, the size of an electric can opener.

Ed's ripstop nylon saddlebag, shredded, now consisted of a torn canvas strap and some threads. All of his painstaking class notes were floating through the air like ungainly, oversized snowflakes. They littered the platform, landing on passengers, on the train tracks, on Ed and Gaia.

The noise of the train faded—it hadn't even slowed down. The few people coming down the steps simply passed around Gaia and Ed, clutching each other halfway down the stairs. The scene would need to be much more unusual to merit attention.

Gaia swallowed, clutching Ed. Slowly he braced his arms on the steps and eased himself upward to sit next to her on the step. She didn't release her hold to make it easier for him. She felt like she could never let him go again. She stared into his eyes, and he returned the look.

"You still have my handprint on your cheek," he said in a shaky voice.

"You still have mine on yours," she told him, her voice warbling stupidly. The enormity of what had almost happened tried to filter into her brain, but she resisted it.

Ed gave her a crooked grin, though his face was still white with shock, almost greenish around the edges. "Love pats," he said.

Gaia had the sudden certainty that she was going to throw up. Emotion was rising painfully through her chest, and it was terrifying and nauseating. *Oh God.*

"I almost lost you," she blurted out, unable to articulate the kind of disaster she knew his loss would be. Having lost Mary, she now realized that losing Ed would be unbearable. It was as if a stained glass window had shattered inside her mind, showing her the white light of her feelings, her connection to Ed, her best friend. "Ed," she muttered, overwhelmed. "Oh God." Now she was trembling more than he was, and she felt his arms come around her strongly, reassuringly.

"Tell me you love me," Ed said softly.

The thought *I would rather be torn apart by wild animals* crossed her mind, but she shoved it down. This was the test. If she passed this test, she could choose life. If she didn't pass this test, she might as well have thrown herself into the traffic ten minutes before.

Oh God. Help.

She couldn't look at him. "I love you." Her voice cracked, and she gave a wet little cough. Ed's arms tightened around her.

"I love you, too," he said back, and kissed her hair. Then she started to cry.

COURAGE

GAIA HAD COME THROUGH THE FIRE AND EMERGED TEMPERED, NOT CHARRED.

ENOUGH CHITCHAT

Gaia frowned. "What is that?"

Ed, looking surprisingly presentable in a navy blazer, white shirt, and tie, rolled up to her at the handicapped entrance of the Riverside Chapel.

The thin, Wednesday morning light barely dusted his shoulders and glinted off the wheels of a clunky, old-fashioned wheelchair.

"Rental," Ed answered glumly. Then his face brightened. "But the 'rents ordered me a new one. A racer."

"Good. You needed a style update. Your last chair was so 1999." Gaia pulled her jacket more tightly around her.

"Yeah. Is that enough chitchat?" Ed asked.

"Yes, I think so," Gaia replied reluctantly.

"Then let's hit it."

And they went into the chapel to attend Mary Moss's funeral.

The Mosses, both parents and Mary's three siblings, sat in the first row of the small chapel. Other relatives took up the next four rows. Ed and Gaia sat together in the fifth row, with Ed's rental chair practically blocking the aisle. He moved backward a few inches to let Gaia out when it was time for her to speak.

Obviously uncomfortable but moving with her innate grace, Gaia climbed the two steps to the podium to the right of the altar. She tapped the microphone experimentally and sent a buzz through the room. Ed winced, then quickly smoothed his face into what he hoped looked like supportive expectation.

With her repulsive jacket stuffed under the pew, Gaia looked pretty close to presentable. She wore some sort of dark skirt thing, with a thin, pale blue sweater on top. No jewelry flashed under the lights, but she had actually brushed her hair this morning, and it hung in clean, soft, golden waves down her back. She was gorgeous.

"Ahem. I, uh, just wanted to say a few words about my friend Mary. Who we're all here to remember today. On this . . . sad day." Gaia drew in a deep breath.

"Actually, I only knew Mary a really short time. But

she made an impression on me that very few other people have made." She looked out into the chapel and met Ed's eyes.

"Mary was an incredibly strong person," Gaia went on. "She was incredibly brave. Most people can't face their problems, their faults." She looked down. "But Mary could and did. And she beat them. She showed me it was possible to do if you have courage."

In the front row Mrs. Moss gazed up at Gaia, her eyes brimming with unshed tears. Gaia tried not to look at her again.

"Not only that, but Mary showed me how to have fun. How to enjoy life. How to work with what you have and do the best with it. We had some great times together." Gaia swallowed. "Times I'll remember the rest of my life. And she showed me something else: how to *be* a friend. How to have a friend. What it feels like when someone cares about you." Looking right at Ed, Gaia said, "Those were lessons I wasn't ready to learn before. But I'd like to thank Mary now for teaching them to me." Her voice wobbled, and Gaia frowned and cleared her throat. Then she looked out at the group.

"Now Mary is going to continue in our memories," Gaia said. "I hope you all have good memories of her, as I do. I remember her laugh, her crazy red hair, her daring fashion sense." Some people in the audience smiled. "But I don't really need to remember Mary on purpose. Because every time I actually manage to be a friend to someone or let them be my friend, I'll know that Mary is right there with me."

Not knowing how to end or if she should say thank you or what, Gaia simply stopped speaking and stepped down from the podium. As she passed the first row, Mr. and Mrs. Moss smiled at her. "Thank you," whispered Mrs. Moss. Gaia nodded at her.

Safely back in her own seat, Gaia felt breathless, as if she had just run a hundred blocks. The minister stood up in the front of the chapel and started speaking, but Gaia couldn't concentrate on what he was saying.

Ed reached across the arm of the pew and took Gaia's hand. Without looking at him, she squeezed back and held on.

TO: L 43671.1011@alloymail.com

FROM: ELJ 239.211@alloymail.com

Subject was observed at memorial service sitting with young male. They were observed holding hands. Later, subject was observed wiping away tears with sleeve of sweater. Young male subject (in wheelchair) hugged her. She did not resist.

SOMETHING OF KATIA

In the back of the chapel Tom Moore turned up the collar of his coat. Something in his chest tightened when he saw the golden head of his daughter lean against the shoulder of the young man in the wheelchair.

Gaia had gone to Mary Moss's funeral. Gaia and her handicapped friend had apparently made up. Gaia had been seen to cry, to lean on someone, again.

An overwhelming sense of joy and relief flooded Tom. This past week his guts had been almost chewed out by his worry about his daughter. His unfeeling, automaton-like daughter. His daughter whose emotions had effectively been destroyed, whose sense of loyalty, of compassion, of humanity had been obliterated, surely and effectively, by decisions he alone had made.

Who knew what would have happened if she had actually been the one to kill Skizz? Tom winced at the thought. Gaia was capable of great courage. But she was also capable of great rage. It had been the right decision to take Skizz out of the equation. A difficult decision, but the right one.

But there was no use dwelling on that. Gaia had come through the fire and emerged tempered, not charred. It was more than Tom had hoped for. It was more than he deserved.

As he stood and made his way quietly to the chapel door, Tom Moore gave thanks that his daughter had some remnants of her mother still existing with her. Katia lived on, in Gaia. And for that Tom was grateful.

WANT MORE?

HERE'S A PEEK AT

THE NEXT FEARLESS BOOK:

LIAR

BY FRANCINE PASCAL

GAIA

I read somewhere once that there are four stages of grief. Or maybe five. I can't remember. Which is kind of strange because I have a great memory. Photographic, in fact. All the shitty things that have ever happened to me are permanently burned into my mind, like a continuous movie. And it's not a movie you would want to pay eight bucks for, either—no heroes or happy endings, just a lot of sadness and destruction.

Anyway, the first stage is denial. That's one I can understand. In fact, it's probably the reason why I don't remember the stages of grief in the first place—because for a while there, I didn't want to believe that grief even existed. If I can't feel fear, then why should I feel grief?

I mean, it makes sense, right? I don't even have to deny fear. It just doesn't exist. Things are much easier to deal with if they don't exist.

The next stage is anger. (I think.) That's also another one that makes perfect sense to me. For example, when I finally realized that my friend Mary Moss was truly *gone*, that she was never coming back, *ever*—I got pissed.

So I went on a little mission. I decided to murder somebody.

That somebody was Skizz, the asshole coke dealer who ended Mary's life. Luckily, another somebody beat me to it. *Barely.* Skizz died in front of my eyes.

Even more luckily, I was reborn.

I know that sounds really lame and cheesy, but it's true. I realized that by going on this mission—by thinking of nothing else except murdering a scumbag whose life isn't worth the coke he sells—I was losing the one person I have left. Ed Fargo.

This isn't an exaggeration, by the way. I'm not being melodramatic. Ed *is* the only person I have left in the world.

I know what you're thinking. Don't I have *anyone*?

What about my mom, for instance? Nope. Gone.

My dad? Also gone. Missing in action the night Mom died.

George, my guardian of the moment? Nice, sweet, sincere—but not really there for me.

Ella, the evil bitch who happens to be George's coguardian? Best not to go there.

Which brings me to Sam. Sam Moon, the guy who haunts me, the guy I obsess over; the boy goes out with Heather Gannis. . . . Okay, it's best not to go *there*, either. But for a brief moment I thought Sam and I had made a breakthrough. That is, until he showed up at my door, took one look at the Wicked Witch of the West Village (Ella, in case you haven't guessed), then bolted. Not that I can blame him for running away from *her.* Still, it was kind of weird. And I've only seen him once since. I basically told him to screw off.

Of course, that was when I was still in the "anger" stage.

I'm pretty sure the last stage of grief is acceptance. Which is where I am now. I accept that Mary's dead. I accept that Sam Moon and I will never happen. I accept that my life sucks, that danger stalks me like a psychotic villain, that I'll live the rest of my life with no friends except a guy without feeling in his legs.

I guess that means I'm fully recovered, right?

GAIA'S PROBLEM

A LITTLE CHARLES MANSON AND

A LITTLE MOTHER TERESA . . .

THE BEAUTY OF ED

Gaia stared blankly at the book on her desk. She almost laughed. What was she thinking? Did she really believe she would spend Friday evening in this lame little bedroom and actually *read*? Maybe she was finally pulling herself together after the trauma of Mary's death—but still, normalcy came in stages. It came in baby steps. And reading *The Great Gatsby* in the Nivens' house felt like a giant step clear into somebody else's life.

Besides, nobody did homework on Fridays. Not even the ultranormal. Not even studious people like . . . well, like Sam Moon. Not even if *The Great Gatsby* was the great work of literature everyone said it was.

Time to bolt. Bolting was a specialty of hers.

Gaia sighed and brushed a few tangled strands of blond hair out of her face, then pushed herself away from the desk. Part of the problem was that Ella was home, and even though Gaia had avoided her (Ella was locked in her bedroom, listening to some horrid Celine Dion CD), the knowledge that they were under the same roof was enough to make Gaia want to puke.

She stood up and stretched, peering out the window. It was cold and dark—but that had never stopped her from going out before. Maybe she'd go to the park and try to hustle a chess game. Or maybe she'd swing by Ed's and see if he wanted to see a movie. She grinned. That sounded perfect, actually. Ed would definitely be up for something. He hated being stuck in his bedroom almost as much as Gaia hated—

"I'm sorry about your friend."

What the hell?

Gaia whirled around, her blue eyes smoldering.

Ella was standing in the open doorway—decked out, as usual, as if she were going to model at a teen fashion show. Today's outfit consisted of a tight baby T-shirt that wouldn't fit a dwarf, black leather miniskirt, and boots. And her red hair was in pigtails. Freaking pigtails. It was almost funny.

"Don't you knock?" Gaia asked.

Ella stared back at her blankly. "Not in my own house," she replied.

Touché, Gaia thought. That was classic Ella. Always reminding Gaia of her place. Always making sure Gaia knew who was in charge. And this was Ella's house. Not Gaia's. It never would be. At least that was something they could agree on.

"So what do you want?" Gaia demanded impatiently, turning toward her closet.

"I just wanted to tell you that I'm sorry about your friend," Ella repeated. Her tone was colorless, without emotion. "You know. The one who died."

Gaia froze. She scowled. *Sorry about your friend?* Please.

Ella didn't give a shit about anyone but herself. And she sure as hell had never offered any kind of sympathy toward Gaia before.

"What do you really want, Ella?" Gaia asked, looking her directly in the eye.

"I told you," Ella replied.

"You're . . . sorry," Gaia stated dubiously.

Ella's face darkened. "Look, just forget it. I . . ." She bit her lip, hesitating. Finally she shook her head. "Forget it," she said again. "This isn't going to work." She turned and strode down the steps.

A moment later Ella's bedroom door slammed.

Gaia's jaw fell open. In all the months she'd been stuck in this freakish house, that was by far the most bizarre encounter she'd ever had. And disquieting, too—much more so than any of their arguments. That's because their arguments made sense. Even when Gaia had smacked Ella in the face a couple of months ago, there had been some kind of logic involved. Ella had said something particularly loathsome. Therefore Gaia had found herself throwing a punch. *A* led to *B*, which led to *C*. Gaia had regretted hitting her; she'd promised it would never happen again—but Ella had provoked the incident. It hadn't come out of *nowhere.*

Not like this.

So. That posed a very disturbing question.

Could it be that Ella actually *meant* what she said? That she was sorry about Mary?

No. Gaia shook her head. Of course not. This was the woman who treated Gaia like dirt . . . who was using her unsuspecting husband for some sinister purpose Gaia had yet to determine—but that probably involved embezzlement and sleazy affairs with one or more men. Ella was evil. Plain and simple. This was just another manifestation of Ella's multiple personality disorder: slipping from mask to mask without ever revealing her true face.

Still, what had she meant by *"This isn't going to work"*? It sounded like the kind of thing that somebody would say if they were trying to mend a relationship. But she and Ella didn't have a relationship of any kind. At all.

Gaia took a deep breath. She took two quick steps across her room and picked up the phone, then punched in Ed's number.

After two rings he picked up. "Hello?"

Ed's voice could always make Gaia smile. It was so open, so friendly—but with an edge, too.

"Hey, Ed," she whispered.

"Hey, I think we've got a psychic connection," Ed remarked dryly.

"Why's that?"

"Because I was just about to call *you*. My new wheelchair came today while we were at school. I wanted to show it off.

It's radical. I'm talking state-of-the-art. Power steering. It goes from zero to sixty in four hours. Faster down a flight of subway steps, of course."

Gaia wanted to give Ed credit for being funny, but she couldn't muster a laugh. "Sounds good," she mumbled. "Actually, I was . . . um, I was just calling to see if you wanted to go see a movie. Or rent one, maybe."

"Sure." There was a pause. "Are you okay?"

"Yeah," she said automatically. But then she frowned. In the past she would have shrugged off Ed's questions or told him to mind his own business. But after the events of the past week—after she'd nearly killed Ed and destroyed his wheelchair on the aforementioned subway steps—she was determined not to hide from him anymore. He was her one friend, so she might as well treat him like one.

"Nothing's wrong?" Ed prodded.

She flopped down on her bed, twirling the phone cord in her fingers. It took a few seconds to get the words out. "Actually, there *is* something wrong."

"What's that?" Ed's voice registered both surprise and happiness. Not that there was something wrong, but that Gaia was telling him so.

"Ella."

"Something new?" Ed asked.

"She told me she's sorry about Mary."

Ed was silent. "And that is bad because . . . ?"

"Come on, Ed. I would have felt better if she'd punched me in the face. I'm comfortable with our mutual hatred. Her pretending to care really gave me the creeps."

Ed fell silent again.

"Hello? Ed?"

"Maybe she *is* sorry," he suggested.

Gaia rolled her eyes. "Believe me, she isn't. The woman is completely evil."

"Mmmm," he said equivocally.

"What, mmmm?" Gaia asked, frowning. If she was going to be open and honest, the least Ed could do was agree with everything she said.

"Listen to me, Gaia," Ed said. "Nobody's completely evil."

"Oh, no?" she asked, raising her eyebrows. "Why's that?"

"Well, I guess there's Charles Manson. But ninety-nine-point-nine percent of people aren't completely anything. See, it's like . . . you've got Charles Manson on one side of the spectrum, and Mother Teresa on the other. The rest of us are in between. Aside from a very few extremes, nobody's *all* good or *all* bad."

"I didn't know you were such a philosopher, Ed."

"Being in a wheelchair makes a person philosophical," he replied. His tone wasn't self-pitying; it was matter-of-fact. That was one of the things Gaia loved about Ed most: He never let people feel sorry for him because of his accident.

He took people's pity and threw it right back in their teeth.

"So you're saying that everybody's got a little Manson and a little Mother Teresa inside them?" Gaia asked.

"Exactly," Ed stated confidently.

"I'd say Ella's snuggled up pretty close to Charles Manson," Gaia theorized.

"Maybe Ella is mostly Manson," he agreed. "But today she let her pinprick of Mother Teresa shine through."

Yeah, right. As much as Gaia wanted to tell Ed that he was full of crap, she laughed instead. That was the beauty of Ed. He could take any asinine theory and improve a person's mood with it.

"So are we gonna rent a movie or what?" Gaia asked cheerfully.

"Sure. Meet me at the Blockbuster by Thirteenth and Broadway."

"Yup."

"And maybe after that we can go to Alice Underground and buy me a blazer."

"Why would we want to do that?" Gaia asked.

"Because I need to wear a jacket and tie to an engagement party."

Gaia picked at her thumbnail. "Who's getting engaged?"

"My sister. She's marrying a guy named Blane."

Gaia sat up on the bed. "Your sister? Really?" she asked, genuinely surprised. Ed hardly ever talked about his sister.

Gaia got the feeling the mysterious other Fargo sibling didn't take many opportunities to hang around Ed.

"Yeah. Blane."

"Weird."

"Yeah, so I'll see you at Blockbuster in twenty minutes," Ed said.

"You got it." Gaia hung up the phone. She sat on her bed for a few seconds, staring into space.

Amazing. She couldn't even remember why Ella had freaked her out so much. Maybe Ella *was* letting her Mother Teresa shine through.

Sure. And maybe Gaia would end up marrying a guy named Blane, too. It was great to be back in the denial stage again.

TWO TO TANGO

Sam Moon exhaled deeply, watching his breath billow in the frigid January air. He'd been freezing his ass off in the alley by Gaia's brownstone for almost half an hour, and his toes were beginning to burn. He stomped his boots on the pavement to get the circulation going. But all *that* did was rattle his bones—

"Whoa!"

His legs went out from under him. All of a sudden he was slipping wildly out of control. His overcoat flapped like a cape. His arms flailed. He lunged for a nearby railing to steady himself, just barely keeping balance, and hoisted himself to his feet.

A scowl crossed his face.

Jesus. His lungs heaved. He ran his frozen fingers through his tousled hair and shook his head, then glanced down at the ground. He couldn't even see any ice—just a layer of glistening blackness over the concrete slabs of the sidewalk. Great. Even the *sidewalk* seemed to be laying a trap for him.

Traps. He shook his head and glanced up at Gaia's front door. He knew all about them. All about deception. Oh, yes. A sickening queasiness began to gnaw at his insides. The last time he'd opened that door, he'd felt like he'd walked into the biggest trap of his life. . . .

"No," he whispered out loud.

That image was so clearly etched into his mind: the image of Gaia's foster mother, standing just inside the doorway, smiling seductively at him over Gaia's shoulder. Just *thinking* about her made him want to vomit. He couldn't believe he'd allowed himself to be seduced by her. He couldn't believe she would *want* to seduce him. He couldn't believe she'd continued to hound him with e-mails and calls and all the rest of it. . . .

But the most nauseating part was that the blame didn't fall solely on her. No. He was to blame, too. After all, their sordid encounter fit the stupid cliché, didn't it? *It takes two to tango.* He'd slept with Ella willingly. He'd allowed her to sweet-talk him at that bar, to dance . . . to take his mind and body to some other place. Of course, at the time he'd had no idea that she was Gaia's legal guardian—but still, he'd consciously cheated on his girlfriend. His beautiful, unsuspecting girlfriend. The one he should love but couldn't.

For a moment Sam's mind changed gears. That very beautiful, unsuspecting girlfriend may or may not have cheated on him. That was partly why he'd been at the bar in the first place. *Bullshit,* he growled at himself impatiently. Heather wasn't the cause of his torment. Gaia was. Gaia always was.

His jaw tightened. Now he had to confront Ella. He had to make sure she left him alone, that she stopped hassling him—and most of all, that she never, *ever* told Gaia what had happened.

Out of the corner of his eye Sam caught a glimpse of an NYPD cruiser, rounding the corner and turning onto

Perry Street. It slowed as it rumbled past him. Two craggy, tough-looking members of New York's finest gave him a once-over. Sam averted his eyes. Maybe they thought he was a stalker. He almost laughed. He *did* look a little sketchy—disheveled after his near fall. But suspecting him would be pretty ironic, wouldn't it? He was here to *stop* a stalker: the woman who was harassing him with e-mails and phone calls. He was here to insist that she stop, to issue his own version of . . . what was it called? A restraining order. That was it. He was going to demand that Ella leave him alone. Forever.

Yes. For once in his life Sam Moon was going to set everything straight. He took a deep breath and turned his attention back to the closed door. He was tired of waffling and wavering, of dating Heather but desiring Gaia, of acting out his anger and frustration by behaving in ways he only regretted. It was time to make some decisions. To go after what he wanted. To follow his heart—

His heart nearly stopped as the front door swung open. He sucked in his breath.

It wasn't Ella. It was Gaia. She bounded down the steps . . . right past him, without even so much as a glance in his direction.

Gaia!

He wanted to shout her name. But he couldn't. He'd been robbed of speech. He stood there, paralyzed—unable to move, unable to breathe, unable to do anything but watch as she trotted down the street, her blond mane streaming from under her ratty black wool hat. Even from behind, she was like some kind of . . . well, *vision*—not like any other girl he'd ever seen or known.

Every time he laid eyes on her, he was entranced by that intangible quality that separated her from everyone else—the way she carried herself that he could never quite place. It wasn't just that she was beautiful: tall and strong, like those mythical women of the Amazon. It was more that she had no *idea* she was beautiful.

Generally speaking, girls in Manhattan tended to know they were hot. They strutted around in the latest trends, self-possessed and perfectly put together . . . like Heather, in a way. Or Ella. Not Gaia, though. Gaia—

The front door opened again.

Without thinking, Sam ducked behind the railing.

It was Ella, of course. Sam shook his head, furious at himself. He was here to *confront* her! So why the hell was he crouched down, hiding from her in the freezing cold like a frightened animal?

Actually, he didn't want to answer that question.

AN EXPERT

Tom Moore sat perfectly rigid as Gaia strolled past his parked brown Lexus. If she turned her head only the slightest bit, she might see him. He silently swore under his breath. He knew he shouldn't have driven here. And he shouldn't have parked so close to the Nivens' house. But he'd had no choice. This was the only spot available in an eight-block radius. In New York City parking spaces were like taxicabs: They were impossible to find when you needed one. Besides, the car was equipped with certain devices essential for today's mission—a satellite link and fax machine—that he couldn't carry on his person.

Don't look at me, Gaia. Don't look. . . .

He slouched down low in the driver's seat, staring at her. Every day she looked more and more like her mother.

A lump formed in Tom's throat. He shook his head. Here he was, not ten feet away from his daughter, and he still couldn't touch her. He couldn't call her name. But that was nothing new. He'd learned to live with frustration. That was part of the job. He was a professional. Not a day went by when an agent didn't suffer in some way. But the best of them compartmentalized the suffering—locking it safely away with the rest of their souls, where it couldn't affect other matters.

Tom was an expert at compartmentalizing.

Gaia crossed to the opposite corner. Tom couldn't help but notice that her walk was like a taller, lankier version of Katia's—strong and sensual at the same time. . . .

His eyes flashed back to the house. Ella was leaving. George would be home in a matter of minutes. But maybe he could follow Gaia for a little while, just to make sure she was okay. Yes. There was no telling when Loki would strike—

What am I thinking?

Following her would be inconceivably stupid. For one thing, he'd lose his parking space. For another, Gaia might notice him. No, she *would* notice him. She'd been trained to detect tails; he himself had conducted the relentless drills, day after day in their old home in their old life . . . so long ago.

But George's words from their last meeting kept echoing through his head. They blasted away at his common sense, reducing it to rubble. *"Loki's interest in our girl has taken on a new twist. There's reason to believe he wants her—for himself."*

Tom shook his head. Screw common sense. No way would he let Gaia out of his sight. He grabbed the key out of his pocket and jammed it into the ignition.

THE DEAD GIRL

Ella paused on the sidewalk. She was fumbling for something in the pocket of her faux fur coat . . . a cell phone. She flipped it open and began walking briskly in the opposite direction Gaia had headed, away from Washington Square Park.

". . . doesn't need to be monitored every second," she was saying.

At least that's what Sam *thought* she was saying. Her voice trailed off, lost in the ambient noise of the city.

He hesitated. This was stupid. Even worse, it was shameful. He was *going* to confront her. Summoning his courage, he stood up straight and marched purposefully after her.

Ella suddenly stopped in midstep.

"The dead girl's not an issue anymore," she stated. "Gaia's problem was solved. *You* solved it."

Sam's pace slowed . . . then he stopped altogether. At the mention of Gaia's name, he found he couldn't continue. His face twisted in a scowl. *The dead girl? Gaia's problem?* He shook his head. Could it be that Ella was talking about Mary? No. No way. Mary wasn't Gaia's *problem.* On the other hand . . . what could she possibly mean?

Ella snapped the cell phone shut and scurried across the street.

Sam swallowed. *Follow her, dammit!* He clenched his fists at his sides and darted after her, splashing into a puddle of brownish slush as he leaped off the curb.

SHADOWY

Gaia paused on the opposite corner, struck by the sound of an engine. She'd noticed it a few seconds ago—loud at first, which meant that the driver was in a hurry, then very soft. Which meant that the driver was being cautious.

Or following someone.

The chances that the driver was following *her* were probably small. Still, it was good to have a healthy paranoia. She turned and peered through the early evening twilight at a brown car, idling on the opposite curb. Her eyes narrowed. The driver was a man. . . . She couldn't make out any of his features, just a shadowy silhouette. Instinctively she stepped forward. The car suddenly jumped to life, pulling out into the street. Shit. But then her eyes zeroed in on something else. No, *somebody* else.

What the—

UNANSWERED QUESTION

A horn blast tore through the air.

Sam snapped his head around. His feet became jelly. He hadn't looked before he'd rushed into the street. He heard the tires screeching and perceived only a massive blur, framed by the dark gray drabness of the winter landscape. He knew it was a car, though, and that it was going too fast to stop in time. In seeming slow motion the blur consumed his entire field of vision . . . drowning out all other sights and sounds until there was nothing.

He was about to ask himself a question, but he never had the chance.

IDIOT KID

"Jesus Christ!"

Tom Moore furiously stamped the brake, but the pavement was too slick. *No, no, no.* The car wouldn't stop. It was careening out of control. That kid, that *idiot* kid—why had he run out into the middle of the street? The tires whined. Tom cringed involuntarily. But at the moment of impact he was struck by two simultaneous realizations: one, that he *recognized* the kid; two, that Gaia was flinging herself in front of the car and shoving the kid to safety.

"No!"

The word erupted from Tom's mouth the instant the hood struck his daughter. Flesh and metal connected with a sickening thud. Tom watched dumbstruck as Gaia's body hurtled up into the air and then slammed into the windshield. He threw his hands in front of his face. But miraculously the car lurched to a stop.

Gaia rolled onto the pavement, disappearing from his view.

Silence.

Time came to an instant standstill. The world ceased to turn. Tom didn't hear a sound. He couldn't breathe. His mind shut down but for one horrible thought.

I've just killed my own daughter.

But then something else crept into his consciousness . . . a noise. Shouting. The kid. He was back in the street, grabbing Gaia and propping up her head. Tom could just barely see her over the hood. His heart rattled like a machine gun. His body felt like it was on fire.

What have I done? What have I—

And then he saw it. Yes! Oh God, she was alive. A warm rush of relief seeped through his veins as he saw the wisp of frozen vapor drift up from under his daughter's nose. She was breathing. She was alive. Thank God she knew how to relax during a collision, to let the force of impact throw her body as if she were a sack of potatoes. One of the first lessons of martial arts was minimizing injury. She would be bruised, maybe even have a few cracked bones . . . but she would survive.

He gazed at her transfixed, watching in blessed relief as Gaia lifted her head and blinked her eyelids, pulling the world into focus. He read the single word on her lips:

"Shit."

He let his breath go. That was his Gaia.

He shoved his panic aside and thrust the car into reverse, simultaneously reaching for the car phone. As the car jumped backward, he punched in three numbers: 911.

"Emergency," a voice answered.

"I'd like to report a hit and run at the corner of West Fourth and Perry Street," Tom hissed. "You better call an ambulance."

He pulled the car around the corner. He'd abandon the car just west of Bleecker and return to the scene of the accident to make certain Gaia was all right. It wasn't a hit and run exactly. More of a hit and hide.

THE HORROR

At first the sequence of events didn't register in Sam's brain. Everything seemed to swirl together like some nightmarish impressionist painting. One moment he was about to get hit by a car; the next he was lying on the sidewalk, staring at Gaia as she lay in a heap on the street. And now he was holding her. Cradling her in his arms. Praying that she was alive, that the bastard who'd hit her hadn't killed her . . .

"Come on, Gaia," he heard himself whisper. But the words seemed to come from some other place—as if he were standing off to the side, watching the horror as it unfolded. "Come on—"

She moaned. A flicker of hope sparked inside him. He pushed tangled hair away from her lovely face. "Gaia, please be okay," he whispered. She had a cut along her cheekbone. He held her closer, bending so close to her, his lips nearly touched her forehead. "Please," he whispered again.

Suddenly he felt her body stiffen. Slowly, mercifully, she lifted her head and opened her eyes. Oh, Christ, she was going to be okay. His heart seemed to levitate above his chest.

"Shit," she muttered, curling her body in pain.

Sam's head snapped up at the noisy strain of a car engine backing up in a hurry. Before he could clear his head, the car had disappeared around the corner, speeding crazily in reverse down West Fourth Street. Dammit. He wished he'd had the sense to get the bastard's license plate number. What kind of shameless asshole would hit an innocent girl and speed away?

Plenty of people in New York City, Sam answered his own question. People ran over each other every single goddamn day. And nobody cared. Nobody wanted to get involved. Nobody wanted to take responsibility.

He urgently scanned the street for Ella, for an onlooker, for *anyone.* Gaia needed an ambulance. But the sidewalks were deserted.

"Sam?" Gaia whispered.

He gazed down at her, startled. A drop of blood trickled over the ledge of her chin onto the sleeve of his coat.

"I'm here," he murmured. "Just hold on. . . ."

Sirens were approaching. He could hear the distant wail, drawing closer and closer.

"Sam?" Gaia repeated. She squirmed in his arms.

He hugged her as tightly as he could. "Shhh," he whispered. "They'll be here—"

"Do you think you could let go of me?" she finally managed.

His eyes widened. She squirmed harder.

"But I—I—just . . . I didn't," he started stammering incoherently.

"I'm *fine,*" she grunted. Her eyes were open now—alert, awake, fixed on him with a cold intensity. "Just let me go."

The sirens grew louder.

Let you go? Sam stared at her, slack jawed. Didn't she know that she'd almost been killed? His grip on her loosened—and in that instant Gaia pushed herself away and staggered back toward her house.

"Gaia!" he shouted. "Gaia, please don't go—I need to—Gaia!"

But if she heard him, she didn't show it. She stumbled up the stoop and through the door and slammed it behind her, leaving Sam alone on the frozen pavement.

The street was eerily silent. "I need to thank you," he finished to nobody at all. "Thank you for saving my life."

ABOUT THE AUTHOR

New York Times bestselling author Francine Pascal is one of the most popular fiction writers for teenagers today and the creator of numerous bestselling series, including Fearless and Sweet Valley High, which was also made into a television series. She has written several YA novels, including *My First Love and Other Disasters*. Her latest novel is *Sweet Valley Confidential: Ten Years Later*. She lives in New York City and France.